PRAISE FOR W. MICHAEL GEAR'S COYOTE SUMMER AND THE MORNING RIVER

"A thinking [person's] historical novel, with crisp, authentic dialogue and strong characterization."

— *AMARILLO GLOBE-NEWS* ON *COYOTE SUMMER*

"[A] solid Western...A well-plotted page-turner that distinguishes itself from other Westerns in its depth and quality of its historical reconstruction."

— *PUBLISHERS WEEKLY* ON *COYOTE SUMMER*

"Gear presents the early American West with a rare, salty accuracy of detail."

— *KIRKUS REVIEWS* ON *COYOTE SUMMER*

"A bold novel of the birth of the American fur trade in 1825...A good, strong story, the ending will leave you wanting more...which you will get in the sequel."

— *AMERICAN COWBOY* MAGAZINE ON *THE MORNING RIVER*

“Gear writes superbly rolling prose with flair, confidence, wit, an ear for sounds, and an eye for details...And he has another gift: the ability to teach his readers as he entertains them.”

— *ROCKY MOUNTAIN NEWS* ON *THE MORNING RIVER*

“This is a wonderful book...Well-researched fur trade setting, cultures in interaction and sometimes conflict. [Gear has] a special understanding of American Indian mysticism which provides the stamp of reality.”

— DON COLDSMITH ON *THE MORNING RIVER*

COYOTE SUMMER

SAGA OF THE MOUNTAIN SAGE

BOOK 4

W. MICHAEL GEAR

Coyote Summer
Paperback Edition

Wolfpack Publishing
9850 S. Maryland Parkway, Suite A-5 #323
Las Vegas, Nevada 89183

wolfpackpublishing.com

Paperback ISBN 978-1-63977-825-6
eBook ISBN 978-1-63977-826-3

Once more, to my beautiful Kathleen.
Heart of my heart
Love of my love!

AUTHOR'S NOTE

Coyote Summer is a historically accurate novel set in the fur trade in 1825 and depicts cultural practices, language, and behaviors which modern readers may find disturbing.

COYOTE SUMMER

CREE
BLACKFEET
(PA'KIANI)
ASSINIBOIN
HIDATSA
ATSINA
MANDAN
MOUTH of the BIG HORN
YANKTONAN
CROW
(ANI)
Arikara
Village
GRAND
DETOUR
Fort
Kiowa
YANKTON
DUKURIKA
TETON SIOUX
KU'CHENDIKANI
PONCA
PLATTE
OMAHA
RIVER
Fort
Atkinson
PAWNEE
Kaws Mouth
KANSA
OSAGE
Coyote
Summer
Miles 0 100 200 300

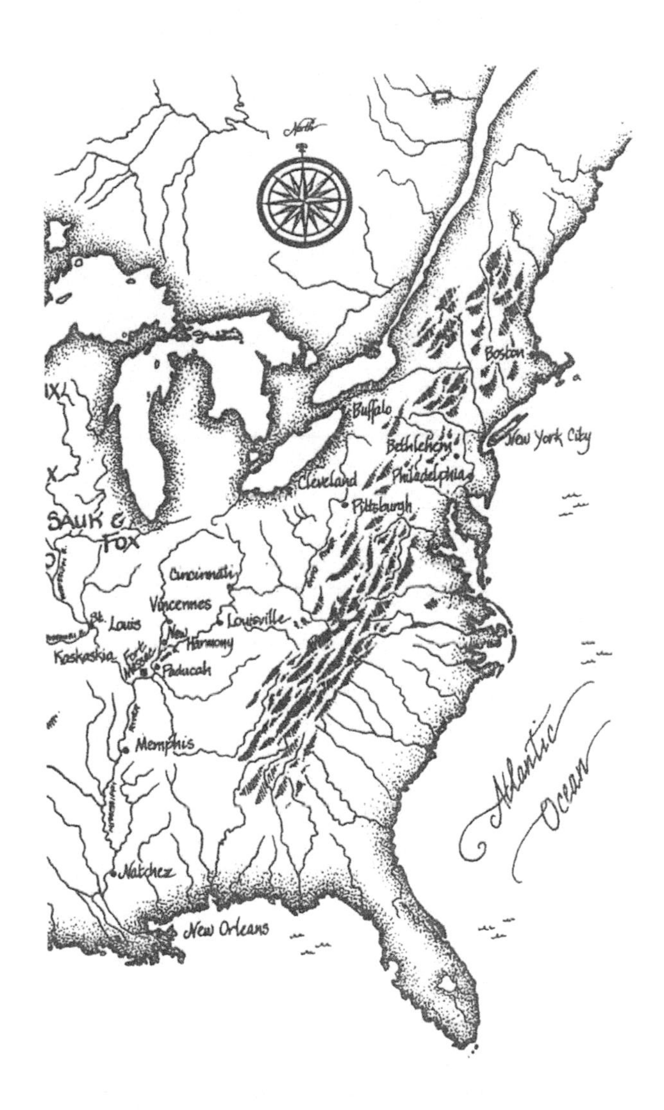
North
Boston
Buffalo
New York City
Bethlehem
Philadelphia
Cleveland
Pittsburgh
SAUK &
FOX
Cincinnati
Vincennes
Louisville
St. Louis
New Harmony
Kaskaskia
Paducah
Memphis
Natchez
New Orleans
Atlantic Ocean

North
Missouri River
Milk River
Musselshell River
Mouth of the Big Horn
Yellowstone
Crow Village
Big Horn River
Tongue R.
Powder River
High Wolf's Camp
Ainkahonobita
(Red Canyon)
Hot Springs
Red Wall
Snake River
Slim Poles Village
Green River
Willow Valley Rendezvous

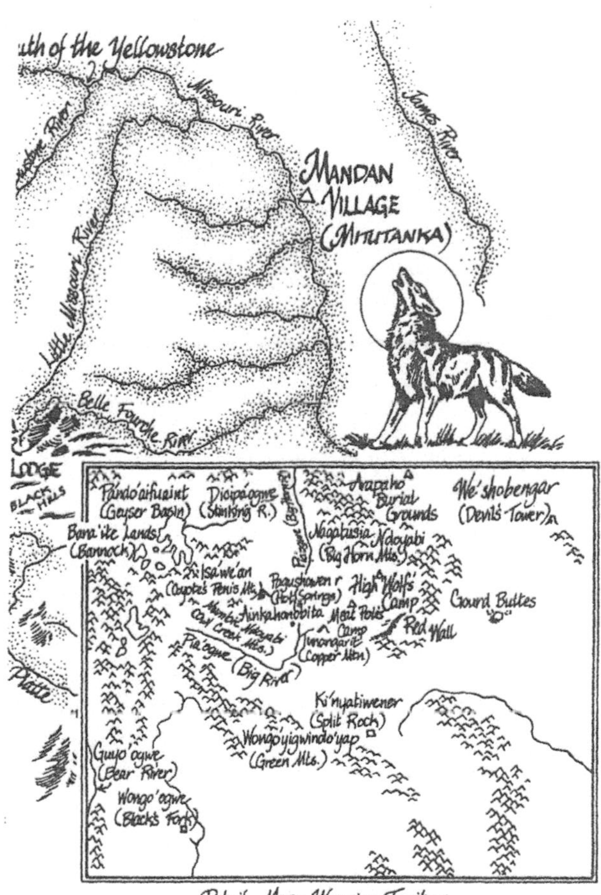

Detail Map: Wyoming Territory

CHAPTER ONE

...I conceive that in all deliberations; that is to say, in all alternate successions of contrary appetites, the last is that which we call will, and is immediately before the doing of the action, or next before the doing of it becomes impossible. All other appetites to do, and to quit, that come upon a man during his deliberations, are called intentions and inclinations, but not wills, there being but one will, which also in this case may be called the last will, though the intentions change often.

—Thomas Hobbes, *Leviathan*

Willow sat bolt upright in her robes. Beyond the protection of the rock overhang, the wind whistled through the rocks and whimpered in the branches of the trees. Over the deep breathing of the sleepers, she could hear the blowing snow patter on the leather shelter wall. What had awakened her? Some subtle call to her souls?

Richard?

His image sifted through her thoughts, more unsettling than the dreams that had haunted her sleep.

Willing her souls to silence, she closed her eyes, stilling everything, seeking...and finding nothing.

He called to me.

She settled into the soft bedding again, and listened to the gusting night wind in the canyon below the *Dukurika* Shoshoni camp. Her father had located it high on the southern slopes of the Powder River Mountains. Where was Richard? At the mouth of the Big Horn? By now, Richard, Travis, and the rest should be building their post, perhaps with the *Maria* frozen into the ice. Or would they have drawn the boat up on shore?

She snuggled deeper into the warm hides, a smooth otter pelt against her cheek. In her imagination, Richard's brown eyes softened, that faint quirk of a smile on his lips. She could imagine his hand, reaching out to her with such gentleness.

Oh, Willow, how did he charm you so?

She tucked a fist under her chin, trying to understand. Everything about Richard was a contradiction. That incredible gentleness with which he looked at her; the terrible violence with which he'd fought Trudeau. A warrior who had taken trophies in battle, stolen horses, and fought with great courage; he had marveled at the colors in a sunset, or would mourn a wounded songbird. He had fearlessly looked into the eye of her soul and remained unaffected by her Power. But his desire to join with her under the robes had terrified him.

Richard, my Richard, you were always afraid of the wrong things, the inconsequential things. The terrible longing ached inside her chest.

She took a deep breath of the cold night air. A smart woman would take her time, find herself a good man, and resume her life. She would have children, raise them correctly, and praise her man for his hunting talent and all the other skills he excelled at. She would keep the fires warm and the food cooked, and finally smile with relief when her children turned into adults and moved off to start lodges and families of their own. *Tam Apo* had made the world that way. Such things were expected of a smart woman.

It's not a bad life, she reminded herself sternly. *I had started just such a life with my husband.*

Why did she resist doing it again?

"Because if my husband was stupid enough to dull an ax on a rock, I'd break a club over his head," she whispered.

The Whites had changed her opinions, showed her different strengths, and, at the same time, different weaknesses. She still couldn't understand how they could put God into a building. And the way they thought of women disturbed her deeply.

The truth is, Willow, that you've stepped between peoples, and now, neither one satisfies you. And the final question remained: *What do you really want?*

She tossed and turned, gnawing at the answer, and finding none. But in the process of shuffling longing against reality, she understood that when the winter broke, she would travel to the mouth of the Big Horn.

It's only to go and see them, she insisted to herself. *I'm curious, is all. I just want to know how they are doing. See what they've built.*

As the long hours of night passed, she began planning her route, and what she would take.

The wind howled throughout the endless night, and Richard alternately slept and struggled within his death trap. That afternoon, he had killed a yearling buffalo bull. He had skinned it, and as night had fallen, folded it hair-side in, and crawled inside. Only, when he'd awakened hours later and tried to turn over, he discovered that the deep cold had frozen the thick wet hide solid. It now clamped him like a vise.

The warmth of his body should have been sufficient to loosen the hide, shouldn't it? But the relentless cold had frozen the thick skin into something like iron.

If only I hadn't tucked myself in so tightly. He tried once again to draw his arm back so he could reach his belt knife. No amount of straining helped. The wet green hide, covered with stringy tissue and bits of muscle, cocooned him like an iron maiden.

Another gust of wind stirred the air. He shifted as much as he could in the glovelike tightness and stared past the frost-matted buffalo hair above his head. A faint light was visible. Morning had come. Trembling with effort, he gasped and relaxed.

What if it shrinks? I'm going to be squeezed to death.

The image of rawhide, sewn wet around a cracked rifle stock and allowed to shrink dry, reminded him of just how strong even thin hide could be. He'd seen Indian hammers held together the same way.

Panic lent him renewed energy as he pushed down with his legs. Despite his wiry strength, he made the barest of progress as he wedged his feet down.

Panting, he strained to reach his hip, fingers brushing the knife handle ever so briefly. He just couldn't get his arm back far enough, despite cramping his muscles.

Closing his eyes, he sucked deep breaths to fight the sick feeling in his gut. If only there were a way to get some leverage. Out of the question since he lay curled on his side like a baby.

Worse, his bladder began to nag at him. His urine would only add to the trouble, spreading out, chilling and leeching warmth from his tired body.

I won't have time to be squeezed to death. As I get hungry, I won't make heat. The cold will get me first.

If only the buffalo wool didn't insulate so well. But then he'd have frozen to death.

Think Richard. Use your noodle. Where's the way out?

"If it had snowed hard last night, or if that airhole had been downwind, the snow would have covered it and I'd be dead already. God, what a fool I've been."

As the light grew brighter, Richard continued to twist and push, and finally drifted off to sleep, defeated.

Curious fragments of dreams tortured him. Images of his father mixed with those of Travis, Dave Green, and Baptiste. Out of the twisted collage, he could hear the old Sioux *wechashawakan* laughing at him. Woven in were images of dead men, their bodies blasted apart. The listless eyes of the Blackfoot boy stared at him, uncomprehending, soul-dead before Richard's rifle shot blew the brain out of his head. In the background, Laura was sobbing, the dull ache of her grief almost palpable.

Sound, coupled with curious vibrations, brought him awake. His heart, already pounding from the dream, beat harder. There, that sound! He could feel a sensation, like scratching, through the hide at his back.

And then, something puffed—an animal's exhalation. Listening carefully, he could hear soft feet on the snow. The sniffing sound came again.

Craning his neck, he could just see the black tip of a nose at the airhole. Then came the sound of scratching again, like a dog's.

Wolves!

"Get away!"

Silence.

A shadow moved across the airhole. Richard twisted, surprised that he could move further than before. Hopping and jerking like a fish on the bank, he forced his left hand around to his hip, fingers slipping off the wooden knife handle. Just a little more. He grunted with effort, body trembling. Ignoring a painful cramp, he got a tenuous grasp on the knife handle. He exhaled, driving all the air from his lungs, and wrapped fingers around the handle. With a mighty jerk, he pulled the knife partway from the sheath.

One more time.

He gulped air, charged his lungs, and exhaled until he wheezed. He jerked again. A little further.

That's it. Come on!

He wrenched the blade free, and gasped in relief.

Careful now, don't cut yourself.

He wiggled, changing his grip on the knife, slipping it up along his body. The blade had bent, and God alone knew what he'd done to the sheath. Well, at least he hadn't cut his hip open in the process.

He had to hold it by the curved blade—cramped as he was—and work the tip into the thick hair above his shoulder. Using it like a drill, he twisted the point back and forth. Hair rasped and gave, the hide making a hollow sound. In sudden victory, he slid the blade through and into the air beyond. Changing his grip to the handle, he sawed. Ice-stiff, the hide resisted. Richard worked diligently.

As the slit lengthened, he pressed upward, levering himself around, and managed to get a better grip on the knife. His fingers cramped and ached; his bladder shot pains through his pelvis.

Come on. Almost there. His slit was nearly a foot long now, and the hide had some resilience. If only he weren't running out of room. The further he got from his original hole, the more the hide restricted his movements, and the slower his progress, until his cuts were mere jiggles of the blade.

He backed the blade through the clinging skin, twisted it around, and began cutting upward, working within inches of his chin.

Stopping to rest, he cocked his head. The wolves were silent. Had they gone, or were they watching—waiting?

He flexed his fingers, and resumed working until he once again ran out of space.

How far had he cut? Two feet?

Richard shifted around as far as possible, braced his shoulder, and pushed. Light filled his trap. Laughter bubbled up with excitement, and he pushed again, seeing a good four inches of gap. He pulled his feet up, got the leverage, and shoved with all his might. With a knee for a brace, he grabbed the knife, sawing desperately until he could wiggle around and pry the hide apart with his hands.

Like a worm from a nut, he poked his head out and twisted, half sprawling atop his death trap.

He staggered to his feet and stared around. The wolves were there, fifteen of them, no more than thirty yards away; They watched with wary amber eyes. The buffalo had been gnawed to bloody bones. They'd ransacked his meat pack, chewed the antelope hide to ribbons, and the gut pile was gone.

Richard attended to his bladder, laughing and chortling to himself as he stared up at the slanting sun so low in the southwest. He'd been trapped in there for almost an entire day. The wind had brought warmth, enough so that the sun's heat could soften the bloody skin atop the hide. Not much, but just enough.

And but for the wolves, I would have slept through it, missed my opportunity.

Richard relaced his pants and picked up his rifle and possibles. He stared at the buffalo hide where the snow had drifted around it. It looked like a pastry dough folded in half, hardly the terrible trap that he'd just escaped. But if the wind hadn't come, and the cold hadn't broken...He shivered at the thought.

"By God, I'll never do that again." He turned to the wolves, who'd backed ever farther. "Sorry, coons. I'm not your meat this time—but it looks like you've had a fill of mine." Then he bowed to them. "Thank you for waking me up. I owe you my life."

From their expressive eyes and cocked heads, he could almost believe they understood him. Then a small gray one wheeled and trotted over the rise, bushy tail bobbing. One by one, the others followed, some casting final glances back at him.

Richard stepped across to the carcass, and used his bent knife to chisel meat scraps from the bones. Measuring the length of afternoon light, he went about the task of twisting up sagebrush, and dipped into his little tin of charred grass. With the strike-a-light, he started a fire and collected snow in the tin cup.

The idea of eating meat with wolf spit on it caused only a moment's hesitation before he chopped it up and put it in his pot to boil.

As darkness fell, he pried the slit hide apart with his rifle barrel and crawled into his cocoon. This time he'd sleep warm and be able to escape the next morning.

"What's you brooding so, foah, Travis? It ain't like you." Baptiste inspected him with curious eyes, the long stem of his pipe clamped in his teeth.

They slouched against the willow backrests in Two White Elk's lodge, a crackling fire in the hearth. Two White Elk's wives were playing a game of tickle with the children. The old woman sat in her place before the lodge door, studiously sewing a pair of moccasins and humming a song under her breath.

"Wal, who else would it be like? If'n I'm a-doing it, it otta be like me." Travis snorted, his cold pipe cradled in his hands. He rolled the stem back and forth in his fingers, staring into the stained bowl, then relented. "I keep wondering, is all. Hell, I shoulda sent Dick back on Atkinson's boats. That coon'd be ter Saint Loowee by now."

Baptiste stretched a buckskin-clad leg toward the fire and shrugged. "Cain't tell. A man does what he does. So, why're you stuck on Dick when you could be crucifying yourself fo' all the rest, too?"

"The rest of us, we knew what we was signing on fer. They's old hands, every one of 'em. Dick, why he was just a Doodle, and it was plain dumb luck got him inta this fix."

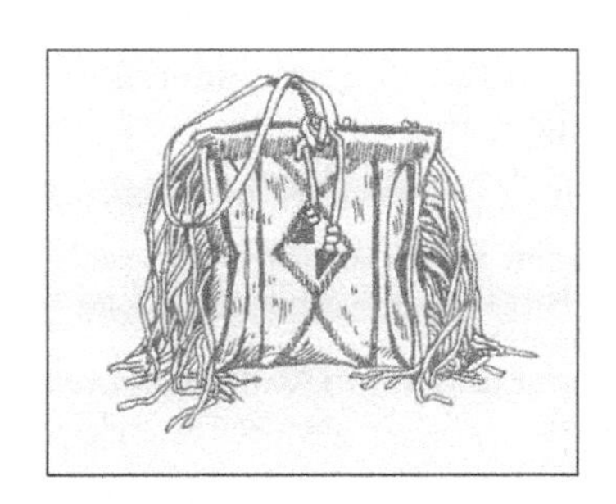

Baptiste leaned back on the robe-covered backrest and sucked on his pipe, then let two streamers of blue smoke twine out of his nostrils. "You give him a chance, Travis. Let him choose. He figgered to stick it out with us. And by that time, he know'd the risks. Reckon if'n he's gone beaver, he done made that choice hisself."

"Hell! I made it fer him. Sure, I told him ter go, and then I looked him in the eye with that look I got, the one that says, If'n ye don't choose right, yer shit. And Dick never wanted no one to think he's shit."

"And what makes you think he's gone beaver? Hell, maybe he holed up somewhere and rode her out."

Travis pinned Baptiste with a hard eye.

"All right." Baptiste scratched his ear. "Believe what you wants. But figger this. He might have been a pilgrim to start with, but he had some fine larning on the way upriver. Now, shoah 'nuff, that coon had some queer ideas, but he had a plumb smart head on his shoulders. He larned quick, he did. Took to it like a fish to water when he warn't locked up in nonsense thoughts."

"Yep. That he did. I just wish ter hell I'd sent him back on Atkinson's boats."

"You couldn't ,and you knows it. Travis, life gives men a chance if'n they'll take it I took it and so far I'm prime beaver. Dick took it, and he made his own way. So far as I recollect ain't nobody told him it would be poseys and fat cow. Ain't nothing fo' certain, Travis. Not fo' you, me, nor any other coon. So Dick's gone under? By God, Travis, he lived afore he did."

"That he did."

"Ain't that what it's all about?"

"Yep."

"And yor going up to find Willow come spring?"

"Uh-huh."

"Wal, I reckon I might's well ride along. Keep you from moping when yoah eyes otta be peeled."

"Did I ever tell ye that yer a sassy neck chopper?"

"Reckon so." Baptiste paused. "I got other news."

"What might that be?"

"Heard tell from ol' Badger Hair that he run inta a trapping party down south, that they told him Ashley's gonna have him a rendezvous."

"A what?"

"A rendezvous. Remember all them packs of beaver he took downriver?"

"I ain't likely ter fergit."

Baptiste leaned forward, a keen light in his eye. He tapped the buffalo robe with his finger to make his point. "Wal, he's a gonna use all that beaver to buy supplies. Powder, shot, foofawraw, traps, all the things a coon needs."

"That ain't news, Baptiste."

"Depends on how you reads sign. He ain't taking it to no post. He ain't putting it on no boat. Instead, he's outfitting a brigade. Gonna bring it all on hossback to someplace down on the Green River, or some such. He's got trappers out all over the mountains a-trapping plews. They's all coming together next summer fo' a rendezvous, and Ashley's gonna trade fo' fur. Like bringing a whole post *to* the mountains, coon. And this child's gonna be there with a load of fur. No boats, no river...and no Saint Loowee. Just trade at the Rendezvous, and Ashley worries 'bout getting the shitaree back."

"It'll never work."

"I figger it will, and I'm fixing to ride down there and see fo' myself. So, let's go see Willow and her kin, trade what we can in the meantime fo' plews, and give it a throw."

"Yer sassy all right!" But deep down, he could see how the whole thing might work. Assuming Ashley made it across fifteen hundred miles of hostile plains.

"Shit! I ain't nothing you didn't teach me to be. And God alone knows what you taught Dick." Baptiste gave him a smile. "So I ain't burying him till I knows better."

"But I'll say ye ain't betting on seeing him again either, lessen it's as a pile of bones."

High Wolf's people held the *Ap'ene Kar,* the midwinter Father Dance, on the flat caprock above the camp. Here, on the edge of the canyon wall, the horizon was visible, as well as the entire vault of the sky.

Wood had been carried in, the firepit cleaned out, and a new fire laid. Beside it, the sacred cedar tree had been placed. Rock Hare, Many Elk, and High Wolf had gone out four days before, ritually scouted, and finally "killed" the tree. Then they'd offered prayers to the tree's soul, chopped it down, and dragged it to the dance ring where, propped on all sides, it now stood.

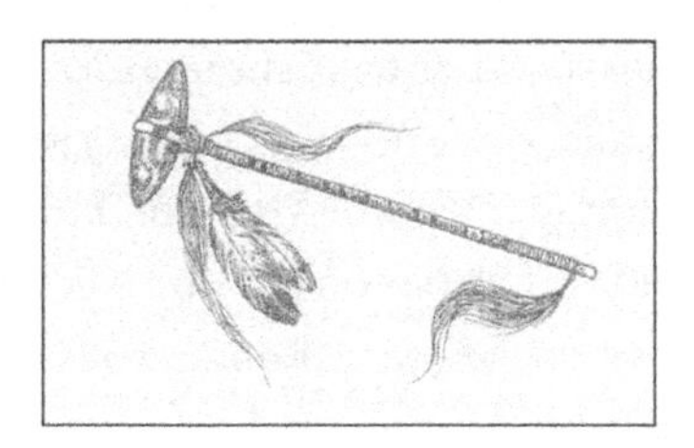

The people had tramped the snow flat, and the few scrubby sagebrush that might impede the dance had been twisted out. Then, just as the sun slid behind the western horizon, the fire had been lit.

Now the people stood in a circle around the roaring fire. They were dressed warmly in sheephide coats, thick moccasins, and warm buffalo or elkhide robes. Excitement gleamed in the eyes of the children, and men and women held hands. The last glow of sunset had left the western horizon. Stars packed the crystal-cold night sky. All eyes had turned to the horizon where a new glow could be seen across the ragged snow-mantled peaks.

As the first sliver of moon cleared the peaks, Eagle Trapper thumped a long drumstick on the big round drum. The instrument was as wide as a man's arm, the head stretched tightly over the wooden cylinder and bound with rawhide strips. The resonant bass carried in the night, echoing from the canyon below. Even the stars seemed to dance to the beat. The dark trees absorbed the rhythm as it mingled with their snow-packed branches.

With the first throbbing beats of the drum, fires of memory stirred between Willow's souls. Excitement tingled within her. How long had it been since she'd danced the *Ap'ene Kar?* The bonfire devoured thick sections of pine that popped and showered sparks into the frigid night.

Each day during the last moon. High Wolf had climbed to the high places to watch the sun rise across the peaks, and marked off another notch on a slim section of elk antler he carried. Over the years, he had learned which peaks were illuminated on which days. So he counted his notches to be sure of the days in case clouds obscured the horizon on this, the most holy of days.

High Wolf always held the *Ap'ene Kar* on the winter solstice. Some *puhagan*s held the Father Dance during full moon, but High Wolf's vision had told him to hold it during the longest night of the year.

Willow stood in the circle with the rest, swaying in time with the music as Eagle Trapper beat the drum and sang the greeting song. From the shadowed depths of the forest came High Wolf, dressed in his finest clothing, his face painted in white and black streaks. He carried sage bundles in his hands, and shook them like rattles, in time to the drum. With each shake he sent the plant's healing Power in all directions. The people parted and he walked into the center of the dance ring. There, he lifted his head to the cold night sky. For a moment, he seemed to reflect on the cold heavens. Then he opened his mouth and began to sing the familiar old songs.

Willow and the rest closed the ring, men alternating with women. Her feet seemed to move of their own accord to the rhythm of the song. Around her, the people lifted their faces, sang, and danced in the shuffling step of the Father Dance. Across the ring, Red Squirrel was holding little Pika's hand as the child frowned and tried to imitate his mother's dance step.

That was how I learned.

Willow smiled at the thought, remembering White Alder's gentle hands on her shoulders. It seemed like forever since that day. Willow sang louder, her heart at peace—as if time had ceased for this one glorious moment.

In the beginning times, Coyote had been instrumental in the first Father Dance. He and the Hoodwinked Dancers had used it to banish disease and bring good health.

Tonight, it would do that for her people, and—High Wolf said—for the new year that would begin tomorrow at dawn. As the dancers circled in their shuffling step, High Wolf danced out from the center to shake his sage bundles at each person in turn, bathing them with the sacred essence. Willow's heart thrilled when her turn came. How long had it been since High Wolf had purified her and driven away the little evils that clung to her?

Too long.

For that brief moment. Willow surrendered herself to the swaying beat of the drum, her souls twining up into the night sky as if to join the very stars. A lightness filled her breast, as if her own fire burned there and drove away the darkness.

High Wolf stopped the greeting song with a high yip. For a long moment the mountains were bathed in silence. Then Eagle Trapper hammered the drum, and High Wolf began the Water Song. As his lilting voice rose and fell, the dancers picked up the beat and resumed their endless circling.

Willow might have left her body, floating in the cold air, seeing the world through happy eyes. *Home...I'm home again. The world is set right once more.*

She hadn't realized how much she'd needed this healing, how parts of her souls had become disjointed. In a world turned strange and uncertain, she could forget her worries and follow the familiar patterns of a life nearly forgotten.

I am one with my people.

For the dance went back to the beginning of time. She stood now as each of her ancestors had once stood.

In her *mugwa*'s eye, she could see them, feel them, dancing as she danced. The continuity reassured her. Time might not have been. No past or future, only the eternal now of the dance, of her souls swaying with the music.

One by one, they sang and danced the Water Songs, and High Wolf told the stories about Coyote after the Creation. How he found the first women, desired them, and how he had to break the teeth out of their vaginas before he could copulate with them to create people.

For once, Willow didn't smile at the story. Was that why Richard feared laying with her?

Even in the silliest of stories, you will find truth if you look hard enough.

She shook her head.

So, where does the truth hide in Richard's stories about Adam, Eve, and Mary?

High Wolf paused beside her, staring at her from the corners of his eyes. "Such a look, *peti.* Tell me, which malignant spirits are you wrestling with this time? And on a night of healing, too."

She lifted an eyebrow. "I'm sorry, Father. I was thinking about stories, and how, even if you don't believe they happened the way they were told, they still teach you things. Even now, at my age, I find something new in them."

He gestured for her to accompany him and walked away from the circle of rapt listeners. Many Elk had taken the place beside the fire and the sacred cedar tree, and was now telling the story about Cottontail Rabbit shooting the sun. In the leaping firelight, the faces of the children beamed with excitement, while the adults smiled knowingly at each other.

High Wolf led her to the edge of the canyon, and

stopped. He stared over the chasm to the southern horizon, masked as it was by a black picket of conifers. "Willow, tell me what a person is."

She tugged her buffalo robe tight against the chill, and followed his gaze across the distance. "A person? Um...a human. Two-legged. A man."

"Not a woman?"

"Maybe a woman."

"Not a child?"

"Maybe."

"An elder?"

"Yes, of course."

"An infant?"

She shrugged. "Sometimes...after it's lived long enough to gain a *mugwa*."

"Then, all these things—infant, child, youngster, man, woman, elder—are persons?"

"Of course. What's the meaning of this?"

"To teach you something, *peti*. That everything changes."

"I see."

"Do you?"

She exhaled wearily, watching her white breath rise. "Our perception of truth, of life, of the world itself, changes as we do, *appi*."

"Nothing is fixed, Willow. Not the stars, the sun, the mountains, or the very rock in *Tam Segobia*'s breast. Tell me, did you expect to find everything pegged in place, unchanging?"

"No, never, but I know someone who does."

"Then he is a fool."

"No, Father. Not a fool. He has just been taught wrong, that's all. Like a child who has been told all of his life that water runs uphill, he can't quite allow himself to believe what he sees with his own eyes. When I left, it was driving him mad."

"The measure of anyone. Willow, is how they adjust to the changes in the world. How about you, Daughter? Have you learned to live with the changes?"

She took a deep breath, searching her souls. "I don't know, Father. Sometimes, like tonight, I am so happy to be home, sharing with my people. Then, at other times, I want to beat Rock Hare over the head with a digging stick, or slap Lodgepole for some of the nonsense things she says about White men, or *Ku'chendikani.* She's stupid, Father, like a grouse who thinks she's seen through a hawk's eyes."

He nodded thoughtfully, eyes still on the sky. "The girl who left here five summers ago to marry a *Ku'chendikani* was very different from the woman who has returned to me. You are still my *peti*, Willow. But now, I sometimes wonder who and what you are. I look at you, and sometimes, as tonight at the dance, I see the girl I knew. And other times, like now, I hear a stranger talking with my daughter's voice."

"I've changed, Father."

"And I must try to adapt. But so must you, Willow. You fit here, among our people—but at the same time, you do not. What are you going to do, Willow? What are your plans?"

She lowered her head, shrugging her frustration. "I don't know, *appi.* I only know that I've changed. You're right about that. Sometimes...it's as if I were a leaf on the wind. Blowing, swirling, tossed here and there—and never knowing where I'm going to land."

High Wolf pursed his lips, eyes narrowed in the darkness. "I would not say such things aloud, girl. Those are not words to reassure those who already wonder at your strangeness."

"Am I strange. Father?"

He nodded. "I think you are a leaf on the wind—and it's blowing in a terrible storm. I just hope that it is not going to harm my people."

The joy, sparked within her during the Father Dance, had faded like the last embers of a dying fire. Each time she reached out to grasp a piece of her past, it seemed to dissolve like mud held underwater in a tightly gripped fist.

And soon, Willow, there will be nothing left to squeeze.

CHAPTER TWO

Nature is to be viewed as a system of stages, in which one stage necessarily arises from the other and is the truth closest to the other from which it results, though not in such a way that the one would naturally generate the other, but rather in the inner idea which constitutes the domain of nature. It has been an awkward concept in older as well as more recent philosophies of nature to see the progression and transition of one natural form and sphere into another as an external, actual process which is generally relegated to the darkness of the past.

This externality is precisely characteristic of nature: differences are allowed to disintegrate and to appear as existences indifferent to each other; and the dialectical concept, which leads the stages further, is the interior which emerges only in the spirit

—Georg Friedrich Wilhelm Hegel, *The Philosophy of Nature*

How great is the gulf between man and beast? When the extraneous trappings are stripped away, how different is the human being from his kin in the animal world? Is it a matter of size, or fur, or the shape of a foot? To those who know the rudiments of survival

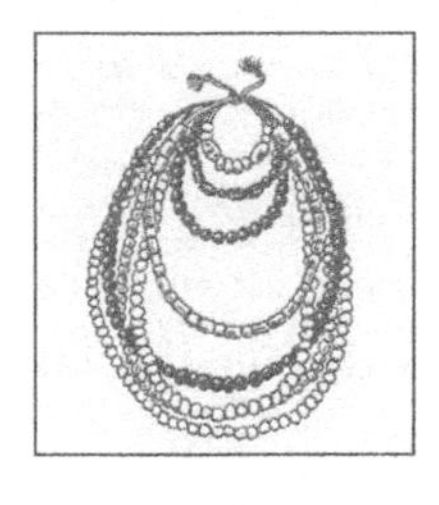

in a state of nature, they might say that the difference lies in dreams.

Richard huddled in a mat of moldy brown cottonwood, currant, and willow leaves that had blown into this protected warren last fall. His knees tucked tightly to his chest. He slept like a rabbit in a hole, just another creature hidden in the thermal shelter of the snow-cloaked brush under the embankment. Dried threads of last year's grass waved before his face, swaying with each breath. Muted sounds died in his throat. His closed eyes darted under their lids, seeing the dream with such clarity...

I have transcended myself, floating in the air like some sprite, looking down on my flesh from above. I should be awed by this experience, but for the moment, I am too concerned with what I see. How pitiful I look now, how empty and sodden.

My body is sprawled on its back in the snow, my skin alabaster pale and slightly blue. I look into my eyes, frozen open with milky gray exposed behind wide pupils. My limbs jut out like boards and my fingers clutch at nothingness, flesh puffy white. My mouth hangs open—stopped in mid-scream. I peer inside, and see ice around the stiff tongue, crystals sparkling on my teeth, all illuminated by the snow filling the throat.

Could this frozen meat really be me? I pull back, refusing to accept what my swimming senses tell me is true.

I must see this as something else, not really Richard Hamilton. I can't help but stare at this abandoned corpse as if it were a stranger's. The oak-hard flesh has taken on a pearlescent hue that contrasts with the frosted nipples. Crystalline ice glints in the curly chest hair, like little diamonds in the blue light.

He's cold, so damnably cold. I can imagine the bones inside, frost-cracked and splintered, with pink marrow puffed out. His heart must have stopped in midbeat, the blood solidified as it jetted. Cold...cold...forever.

I am fascinated by the gruesome expression of death and the corpse's stark contrast to the purity of the snow. Richard... Richard Hamilton...how did you come to this? Is this all that's left of life? Why, Richard? What's the purpose?

At that moment I sense the change. I glance around, seeing nothing but hazy white fog around me. The cold presses down like a weight, bitter and powerful.

The silence is broken by the faintest groaning sound—like ice being crushed between molars. Fear tickles within me, for the sound comes from the hollow just below the ribs. I see movement, and a crack ruptures the bluish-white skin. It opens slowly, pulling the stomach apart, running down toward the ice-encrusted navel and widening to expose an inky blackness.

I try to back away from the midnight eternity, wishing only to turn and flee. Instead, like a fly trapped in honey, I can only stare at the gaping tear in the corpse's belly. That is when I discern the faintest of white sparks—a tiny twinkling that becomes a minute star gleaming in the blackness.

With unexpected suddenness, the star splinters. Glasslike shards of light explode in all directions, and there, in its place, a slender stem of green rises out of the darkness. The shoot grows with slim grace. A single spear of verdant life that ascends from my dead body's gaping black gut to unfold tendrils. From them leaves uncurl, vibrantly alive. At the tip, a bulb forms, swells, and finally bursts forth in a bloodred rose that pulses with color and fragrance...

Richard jerked awake in his leaf-filled hollow under the bank. Afterimages of the dream burned in his memory—as intense as if he'd really seen it. How macabre! He snorted in irritation and threw his stiff hide to one side. Powdery snow cascaded from the branches and onto his warm flesh.

Gasping, he ducked out from under the overhanging brush and into the creek bottom. From a leaden sky, snow fell in tiny crystals, adding to the endless white.

"God help me." Richard rubbed his face with blood-stiff mittens and shook his head. The warm spell had lasted no more than three days. Time enough for him to travel southward to this tree-sheltered valley with its plentiful supply of wood. The day before he'd shot another buffalo, a young cow, and skinned it for the hide. He'd managed to cobble together a warmer outfit.

As his dream self had just done, he glanced down. His living body was encased in wrappings. Cut so carefully, each piece had been tied on—hair-side in—like a medieval knight's armor. He'd crafted thicker moccasins from the heavy hide that covered the buffalo's forehead, and stuffed them with more buffalo hair for warmth. He'd added another layer to the hat Travis had made for him.

"I look like an overstuffed doll." Bits of dried and frozen flesh still clung to the hide, having resisted his attempts to scrape it clean.

He kicked his sleeping robe out of the leaf mat he'd piled atop it, and considered the thing. In the beginning, he'd worn it, hair-side in, like a cloak, and, green hide as it was, it had frozen into his general shape, conforming to his head and shoulders. The result was something like wearing a part-time tent—heavy, immobilizing, but warm.

In the ash of last night's fire, he found embers and stoked them to life. On the flames, he cooked a mixture of liver, heart, and backstrap for breakfast. Snow obscured the mountains to the west, but he knew pretty much where he was. The highest peaks were behind him now. But progress had slowed. As he traveled south, the terrain grew ever rougher.

"I'm all right," he told himself. "As long as I have a rifle, a knife, and can make fire, I'm all right." His lips pursed as he watched the meat cooking.

Travel had become a ritual. Walk too fast, and the cold air burned his lungs, or he started to sweat. Go too slow, and the chill ate into him. Each night he found a sheltered spot to make camp, start his fire, dry his moccasins, and cook his meat. He'd char grass stems to replace the ones in his tinderbox, and eat his meal. Shelters were cobbled together from brush, or dug into the leaf mat under fallen trees—anything that broke the wind and provided a little extra warmth.

Sleep itself had become an art. Some inner sense woke him if his feet became too cold, and he'd stamp them back to life. God preserve him if they froze. He'd heard enough stories in New England about blackened flesh and amputation.

"Just be careful," he told himself over and over. "Don't take any chances. You're still alive. Though no one would believe it. Hell, I don't myself."

The important things were fire, knife, and rifle. With those, he was beginning to believe he could survive anything.

He broke camp, walked over to the stream, and studied it. Most of the channel was frozen over, snow glaring on the ice.

"Take no chances." He repeated the phrase—his mantra of survival—as he turned westward, seeking a safe ford. If he got wet now, in cold like this, he could freeze before he could make a fire.

By midday he had found his crossing—a place where a gravel bar had braided the channel—and crossed the shallows without mishap. But which river? The Powder?

The clouds were breaking overhead as he trudged up

out of the valley. The eternal Big Horns lay to his right. A giant slab, like one of God's shoulders, rose into the cloud-shrouded heights, and behind it, the mountain's slope lessened.

"Travis said the slope wasn't as bad the further south you went." Well, he'd have to go a way farther before he could scale the likes of that.

Richard followed the ridges; there the climb was easier, and the snow not as deep.

Snow had become as normal to him as sunlight or wind. He lived in a world of powdery white, wary of its glare at midday, frightened of its hidden danger. At times the wind kicked up, and the world vanished in a hurricane haze that staggered him. It blew fine granules of snow into every nook and cranny, seeking to rob him of warmth and life.

On sunny days he cast a shadow that brought insane laughter bubbling into his throat. What he saw resembled no human shape, but something headless and monstrously humpbacked, wrapped in stiff hides and tied together with brittle tendons and stripped ligament.

"'Just like ourselves,' Socrates said, 'For, first of all tell me this: What do you think such people would have seen of themselves and each other except their shadows?'" Richard finally understood, too, the incredible richness of Plato's Allegory of the Cave.

And what sort of being is this monster cast upon the snow?

He'd look at his shadow and ask, "What is your nature, dark being? A repository of the highest human thoughts, or a terrible beast that slays to eat, gorging himself on raw flesh and hot blood? A killer who stalks the wilderness?"

Then he'd bark an insane laugh, crying out, "By God, *both!*" And in that lay the ultimate irony. "What," he'd croak, "is the measure of man?" And "Know thyself!" More maniacal laughter would follow.

One hill led to another, each a little steeper than the last. On the heights, he'd brace himself against the cutting wind and study the route ahead. Sometimes he had to work over sections of rimrock—chipped and worn from time—before picking his way around tumbled boulders that had fallen from above.

The slopes were brush-covered, and occasionally, he jumped herds of deer that bounded off, only to stop and stare at him, their huge ears spread wide.

"Where am I going?" he asked himself. "Boston. That's where. Home." Wasn't it odd that the house on Beacon Street conjured only the most contented of memories?

If I were there now, I would sit by the fire and have Jeffry bring me a hot pot of tea. I'd stretch out in the big chair, roast my feet, and sip tea as I read. I'd be so warm. So wonderfully warm.

Phillip's fleshy face, the bulbous nose and sagging jowls, filled his mind. His father's hawkish gray eyes looked at him, curiously wounded.

"Don't never go agin' yer pap," Baptiste spoke from the past. *"Don't matter what's ahind you. I reckon it can be patched. If'n not, I reckon I'll trade you, 'cause you got a pap and I don't."*

"Can we do that, Father?" Richard asked Phillip's spectral image. He placed Phillip in a chair across the fire, and the old man frowned as he fingered his watch chain. *"Perhaps, Richard. I should never have sent you west, risked your life that way."*

"And had you never sent me, I would never have known what an arrogant fool I was, Father."

"We have both been fools, Son. You in your way, and I in mine."

"I never understood, Father. How lonely you've been. Blaming yourself for Mother's death. Never able to free yourself of the guilt." Richard blinked against the glare on the snow. What a terrible weight a woman could place upon a man's soul. And if he arrived at the *Dukurika* camp, and Willow wasn't waiting? "If she, too, lies dead out here someplace, can I ever forgive myself?" He shook his head. "Oh, Father, I do understand. God help me, give me another chance. Make Willow be waiting for me, alive, healthy. Let me see her again. With all my soul, I beg you."

Frowning with concentration, he pictured her face: There was her wry smile; her long black hair; and the sparkle in her gaze. Closing his eyes, he sniffed at the cold air, seeking her scent. He remembered the way she'd felt in his arms that day he'd killed Packrat. Her breast had brushed his arm so softly and caused a quaking of his soul.

"Remember how she pressed against me when we lay side by side in the water at the Grand Detour?" How he'd thrilled as his penis slipped along the curve of her hip. "Why didn't I mate with you when I had the chance, Willow?"

And if he found her again?

I'll wrap you in my arms and drown myself in you, Willow. I'll lie under the robes beside you, and hug you close. I'll look into your eyes forever, and marvel at their secrets.

He dared not anticipate the other images—fleeting sensations of the soul as he kissed her, ran his hands over her full breasts, and shivered as her warm skin touched his. When he had such thoughts, especially at night, his erection no longer embarrassed him.

And why is that? Tell me, Richard What's changed in you, in your principles?

"Reality," he'd whisper. "Somewhere along the way, the blinders fell off and I became a man."

And if you lie with her? How will you live the rest of your life? With Willow?

"No. I don't belong here. My place—my world—is in Boston."

And if you return and marry Laura? Will you look into her blue eyes and tell your wife that you've had carnal intercourse with an Indian woman? Or will you live with a secret?

"I don't know."

Then why is it suddenly morally acceptable to fuck Heals Like A Willow?

"It's not fucking. One doesn't 'fuck' the woman one loves."

Ah. Love, you say? Tell me, philosopher, what is love? Eros? Agape? *Or* Philos?

He balled a fist, looking at his inquisitive shadow. "Oh, don't try and twist me up in all the philosophical investigations of love. I know the arguments from Abelard to Zeno, just as surely as you do."

But what is it that you feel for Willow?

"Something of the soul, a sharing, a longing for her to be close, to share my life, to share hers."

But only for the moment.

"You know reality as well as I do, shadow."

Then you have fallen into the trap of utilitarian ethics. Since when did you become a follower of Bentham? Pleasure is good? What happened to your loyalty to the idealist ethics that you embraced from Kant, Fichte, and Hegel? You are no better than Menon trying to argue virtue with Socrates.

"Damn you! The problem with you—and all your book-bound philosophers—is that you are safe, surrounded by your cities, and laws, and constables." Richard squinted up at the pale white sun that hung low in the west. "Life is more elemental here, shadow monster. You seek Truth?"

Why else do I examine you?

"Truth, my friend, is food, shelter, warmth, companionship, and living to see another sunset. There, damn you. How much more elemental can you get? That's Truth."

You disappoint me, Richard. You used to be better than this.

"You can argue abstracts all you want over ale with other philosophers in safe, cozy Boston. This is the wilderness. The rules are different here."

What did you just say?

"I said the rules are different. We've forgotten what it means to be alive in the real world. Don't you see? Boston, America, Europe, the whole of it is removed from nature, living within the artificial security of the state and all its conventions and institutions. I am a man in love with a woman. What could be more right than that?"

And he paused, reaching the crest of a tilted slope and staring out over a sheer red cliff that dropped nearly two hundred feet to the gentle valley below. It extended north-south, as far as he could see. In the glaring light of sunset, the crimson sandstone blazed like blood.

In the distance, the cliff continued like a monstrous, crested wave of stone—a giant breaker turned to crimson rock. Nowhere did he see a trail down that sheer wall.

"Dear Lord God," he whispered, as if the sight and declaration were both gifts from the divine.

He took a deep breath, studying the land. Far to the south, he could see the dark bulk of yet another mountain, separated from him by an endless sea of choppy ridges. Across the valley, to the west, the sloping flank of the Big Horns rose to meet the afternoon sky. Juniper and pine dotted the long incline, the snow field mottled here and there by patches of gray brush and the infinite speckling of sagebrush. Turning, he looked to the north, where a thick bank of gray clouds masked the high peaks. Wispy stringers, the kind made by falling snow, feathered out from the bottom of the storm front.

He'd been so lost in his argument with himself, he'd failed to pay attention to the time, to the building storm in the north. Night would fall soon, and that brooding cloud-bank would roar down from the peaks.

"I think, Richard, that we'd better leave ethical dilemmas for the future and worry about getting off this ridge."

He turned southward, scrambling along the rocky crest of the cliff. Was it better to drop back down the eastern side to the sage-filled valley? But the wind was coming from the north. He'd find no adequate shelter there, not from a storm like this one fixed to be.

The sun had slanted behind the mountain, casting rays of yellow across the sky in contrast to the blue and purple shadows that loomed ever longer. The bloodred of the sandstone slowly dulled to maroon.

He'd followed the ridge's spine before he found the cleft: A crack as wide as his shoulders had split the forbidding rock like God's meat cleaver. Dirt, tumbled rock, and snow filled the slanting bottom. It appeared to offer a way down the red wall—or did it? What if he made it halfway down and it narrowed?

Richard growled to himself, plagued by indecision. "I can't afford a mistake...but then, I can't stay up here."

The light continued to fade as the storm dropped down from the peaks.

"God help me." He lowered himself into the crack, trying to brace himself against the sides. His frozen buffalo-hide cape cramped his movements. So did his cumbersome rifle and possible. He took a moment to shrug out of the cape and pitch it headlong down the gloomy fissure.

He was being swallowed by solid rock as he dropped into the darkness. Under his feet, stones slipped atop the frozen dirt. The walls narrowed, close as a coffin. *Blessed God, if this leaves me stranded on the cliff, I'm dead.*

With cold stones rasping his shoulders, he shimmied down the precarious slope. The next thing to go were his mittens. He tossed them down the chute. "I'll pick them up at the bottom," he promised. "Better to take the chance of losing one than to fall and break a leg." The Hawken had turned into an impediment.

If only he could pitch the rifle as well. Keeping a grip on the cold Hawken numbed his fingers and slowed his descent. Feeling with his feet, he placed each step carefully on the tumbled rock wedged in the bottom. If only he could use both hands.

"Don't slip, Richard."

And be careful.

He was deep into the crack now, and wedged his elbows to look back. A tightness formed in his throat. The earth had closed around him, cold and unforgiving as a tomb. He closed his eyes, gut sinking.

I've made a terrible mistake!

If only he didn't have to hang on to the rifle. Bracing himself, he lifted the heavy Hawken and slid it down the back of his shirt, thrusting the muzzle past his belt. The barrel burned cold against his hot skin, and the butt rested along the side of his head, but his hands were free.

Step by careful step, he lowered himself, unwilling to look down. He tested each handhold, cursing the hard wrappings of hide that hindered his movements. Feeling his way through the thick layers of moccasin he prayed each step would hold.

No doubt of it, the crack was narrowing. How far had he come? Fifty feet, seventy? Looking out, he could see the dusky sky growing darker by the second. The rock bore in on him like jaws, crushing his spirit with its ponderous weight

Swallowing hard against the dryness in his throat, he eased himself down, blocked his foot on a wedged rock, and shifted his weight onto it. Below him, pebbles rattled for what seemed an eternity.

What if this ends in a straight drop?

Don't...don't think it.

His possibles rasped with each movement. Wind-blown snow had collected here, adding to the treacherous footing. Craning his neck, he could look down between his legs. Perhaps twenty feet below him in the gloom, the crack opened out. But from there it was still a long way to the valley floor, and growing darker by the moment.

He wiped at the fear-sweat that had begun to dampen his face. He took another purchase, only to have his foot slip. Jamming his arms out, he clawed at the snow, and saved himself at the last minute. The rifle butt hammered the side of his head hard. Clinging to the rock, he trembled, panting.

You've got to move!

But terror had locked his muscles.

Come on.

Trapped!

Dear God, I'm trapped in the middle of the earth!

The ache in his cold hands finally overcame claustrophobia. Mustering courage, he tried again, kicking a foothold into the snow before slowly shifting his weight. Crabbing around, he lowered himself. His hands throbbed as he clutched the snow. His fingers were turning numb.

"You've got to go, coon. Lose the feeling in your fingers, and you'll slip for sure." Hitching his possibles around, he backed down, and thunked his temple painfully with the gunstock.

Why'd I do this? Better to have taken my chances on top.

Panicked, his clothing scraping the rock on either side, he scrambled another body-length down. The awkward rifle was pulling his shirt out so that cold air stole his warmth. What a terrible place to die, wedged here in cold, eternal shadow.

You're a fool, Richard. A damned fool!

He climbed over a rock that choked the crevice, then stole a glance over his shoulder. The crack ended just under his feet—and his heart sank. Runoff from the crevice had worn a narrow channel into bedrock the width of his hand, but to either side the anticipated ledge was nothing more than a bulge in the cliff. Richard carefully rolled over, only to have the rifle butt smack him painfully in the face.

He pulled the gun from his sagging shirt, and, puffing with exertion, leaned over to look down. The drop was at least fifteen feet before the ground began to slope. His cape hung in a juniper tree that clung to the scree. Wedging his elbows, he peered into the evening gloom. The first snowflakes came twisting out of the gray sky.

What now? He shivered from the cold, scared stiff by his predicament.

"You can do this, Richard."

Fifteen feet isn't so bad.

And the slope would give. Richard picked a place that didn't look as if it had too many rocks. He closed his eyes, unable to will himself to jump. His guts had that watery feel, and every nerve prickled. All he had to do was step out, and fall—but some stubborn instinct deep in his brain panicked and refused.

Richard, you must.

He resettled his possibles, gripped his rifle tightly in front of him...and jumped. For a split second, his stomach rose and tingled. Air rushed past him.

The impact stunned him, and he rolled. Lost the rifle. End over end, he tumbled down the frozen scree. Lights flashed in his eyes when he hit his head. With each thumping jolt, his breath huffed. A small juniper stopped him, and for a second he gasped, dazed, aware of the pain that shot up his legs. He lay there, terrified of what he'd done to himself. Then, choking with fear, he felt his ankles, moved his feet. Hands, arms, everything all right. Nothing broken.

He practically cried from relief, picking himself up to make sure he could walk despite the aches. The strap on his possibles had broken, and he limped back up the slope to pick up the spilled strike-a-light, tinder tin, awls, and other necessities. The rifle, he found it half-buried in snow. He grabbed it up, and started to run his fingers over the wood when his heart stopped in his chest. For the moment, all he could do was stare. The cock, made from cast iron, had been snapped off clean above the mounting screw, the metal edge pale and jagged.

He dropped to his knees, searching the scuffed snow with trembling fingers until he found the piece, flint still cradled in the leather-lined jaws.

Fear gave way to futile anger, and then to the horrible realization: The broken piece couldn't be fixed.

In mute defeat, he stood there as the snow settled soundlessly around him.

CHAPTER THREE

Now then, I want to give the proof at once to you as my judges, why I think it likely that one who has spent his life in philosophy should be confident when he is going to die… The fact is, those who undertake philosophy correctly are simply and solely practicing dying, practicing death, all the time, but nobody sees it. If this is true, then it would surely be unreasonable that they should earnestly do this and nothing else all their lives, yet when death comes they should object to what they had been so earnestly practicing.

—Plato, *Phaedo*

Breath puffing. Willow ran forward, feinted, and jammed her hip into Red Squirrel's with enough momentum to throw Red Squirrel off balance. In that instant, Willow caught the double-ball with her shinny stick and batted it in White Alder's direction.

With a growl, Red Squirrel launched herself at White Alder, her shinny stick held out like a baton.

They played on the snow-covered flats above camp, just back from the rimrock. The game was double-ball shinny, played on a field marked out over the distance of a bow-shot. The ball was sewn out of leather, stuffed with buffalo hair, and looked something like two wasp wings tied in the center. To win, one group of women had to fling the double-ball across the opponent's goal line.

Good Root had stolen the double-ball away from White Alder. Willow dashed forward. Snow flew as she blocked Lodgepole, twisted away, and scrimmaged with Good Root for the double-ball. Willow managed to snag it, and started forward, only to have Red Squirrel butt her from one side. As Willow staggered. Red Squirrel whooped and flicked the double-ball off Willow's stick to Good Root.

Huffing and gasping, the women ran in pursuit. Despite her aching lungs, Willow thrilled with the competition. It had been years since she'd played, but many of her old skills weren't forgotten. She caught up with Good Root, used a side-armed strike, and knocked the double-ball from Good Root's stick.

Sweet Grease cut in, snagged the ball with her stick, and flipped it across the trampled snow back to White Alder, regaining the ground they'd just lost to Good Root.

Willow sprinted back the way she'd come, angling to one side and shouting to her mother. White Alder saw, made the pass, and Willow artfully caught the ball. From some last reserves, she tucked a shoulder, bulled Red Squirrel out of the way, and sent the double-ball bouncing across the boundary.

Yipping like coyote pups, her team came together—

jumping, ripping the air with their shinny sticks, and pounding each other on the back. Lodgepole, Red Squirrel, Good Root, and their girls muttered among themselves, as they bent over and panted for breath.

"Good game," White Alder wheezed. Then she, too, bent over, panting for breath.

Willow grinned at her teammates, flushed with excitement. She wiped the sweat from her forehead, and sucked air into her starved lungs.

"You haven't lost any speed," Sweet Grease told her, patting Willow's shoulder. "We haven't beaten Lodgepole in how long? Three winters?"

"Three at least," White Alder agreed, straightening and flipping one of her braids over her shoulder. "It feels...well, real good. Good indeed, after all these years of listening to those old grouse clucking to each other." White Alder winked. "Good to have you back, *peti*."

Willow nodded, and started toward the sweat lodge, plodding through the deep snow on trembling legs. In the chill air, she'd begun to cool down just as they reached the domed lodge back within the trees. There, a fire burned like a sooty eye in the packed snow. Hot stones were piled in the middle of the blaze. The little girls, too young to play with the adults, had kept the fire hot.

"That Willow," Lodgepole grumbled as she walked up, "she's half wildcat."

"All wildcat," Red Squirrel complained as she pulled her dress over her head. Steam curled up from her sweaty skin. She winced, and massaged her left breast. She glanced at Willow, and grinned. "That was a hard elbow you hit me with. If Rock Hare gets too friendly tonight, I might just make him sleep in the snow."

"He doesn't need to play with your breasts to do what

he's going to want to do," Sweet Grease said as she pulled her own dress off. "But then, given where I'm going to have bruises tomorrow, Black Marten might just have to sleep in the snow with Rock Hare."

Willow chuckled as she shucked out of her dress and ducked into the dark interior of the sweat lodge. The winning team got the rear of the lodge; the losers had to tend the hot rocks and steam.

Willow sat cross-legged beside her mother as the glowing rocks were carried in on smoking branches. Good Root recited the prayer for health, called for the blessing of the steam, and closed the flap to seal them into the darkness. Water trickled musically, then steam exploded in a violent hissing.

Willow closed her eyes, sighing as the steam clouded around her, soothing her tired muscles and aches, cleansing her body and souls. White Alder began to sing the sweat-lodge song, and one by one the women joined her, offering thanks to Power for the healing steam. When the song finished, they sat in silence until White Alder said, "Them two men from Black Storm's camp finally left today."

"Good," Red Squirrel muttered. "They were nothing more than walking appetites. It seems we've had to feed half the men in the mountains this winter."

"They always bring something with them," Sweet Grease reminded.

Willow ground her teeth, grateful for the darkness. The pressure had been growing. Nothing overt, just the ever more pointed references about the suitors who came, looked her over, and made their oblique offers. She let each one know that she wasn't interested.

Why, Willow?

She clamped her eyes shut, fists knotted at her sides as the sweat beaded and rolled down her skin.

"That Three Moons," Lodgepole said, referring to one of the men who'd left that morning. "If I were younger, why, I don't think I'd complain if he crawled into my robes some night. Quite the handsome sort, and did you see that smile? And the way his eyes twinkled when he told a joke?"

"I did." Good Root sighed. "And besides that, I caught a glimpse of him one morning. His *we'an* would take a two-handed hold."

"Is that all that you look for in a man?" White Alder growled.

Lodgepole chuckled. "Of course it is. Why do you think they called her Good Root? She's wanted one all of her life—and ended up married to Eagle Trapper!"

"His root is just fine," Good Root snapped back. "Five children prove it!"

Willow cocked her jaw, grateful for the lull as more water was sprinkled on the rocks. The curling steam thickened around her, stifling and hot. Water was trickling down her face, dripping from her nose, salty on her lips.

He *was* a handsome man. No, more than that, Three Moons would be the answer to any *Dukurika* woman's dreams. Tall and attractive, broad of shoulder and strong of arm, he'd been more than genial, he'd delighted everyone. His smile brought warmth, and the amiable gleam in his eyes had promised things most men would never have thought of: attention, helpfulness, and tender hugs on difficult days. Even White Hail had warmed to him, and they'd become fast friends. Willow had been surprised to discover that White Hail had told Three Moons stories about her husband, about the sort of man he'd been.

Three Moons's charm had even conquered High Wolf. More than once they'd sat up late at night discussing the stars, and the ways of animals, Three Moons asking the old *puhagan* serious questions.

Would it have hurt to have been polite to him?

Willow wrinkled her nose, letting her shoulders sag.

"Enough," Lodgepole finally stated, and threw the flap back. "I'm going to rub myself dry and go see what those lazy men have come back with. No doubt they've killed something big and want to brag about it."

"They don't want to brag about it to us," Red Squirrel declared as she slipped out into the afternoon. "They just want us to cook it for them."

"Sure they do," Good Root agreed as she ducked outside. "But they want us to praise them and their skill at the same time. It makes them feel better. And for some reason, men need all the praise they can get."

One by one the women stepped outside to scrub their hot skin with crusted snow. Sweet Grease settled the flap after she left. Only White Alder and Willow remained in the hot darkness. White Alder leaned forward and sprinkled more water on the hot rocks. As the steam worked its magic on their sweltering bodies, the voices of the others became ever fainter as they walked back to camp.

"I need a little longer in the steam," White Alder said. "It's good for my bones. My joints and muscles don't hurt as bad the next day."

"You amaze me," Willow said gently. "My mother, and you look and act more like an older sister."

"Huh! Well, you should feel me on the inside, girl."

"I did, once, long ago. I can't remember what it was like."

"Being in the womb? I don't think anyone does. It must be pleasant. I think that's why childbirth is always so difficult. Who wants to leave that nice warm place and come outside into the cold?"

Willow rubbed her hands over her arms to slick the water off. "Is that what people think I'm doing? Staying in the womb? Do they think I don't want to come out?"

"You tell me, girl. What do you want, Willow? I have to admit, I think I fell in love with Three Moons myself. At least a little. And I thought no man would touch my soul while your father was around."

"I liked him, Mother. He'd have made a wonderful husband."

"But not for you?"

She shook her head, and realized her mother couldn't see her in the darkness.

Perhaps White Alder didn't need to. She said, "You have not slept well these last days. Last night, I listened to you. You were talking in a language I have never heard. None of the words made sense."

In English, Willow said: "Did the words I spoke sound like this? Is this the tongue you heard me speak?"

"What was that?"

"Did I sound like that in my sleep?"

"Maybe. I think so. Maybe not. It's all grouse squawking to me."

"Richard. I expect I was talking to him."

"Ritshard. You said that word. He's the White man, isn't he?" After a long silence. White Alder asked, "What happened to you, girl? Can I help you heal this thing inside you? Can your father?"

"No, Mother. It's not a thing to be healed. A *puhagan* can't blow it away with his fan, or suck it out with a hollow tube."

"Your father says you've been between worlds." In the darkness, Willow could feel her mother lean close, her voice a mere whisper. "He says that Power is growing inside you."

"Why do you lower your voice?"

"Because not all people have your father's tolerance. Is that what it is, Willow?"

"I don't know. Mother. Can't I just be left alone?"

White Alder leaned back to her place, silent again. At last she said, "I think you know how people are by now. What do you think? Will they leave you alone? You, a strong, healthy young woman?"

Willow clamped her eyes shut.

You've got to make a decision. Soon. Would life with Three Moons be so bad?

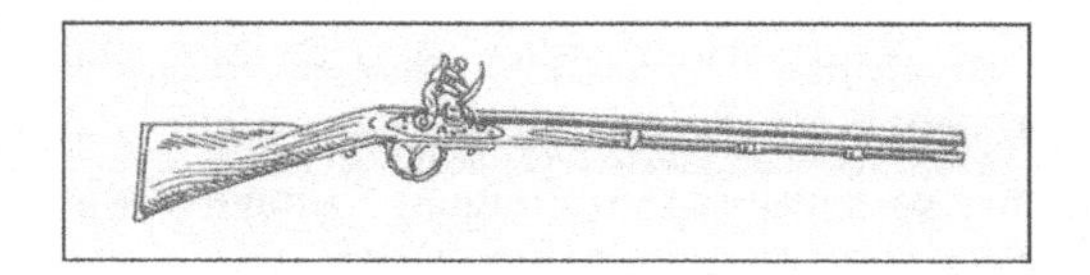

If only Richard didn't haunt her dreams. She could see him so clearly, hear him as if he were just beyond the dream soul's reach.

"It's the future that bothers me, Mother. But, yes, I'll make my decision soon. One way...or another."

The morning dawned brittle with cold. Richard awoke, horrible dreams spinning away in his mind. He uncurled from his robe and looked out at the world from under the base of a spreading juniper tree. He'd taken refuge there, sheltered from the wind and blowing snow by the shaggy branches.

He turned his attention to the cliff he'd fallen down the night before. Snow made patterns, delicate as lace, on the shadowed red rock. Eight inches of white covered the ground, creating a wilderness of beauty. Hard to think that death stalked those frigid blue shadows.

Still unwilling to believe his disaster, Richard picked up the frosted rifle. He closed his eyes, wishing with all his might—and opened them. The snapped metal still mocked him with its gleaming gray.

Every time he looked at the broken gun, his stomach turned.

He unwrapped himself from the frozen folds of his buffalo robe and winced at bruises suffered in the fall. He shook the powdery snow from his robe and shivered as white breath curled around him. His legs were tender, strained from their hard landing. He had a scab on the side of his head from the fall.

Heavy, deafening silence pressed down, unmarred by so much as a whisper of breeze or the flutter of a leaf. Nothing moved in this world of white. The land seemed to be waiting, watching.

Cold, desperately cold.

Richard slung his possibles over his shoulder—the strap knotted where it had broken—and tried to pull his frozen robe tighter. He pulled a piece of meat from his pack, shaved some with his bent knife, and popped it into his mouth. Chewing the tough stuff aggravated the bruise on his head. His rifle leaned against a branch. Leave it behind?

No, he resolved. *Maybe somewhere, somehow, I can fix it.*

With what, fool?

Nevertheless, he hefted the Hawken, feeling its weight. He'd clubbed men to death with it. Perhaps he could...He snorted at his ridiculous thoughts. As if a buffalo was going to walk up and let him club it to death.

Snow crunched under his moccasins as he turned, looked back at the red wall's sheer heights, amazed he'd survived the descent. If, in reality, he had. Breaking the rifle might have killed him as dead as a broken neck.

He rubbed frost from his frozen beard and looked up at the mountains. Where did he go to find Willow? Damnation! Her people could be anywhere.

Well, let's head south a little farther, and skirt the worst of the terrain.

He limped steadfastly forward, snow protesting underfoot. He was a mote—a single brown speck in an eternity of white. When he looked back, only footprints remained as mute evidence of his passing.

Alone.

He clamped his jaw. Nothing could prepare a man for this feeling of futility.

Don't give in to it, Richard. If you do, you'll sink down in the snow and die here.

The Hawken felt heavier, dead weight. Tears came to his snow-burned eyes. The rifle had come to be more than a piece of machinery, more like a friend who had buoyed, comforted, and fed him.

He clung to the cold steel and endured the relentless reality of punching one step after another through the dragging snow.

One step after another.

The massive weight of the wilderness bore down on him, fit to smother his fragile spark of life.

At midday, he cut deer tracks, stared absently at them, and plodded onward. Here a mouse had dotted the white as it scurried from one protective patch of sage to another. Later he saw where a coyote had trotted across the wide valley, but no sound broke the oppressive silence.

That night, Richard camped in a hollow created by an outcrop of rocks. After kicking the snow out of it, he built a small fire and squatted over it, nursing the flames with bits of sagebrush. As he dried his moccasins, he worshiped the fire. Extending his hands to the heat, he closed his eyes and let the warm smoke rise around him to bathe his face. If he lost his strike-a-light, he'd have nothing. Reaching into his meat pack, his fingers groped around the bottom.

Frowning, he lifted the pack and looked inside. Only bloody leather remained.

When did I eat it all? No, there's got to be more.

The slow realization dawned that he'd eaten all day as he walked. Pulling a piece of meat, slicing it, and chewing to keep his strength up, to keep his belly full.

"Richard, you didn't think." Instead, he'd drowned in self-pity over the broken gun.

Mistakes, too many mistakes. A smart man wouldn't have tried to descend the red wall. He'd have taken a chance on the storm, then gone around, looked for a safe way.

Too late...too late for everything.

Hollow-eyed, he stared at the glowing embers.

What now, Richard?

He swallowed hard and took a deep breath before answering, "Can't give up. I'll make do."

No, you won't. You'll die out here. Die...all alone.

He jammed a balled fist into his mouth and clamped his eyes shut, desperate to keep from sobbing.

That night, horrible dreams haunted his sleep...

Willow lay dead, scalped and gutted. Maggots wiggled in the wounds that mutilated her body When he touched her. the skin broke like a bruised tomato's, and putrid fluid ran out to stain the grass.

Phillip Hamilton knelt in his office, back bowed as he wept for his dead son. Guilt, so much guilt for one old man to bear. Finally he looked up, unseeing, into Richard's eyes and lifted that long-forgotten pistol to his temple.

"No! Father, no! I'm alive! You hear—alive!'

No shot accompanied the discharge of the pistol. Only a curl of flame and smoke that destroyed the image.

From the angry mists, a face formed: old One-Eye, the Sioux wechashawakan. He was watching Richard through that gaping socket where his right eye had been.

Wolves and coyotes circled in the darkness, watching, waiting, while the old Sioux medicine man laughed...

"I do not know if you will live, White man, but you will find your answers out here in the snow.'

Richard cried out, Tell me!'

But the image of the old medicine man blurred into a huge wolf, black as midnight. "The answers are in this world, and the next—if you are brave enough to seek them.'

"I am," Richard cried. 'I won't give up. I won't!'

He started awake just before dawn. In the distance, wolves were howling, their unearthly cries twining with his dreams until that world and this were indistinct.

He shivered in the cold, his thoughts in a Gordian knot. How did a man tell the difference between dream and reality? And, if he couldn't, did it really matter in the end? Was one reality more important than the other?

Richard shivered and stirred the embers in his fire. For long moments, he huddled over the flames, head cradled in his hands. The dreams had grown so powerful, the images frighteningly real. "Am I losing my sanity?"

His forced laughter sounded oddly harsh to his ears. Then, shaking it off, he scooped a handful of snow, picked up his possibles, and started along the slope. Plodding through the snow, he climbed as he went, seeking a high point to look for...what? Game? Smoke from someone's fire?

"I won't give up. I won't."

One step crunching after another. One, two, one, two...He dropped into the litany, plagued only by guilt and his nagging belly. Thoughts of tender roast beef, of steaming turkey, freshly baked bread, of chocolate and mint, swirled like fog through his mind.

"A chicken," he mused. "Roasted in a big pan, basted with butter, with onions and leeks, and lots of salt and pepper.

At midday the sun still hung low in the south, no matter how hard he wished it to rise higher and warmer. Step by step, he slogged through the snow; each swing of his feet nibbled at his reserves.

Food. I must find food.

He plucked leaves from sagebrush, and chewed them, then made a face as his mouth filled with the bitter flavor. Within minutes his head began to ache, and he spat to clear his mouth. He'd heard somewhere that headache was the first sign of poisoning. Who'd told him that? Henri, Baptiste?

Rosehips? He squinted across the sage-studded hills, seeing nothing that resembled brush. When he crossed the drainages—mocked by rabbit tracks—the serviceberry bushes and chokecherry stems were bare.

Food, I'll die without it.

But where would he find it? How long could he continue?

That night he used a fallen cottonwood in a brushy creek bottom for shelter; its branches fed his fire. Hollow-eyed, he watched the flames, and relived that last meal in Boston.

I skipped breakfast. Told Father that the sooner it was over, the better. I didn't eat. If I could just lick that plate now, I'd be eternally grateful.

Phillip had watched him with grim eyes.

If I could do it again. Father, it would be so different.

The next morning he started out, shivering and lightheaded. One step after another, he pushed on doggedly through the snow, slipping back and forth from a snowdrifted waste to a hot plain where he followed Travis Hartman's wavering form in pursuit of horses.

Blinking, he found himself sprawled face-down in the snow, shivering. Had he fallen? Sitting up, he gazed around, trying to determine where he was. Flickers of light, like dancing sparks, filled his eyes.

Lightheaded...I'm dizzy.

"Come on, Richard. Stand up. Let's go." He struggled to his feet, using the rifle barrel for a support. Another racking attack of shivers left him shaken and wobbly—and completely frightened by his weakness. He wiggled his toes. They felt cold, nothing like the misty warmth he'd heard tell of.

"Dear Lord God, don't let my feet freeze." He steeled his resolve and walked on, setting a distant knob as his pilot. He frowned, aware of the way the world turned watery. He couldn't think.

He squeezed his eyes shut for a moment and took stock. He was traversing a long slope, sage-dotted, and rising up to the west. He'd climbed high enough to have a good view of the land. To the east, endless ridges of bent and folded rock dropped away to the hazy Powder River basin. Southward lay the distant black peaks of yet another mountain range. The sky was so clear, azure to the north, unmarred by clouds. All about him, diamond sparkles reflected the weak winter sunlight.

He shifted the Hawken, hearing gurgling noises from

his hunger-cramped stomach. He'd been climbing for two days now, crabbing his way along the slopes. Just how high were these long hills?

Richard sighed, feeling slightly faint and nauseous. Resolutely, he tramped forward, watching his feet drive through the white crust to leave sharp-edged holes.

Food, Richard. You must eat, or die.

In the distance a herd of antelope watched, ears pricked. Finally a nervous doe flashed her rump patch and they vanished, spurts of snow flying from their feet

The sun was dipping low in the southwest, evening close, and the night's unbearable cold with it.

Tomorrow, I won't wake up. Too many of my reserves are gone.

He'd walked past the dead elk. Then stopped to stare at it. It had been an old bull. The guts had been eaten out by the wolves and coyotes; strips of hide hung from gnawed bones. White smears of raven droppings streaked the antlers. It stank to high heaven.

"Meat's meat, coon," Travis's voice reminded sardonically.

Moose or mouse? Wasn't that what Travis had said?

No, not carrion. Richard pinched his nose at the smell, and started on, making three steps...four...then he halted, blinking hard against the sensation of floating.

"Meat's meat, coon."

"How do I want to die? It won't be hard. I'll just lay down in the robe. Close my eyes. I've been shivering for months now. And then a person gets to feeling warm... warm and sleepy."

Willow's face hovered in the wavering afternoon light. Such a beautiful woman, her eyes glowing, her smile lighting for him. How terrible never to see her again.

He hung his head, turned around, and walked back to

the elk. "Meat's meat," he muttered hoarsely to himself. "Come spring breakup, Mandan eat drowned buffalo that float downriver under the ice. Eat it with spoons."

He used the rifle barrel to beat snow off the bones, and pulled his knife, looking for whatever the scavengers might have left. Around the putrid carcass, the trampled snow was covered with a powdering of loose hair ripped from what was left of the hide.

He screwed up his face and shook his head. "I can't do this. I can't."

He started to run away when the voice said, *You'll live, Richard.*

He swallowed hard, the empty knot of his stomach, the weak shivers in his limbs, reminding him of his weakness.

He took a deep breath and studied the knife in his hand. The blade was irrevocably bent. In weary defeat, he dropped to his knees in the snow and began hacking strips from the exposed pelvis and back ribs.

Next, he cut the ligaments around the joints and twisted the big leg bones loose before finally severing the tendons. One by one he laid them on the hard-packed snow, and with the rifle barrel, cracked them open.

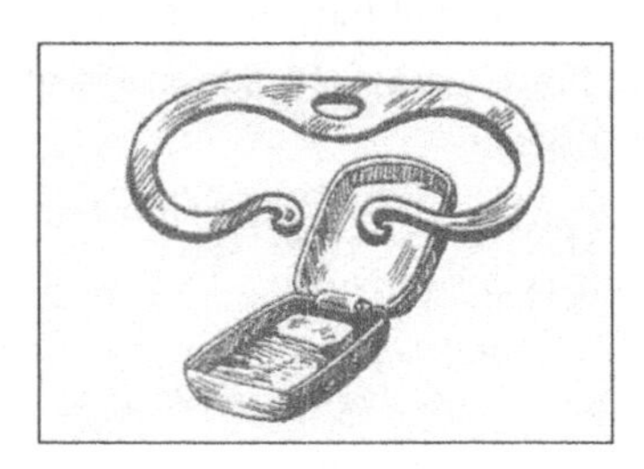

Splintered bones all around him, Richard ate. He started slowly, placing a lump of marrow far back on his tongue, choking it down fast. Then another. As to the taste, well, he'd eaten cheeses that smelled worse, and maybe tasted almost the same. Yes, that was it. People paid handsomely to provide a taste like this for the finest social gatherings.

He ate more, filling his mind with Boston, hearing the sounds of a minuet being played in the background.

From the skull he extracted the brains; and the tongue—surrounded by bone—hadn't been eaten. He didn't think as he chiseled his way through the frozen hide, more clumps of hair coming off in patches to blow about. The neck meat was still there, and he hacked it from the vertebrae and thick waxy tendons.

He looked up suddenly, wary of the coming night. He stood, his pack full again. Strength and warmth returned as the cheese-tasting marrow began to digest.

"I'll live," he vowed. "For one more day, I'll live." Now all that remained was to find a sheltered spot. Start a fire, and boil the prizes he'd chopped off the dead elk.

CHAPTER FOUR

Certainly the older accepted ideological perspective provided the basis for the relation to the concept, and in the same way, the relation to the spirit, but it focused only on the external purposes and observed the spirit as if it were intertwined with finite and natural purposes. Because of the vapidity of such discrete purposes, purposes for which natural things were shown to be useful, the teleological perspective has been discredited for demonstrating the wisdom of God. The idea that natural things are useful carries the implicit truth that these things are not in and for themselves an absolute goal; nevertheless it cannot determine whether such things are defective and inadequate. For this determination it must be postulated that the immanent moment of its idea, which brings about its transiency and transition into another existence, produces at the same time a transformation into a higher concept.

—Georg Friedrich Wilhelm Hegel, *The Philosophy of Nature*

The dream was so vivid that Heals Like A Willow jerked upright from her robes, gasping. She placed a hand to her throat, and stared around in the shelter's darkness. Only small patches of starlight could be

seen through the gaps where the leather didn't fit tightly.

Willow swallowed hard, whispering, "Richard? Where are you?"

"What is this?" High Wolf asked from the darkness. "Is everything all right?"

"Someone cried out," White Alder growled, sitting up.

Willow sighed. "Go back to sleep. It was only me. I had a dream, that's all."

People settled into their bedding, mumbling to themselves. In the darkness, Willow could feel their unease. She was making them as uncomfortable as they were making her.

Willow pulled her loose hair around, twisting it into a rope before rubbing the sleep from her eyes. She slipped a sheephide cape over herself and tucked it tightly around her shoulders before she stood and stepped out through the flap.

The night air made her skin prickle as she watched the twinkling stars. A shiver unrelated to the cold ran through her.

She heard the flap pulled back again as High Wolf ducked out to stand beside her. He wore his coat, and had a cape over his shoulders. He, too, stared up at the stars. With each exhale, his frosty breath puffed like a buffalo bull's.

"I'm all right," Willow said gently. "Go back to sleep."

"Dreams are strange things, Daughter. The *puha* flows inside you. I think you know this."

"I know," she said wearily. "It's all right, *appi.* It wasn't a Power dream. Just a...well, about the White man."

"Ritshard."

She nodded.

"He has *puha* flowing within him?"

"He has something," she admitted. "I told you about looking into the eye of his soul."

"When these things happen, souls join. You were aware of this?"

She kicked at the snow. "I was proud, Father. I had destroyed the Pawnee, broken his will to live. To use Power that way, it just came upon me. I was worried about the White men, not sure what to think, and I didn't trust them. I thought I would show Richard my Power, make him and the rest of the White men wary so they wouldn't hurt me. And, in my pride, I looked into the eye of his soul."

"And he looked back." High Wolf scratched the back of his neck. "Most men would fear a woman seeing into their soul."

"He didn't."

"And you didn't fear when he looked into yours?"

"No, Father. But something changed. I started to love him. I understood from the beginning that he and I were different. I was wary, careful, but he filled my heart. When I couldn't stand it any longer, I left."

"I see. And what are these dreams?"

She closed her eyes. "I hear his voice calling to me, telling me things I can't quite understand. I see him, cold and alone out in the snow. I sense his fear, his hunger, how desperate he is."

"He is calling you. These things happen, but mostly to men." He glanced at her from the corner of his eye, then at the shelter, lowering his voice. "It would make many people nervous to hear such things from a woman's lips. It would make them think that you are as dangerous as Water Ghost Woman."

"And you?"

He shook his head slowly. "I know your heart, Heals Like A Willow. *Puha* can be used for anything you wish. You used it against the Pawnee, but he should have expected you to protect yourself. I know the shape and color of your souls, and I trust the way you use *puha*—although I don't tell everyone about it. People talk, and the next thing you know, someone is shouting, 'Witchcraft!' You are not a witch, Daughter. You don't yearn for the things a witch does."

"What about the dreams, Father?"

"What else do you see in the dreams?"

'That he needs me desperately."

"He is with his boat, up where the *Pia'ogwe* empties into the *Gete'ogwe*—"

"No. Father, my *navuzieip* has traveled to him and seen him. He is alone—in the snow. I see red sandstone... a rim..." She frowned. "Like the Red Wall. Something terrible happened at the Red Wall."

"You're sure? Could it be *Ainkahonobita ogwebi,* the Red Canyon?'

She shook her head. "No, *appi.* It is the Red Wall. I was just there with White Hail. I know the place." She shook her head in confusion. "Or did I dream it because I was just there? What is true, and what is a trick?"

"Dreams are strange that way. They *can* trick you, Willow. You have to ask yourself, was it a Power dream? Did you really see the place?"

She nodded. "Yes. And more. I saw Richard dying. I saw him freezing to death, and his *mugwa* had come loose, already on its way to the Land of the Dead."

"Then he is dead?"

"No. Because my *navuzieip* was there, Father. Trying to save him. That was when I awakened everyone in the tent. It terrified me because I knew his soul was gone—just like my husband's was. And I couldn't save him. I had to just sit there in the snow, and hold him while he died in my arms. Powerless...so horribly powerless. I couldn't stand that again, *appi*."

He cleared his throat, staring at the stars. Willow listened to the distant hooting of a great horned owl, followed by the faint ululations of a tribe of coyotes high on the rim.

"You could go after him," High Wolf finally said. "If you are a true *puhagan,* you could send your own soul to the Land of the Dead to bring this Ritshard back."

"And if I am not a true *puhagan,* Father? What then? You know what will happen to me."

He sucked his lips. "It is not something to undertake lightly. Heals Like A Willow. If you are not *puhagan,* your *mugwa* will not return from the Land of the Dead. *Peti,* you'll be as dead as the White man. The journey to the Land of the Dead is full of traps." He glanced nervously at the shelter behind him. "I will tell you what I know, though, Wolf help me, I may be telling you how to destroy yourself."

"I am listening, *appi*." She faced him bravely, ready to hear what no woman her age should know.

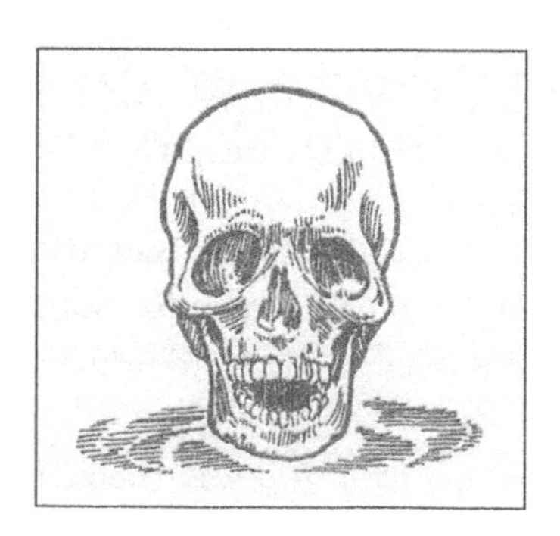

The wind came from the west: a terrible wind, the likes of which Richard had never imagined. By itself, it would have been miserable, ripping the slightest warmth away, chilling the skin until it iced, freezing tears on eyelashes. But this wind scoured the ground of snow and drove it headlong. Howling wreaths of white roared across the land, turning the very air opaque.

Richard huddled in the lee of a sandstone outcrop, his buffalo robe pulled tight, and waited in dumb misery as the wind screamed like banshees and the world disappeared into a racing wall of solid white. Through the gap in his robe, he could see swirling dervishes, ripples and eddies in the air.

It's like a river...a river of snow.

He tucked himself tighter into his robe, huddled down as far as he could behind the rocks, and watched the fine crystals settle around him like baker's flour. Here, at least, he was out of the main blast. Travel was unthinkable. A man wouldn't be able to see five feet in front of him. The universe had suddenly gone colorless, worse than any of the fogs he'd ever seen in Boston.

He shook his head, dog-weary and cold. Perdition might have been this way: torn by winds so violent only the devil could have conjured them; bone-splitting cold, so intense that a man's spit crackled when it hit the ground; scrubby trees, rock formations spawned of a demon's dreams, and prickly pear to plague every step. Starvation and disaster loomed on every hand.

He bowed his head. *I was a gentleman.*

Or had that just been an oddly alien dream?

What are you now, Richard?

In numb misery he shivered and hugged himself. "I'm nothing. I'm no different than a vulture...or even a worm.

I've lived off rotten meat—a scavenger of corrupted flesh." He snorted his derision. "And I was a gentleman?"

Another howling gust tore past, and more twirls of snow dusted down to cake him.

"I tried so hard to keep something of myself. To cling to something from the past, some bit of who I was."

He'd tried, and failed. Everything was stripped clean, like the scavenged bones he gnawed with his teeth. All that Richard Hamilton had been was gone. Only a little thread of life remained.

The worst part is, you 're losing that as well.

He shifted, working his toes from habit rather than worry about frostbite. It was too late for his face; his cheeks were peeling, and the skin on his nose had turned black. The single most damning sign of doom was his stamina. Where once he'd been able to walk all day, now he could only take one hundred steps, maybe less, before he had to stop and rest.

The snow and cold had sapped his warmth, his endurance, and was playing with his very sanity.

That morning, before the wind rose, he'd found another carcass, a buffalo—not so long dead as the elk, but rancid nevertheless. And from it he'd plundered bones, withered hump meat, and scraps from the neck. The scavengers didn't seem as drawn to the neck meat. Like men, they knew the best parts were the guts, rich in energy and nutrients.

I'm losing, Willow. Bit by bit, I'm feeling my life slip away. A man can't live on bones. He just can't.

The wind howled, deafening, like the laughter of God.

A pink morning sky shadowed silhouettes of pine and fir that surrounded the little meadow. The vigorous winds had died during the night, and in their wake, the air had turned from frigid to medium cold.

White Hail lifted Willow's pack and gave her an inquiring glance as he walked to her horse. The half-cocked jaw gave him a permanently skeptical look. That gleam of wild youth was gone from his eyes, replaced by sober reflection. The finely tailored sheephide clothing he now wore was decorated with *Dukurika* patterns. He helped Heals Like A Willow center her pack on the brown mare's rump. As she tied the straps, he worked the flat of his hand under the leather to ensure that nothing would gouge the horse's kidneys.

The horses had spent their time here, on this little meadow in the timber. Aspen poles had been lashed across trees to block the trails leading in and out of the clearing. A spring that fed summer's lush grass also provided winter water for the horses. It had trickled across the flats in scalloped ice sheets. What had once been a pristine meadow had now been trampled with horse tracks and dotted by black mounds of manure.

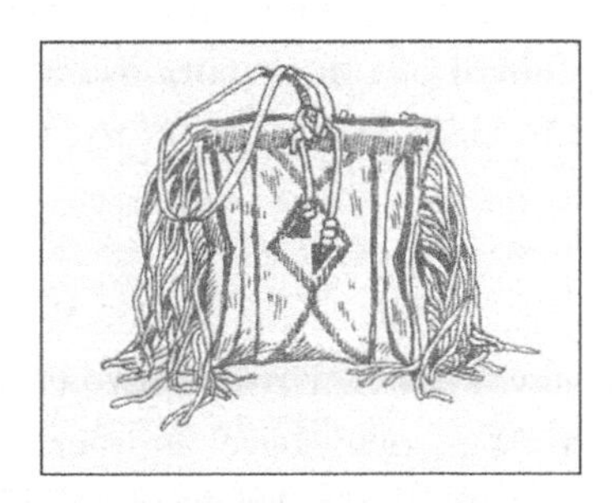

As they packed the horses, White Hail said, "A man with any sense would knock you alongside the head, tie you up, and call in the *puhagan* to drive the insanity out of your souls. Only when you came to your senses would a wise man let you loose."

Willow's deft fingers tied the last of the knots. "If a man was really wise, he'd leave me alone. If he was a little less wise, he'd sneak up behind me, because if I have any warning, I'll fight like a cornered bobcat. Ask the Arikara. Now, if he'd tied me up, he'd be a fool to let me loose because I'd kill him the instant he did. So a wise man wouldn't try any such thing."

"Willow, I wasn't—"

"And to discuss your final point, you may call the *puhagan.* Among the *Dukurika* there is none so widely acclaimed as High Wolf...who, you will remember, is the man who carried my pack up here."

White Hail huffed his weary resignation. "Sometimes I wonder what my brother saw in you."

"Haven't I warned you, White Hail?"

"Time after time. The fact is, I'm starting to believe you." He grunted, checking knots. "Half the time I think you're more like a man than a woman."

"Don't be silly, *teci.*"

"The only person silly is you, *papinkwihi,* chasing out after a White man who called from your dreams. He's supposed to be north of the mountains on the river, yet you say he's south. How do you expect to find him even if he is?"

"I'll know."

"Willow, it's the middle of the winter. Yes, it's warmed up, for now. It always does. Usually just before a terrible storm blows in. We could have another bitterly cold spell." He glanced up at the bright morning sky, hands raised. As if talking to *Tam Apo* he said, "Why am I telling her this? She knows how foolish she's being."

Willow turned, glaring hotly. "You *don't* need to come.

Go back to the camp and stay warm. Rock Hare and Eagle Trapper are going hunting tomorrow. They'd like your company. Well enough, I might add, that they keep hinting I ought to marry you and keep you here."

"Well, why don't you? And forget this crazy trip out into the cold. The White man will take care of himself. They have their own Power."

"Ah! Now you're as much an expert on White men as Lodgepole is?" Willow scrambled up on her mare, grabbing up the reins as the animal sidestepped and tossed her head, clearly irritated at the idea of going anywhere. White Hail growled to himself, then pulled himself onto his *Pa'kiani* mount. He checked his pack one last time and kicked his horse around.

He threw a glance over his shoulder and sighed as the trees closed in behind him to block the little meadow from view. He had to admit, life among the *Dukurika* had its advantages. If only Willow weren't so headstrong.

"Well," he told himself, "we'll go ride around, sleep in the snow, and suffer wind chill for a couple of weeks. After that, maybe she'll give up this madness and decide that I'm the right man for her. By spring, she'll have forgotten she ever knew a White man."

Indeed, it might just work out that way.

On the heels of the vicious winds had come warm weather. "Warm," Richard discovered, was a truly relative term. That bone-brutal cold might have been blown eastward, but come nighttime a man had better have a warm fire and a shelter of some sort.

Another danger came with warm weather. On the southern exposures, the snow softened into daytime slush. His moccasins became soaked, chilling his feet; the untanned leather he had tied on like patchwork shrank and hardened each time it was dried over the fire.

The gnawing ache in his belly remained constant. Day by day, he limped onward, not traveling so much as searching for food.

With building excitement he found a rabbit's hole. After trimming a juniper stick, he waited half of the day crouched in the soggy snow over the cottontail's hole, knowing the rabbit had to come out sometime.

The world had funneled into this one spot on earth. His mind went blank, concentration centered on the reality of his prey. Nothing existed but the eternal now. A strange peace filled him. The universe contained only himself and the rabbit. As he tightened his grip on the stick, his teetering imagination played and replayed the way he'd strike—and when he did, the triumph would shake the world.

You'll get one chance, Richard.

When it happened, he almost missed it. It took a moment to realize that the rabbit's nose had appeared, wrinkling and twitching. The cottontail hopped a body-length from the hole.

Now! His muscles had grown so slack and cold that he wobbled as he struck. The blow glanced off the rabbit's back. But it stunned the animal enough that he could leap on it. He'd never known that a rabbit could scream until the moment when he grabbed its head and twisted to break its neck.

Fingers clumsy and shaking, he slit the soft white belly open, heedless that it still quivered, and licked up the blood. He swallowed the liver, heart, and kidneys on the spot—strength, enough to get him back to his little camp, stoke his fire, and roast the rest. The stomach and intestines, along with the lungs, he chopped up and boiled with twig ends he'd seen deer eating. It made a thin and bitter stew.

That night, surrounded by lonely darkness, he gazed vacantly at his fire, chewing slowly to savor every bite of the tender meat. His stomach was full for the first time in three days.

The fire popped and spat. Canted from sticks, his moccasin outers hung, steaming. The rabbit hide was propped in the smoke to dry and be stuffed inside his left moccasin as a liner. Richard cocked his head, staring up at the clear night with its quarter moon. Coyotes yipped in chorus to the distant howl of the buffalo wolves.

"You've got nothing on me, coyotes," he whispered softly. "I got the rabbit today. Maybe tomorrow I can be like wolf and bring down an elk." With his teeth, he cracked the last of the rabbit bones to suck the marrow.

He flipped the bone splinters into the coals and lost himself in the flames. Faces formed in the leaping light: Professor Ames, George Peterson, Thomas Hanson, and Will Templeton.

"Remember...remember those times? Do you, old friends? The wonderful ale. Lamb chops...roast joints of beef. Fish chowders and hot biscuits, freshly baked, steaming with melted butter. And the conversations—remember them? Anselm and Aquinas, Plato and Epictetus. Locke, Hume, and Fichte. Descartes, Voltaire, and Rousseau. What is the nature of man? Of ethics and morality? Of the individual in the state? Is existence phenomenology, or is phenomenology existence?"

He chuckled. "I killed a rabbit today. Thus, today, existence is rabbit. Three days ago, it was a dead buffalo. I didn't get much from it. Coyotes were there first, and then the ravens. That day, existence was buffalo bones and what I could scrape out of them. Marrow mostly. You see, it's a funny thing, but that's all that's left when the coyotes and wolves get there first. They chew the ends off the ribs...things they can break. But I'm a man. I have a rifle barrel, and I can break the bones. I...am a man... human. I have a rifle."

He rubbed his painfully frostbitten nose. Pulling off his filthy mittens, he reshuffled his robes, digging deep along his side to scratch a sudden burning itch. In the process, he couldn't help but smell himself. Yep. Bad, all right. Funny how a person could take his own stink when another's would make him want to throw up.

"Do you remember"—he followed up another itch—"hot, steaming baths poured into the wash tub? Remember those?"

He grinned as he recalled the whitewashed wooden walls, the warm Franklin stove with its kettles blowing pale steam from the spouts, and Jeffry, so stiff and proper as he poured the water by lamplight and lectured on the way a gentleman should dress.

"You've no idea what I'd give for a bath like that." Richard pulled his hides closed, scowling in irritation.

Hell, I know better than to scratch an itch. Scratch one, and another starts. Scratch it, and the next thing you know, you're scratching like a street cur. One scratch into a universe of scratching—what a teleology!

He squinted up at the stars, forgetting the burning itches that now peppered his skin. "Damn lice." Every now and then he caught one in his beard and pinched it to death. "It'll warm up sometime. I'll find water. Take a bath then."

I won't quit. I'll survive this, Willow. I promise. And to hell with you, Coyote!

For a moment, he thought he heard voices—and was

on the verge of standing to stare into the darkness when they vanished.

"Philosophy lecture," he added, suddenly placing the sound. "A year ago fall...on Enlightenment." He smiled and tossed a stick onto the embers. "The real is the rational."

"Can you prove that, Mr. Hamilton?" Professor Ames asked, a slight frown on his forehead, glasses pinched to his nose.

"I...I don't know, sir. I could once...a long time ago.

He stopped, staring owlishly around.

You're seeing things. Dear Lord God. *And on a fall stomach, too.*

He rubbed his cold face, then stretched his hands out to the flickering fire. "Take hold of yourself, Richard. You must, for if you don't, you'll go crazy and die out here."

But why is that so bad? Can you prove *to me that death is that terrible? The cold would be gone. The fear of frostbite, the hunger...none of it would concern you.*

"I can't die. Can't. Willow's here, somewhere. And then I've got to get back to Boston. Remember? Find Willow—and go back to Boston."

You have no evidence that death is such a bad thing, Richard. Just a loosening of the soul, and then all this misery will be over. Do you hear? It will all be over. Over...forever.

"It would, wouldn't it?" He nodded to himself and picked up his broken rifle, tucking it to his chest. Eyes vacant, he rocked it back and forth, as a mother would her baby.

CHAPTER FIVE

My memory of past errors and perplexities, makes me diffident for the future. The wretched condition, weakness, and disorder of the faculties, I must employ in my enquiries, increase my apprehensions. And the impossibility of amending or correcting these faculties, reduces me almost to despair, and makes me resolve to perish on the barren rock, on which I am at present, rather than venture myself upon that boundless ocean, which runs out into immensity. This sudden view of my danger strikes me with melancholy; and as 'tis usual for that passion, above all others, to indulge itself; I cannot forebear feeding my despair, with all those desponding reflections…

—David Hume, *A Treatise of Human Nature*

Meat Pole and his small band of *Dukurika* traditionally camped below a sandstone rim on the southern slope of the Powder River Mountains. There, surrounded by giant boulders cracked off the rim, and sheltered by pines and juniper, they were protected from the prevailing winds. From the heights, they could watch the surrounding mountain slopes for elk, sheep, and deer.

A small seep provided enough water for their needs. In the dry sand, and in the gaps under the rock, they stored their winter food in steatite bowls and crude clay pots. Winter meat was cached in the shadows of the rock, where it stayed frozen until needed. Sloping shelters of hide and brush kept their bedding dry.

Willow and White Hail had arrived just before dark. They'd picketed the horses in a hollow under the rim where the animals could paw for grass.

Meat Pole had greeted them cordially. In the wavering yellow light of the fire, his people sat wrapped in their fine robes, excited by the prospect of stories and news of other bands.

Willow remembered Meat Pole from years past, but when had he aged so? And how long had it been since she had last seen him? Four years, five? Perhaps it had been the summer she met her husband.

Or is it just that I have changed so much?

Meat Pole was the band's leader, or *tekwhani.* Short, squat, and thickset, he looked to be about four tens of years in age. His broad face, prominent cheekbones, and square jaw were classically *Dukurika.* He wore a hide cape made from the shoulders of a massive silver-tip grizzly bear, and the claws hung over his chest in a long necklace.

His people wore fine, tailored hides, tanned as soft as a baby's cheek, and decorated with colored quill work, bone beads, and strips of silken fur taken from otter, fox, and marten.

The band consisted of four men, five women, and a cluster of children. The dog pack slept in curled balls of fur around the camp's periphery.

From the feast they'd been given, Willow decided that Meat Pole's band was faring well through this colder-than-normal winter. Willow and White Hail finally finished their share of the roasted mountain sheep, biscuit-root, and serviceberry pemmican. Each portion had been served in dishes crafted from sheep-horn bosses. They sat beside Meat Pole, in the place of honor. Immediately behind them, the sandstone rim reflected the fire's heat and light. Just over her shoulder she could see the painted figures of mountain sheep, wolves, and elk. The paintings had been done in charcoal, blood, and fat. Some had faded, especially the yellow, red, and purple colors created from flower petals.

Meat Pole leaned back and belched after he lay his horn bowl down for one of the dogs to lick clean. "Thanks to the animals, our bellies are full." He smiled happily and glanced at Willow. "We have heard rumors that you just returned to High Wolf's band."

Willow licked her fingers clean and wiped the grease from her lips with a sleeve. "That is true. And it's quite a story."

"You will make us very happy if you tell it from the beginning to the end."

When Willow had related her journey east, and answered the many questions about the White men, White Hail told of his rescue from the *Pa'kiani* and the trip to High Wolf's camp. Then they had to answer questions about High Wolf, and his band.

Finally Meat Pole lifted an eyebrow, asking, "What brings you here in the middle of winter, Heals Like a Willow? This is not the time to travel. Snow is deep, and hard on horses. It is a time for snowshoes."

At last!

Willow crossed her arms, tucking her hands into the folds of her coat. "I have come looking for someone."

Meat Pole nodded, cocked his head, and said, "Ask. Perhaps we know this person?"

She smiled briefly. "I doubt it, honored *Tekwhani.* I am looking for a White man who is lost somewhere around here."

Willow held her breath, hardly daring to hope. People whispered back and forth, glancing curiously at her.

"I have not heard of a White man." Meat Pole paused thoughtfully. "He has a horse? Would we have heard his *atti,* his thunderweapon? I have heard that White men only hunt with guns."

"I don't know if he has a horse. I would think he had a gun."

Meat Pole frowned, then looked at young Spotted Falcon, who sat beside his wife, Green Shoot, a woman of Willow's age. "The only unusual thing we know of is what Spotted Falcon saw several days ago."

Was this finally it? Willow turned her attention to the young man.

Spotted Falcon shifted uncomfortably. "I was hunting to the south, along the long ridges. The elk winter there, and sometimes the buffalo. We did not need meat, but I thought I would go see anyway. You know how it is."

"And what did you see?" White Hail asked, nodding solicitously.

Spotted Falcon glanced away, obviously uneasy. "They were tracks...and I only saw them from a distance. From a higher ridge. To have gone down, I would have had to cross a deep drift, and then climb it again on the way back."

Willow shot a glance at the piled snowshoes that leaned against the rocks beside the dog travois frames. A drift would not have slowed Spotted Falcon in the slightest. "Tell me about these tracks."

He scratched his ear, thought for a moment, and said, "Well, they looked like a man's tracks. You know how a man's tracks are different from an animal's?"

"I do."

A *Dukurika* hunter like Spotted Falcon would have no trouble reading tracks, even from a distance.

"The strange thing is"—Spotted Falcon now tugged on his ear—"the tracks didn't go in a straight line. You know how a man walks? He goes in a mostly straight line. Men usually know where they are going and walk with a purpose."

"And these tracks didn't?"

"They wandered in and out and around. This...this frightened me. That country down there, Pandzoavits lives down there, somewhere. The way these tracks looked..."

"I see. You are a wise man." Willow glanced at White Hail, reading his veiled expression. Her excitement was building. Could it be? "But a lost man might make such tracks?"

Spotted Falcon shot a quick glance at Meat Pole and shrugged. "He might. If he wasn't well, or was hurt, he might."

Willow bit her lip, frowning, remembering the visions her *navuzieip* had seen. Richard had called to her in desperation.

"Perhaps tomorrow," she declared, "we will ride down there, look and see."

"And if it was *Pandzoavits*?" Meat Pole asked.

Willow lifted an eyebrow, and looked at White Hail. "This *Ku'chendikani* warrior has obsidian-tipped arrows. He claims to be a great warrior. I'll distract *Pandzoavits,* and White Hail can shoot him in the anus with one of his arrows."

Chuckles broke out among Meat Pole's people. Everyone knew that the anus was the only vulnerable spot on a rock ogre's body.

White Hail only gave her a wooden look.

"You had better be quick, Heals Like A Willow," Meat Pole said. "If *Pandzoavits* catches you with his sticky hands, he'll turn and run. Even a great warrior like White Hail might not get a shot."

White Hail stroked his chin and arched an eyebrow. "*Tekwhani,* I know Heals Like A Willow. I think a rock ogre would have his hands full. He could try and eat her, but I have come to find out that Willow doesn't digest well."

It was only later, when Willow had retired to her blankets, that White Hail came to crouch over her. He asked, "Do you think these tracks are Ritshard's?"

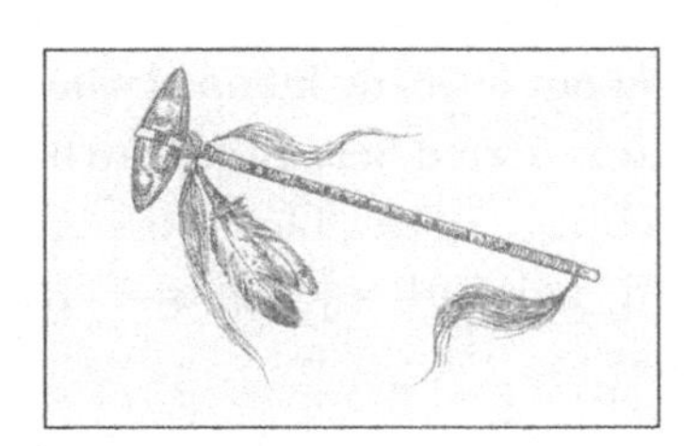

"I don't know. Maybe. If they are, we will need to hurry."

White Hail bowed his head for a moment. "You know, it's cold tonight."

"Yes, it is."

"I could make you warmer. These people"—he jerked his head toward the shelters—"they think we're together."

She sighed wearily. "What speaks for you, White Hail? Your *we'an,* or your pride?"

"Just once, can't you and I—"

"White Hail, go find your robes and *sleep*."

He stood slowly. "You will fill my dreams anyway. Is that so different from filling my bed?"

"I can't control your *navuzieip*. If you long for me that desperately, I think it would be best for you to return to Red Calf and soothe your needs." But her last words were wasted on his retreating back.

Richard fell face-first into the snow. Had he tripped over a malicious sagebrush, or just collapsed? He lay for a moment, outstretched, aware of the cold soaking into his body. His arms trembled as he pushed up and sat back, on his knees.

Little yellow lights danced through his vision like fireflies as he looked out over the humped side of the mountain. The slope was dotted here and there by junipers and textured by sagebrush. Rocks, blown smooth by the wind and baked hard and dark by the sun, thrust roughly through the snow.

To the south, past the guardian ranks of ridges, stretched a broad, snowy basin, hilly in places, lumped here and there by tree-cloaked hills. In the west, ragged snow-capped mountains, like teeth in a dog's jaw, jutted into the morning sky. He could make out the intricate details of canyons, rocky slopes, and patches of timber. So clear, yet so distant.

How beautiful it was, mountain and basin softened by pastel blues and pinks cast by the low sun. The land dreamed, spinning images that he could but barely catch.

I can hear it, now. The clutter is gone. All of the thoughts drained away. I've lost so much of me that I'm empty. Only the land is left. It fills the universe.

He used his Hawken as a crutch, pulled himself stubbornly to his feet, and teetered there on the awkward tripod.

Weak. When did I get so weak?

Since the rabbit, he'd had nothing but boiled twigs and stripped pine bark to eat. Three days? Frowning, he couldn't remember.

Why do you try, Richard? The struggle is pointless. You've nowhere to go. For days you've been wandering around these foothills. Sometimes east, sometimes west, afraid to climb because you know the snow is deeper up there, and you haven't the strength to wade through it.

"I just need food," he insisted dully. "If I could kill something..."

Like the deer this morning? The ones who stopped to stare—fearless of the man with the broken rifle?

"Not them...maybe some others."

Throw your rifle away, Richard. It's just weight, sapping your energy. And you have so little to spare.

"No. I can't. As long as I have a rifle I'm a man. Do you hear me? *A man!*"

He staggered, mouth hanging open. Reaching up with a trembling hand, he rubbed his face, barely aware of the flaking skin, the hollow cheeks and sunken eyes. "A man," he rasped in final defiance, and grunted as he wobbled onward, the rifle acting as his trusty support.

Vision had become a tricky thing, wavering, shifting, sometimes glassy. At midday like this, colors, mostly red or yellow, flickered at the edge of his sight. Sometimes people hid in them. Professor Ames, Laura, or Will

Templeton. Often it was his father, trying desperately to tell him something.

Willow came to him frequently, usually in dreams. Like a succubus, she'd wrap herself around him, incredibly warm and soft. He'd bask in her glory, drawing strength from her body and soul. Rising, they would dance around and around in the streets of Boston while smiling people clapped and quartets played the latest compositions from Vienna, Berlin, Salzburg, and Paris.

"Dance, Willow!" he cried hoarsely as he wove awkwardly through the sage. "Dance with me tonight."

He fell again, and struggled to rise.

Where are you going, Richard?

Damn that voice! It spoke out of the very air. More than once he had caught himself blinking up into the sky, trying to catch the culprit.

"I'm going...that's all. Going to Willow—as if it's any concern of yours." He began to shiver again, waiting until the spell passed before chancing the next step.

"Damn the shakes. They take so much out of a man."

You're losing, Richard. The race is nearly run. Stop, now. Rest a while.

He managed to make it to a rock outcrop on the spine of a wind-blown ridge, and settled there. In the sunlight, his back propped against the lichen-covered stone, he stared dully down the long slope of the hillside he'd been traversing. A golden eagle hung on the air currents, washed by the wind. How stately, majestic in the ease with which it flew, barely moving a wing.

When I die, I'm going to fly like that. Sail on the winds, eastward, ever eastward, across the Missouri, then across the Mississippi, and over the forests and up the clear Ohio. Then I'll soar north along the Allegheny and eastwards, over the granite-domed mountains, across the Berkshires, and into Boston. There, you will find me, Father. A huge, dark hunter, perched spectrally on your window.

He hung his head, half in dream. The chilled breeze bobbed the sparse grasses poking through the crusted snow. The sun's warmth caressed him, stroking the weariness within his starved muscles, sending him deeper into the dream, into Willow's arms to twirl around and around. They skipped off rocks and sage. Spiraled over endless heights like the eagle as they embraced each other and rose through the clouds.

Richard stared into her eyes, falling into their depths the way a pebble sinks into a bottomless pool. Her soul wrapped around his, soothing and healing.

Willow...oh, Willow, how I've come to love you.

He jerked upright, blinking, surprised at how little remained of the day. Cold was creeping into the air, its defiant tendrils ignoring the sun's slanting rays.

Fire. I've got to make fire.

He tried to stand, and couldn't. Instead, he crawled out like a baby to strip branches from the sagebrush. When he pulled his tinder from its tin and tried to hold his strike-a-light, his arms trembled. It took many tries before he struck a spark, and bent down to blow it to life.

One by one, he fed grass stems, then sagebrush twigs until his fire crackled. Ritually, he charred tinder for his strike-a-light and packed it safely in his tin box.

With resignation, he pulled his knife and began slicing up the empty hide bag he'd used to pack his meat. If nothing else, the caked blood would give him something, and the hide—gluey when boiled—might stick his soul to his body for one more day.

And if you do not find food tomorrow? What then? Eat the rest of your clothing?

As he placed his pitiful stew on the flames to boil, he nodded acceptance.

Let yourself go, Richard. As it is, you can barely walk. But dead, your soul will soar free.

How good it sounded. Free! Able to sail up to God, and demand answers for all the myriad questions that plagued him. A solution to the doubts that infested his mind.

You don't need to linger, Richard. Just take the tip of the knife and open a vein. It won't hurt.

He made a face, trying to focus his blurry eyes. Pulling back the edge of his mitten, he looked at his wrist, grimy with dirt and old blood. The knife lay cool and heavy in his right hand. It felt oddly vivid in contrast to the rest of the world, which had grown so hazy.

It wouldn't hurt. Not like the beatings he'd taken. Hard to think that up until François waylaid him, a barked shin or pinched finger was the worst pain he'd ever experienced.

He took one last rubbery gaze around his little camp—a feeble way of saying goodbye to the things that made up his world. The possibles, the broken Hawken, his smelly, stiff buffalo robe.

He shook his head and squinted. A pair of eyes gleamed in the darkness, reflecting the fire's glow.

"What do you want. Coyote? Ready to take my carcass? Huh? Is that it?"

Coyote the Trickster. The cavorting counterpart to Wolf just after the Creation. Willow had told him the stories. The *wechashawakan* had tried to warn him that night in Wah-Menitu's village. And now the beast waited for him to kill himself. Later, after the fire burned out. Coyote would slip in, his pointed nose quivering as it smelled the blood. Tentatively, he would lick at the frozen edges of the pool, and then deal with the problem of ripping away all those pieces of rock-hard hide tied to Richard's cold body.

"But you ain't getting much, you son of a bitch. My belly's all gone gaunt. Not a lick of fat left for you. Tricked again, Coyote."

Tricked...by what?

"What was I going to do?"

Going to open a vein, the voice reminded.

Richard nodded absently, the knife forgotten in his hand. He frowned and looked down into the fire. Curls of smoke rose in the playful light.

An image formed in the embers: a face. Whose? The lines solidified into familiar features. Tonight, Travis watched him from the coals of the fire, all those hideous scars crisscrossing his cheeks and ruined nose. "Travis wouldn't open a vein. He'd just be a tough. Make do. Hell, he'd slither out there and kill that damned coyote. 'Meat's meat,' he'd say."

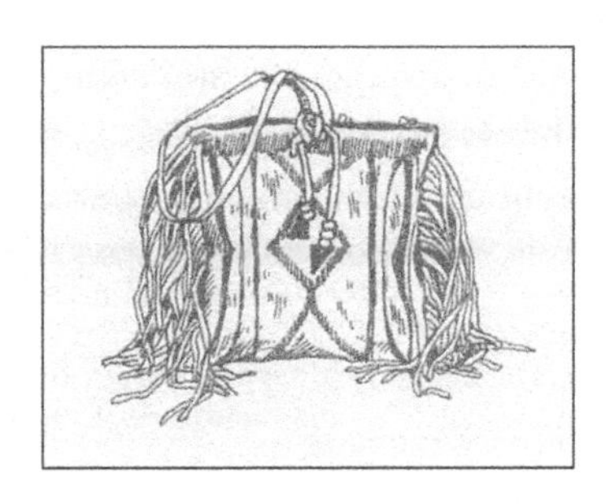

Richard glanced down at the knife, slowly shook his head, and struggled to slip it back into its sheath. Damn! If he could just control his muscles. Anything but the trembling. He hated the loss of memory and the weird hallucinations.

"Yer doing fine," Travis insisted from somewhere. "Buck up yer grit, and see to 'er, coon."

"Yes...see to her." He stared dully into the flames, then remembered to pull his pot away from the heat. The hide soup was half boiled away. For the moment, he'd just let it cool, and then go get more snow to melt into it

He fell asleep before he remembered.

The next day, he didn't attempt to travel. Instead, he tottered out for more sagebrush, levering the plants from the ground with his rifle barrel since he didn't have the strength to twist them off their roots. For breakfast he ate the last of his hide bag.

He was blessed by another sunny day.

As it warmed up, Richard sat with his back against the rocks, blinking, trying to remember where he was. How could Professor Ames have found him? He looked up at the white-haired professor, and they talked for a while. But Richard couldn't quite remember about what. And when he turned to ask, the professor was gone, only rocks sitting where he'd been but a moment before.

You're losing your mind, Richard.

No, not losing it. It just floated, hovering there in the silvered air, seeing all around. He smiled at the sensation, distantly aware of his cracked lips.

Night was coming. This time, he didn't care...

"I have to admit," Heals Like A Willow said as she rode along, "I don't know why you insisted on coming. You're making your *mugwa* crazy."

White Hail chuckled in his maddening way. "Someone with sense had to accompany you. It's the middle of winter. A time for sitting by fires and telling stories." He gestured toward the west and the hazy cloud-bank hanging over the Wind River Mountains. "You saw the sunset last night. Orange and pink over the peaks. You tell me it isn't going to snow. And I don't need to be a *puhagan* to know the signs."

The horses bucked deep drifts on the northern side of the ridge before cresting out onto a knob. In places angular rock had been exposed by the wind, and amber clumps of needle-and-thread, wheatgrass, and threadleaf sedge thrust through the crusted snow. From this high point, they could see across the basin to the south, past *Ki'nyatiwener,* the Hawk-Stand Rock, to *Wongo'yigwin-do'yap,* the Pine-Stand Mountains. To the west, most of the view was blocked by the bulk of *Tunangarit,* the mountain known as Thundersitter. Willow pulled her mare up, shielding her face from the wind, searching the rolling hills below.

They'd followed the winter trails: ancestral routes that wound along the ridgetops. Willow had listened to her heart, steering by some faint urge that brought her this way. White Hail decried it all as foolishness, but something in her souls pinched at the idea of going any other direction.

The information gleaned at Meat Pole's camp was the only hint, tenuous as it was, that Richard might be in the area. So they'd come south as Spotted Falcon directed, and now Willow scanned the country below, looking for anything out of the ordinary. The rolling hills dropped away in a series of rocky humps as the mountains sloped down toward the Wind River Basin. Out to the west, beyond Thundersitter, the clouds had a soft, hazy look, the kind that fooled like Coyote, for the haze was that of wind-packed snow blowing down around the peaks.

"I don't think we want to be out in the open tonight," White Hail told her, attention on the western sky.

"No," she said. "I think not."

"We could turn around, try and make it back to Meat Pole's camp."

Willow tightened her blanket, squinting against the gusts as she searched. "I suppose we could. I'd rather make camp down lower, maybe in that valley down there to the right. Wood would be plentiful, and we'd have shelter from the wind."

He added, "We wouldn't have to leave until spring."

Willow met his level stare. "Why are you tormenting yourself, White Hail? You didn't have to come to High Wolf's camp in the first place. You didn't have to stay there with your heart in your throat every time a man came and asked to marry me. You didn't have to come on this trip. And if I find Richard, it will only sicken your souls. I have done nothing to encourage you."

"No. You've been honest." He gave her that familiar grin. "But I have hope."

"Go home to your wife and child."

"Red Calf is no wife." He glanced away. "I have come to understand that. I'm not very smart when it comes to women."

"No, you're not. You're better at stealing horses and getting caught by Blackfeet."

"And you, Willow?" A gust of wind flattened his sheep-hide coat against his shoulders. "You're good at getting caught by Pawnee, and involving yourself with silly White men, and the even sillier idea that there's one out here—let alone the one you really want to find. Face it, he's up at the mouth of the *Pia'ogwe.* This is crazy! Some evil spirit's dream that has...Willow? Are you listening to a single word I'm saying?"

She canted her head to keep the wind from tearing her eyes. What *was* that? Blinking, she could see dark dots moving against the snow: wolves padded around a rockpile on a lower ridge to the southwest. Something about the way they acted—hanging back. Why?

"Willow," White Hail insisted, "when that storm arrives, it's going to get colder than a rock ogre's heart. Come on, let's find a... Where are you going?"

"*This way.* Are you coming?"

What would keep a group of wolves so interested, but at such a distance? Were it prey, they'd close in, bring the beast to bay, and kill it. No, this had to be something different, and Willow had always had an affinity for Wolf, the most sacred of *Dukurika* spirit animals.

"Willow? *Tam Apo,* but you're stubborn! *Willow!*"

Richard floated, savoring the warmth. Visions spun around him, Harvard trees lush with spring leaves, and the brick buildings looking so rosy in the sunlight. He strolled along familiar shady walks. Professor Ames walked beside him, casting curious glances his way.

"So, Richard, did you find the answers you were searching for?"

"Some, sir, but not all. It took a long time to discover the errors in our philosophical framework."

"Errors, Richard. Indeed?"

"Yes, sir. Philosophers, especially those in our modern

era, are incredibly vain. We are forever flawed by our own arrogance."

"Arrogance?"

"A form of the same arrogance that I left Boston with, sir: the notion that we have a unique understanding of truth. Which is not to say that our philosophy is meaningless, only that we have but a part of the whole. Human nature, it's so varied, forever depending upon the initial assumptions we make about life. Our philosophy is the product of Greek, Roman, and Hebrew thought, modified in the crucible of the Middle Ages, and recast by the Renaissance and Enlightenment. There is a great deal more to investigate, but none of us is willing to explore the alternatives. Our rationality has become a prison, as much a syllogism as Plato penned in the Dialogues of Ion."

"But, Richard, philosophy is a means of liberation."

"Are you free, sir?"

"I am. I have the ability to think, to investigate."

"That is the trap; for, you see, sir, you can only investigate within the framework of your experience, what you've been taught. I am seeking to find a different framework."

"Indeed. And have you discovered such a framework?"

"In part, sir. So much of what we believe has

become cluttered with elegantly formulated arguments and proofs. Before I could see clearly, I had to strip away all the illusions and diversions. They all sound so logical in Boston, London, or Berlin. But, sir, Truth isn't found in elaborate philosophical constructions; it's in the essential fundamentals of life. We are all animals beneath our dress, manners, and the conventions of society."

"Animals, Richard, really? From Aristotle on, great minds have argued that humans are distinct from the animal world, that our values, abilities, even the divine spark of creation have placed us above the base realities of animal existence."

"Before anything else, sir, we need food, water, shelter, to protect ourselves from beasts, and to mate. Those five facts are the foundation of human reality. Society has placed us in a cage of our own construction, and from it we look out of windows, catching but the briefest glimpses of nature. And then we retreat to our warm drawing rooms and lecture halls to debate that momentary glimpse, fooling ourselves all the while that we see from above, like God, and know Truth."

"Your thesis will not find a warm reception among your peers, Richard. How do you expect to prove such assertions?"

"They can only be experienced, sir. You see, that's the flaw in enlightened reason. It becomes a mental exercise, totally logical—a sophisticated syllogism: 'Socrates is a man. A man has two legs. My cat is named Socrates. Therefore, my cat has two legs.'"

"The logical flaws in a syllogism will always be detected by a critical examination, Richard."

"Will they? Doesn't finding the flaw in that example hinge on knowing both men and cats? Professor, let me postulate an axiom: Nature cannot be fooled by logical architecture, no matter how grand its construction."

"So, you have Truth, and it consists of man being an animal?"

"No, sir. I have only discovered the foundation from which to work. Something is missing—the final nail that will pin it all together. Human nature is so complex."

"Yes, so complex..." Ames began to laugh, and slowly faded into a gray mist.

Dear Professor Ames, more like a father than a teacher. If only his own father had had that gentle look, that warmth of personality. But Phillip Hamilton had been forever cold, unforgiving, and strict.

Richard cried out into the haze, "Father, why couldn't you have smiled at me? Why couldn't you have shared part of yourself with me? What did I ever do to hurt you?"

The disembodied voice, backed by the ticking of a ship's clock, sounded sad and weary. "I wanted you to be a man. I failed, boy. Despite your self-proclaimed philosophy, don't you understand the suffocating guilt? It devours us, boy, it's been eating at you and me until we have nothing left to share with each other except misery."

Guilt? Dear God, what a horrible monster that was, forever lurking in the human heart. He could sense it, black and terrible, a miasma rising in his breast. Oh, he knew it all right, had seen it in his dreams devouring Boston, and settling over Willow's dead body.

It came from me, from inside.

"I'm so sorry, Father." An ache filled his chest. "I understand now. For I have my own guilt, Father. My own needs for atonement."

"Richard?" Phillip's voice barked, "What have you

done now? Where is the money, Richard? Have you failed me again?"

The old fear didn't rise to choke him. "Yes, Father. I failed you."

His father responded evenly. "Please, see that you don't again."

What curious irony. "I won't, Father. I'm dying. I can't fail you again."

And what sorrow that brought. So many things left to do, so many mistakes to correct—and no time left.

"But it's all right. Father. I forgive you for trying too hard. Do you hear me? I forgive you!" He sank down onto his knees then, head bowed. "But, sir, can you ever forgive me?"

The sensation was so gentle that he never knew when he floated away, lost in the warm gray haze. Fragments of memory flitted through his mind on siskin wings, echoes of the boasts he'd made that night in Will Templeton's parlor. Oh, he'd conquered the wild frontier and its wilder men, hadn't he? Like a vulture, he'd lived on carrion, and chewed bitter twigs. He'd killed, taken scalps—and worn them with the pride of a savage.

So much for becoming the vaunted sage of the frontier.

Eyes watched him. Familiar eyes—Will Templeton's, Thomas Hanson's, Peterson's, Fenno's, and the rest. For a short eternity, Laura's blue eyes withered his soul, her disapproval nearly palpable.

Oh, Laura, I'm sorry—sorry for the life that we'll never have together.

The eyes changed—a reconciliation of opposites. Now Trudeau studied him with hard intent. Why Trudeau? He used women, took them against their will. What did he have in common with Laura?

Richard squeezed the image from his mind, only to hear Toussaint repeat, *A man ees what he ees.*

From the watery darkness came a new image. That of a terrible pistol pointed at him. A firm hand curled around the grip, and behind the black maw of the muzzle, Dave Green's implacable face loomed.

"Dear God, Dave. Don't shoot! I'm not the same man I was then. I've changed. Grown. But now it's too late."

And in the distance, François laughed, chortling, "Animal! that's all you are...an animal like the rest of us, *oui?*"

The cloudy gray swirled, and Willow reached out of the mist, her arms open for his embrace.

Richard whispered miserably, "If only I could go back, be everything you thought I could."

Her voice, like fingers on velvet, said, "You have followed your own path. You could do no less."

"But where has it led me, Willow?"

"To the final truth."

The final truth—the last fading moments of life, and a crushing loneliness. Shouldn't there be more? A rising fanfare of trumpets, a swelling of light and brilliance?

"Reckon that's all there is," Travis called from somewhere distant. "Ye done fine, coon. Now, let go and cross the next divide. Almost there. Just a little farther. C'mon, Dick. Ye can do it."

And the terrible gray cold closed around him.

CHAPTER SIX

Thus if I make the assertion that the quality of space and time, according to which, as a condition of their existence I accept both external objects and my own soul, lies in my manner of intuition and not in these objects by themselves, I do not mean to state that such bodies only seem to exist externally to me, or that my soul only seems to be apparent in my self-consciousness. It would be my own fault if I changed that which ought to count as appearance into mere illusion.

This cannot occur, however, according to our principle of the ideality of all sensible intuitions.

—Immanuel Kant, *Critique of Pure Reason*

Willow dismounted, watching the wolves. They hesitated uneasily, then trotted away over the crest of the ridge, paws swishing in the freezing snow. The rock outcrop stood like a rock ogre's cairn, the snow curiously trampled.

White Hail slid off his horse, inspecting the tracks.

"It looks like a man has been crawling here. See, that's a print from a mitten. And here, this sagebrush has been shredded."

Willow hurried toward the rocks, leading her mare. Here and there, she could pick out a footprint in the trampled snow, a pockmark, as if from a stick, and mitten prints.

The rocks jutted from the top of the ridge, lonely sentinels overlooking the rough country to the south. She tied her horse to a thick sage and stepped around the canted stone.

Richard lay propped against a sandstone boulder, eyes closed. His body was wrapped in so many frozen hides, he looked more like a winter-story monster than a man. She crouched beside him, ignoring the stale smells of sweat, smoke, and dried blood. His eyes were sunken, cheeks hollow and peeling. Frostbite had blackened his nose, and filth matted his beard. Beside him lay his possibles, the familiar Hawken, mud-spattered and tarnished. Nothing but charcoal and ashes remained in the cold firepit.

"Richard?" She touched his cold face, and his eyes barely flickered. "Richard! It's Willow!"

"You came all this way for...for *that?*" White Hail asked from behind her.

"Build a fire," she ordered. "He's almost dead."

"Looks like he hasn't eaten in days." White Hail studied Richard skeptically. "I think we're too late."

"A fire, White Hail. Now! And after that, I need you to take the horses and ride down to the valley. Cut me sticks. Long ones, for a sweat lodge."

White Hail placed a hand on her shoulder, his gaze penetrating her panic. "Willow, no matter what, we *must* move off this point. Are you listening? Look out at that storm, and *think,* Willow."

She knotted her fists, studied the dark wall of clouds to the west, and nodded miserably. White Hail muttered under his breath as he walked to her horse and led it over.

"Richard?" Willow cradled his face in her hands. "You must be brave. *Live* for me!"

And her souls froze. Hadn't she said those words before? Over her husband and son, and with the same impassioned pleading?

I couldn't save them. I didn't have the Power. Not again.

Heart skipping, she took a deep breath. "*Tam Apo,* do you hear me? I can't bear it."

White Hail collected Richard's possibles and tied them onto his horse, though he took his time, running reverant hands over the broken rifle.

"Help me wrap him," Willow said, spreading her blanket beside Richard. With White Hail's help, they laid him in soft hides and folded them around his body.

"We'll have to lash him crosswise, like packing a deer," White Hail said.

When they lifted him to her mare, Willow was shocked to discover how light he was.

"Cling to life, Richard. It's not long now. We'll have you warm and fed."

Then Willow took the reins and led her horse down off the point, headed to the drainage White Hail had spotted from above. The storm was closer now, roaring down upon them.

Desperation built with each step as Willow watched her moccasins punch through the crusted snow. With each frantic look back to Richard's bobbing body, she prayed that his *mugwa* would cling to this world.

A half-hand's time had passed before they reached the snowy bottoms. The few solitary cottonwoods that stood in the rounded valley had a pathetic look. Serviceberry, chokecherry, and juniper poked up through the snow.

"White Hail, build a fire. Hurry!" Willow stepped back and began pulling at the knots while White Hail kicked a hole in the deep snow.

Willow tossed the lashing aside, and slid Richard down onto the trampled snow. Her frantic fingers pulled the robe aside and her heart sank. His half-lidded eyes were vacant, his face slack. To her relief, his erratic breathing rasped shallowly.

White Hail was muttering to himself as he stripped bark from the junipers, and built a fire in the hollow he'd kicked in the snow.

Willow stared into Richard's slack face, fear twining through her souls. "Richard, it's Willow. Come back to me."

A painful knot began to swell under her tongue, and tears traced down her cheeks to chill in the cold.

By some bizarre trick of the light, her husband's face superimposed itself on Richard's. Her fingers had rested as futilely on his cold skin. How could it happen again?

Richard mumbled something, the words disjointed, the ramblings a body made when the *mugwa* had come free.

She closed her eyes, steeling herself. If his soul had fled the body, only one way remained to save him.

I can't. I don't have the Power to go among the Dead to find his soul. Why didn't I bring High Wolf with me? He could do this, send his soul in search of Richard's.

When she shivered and looked around, White Hail had the fire crackling. Together, they carried Richard over to it. Then White Hail placed Willow's pack beside her, asking, "How is he?"

"His *mugwa* is gone."

White Hail shrugged. "Then we can do nothing. You'd need a *puhagan* to save him."

"I know." She knotted her fists, eyes closed. What happened to an *omaihen* woman, a forbidden woman, who sent her soul into the afterlife? Would the angry spirits really trap her soul there?

"You tried. Willow," White Hail soothed. "It's not your fault."

How will I live with myself if I fail again? She looked down into his face. *For the rest of my life, I'll hate myself if I don't at least try*.

A new fear was born within as she said: "I'm not finished, White Hail. I need poles, something to make a sweat lodge. Take my ax and see if you can find chokecherry stems long enough."

White Hail took her hand, staring into her eyes. "Willow, if he's lost his soul, there's *nothing* you can do."

"I can go after it."

White Hail's eyes widened. "Go after it? You're a woman! Only a *puhagan* can send his soul out to find another. Don't you understand?"

"I don't have *time* to find a *puhagan!*"

"Willow, you're not Water Ghost Woman! Your *mugwa* has no chance in the Water World."

"This thing will be done now! I will make the journey after his soul. High Wolf told me the way."

For what seemed like an eternity, their eyes locked, wills battling. And in the end, he relented. "Very well, but you'll probably kill us all."

"Then you can leave as soon as you fetch me the

poles. Now, go. Hurry! We've wasted enough time as it is."

Growling to himself, White Hail took her ax and stalked off toward the chokecherry bushes as the wind bore the first flakes of snow.

Willow looked up at the threatening sky and struggled to smother her own rising fear. White Hail's words burned within her: *"You're a woman! Only a* puhagan *can send his soul out to find another."*

Under her breath, she whispered, "I'm forbidden to do this...*omaihen—omaihen...*"

To even consider such a thing was madness. Only the most powerful *puhagan*—and all of them men—could send their souls to the Land of the Dead. But High Wolf had told her what would happen and how to find her way. He'd also told her about the spirits guarding the path—terrible creatures that tested the soul-traveler. Those who failed were destroyed by the most hideous of means.

Yet like the summer moths that flew into crackling fires, she was being drawn, seeing the path she would take. One by one she recalled the things High Wolf had told her. If she could free her soul, it must find the tunnel between the worlds. There in the darkness, monsters would lurk, ready to leap upon her soul if her courage faltered. She would emerge on a mountaintop, and then follow dark paths down into the valley. The whole time she would be stalked by Water Babies, *Nynymbi,* and *Pandzoavits.*

If she made it down into the depths of the Water World, she must find Richard's soul. Here, too, she could fail, for not all souls wanted to return to the living, and the pain, cold, and suffering that living entailed.

She closed her eyes, anxiety rising bright within. On the river, Richard had chosen Boston—and that White woman—over her. Why did she think he would be any different in the Land of the Dead?

Because he's here. Not with Travis and Green at the confluence of the Pia'ogwe *and* Gete'ogwe. He had come seeking her, in the dead of winter. She had to know why.

Whether his *mugwa* accompanied her or stayed with the Dead, she'd still have to find her way back, relocate the tunnel, and retrace her way back to her own body.

Branches cracked as White Hail bulled into the bush. The chopping echoed hollowly around the valley.

Am I strong enough?

How did one measure such a thing? Driving the thought from her heart, she set about collecting snow in Richard's tin cup, then placed it at the fire's edge to melt. Turning to her pack, she undid the straps and pulled out her blanket and robe. With Richard's bent knife, she cut the strands of tendon he'd used to tie the green hides to his body.

First, she checked his feet: cold as clay, but to her relief, unfrozen. Snow was falling faster. She added pieces of sage to the fire. With his rifle, she battered rocks from the frosted ground and tumbled them into the blaze to heat. Next, she began kicking the snow away where they'd build the sweat lodge.

Her nose crinkled at the smell as she cut the last of the hides away and placed a hand on Richard's chest. Cold, so cold, but his heart still beat, slow and irregular.

White Hail plodded into camp, long branches trailing behind him in the snow. He shook his head as he looked at Richard, but began the task of wedging the butts into the ground and bending the poles into a low arch. They built the lodge right over his body. Willow used Richard's thongs to tie the saplings into a low dome-shaped framework. One by one they settled their hide robes over them.

"I hope you know what you're doing," White Hail said, as they inspected the low dome of the sweat lodge.

Willow shook snow out of her hair. "If I don't, you can have my horse and Richard's rifle. The cock is broken, but if you can find a trader, you can get another one."

"Thank you," White Hail told her dryly. "If I live long enough."

Willow rubbed her face, and took a deep breath. With a sagebrush stem, she rolled a hot rock onto one of Richard's frozen hides. Ignoring the smell of burning leather, she ducked into the shelter and dropped the hot rock next to Richard. Snowflakes sizzled as she carried the rocks one by one into the darkness, creating a glowing pile.

"You know what to do?" She took one last look at White Hail.

"I do." He sounded as if his *mugwa* were at risk, too. And perhaps it was, being this close to something so dangerous. "I'll keep melting water, bring you hot stones when you call, and, in the meantime, make us some sort of wickiup." He glanced around in the gloom. Snow was falling in white curtains now, night approaching. "At least we're not up on the point."

Willow ducked into the lodge, settled the robe in place, and pulled the last of Richard's clothing off. She slipped out of her robe, cape, dress, and moccasins.

She shivered in the cold, and pulled the blanket back. "I'm ready for the water now."

"*Tam Apo* guide you." White Hail handed her the tin of water. "I have loved you for a long time, Willow. I will always love you."

She hesitated, seeing the conviction in his dark eyes; but words had been exhausted between them long ago.

With finality, she ducked into the blackness and resettled the robe. She filled her lungs and sprinkled water on the glowing rocks. Steam hissed and exploded to fill the interior, hot enough to scald.

She clenched her fists, the steam's Power prickling on her skin, in her lungs. It bathed her with its cleansing tendrils, twining around her. Then she lowered herself onto Richard's cold body, hugging him tightly.

Richard, how cold you are. The chill sucked warmth from her breasts, her stomach, her thighs, as she pressed herself against him.

She closed her eyes and began to sing, calling upon Wolf and the Spirit Powers to help. The magnitude of what she was attempting awed her. So many strands of her life had come undone. Worry about White men had been gnawing at her. Her dissatisfaction with her own people, with *Dukurika* men who would chip an ax on rock to see sparks. Perhaps, by doing this crazy thing, she could weave them together again, find the balance in her world.

And if I do not succeed, I shall die, which is a resolution in itself.

She sang and prayed, souls rising to the challenge. Outside, White Hail's voice rose in song, adding his support to her call to Power.

The hot steam burned into her, stifling, unbearable. Sweat beaded to run down onto Richard's body.

You can stand it. Willow.

Her lungs sucked for cool air as her flesh crawled and squirmed. Only Richard was cool...cool...her senses swam, the darkness going gray.

She reached out with her life soul, searching, seeking, loosening herself from her body.

There, in the rippling mists of death, lay what she sought, be it success—or oblivion.

Overhead, cottonwoods reflected the firelight, their triangular leaves bathed in the golden glow. Richard leaned closer to his fire, naked heat eating into his chest and arms. Around him other fires popped and burned, smoke mingling with the warm air, redolent with the scents of corn and boiling pork, the pots watched carefully by the *engagés*. Jokes were called back and forth, and Toussaint's rich baritone filled the night with song. The breeze carried the river's musky smells to Richard's fire.

Green sat before his tent, a bowl of stew on his lap as he listened to Henri; the patroon waved his arms in Gallic emphasis as he predicted the next day's travel.

Richard sighed, a terrible weariness like lead in his limbs. How good to be in camp again—cold, snow, wind, and hunger nothing more than a dream. Tomorrow, just after sunrise, they would line out the cordelle and resume the endless struggle to pull the boat upriver.

Richard listened to the boatmen's song, and leaned back from the fire to pull his pipe from his possibles. He tamped tobacco into the stained bowl, and lit a twig. As he drew, he watched the yellow fire drawn downward and filled his lungs with rich blue smoke.

Why had he never sensed this peace on the river before? How could he have been so obsessed with Boston, and home, and all the other trivialities? What a fool he'd been about Laura. She'd never shown the slightest interest in him until he'd become involved in his father's business. How charming she'd been that last night in Boston—and Will had been her accomplice.

Do I blame her?

No, after all, she was doing what they all expected her to do: marry for wealth and station. He smiled crookedly, having never really considered himself a prize before. Poor Laura. For the rest of her life, she would be nothing more than a reflection of her husband.

Willow, however, had been free. Ah, to glimpse her flashing black eyes, see her raven hair gleaming in the sunlight. Within her Shoshoni heart burned a spirit fit for a man. Her supple body had awakened his male instincts, brought him to the verge of bursting the bonds he'd tied himself with.

In his arrogance, he'd made so many mistakes. By now Phillip knew about the money. Richard could see the old man in his office, hands clasped on the polished desk. The color would have drained from his cheeks, and he would have shaken his head before bowing his head and closing his eyes.

Did you think I'd stolen it, Father? Took it and ran off? At the thought, Richard winced. *I was a fool, Father. I just wish...well, that I could have seen as clearly then as I do now.*

So many regrets for such a short life. But here, on the river, they were only melancholy reminders of the past. Come morning, he would rise again, and with the others, face the Missouri and its current. Looking over his shoulder, he could see *Maria* tied by her painter, awaiting the dawn.

Why did I ever want to go back?

He puzzled on that for a moment, then let it go. Better the freedom of the river where life was only work, the capriciousness of current, sawyer, mud, and mosquitoes.

He barely heard the cry—ever so faint in the tranquil night. He cocked his head, listening. There, just at the edge of hearing. A woman's voice...Willow's, calling his name over and over.

"Here, Willow!" He stood up, fire-blinded to the darkness. How many times had Travis reproved him for such stupidity?

She stopped at the edge of the dark-shadowed trees beyond camp, staring at him with frightened eyes. Yes, as beautiful as ever—but naked.

"Willow? What's wrong?" Suddenly worried, he stepped away from the fire's warm security, desperately reluctant to leave that sphere of light. Behind him, the *engagés* had also stood, their songs forgotten.

She looked terrified, legs braced, shoulders hunched, ready to bolt. Firelight cast her perfect body in a bronze glow. Her lips moved, mouthing inaudible words, black hair shimmering around her like a shroud.

Trudeau had come to stand beside him, a feral gleam in his eyes. "She was always a beauty, *non*?"

"Shut up, damn it! Something's wrong."

"*Oui*," Trudeau agreed. "And now, perhaps, I 'ave her forever, eh?"

"Forever? What are you talking about?"

"She needs but step into zee camp. Then you will see, *mon ami*."

Unnerved, Richard took another reluctant step. "Willow? What are you doing out there? Where are your clothes?"

Her chest heaved, breasts rising as she gasped for breath. "Richard?" she whispered hoarsely. "Come to me. Please? Away from the camp."

"Away? That's crazy! Here, let me get you a robe, and then come in by the fire where it's warm."

"No!" She shivered, then tensed as if poised to flee. "Bring nothing, Richard. Just come to me. *Please?* If you love me, come to me. Richard, you must. I can't get back without you."

"Get back? I don't understand."

She reached out to him, imploring. "Richard, if you love me, if you ever loved me, *help me!*"

He took another step, fear ballooning inside him. "Willow, I can't. I belong here."

Her throat worked, head shaking. "No...I mean... You can stay if you want. But I came for you, to take you back with me. Richard, *please!*"

He pointed back at Trudeau, at the crackling fires, and Dave Green, who'd come to stand behind him. "This is the camp, Willow."

Her face contorted, and her fists knotted. "They're all *dead*, Richard. You're in the Land of the Dead! You know that, don't you?"

Dead? He turned, seeing humor in Trudeau's bent smile. Toussaint lifted his eyebrows, shrugging. A knowing twinkle glimmered in Green's eyes.

Willow reached out to him, her arms trembling. "Richard, please. This is so difficult—more dangerous than I ever guessed. If we're to get back, we must go together. I need your help to retrace the way. Oh, please, don't you understand? I *can't* get back alone. I need the threads of your soul to weave the way."

Dead? He rubbed the back of his neck, trying to comprehend.

"Do you love me, Richard? At least tell me that. If I'm to lose my soul here, in the blackness, I must know if you ever really loved me."

His chest heaved, and he nodded. "*Yes.* With all my heart. I never knew how much."

"Then come. Take my hand. At least we can be together here"—she shot a frightened glance into the black forest—"or wherever we end up."

He took another step toward her, fear rising.

Dear Lord, what's happening?

"Trust me, Richard." She reached out to him. Her hair had begun to float like black mist around her naked shoulders.

With each step he took, the terror rose within him. He, too, was trembling; it was like walking out in front of an enemy's rifle. If he took another step, the fear would choke him to death.

Turn around! Run to the safety of the fire, now, before it's too late!

Tears streaked down Willow's cheeks. Her lips were working, but he could not hear her words. He shook his head, on the verge of sobbing. Behind lay safety, the warm fire. He'd do anything for that security. He started to turn back—and saw the look in her eyes: pained disbelief surrendering to abject terror.

I can't let her down again.

With the last of his courage, Richard reached out and entwined his fingers with hers.

Willow pulled him to her, choking on tears, hugging him with a fierce desperation. For a long time they held each other, souls mingling. The terror that had threatened to overwhelm him receded. But what danger lurked around them in those dark trees?

He used his thumb to brush strands of raven black hair from her brow. "I don't understand any of this. What's happening? Can't we go back to the fire?"

"If we do, we'll die, just as they did." She pushed back, running her fingers across his face the way someone would to convince himself it were real. "We're not safe yet. Together, we can do this. Hold on to me, Richard. Under no circumstances should you let go of my hand, do you understand? For no reason—no matter what."

"I won't let go."

"Promise."

"I promise."

And hand-in-hand they turned, walking into the terrible darkness and cold.

Through the long night, White Hail waited and sang. His robes were part of the sweat lodge, and he had only his coat between him and the storm. But one thing he had plenty of was fire. He stomped out another hollow in the snow and built a second blaze. When the chill ate into him, he huddled between the fires and melted the snow from his coat. When he became too hot, he ranged out into the night in search of sagebrush, cottonwood, and juniper. By the armload, he packed it back. Some went to feed the fires, while the rest of it he wove into a rude wickiup just large enough to provide him some shelter. When he completed that, he packed the back of it with snow to seal it against the wind.

His thoughts centered on the sweat lodge, and the battle Willow waged within it.

Between wood trips, White Hail pulled glowing rocks from the fire and bore them into the sweat lodge. As snowflakes landed on the rocks, they sizzled and vanished in tiny puffs. Inside, he'd glance at Willow's dark form where she lay unmoving on the smelly White man. Her skin was clammy to the touch, as cold as the man's. From time to time she'd whimper, and her breathing had dropped to a grating rasp.

"Help her, *Tam Apo,*" White Hail whispered fervently, and then he'd pour water over the glowing red eye of rock. As the searing steam hissed and billowed, he'd recover the cool rocks, back out, and secure the flap to seal the hot Power within. He'd drop his rocks back in the fire to reheat, and scoop up more snow to melt in the tin cup.

As the long night wore on, he continued to sing his prayers to *Tam Apo,* lifting his head to the falling snow. They'd hear in the Spirit World, wouldn't they? They'd send her back, understanding that it was desperation that had goaded her to do this *omaihen* thing. Wouldn't they?

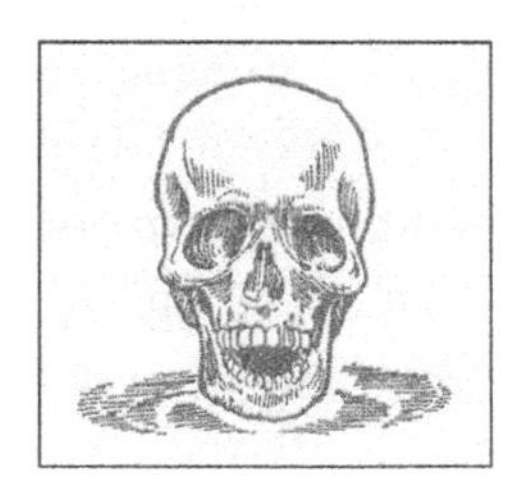

Oh, Willow, only you could be so brave.

Try as he might, he couldn't understand what would motivate her to risk her souls in such a dangerous quest. What if something went wrong? Power had its dark side, and Heals Like A Willow might come back changed, her *mugwa* twisted by *Pandzoavits.* Witchcraft! She might even come back as *Pa'waip* the terrible Water Ghost Woman who copulated with men even as she devoured their souls. The very thought of it chilled his bones worse than the storm.

Oh, Brother, if you could see your wife now, what would you think?

He glanced again at the sweat lodge. It might have been some giant black turtle crouched in the snow.

White Hail shook his head. He could *feel* Power loose on the night, smell it in snow-laden wind.

No matter how this ends, my world will never be the same again.

He poked at the flames with a stick, stirring the coals and watching the falling flakes melting away in the smoke.

If Willow survives, she will have proved herself a most Powerful puhagan. *If she comes back possessed by evil Power, she'll be a very dangerous witch. But if she dies, no one will ever trust me again. I'm tainted by association.*

That was when he began to understand that he couldn't win. Even in the best case, if Willow survived unscathed, she'd never be the exciting young woman who had married White Hail's brother. When he looked into her eyes, he'd see terrible *puha* looking back.

Face it. White Hail, the Willow you once loved is gone.

He could no more bring her back than he could the snowflakes that melted in his fire.

By that time, the fires were down to coals. He slapped his knees, stood, and marched out once again to see what he could scrounge for fuel. Willow would need more hot rocks and steam.

When the first tints of dawn finally cast their gray

light through the clouds, White Hail removed jerky, pemmican, and dried berries from the packs. Willow would be desperately hungry when she returned from the Land of the Dead. She *would* return. She had to.

A wretched headache stabbed like an antler tine behind Willow's eyes. She blinked awake to blurry darkness. It felt as though sand grated under her eyelids. She drew a deep breath—and the steam nearly suffocated her. Thoughts faded as soon as they formed, like water poured on sand.

I am...where?

The familiar sound of wind on hide coverings told her she was in a lodge. Curse the headache! It interfered with her thinking. She shifted, startled to find another human body beneath hers. She reached up to touch the face—and encountered a beard.

Richard! She was lying naked atop Richard, sweat beading and trickling down her sides. In the moist air, his smell nearly gagged her—and her stomach was already upset. Images came whirling out of her *mugwa* like snowflakes from a winter sky: dark caves; eerie trails winding through black timber, shapes darting away from the edge of her vision; the boatmen's camp in the Land of the Dead. A shiver ran down her back at the memory of the soul-wrenching terror.

Lost...in the Land of the Dead. I was holding Richard's hand, lost in the forest...

Yes! And then she'd collapsed, sobbing hysterically as Richard asked what was wrong. She'd cried, "*I can't find the way!*"

That was the last thing she could remember.

But here she was, back in the sweat lodge. Alive. Vague memories stirred: she and Richard being chased through the black forest by shadowy monsters. The bouncing presence of *nynymbi.* Water Ghost Woman, standing by a midnight-black lake, turle at her feet as she raised her spectral bow and point toward the path back with her other hand. Real, or imagined? Some parts of her memory were missing—rubbed out like drawings on loose dirt.

Willow could recall the mountain peak...Wolf...the frigid sucking away of her soul, then voices. Richard and Wolf, arguing over her. Their words had drifted off, like strands of mist in the branches.

She tried to move, only to have Richard's arms tighten around her. "Are you all right?" she asked.

"Are you?"

"Yes. Just terribly tired—and what a headache!"

"Me, too. Weak. Haven't eaten. Dear Lord God, such a dream. So vivid, I can recall every detail. But...I'm not still dreaming, am I? I mean, you're here? Alive?"

She sighed, sinking down on him. "I came to find you. Heard you calling to my souls."

"You *heard* me? Willow, I don't—"

"Richard, be quiet. The questions can wait until we heal you." She raised her voice. "White Hail?"

"Willow! Are you all right?" The flap rose, light spilling in with blinding glare. His cock-jawed expression added to the nervousness in his eyes. Snow was caked on the shoulders of his coat. "You're alive? Willow? Have you...have you done this thing?"

"Yes. I have brought Richard's *mugwa* back from the Land of the Dead."

"Willow, I must know. Are you still...you?" He couldn't mask the fear and uncertainty that brewed within.

"I'm me, *teci.* Nothing possessed my *mugwa.*" *At least, I don't think so.* "I'm terribly hungry, White Hail. We could use food, and fire, and something to wrap around Richard besides frozen hides."

White Hail's expression tightened as he inspected the White man. "Food is ready. I'll see what I can do for the *Taipo*." The flap settled back in place.

"Who's that?" Richard asked warily.

"My husband's brother."

"Husband?" He stiffened suddenly. "You—you're married? When?"

"My dead husband's brother," she corrected, reaching up to press his frostbit nose with a finger. "I'm married to no one."

He smiled then, sighing. "I'm glad. I came to tell you. I was wrong, Willow. About so many things. I wanted to tell you that day you left." He searched her eyes in the dimness. "Can you forgive me for being a damned idiot?"

"Yes." And her heart soared as she ran fingers down the side of his sunken face.

"I love you, Willow. I came to tell you that I love you with all of my soul. I couldn't die until you'd heard me say that."

"I've heard you, Richard."

He shook his head, tightening his hold on her. "For now, I'm happy to be alive, to have you...if you'll have me. The future will take care of itself."

"I will have you, Richard. For as long as I can."

"Thank God," he whispered softly.

White Hail ducked into the lodge, two steaming tins in his hands. "I've made stew," he said, setting the tins down. His hard black eyes fixed on Richard, on his arms about Willow. "But you should know that we don't have much food left." He pointed at the damp robes above. "That's all we have for clothing. You used our robes to cover the lodge. If you're going to dress your *Taipo,* it will have to be with what he was wearing."

CHAPTER SEVEN

Courage then, as has been stated, is the usual condition with regard to things that cause confidence or fear in the circumstances described. A man chooses action, or endures pain, because it is honorable to do so, or because the opposite course is disgraceful.

But to die as a means to escape from poverty, or love, or anything painful, is the act not of a courageous person but of a coward. For it is weakness to fly from troubles; nor does the suicide face death because it is noble, but because it is a refuge from evil…

—Aristotle, *Nicomachean Ethics*

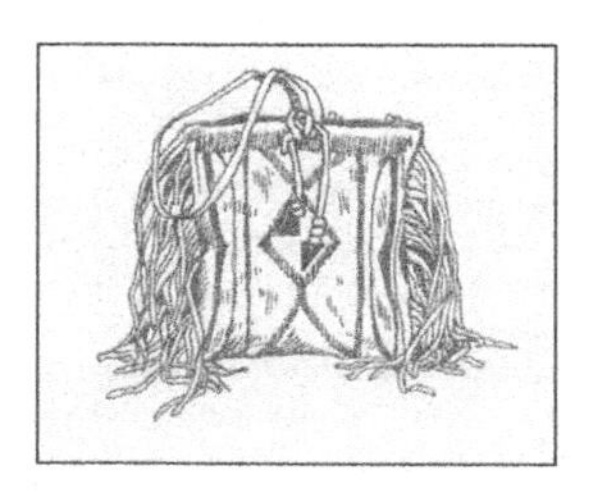

The Shoshoni warrior White Hail rode first, his horse breaking trail through the deep snow. Lead rope in hand, Willow followed on foot, breath puffing whitely as she slogged along in White Hail's trail. Richard clung weakly to Willow's mare. He still teetered on the edge of exhaustion and shivered continually.

They climbed higher, following the windblown ridgeline toward a low saddle in the mountain wall. The northern slopes were timbered with dark green pine and gray-stemmed brush, while juniper clung to the rocky soil on the southern exposures. Wind had sculpted the drifts into scallops, angles, and cornices. Ripples of white undulated around the sagebrush. The world looked as if God had frosted it like a cake—the job so perfect as to be the envy of any Bostonian confectioner.

Richard barely noticed the country, his concentration dedicated to keeping his seat. The mare swayed with each step, often sliding in the deep snow. Sometimes she'd stumble, step in a hidden hole, and pitch sideways to recover. Through it all, Richard had to cling like a tick to a tail. Still lightheaded from starvation, yet the question plagued him: How had Willow found him—and odder yet, how could they have shared a dream in such intimate detail?

That experience *had* to be a dream. Any other explanation defied rationality.

As if I've been rational during the last year.

The cold wind made his eyes water, and he blinked to clear them. Well, what was one more problem to solve? God had been giving him more than his share recently.

He squinted against the wind that tugged relentlessly at him and sought to break his hold on the mare. It whipped Richard's beard and the hair that straggled from the confines of his hat.

Each time the Shoshoni warrior looked back, his flint black eyes betrayed a steely resentment.

Why does he hate me so? What have I ever done to him?

But when they stopped to let Willow rest, Richard

finally saw the worried longing in the warrior's eyes as he watched Willow.

So, he loves her, and she loves me.

Richard closed his eyes, taking stock of himself—and not finding much. His muscles quaked from the effort to hold on to the horse. The odor creeping up from his patchwork of frozen hides offended his own nose. No wonder White Hail looked at him like some sort of bug. Willow seemed completely unconcerned. She walked back, smiling at him and patting his hand. "Are you all right?"

"Tired," he told her, grinning wryly. "If any Pawnee warriors show up, well, I'm not worth a shit."

Her grin met his, and her eyes sparkled like stars. When he looked back at White Hail, the warrior's face was expressionless, but dark fires burned behind his eyes.

Late that afternoon, they crested the low saddle and dropped down into a valley on the northern side of the pass. Fir, lodgepole, and limber pine darkened the slopes; the skirts of the trees were deep in soft-mounded snow. North and west, in the distance, rugged ridges crowded upon each other like concertina folds. Deep drifts lay under each rocky prominence. Far out over the grim basin, torn shreds of cloud drifted westward toward the valley of the Platte.

Willow spoke to the warrior before wading back to Richard. "Let me help you down. We will camp here."

"Sorry. I guess I'm off my uppers, as Travis would say."

She caught him as he tumbled down, searching his eyes with hers. Pulling a hand from her mitten, she felt his cheek, pinching his skin. "Have you been dizzy? Seen—how would you say?—sparks behind your eyes?"

"Yes. Starved, I think. Still a little numb from exhaustion. I'm trying to understand what happened. This Land of the Dead business."

"We'll talk about that later. Come, you're shivering. We'll get a fire started. Sit there, on that log. It won't be long."

"I can do something, get firewood or..."

She pointed a mittened finger. "Sit there, Richard."

Richard shuffled to the log, secretly grateful since his feet barely supported him. Had he ever felt this tired? From the core of his bones out to his hair, every part of him was dead-weary. He dusted off the snow and sat. The warrior gave him a wary look before slipping into the soft shadows under the trees. Sticks snapped as White Hail broke squaw wood. Meanwhile, Willow attended to picketing the horses, stripping off saddles, and making camp under the low-hanging branches of a huge fir tree.

When she came for him, he'd begun to shiver, blinking at the black dots that formed before his eyes. Willow practically carried him into the branch-screened bower.

White Hail had started a fire in a hollow scooped in the duff. He glanced up from the spindle of flame, distaste in the set of his mouth.

Willow guided Richard to a nest of blankets and robes beside the fire. The warrior said something and Willow answered.

"I guess White Hail would rather not have found me." Richard leaned his head back, neck muscles flaccid. "I didn't spoil his journey with you, did I?"

"What he wants or doesn't want is his concern." She glanced across at Richard. "Is it that obvious?"

He smiled. "Maybe I got used to men looking at you that way on the river."

"White Hail is my *teci*, my husband's brother. When

my husband died, White Hail wanted to marry me. I'm smarter than he is, and told him no." She shrugged. "That was another time, another place." She studied him with worried eyes. "Richard, we haven't spoken. What happened? Why are you here? Why were the *engagés,* and Henri, and Dave Green all in the Land of the Dead?"

How can she have been there, too?

He took a deep breath. "Blackfeet. A war party came up from the south, ambushed the camp on the Big Horn. Overran it. Green waited until they swarmed the boat, then set off the powder."

"And Travis and Baptiste?" she asked, voice neutral. But Richard saw her fist clench.

White Hail ducked out to scoop snow into the tin pots. He set them on the fire and began shaving dried meat, pemmican, and something that looked like hardtack into the melting snow.

"Alive. At least, I think so. Baptiste went to join the Crow; Travis and I started south to find you. We were separated back at the beginning of the deep cold. I did all right until I broke my gun. I fell off this cliff. A red sandstone ridge sharp as a knife—just east of the mountains."

"The Red Wall," she whispered. 'That's where I dreamed you called to me."

"I did...in my dreams." Richard stared down at his hands. Once they'd been strong, callused and hard from the cordelle. Now he opened and closed his thin fingers, a bone-deep weakness within them. "Willow, you talk about the camp I saw in my delirium. Green, Henri, the *engagés*...I dreamed that I was there. Was I babbling? Out of my head? How much did I tell you?"

She leaned toward him, eyes luminous in the firelight. "You said nothing to me. You were dying, Richard. I sent my soul to find you, to bring your *mugwa* back to your body. A *puhagan* can do these things. I had to take the chance, even though a woman isn't supposed to. I am *omaihen*."

At the word. White Hail froze in place, a pot half raised.

Willow spoke in *Dukurika,* her words a staccato. White Hail answered in kind. It ended when Willow made the familiar hand sign for enough.

"What was all that?" Richard asked softly. White Hail studiously returned to his chores, as if it took all of his effort to make those routine tasks appear effortless.

"I told him I needed your help to return from the Land of the Dead. Richard, do not mention this among the *Dukurika.* White Hail will keep his tongue, for he owes me his life. From now on, he will fear your Power. We would never have made it back without your *puha.* We did this thing together."

"This is crazy, Willow." He lowered his head into his hands. "But I'm not up to arguing with you right now. There must be some logical explanation for what happened."

When he finally looked up, her dark eyes were slightly hostile. "You have not changed, have you? Everything must still fit into your box."

He swallowed hard, hating White Hail's presence, irritated with himself. He gave her a sheepish smile. "I'm sorry. When inquiry fails, only faith is left."

Faith? The Shoshoni notion of two souls was difficult enough to comprehend. He glanced at her, stung by the old hurt in her eyes. Damn it, did he always have to let her down?

"Old habits die hard, Willow. Suppose you wanted to think like a White man, how long would it take to ignore your Shoshoni instincts?" Richard took the steaming tin Willow passed him. "That's more than my share."

Willow shrugged. "White Hail and I need less. We still have two days' travel to reach *Pa'gushowener.* Until then, you need the food, Richard. Gather your strength. Who knows, maybe we'll kill something on the way."

He pursed his lips, staring down into the steaming tin. His belly won out over ethical concerns. By the time he'd emptied the tin, his stomach was aching. Despite the discomfort, he craved more.

When supper was finished, Willow repacked the tins and slipped out into the night. Richard stared at the fire for a while, then looked up at White Hail, saying, "She's an incredible woman, isn't she?"

The warrior met his English query with silence, no hint of expression in his gleaming eyes. He was a handsome young man, his brown skin smooth over prominent cheeks, his nose long and straight. The crooked set of his jaw pursed his lips into a perpetual expression of mild skepticism.

When Willow returned, she lifted an eyebrow. "You will need to drain your pizzle, Richard. I don't want to get up in the middle of the night with you."

"Drain my...? Oh, yes, I suppose." He eyed the hand she reached down to him. "What are you doing? I *don't* need help."

"You can barely walk. Do you want me to have to pick you up when you collapse in the snow?"

He vented an exasperated sigh, and let her help him to his feet. Together they walked out into the night, and he had to admit his wobbly legs would have failed him but for her support.

He endured, despite chafing embarrassment. Upon

their return to the camp, Willow spread out the robes, eased him down, and slid in next to him.

Richard tried to close his eyes, to make himself drift off, but his mind resisted stubbornly. Had she saved his life? Hell, yes! So what difference did it make to him if she'd done it through her body heat, or through some mystical twining of souls?

I am alive. That's all that matters.

But it's the method of your salvation that cannot be explained with any satisfaction, the little internal voice insisted.

Her head rested in the hollow of his shoulder, her body warmth joining his. When he inhaled, the familiar scent of her hair mixed with the pungent smell of fir needles and smoke; it brought a smile to his lips.

He remembered the way she'd looked that day at the Grand Detour, how her body had felt as it slid against his. He tightened his hold on her, feeling her snuggle closer to him.

Go to hell! he told the little voice inside, and only then did he drift off into fitful dreams.

"Have you considered strangling him?" Willow asked White Hail dryly as they walked side by side through the snow. Sun-warmed and water-rotten, it soaked their moccasins.

They led the horses west down a long valley that would lead them to the very banks of the *Pia'ogwe.* To their left, immediately south, rose the slope of the mountain called *Tunangarit,* Thundersitter. To their right, the valley was hemmed by a bloodred sandstone ridge that jutted up in sheer cliffs. In places melted snow had trickled down the red rock, looking for all the world like dark sweat.

"Strangle him? What are you talking about?" White Hail gave her a hesitant look. He'd almost glanced back at Richard, but caught himself in time.

"Strangling would be best," she said. "You'd have to do it when I wasn't looking, of course. Any other way of killing him would look too much like murder."

White Hail scowled at her, then smiled sheepishly. To avoid her gaze, he looked out at the ragged sandstone ridge. "Woman, you've always been a step ahead of me, knowing the twists in my trail before I did. I can't understand what my brother saw in you."

"Go home, White Hail. When have I been wrong? About Red Calf? About the *Pa'kiani?* About finding Richard? About bringing back his soul? And now I see you becoming more bitter than gall drippings. If you persist, that bitterness will consume you, a festering evil beyond your control. Do you want that, White Hail? Is that the sort of man you would become?"

He paused thoughtfully. "No, Willow. I would rather be the sort of man I once was. What's happened to me? Why do I feel poisoned?"

"It's me. White Hail. The effect I have on you—just as I foretold so long ago when you came to ask me to marry you. *Teci,* I am going to ask you to do something for me, for both of us."

He sighed then. "Yes?"

"Leave. Jump up on your horse, and ride off to find the *Ku'chendikani.* Throw Red Calf out of your lodge, take care of Two Half Moons, and concentrate on hunting. If you wish wealth, hunt beaver for their hides, and trade them when the Whites arrive. There is no rule that says you cannot be brave and wise at the same time."

He considered her suspiciously. "And what will you and the White man do out here all alone?"

"I am taking him to the hot springs at *Pa'gushowener.* High Wolf will take his camp there after the equinox. He always does. He says the hot water helps him to restore his Power."

White Hail gestured his incomprehension. "Why alone, Willow? What if the *Pa'kiani* come? Or the *A'ni,* or some other enemy?"

She reached out, laying a hand on White Hail's shoulder. "I want time alone with him. My *navuzieip* has dreamed it—now I want to live it. I'll tell you another reason I want you to leave, *teci.* He will be my husband. I don't think you will sleep well knowing we are joined under the robes just across from you."

White Hail snorted: "If his *we'an* is as weak as the rest of him, I don't have much to worry about."

"I'll wager his *we'an* is healthier than you think."

White Hail fingered the knife at his belt and slowly shook his head. "That night you went after the *Taipo's* soul, I knew that my life was changing forever. I knew that you would come back changed if you even survived. You have great *puha.* Greater than most *puhagans,* since you can see into souls and travel to the Land of the Dead. For once, Willow, I will do as you say." A crooked smile bent his lips. "And, somehow, I think we will still be friends after this. But as to the White man..." his nose wrinkled. "He still stinks."

"*Tam Apo* go with you," Willow called as White Hail swung up onto his horse. He never looked back as he kicked the *Pa'kiani* gelding into a trot, hooves snowballing.

"What's happening?" Richard asked from where he rode on her mare.

"White Hail is going home to throw out his wife and live with his aunt for a while." She walked back, taking his hand. "I told him that you will be my husband."

"Husband?" His soft brown gaze probed hers. "I would like that, Willow. But do you understand how difficult this will be for us? The uncertainties?"

She squeezed his hand. "Richard, nothing in life is certain. You should know that by now."

His smile warmed. "Yes, I know. However, I think we have something special, you and I."

Richard rode stubbornly, his fingers woven into the brown mare's mane. A terrible fatigue sapped the last of his energy. His stomach knotted with a perpetually ravenous appetite. Willow had fed him all she could spare from her scanty rations, but eat as he might, he remained desperate for yet another bite.

Memories of long-ago meals, untouched food left on plates, tortured him. How fine life had been in Boston, food no farther away than the bell cord or the nearest tavern.

I'll never think of food the same way. These days will always haunt me. Even as he thought of it, the musty taste of rotten buffalo lingered on his tongue.

From Sally's magnificent culinary creations in Boston to scavenging rotten meat in the Big Homs was more than the distance between places.

Who am I now? What am I?

"I'm alive, that's what."

Willow had been pushing herself, walking at a brisk pace as she traveled the sage-dotted ridgetops. Travel was easier since the snow had blown from the rocky crests. Now the ridges led down into the wide valley of the *Pia'ogwe,* the Shoshoni's Mother River. To the south, the Owl Creek Mountains sloped up in a smooth incline, as if God had tilted the plain to form a ramp up to the sky. There, the peak Willow called Thundersitter dominated the southern horizon. To the west of it, the *Pia'ogwe* had cut a sheer-walled gorge through the tilted rock. White limestone lipped the edges—a layer of fat in a gargantuan wound.

At the base of the mountain, the red sandstone ridges huddled in on each other like horseshoe crabs on a beach. Those formations gave way to broken country stretching northward into the snow-shadowed basin. There, brown stone thrust out over yellow, white, and blue clays; the entire landscape, painted by the whim of nature, contrasted to the enamel blue of endless sky and sun-polished snow fields.

Willow turned north as they crested a ridge and dropped into the *Pia'ogwe*'s broad floodplain. The cottonwoods were bare and gray, branches lonely for summer.

Richard glanced curiously at the clear river; bits of ice floated on its dark surface. It was hard to believe that these clear waters would become the same chalk-muddy Big Horn he'd ridden beside with Baptiste and Travis.

Two round-humped hills marked Willow's destination, and even in the afternoon sun, Richard could see the steam rising whitely from the crinkled earth at the bottom of the hills.

"That's *Pa'gushowener*? What's that mean?" he asked.

"It means 'Hot-Water-Stand.' It's a sacred place for us. You and I will camp beside the springs and heal you."

When she led him over the last rise, Richard could only gape. Scalloped formations of rock nestled beneath the rounded red and white hills. Each travertine formation pooled with clear, steaming water through which could be seen beds of orange, red, green, and blue. Only fairy tales could conjure an image like this, yet here it was before his eyes.

"It's magical!"

Willow stopped short, staring at one of the cottonwoods by the river. A large buck deer—tied off by the antlers—hung from a thick branch. The arrow transfixing its breast gleamed in the sunlight.

"What is it? An offering?" Richard glanced around, his starvation-numbed mind suddenly aware of potential ambush.

"White Hail," Willow told him as a wry smile crossed her lips. "That's his arrow. These tracks, fresh...and made by his horse. See, there's the chip out of the left front hoof. Yes, Richard. It is an offering: food. Let me help you down. We'll camp here for the night. Then, tomorrow, we'll find a better place, build a shelter, and fort up."

"Fort up? As in 'prepare for a fight'?" He glanced back at the Hawken tied onto the pack. "My rifle's broken, Willow."

She gave him a thoughtful, sloe-eyed look. "But isn't 'fort up' the word Whites use for a permanent camp? Or should I have said 'build a post'?"

"'Fort up' will be fine."

She took his hands, steadying him as he dismounted. She held him, staring into his eyes. "I've dreamed of having you here, Richard." She reached up, touching her lips to his, and he kissed her, ever so gently.

"For now, I want you to start healing yourself. Go and lie in the hot pool. I'll see to the horse, set up camp, and make a fire. Go on!" She waved him away.

Richard walked wearily to the edge of the nearest pool and stared at his reflection. More of a silhouette, really; he looked like something out of German mythology. He touched a finger to water as warm as any Jeffry had poured in the bath on Beacon Street.

Stripping out of his crusty hides, he shivered in the cold air, then waded into the warm water. The heat, enough to make him gasp, tingled his feet and toes. A wallow had been scraped into the crusty bottom near the edge of the pool. Not only was the water cooler, but the spot overlooked the river. The clear, ice-cold waters of the *Pia'ogwe* weren't twenty feet below. Richard settled himself, lying back to bask.

Even before he ducked his head, sweat beaded to roll down his face. Eyes almost at water level, his imagination found faces and images in the patterns of steam. *Puha*, right here, before him.

Water. The age-old symbol of rebirth. What will you become this time, Richard? Still a philosopher? Or something else?

Cupping his hands, he poured water over his head, then used his fingers and the flaky grit from the bottom to scrub himself clean before moving to clear water where he rinsed.

I could stay here forever, floating in the mist. That triggered his memory. *What really happened? Did I go to the Spirit World, the Land of the Dead, as Willow insists?*

He splashed in the heat, muscles and bones growing lax. "Damn it, it's not rational."

Or is it that you just won't admit what happened? Is that it, Richard? More of your arrogant American certainty that if it isn 't scientific, not in a book, it can't be real?

"That's not it at all. Prove to me, rationally, empirically, that my soul—"

One of your souls.

"All right, prove to me that *one* of my souls went beyond the veil, into the afterlife. Whatever that is. And Willow's soul came to get mine. Good Lord, this isn't the Middle Ages!"

Ah, but something happened to you. Perhaps as it did to Augustine in the desert? To Aquinas, to Meister Eckhardt? To any of the great mystics? Something, Richard. They weren't all *crazy.*

"Maybe they were."

You 're desperate to clutch any straw that might offer an alternative to a phenomenon you can't rationalize.

"Everything in the universe has an—"

"What are you doing?" Willow asked from behind him.

"Arguing with myself about the 'Land of the Dead.' Half of me says it was real, the other half is still skeptical."

"At least half of you is learning." She appeared out of the mist, wading in the knee-deep water. Tendrils of steam curled around her sleek brown legs, wound around her flat muscular belly, and spun illusions over her full breasts. Her long black hair was pulled back over her shoulder and hung down below her rump. It swung with each step, swirling the mist.

Precious Lord God, she looks like a goddess.

She approached gracefully, hips swaying, arms balancing precisely. Reading his expression, she flashed him a smile, challenge in her dark eyes.

"Are you going to run away again?"

"Just stand there, Willow. Yes, like that, with the steam rising around you. I want to memorize the way you look, plant it deep inside my soul, in that place of treasured memories. Blessed God but you're beautiful."

She lifted her chin, a sudden glint in her eye, then, quick as lightning, shifted and kicked water all over him. Before he could recover, she belly-flopped beside him, shrieking delight. She twisted like an otter, black hair wrapping around her, and surfaced beside him.

"That's the only way to do it," she told him. "Just dive in and feel the heat prickle all over your body. Hiyyaa! I'm alive, Richard. Every nerve—singing with the Power of the water."

"What a wonderful phrase." He splashed her back.

She studied him curiously, half seated, half floating. Her toes stuck out like dots in the twilight. "Is it so hard to believe in the Land of the Dead? Where do your souls go when you die? Somewhere?"

He frowned, lips pinched. "I don't know. No one does. I keep searching for an explanation."

She bobbed toward him, taking his hand and searching his eyes. "Can't some things just *be*? It happened, didn't it?"

"That's what perplexes me. How do I prove it? This could be one of the most important discoveries of science, but I must have proof. Not for myself, but for others."

"Other Whites, you mean."

"Yes, other Whites."

"Richard, listen to me. Hear my words. Read my soul." She came close, her body sliding smoothly against his until he could feel her heart beating—sense that joining he'd felt in the Land of the Dead. "The *puha* will defy you if you seek to measure it. You can't *think* your way to it the way you try to do with God. You can't put it in a box. The only proof you have is that you are alive. You may believe or disbelieve, that is your choice. But if you believe, it is only because you *want* to, do you understand?"

With the barest hint of a nod, he surrendered and pulled her closer until his lips could brush hers. "We call it faith, Willow. That's the nail I've been missing—the thing to tie it all together. It took a very brave woman to come after my soul in the afterworld. Thank you for saving my life."

"We did it together," she reminded him soberly, and ran her long fingers down the side of his body. "I could never have returned without your help."

He slipped his arms around her and drew her onto him. Her breasts lay warm on his chest. “You and I, Heals Like A Willow, we’re going to do a great many things together. You just wait until I get my strength back.”

She smiled, relaxing against him. “I’m not a patient woman, Richard.”

CHAPTER EIGHT

The dialectic by which the object, as implicitly null, suspends itself, is the action of the self-assured living thing, which in this process against an inorganic nature thus retains, develops, and objectifies itself.

The living individual, which in its first process is as subject and concept, through its second has assimilated its external objectivity. It is now, therefore, implicitly a genus, with substantial generality. The judgment of this concept is the relation of the subject to another subject, the sexual difference.

—Georg Friedrich Wilhelm Hegel, *Encyclopedia of the Philosophical Sciences in Outline*

The night wind blew in fits and starts, sometimes the barest of breezes, sometimes gusting hard enough to flatten the fire and tear sparks away into the night.

Willow had built a brush lean-to between the boles of two large cottonwoods. It would serve more as a windbreak than anything else. Tomorrow she would build a true wickiup out of brush and poles. To do so she would need willow, sagebrush, and bundles of grass.

The bank here was as high as a tall man above the river's edge, and Willow had placed their camp several paces back from the edge. As a result, they could see the moonlight reflected on the swirling water when the wind wasn't driving rippling waves across it.

Willow smiled as she watched Richard eat. Why was it that seeing a man eat reassured a woman? Was it some sense that *Tam Segobia* had placed in a woman's *mugwa?* Richard sat propped against the saddle. With greasy fingers, he plucked strands of meat from the ravaged deer haunch, chewing with studied enjoyment. He'd been nibbling like this for hours, ever since emerging from the spring.

She returned to scraping bits of tissue and muscle from the deer hide. In the morning, she'd finish slicing the deer's carcass into strips thin enough to smoke and dry.

I've dreamed of this moment.

She stole another glance. His hair shone in the firelight; how soft his beard looked now that it was clean. A fish splashed in the river below their camp.

Tam Apo, *was it so much to ask after this last year?*

Stringy connective tissue bunched on the pale hide. Using a hafted chert scraper, she hacked it loose, balled it, and tossed it over the bank into the river. She worked her fatigued fingers and stood up, amused with herself. "I'm tired. I'm going to wash my hands and sleep."

He grinned up at her. "It's been a long day. And, to tell you the truth, I haven't felt this good for...well...I guess I've *never* felt this good."

She took his greasy hand, and together they walked to

the edge of the hot pool. "I think that hide will make you a good shirt, much better than those pieces you've been tying on like some stunted *Pandzoavits*."

"They kept me alive. I was scared to death of frostbite."

She shook the water from her hands as they walked back to the fire. "You did very well, Richard. I'm proud of you. I'm not sure that even Travis could have done so well."

"Well, you know how these philosophers are."

She chuckled, hugged him, and laid out the robes before unlacing her moccasins. She wrinkled her nose. "We're clean, but the robes still have a smell."

"The sky's clear," he noted. "It's going to be cold tonight. I guess we'll just have to lie in the water again tomorrow." He paused, eyes shining. "I can't stop thinking about you. About the way you looked in the pool this afternoon."

She slipped her dress over her head, the wind chilling her warm skin. "Come to me, Richard."

A faint smile crooked his lips as he peeled his clothing away. Then he slipped in beside her, wrapping his arms around her and pulling her close.

For the moment, she closed her eyes, savoring the feel of his skin against hers, of his rapid heartbeat. As they warmed the robes, she ran her hand along his side to the curve of his buttock. Massaging the skin, she enjoyed the tension her fingers invoked. He sighed, his penis hardening against her hip.

"Willow?" he said, voice husky, "I've never done this before."

"I think I can lead you through it. And Richard, I'll take a great deal of pleasure in teaching you." She rolled onto her back, drew him onto her.

"I won't hurt you, will I?"

She laughed, arms around him in a fierce hug. His breath was warm on the curve of her neck. Her own heart racing, she pulled her knees up and reached down to guide him. He made a strangled sound as his rigid penis slid inside her. Her hips strained to meet his; then she locked her muscles to savor their union.

"Dear Lord God," he whispered, daring to look down at her. Her souls thrilled at the worship in his eyes. She moved slowly, using her muscles and the slightest of undulations.

Now we have shared souls, hearts, and bodies, Richard. Tam Apo *willing, we always will.*

So, that was what it was all about? Richard half floated in the hot water. He lay on his back, only his face exposed to the air. Streamers of mist drifted in front of his nose, and water lapped at his cheeks. The breeze carried across the river from the southwest to ripple the surface of his bathing pond. Pale morning sky was frosted with horsetail filaments of cloud that diluted the hazy sunlight.

Eyes closed, he lay there, buoyed in body and soul. Ravens cawed as they flapped overhead. He and Willow had made love off and on throughout the night, and again as the morning broke.

They'd come here, bathed, and she'd ordered him to remain while she went about the preparation of food, and started construction of a wickiup. Weak as he was, he'd barely resisted, preferring to soak and relive every moment of their night together. Nothing had prepared him for this sense of elation.

Like any young man, he'd grown up with the urges

and the attraction. He'd expected the physical sensations, but in imagination, the act had been somehow mechanical, the only passion animalistically physical. The *engagés* rutting with the Ree women and the Omaha squaw, and Travis dallying with the Sioux squaw had reinforced that idea. Copulation had come to seem nothing more than animalistic grunting.

He'd never considered that sexual joinings could come in two sorts: the sating of desire, and those of mutual intimacy.

Poor Travis, he has only the former.

Surely it hadn't always been that way. He had loved Calf in the Moonlight, married her. He must have felt this swelling joy.

An unexpected contentment ran down to the root of Richard's soul. And for that, he was glad that he'd turned down New Moon Rising's offer to warm his robes that night in the Crow village.

How much better that it was Willow. That first time, she had anticipated his quick ejaculation. *I would have thought that was all there was to it. Enter, explode, and wait until later to do it all again.*

But then Willow's fingers had stroked him to renewed vigor. She'd soothed, taught, and explained what made a woman happy. Under her guidance, he'd explored her breasts, run his hands over her stomach and the firm curves of hip and buttocks. One by one she taught him the secrets of her body and that joining could be done in more than one way.

During their fourth coupling she, too, had stiffened and cried out. Her reaction was stunning. Why had no one told him that a woman reached that pinnacle of ecstasy?

With Laura, his attempts would have been fumbling, shy, and nowhere as satisfying. Laura. He pursed his lips. Once, guilt would have tortured him. Now, he could barely remember her except as a dream.

He searched himself for regrets, and found none. *I would live last night over again, exactly the same way, with the same passion and reverence.*

He had joined his life to a woman, who—in the eyes of Bostonian society—was beneath contempt. He'd forsaken his vow of a virgin bride. How many men had slid themselves into her body before him? Two that he knew of. Definitely her husband—and that same vagina had passed their child into the world. And Packrat—how many times had he mounted her and sated himself inside her? She'd as much as told him that *Dukurika* placed no emphasis on virginity; in *Tam Apo*'s eyes, men and women were supposed to copulate.

He smiled wearily, stretching out his arms and legs and arching his back to float free of the bottom. Travis had once asked, "What in Tarnal Hell are ye in love with? The woman? Or what's atwixt her legs?"

Oh, Travis, how right you were.

Some whim of the mind conjured the serene eyes of Mother Mary, who stared down at him from his right. And from the left watched the haggard eyes of the fallen Magdalene. The two Marys of Christian civilization, eternally unrecognized as an elemental duality, a dialectical abstraction taken to obsessive extremes: the pristine Madonna or the gutter whore, and no common ground between.

Dear God, how we've deluded ourselves. How many people have been crippled by that myth?

One for sure: Richard John Charles Hamilton. He

cocked his head, surprised that he no longer cared, slightly puzzled by the lack of concern.

What if, by chance, he returned to Boston? Married Laura?

What if I do? First, I have to live that long. Second, Willow and I will have come to some bad end. And, should those criteria be fulfilled and I return to Boston, then I will determine the course of action appropriate to the circumstances.

What if he had impregnated Willow?

Then I will deal with it. He paused. *I will live here, now, taking all that I can from this fragile existence.*

Life was too much of an uncertain thin—as ephemeral as clouds on a hot day. If Willow were to have his child, he would take responsibility for it. Travis had been right, no one could escape responsibility.

Again, his reaction surprised him. The usual trepidation no longer plagued him. Why?

And the answer flowed easily from within. *Because I will deal with the eventualities. Because I can.*

But if I die tomorrow, or the day after, I can say that I have lived, loved.

Indeed he had. Her gasps of pleasure echoed in his ears. He could conjure the feel of her body out of the warm water, firm and soft, conforming to him. Man and woman, a sum of parts that made a balanced whole. The magic dazzled, profound in its simplicity.

He opened his eyes to the world, possessed of a new excitement.

In the shadow of death, I finally understand.

To reach this place, he'd had to lose everything—be stripped of the clutter of preconception imposed by his society. *I had to lose myself to find myself.*

"I have become Wolf," he whispered to an imaginary

Sioux *wechashawakan* hovering in the trailers of steam. And a smile crossed his lips.

———

As days passed into weeks, Richard regained his strength. Life at *Pa'gushowener* had a fairy-tale quality. Occasional storms roared down out of the north and left wind-drifted snow in their wakes. Then the skies would turn blue and cloudless and the slow melt would begin. The nights brought a clear cold, ameliorated by their cheery fire, the sagebrush shelter, and two bodies snuggled together under the robes.

During the day they walked the hills, collecting juniper bark to be shredded and twisted into netting. With sinew cord, they set snares for rabbits. With the Pawnee bow and arrows, they hunted the brush along the river for ducks. Willow taught Richard the proper way to net fish, and how to weave a fish trap from sticks and bait it. Together they built an antelope trap in an arroyo, using juniper and sagebrush for wing walls. Willow taught him different ways to sneak up on buffalo, and how killing with a bow differed from using a rifle.

Richard struggled with the rudiments of the Shoshoni language, and spent his evenings listening to the winter stories about the Creation, about Wolf and

Trickster Coyote, who traveled the land with his two penises. In reverent tones, she told him about Pa'waip, the spectral woman he'd glimpsed in their flight from the Land of the Dead, and how she lurked beside streams and lakes, and seduced men before she drowned them and ate their souls. He heard about the *Pandzoavits,* the rock ogres, about Cannibal Owl, Water Babies, and the *Nynymbi.* She told him the stories about *Pachee Goyo,* the Bald One, who hunted the Water Buffalo that lived under Bull Lake. *Pachee Goyo* was abducted by Cannibal Owl but managed to escape when he killed Cannibal Owl with sharp flakes of obsidian.

Each night, they soaked in the hot springs, holding hands and talking of the day's adventures before retiring to the little shelter for supper and trysting under the robes.

Then came the evening when Richard and Willow returned from one of their hunts, the brown mare packed with sage grouse they'd killed with throwing sticks.

She held his hand as they walked, and thought back to the days on the river. "You know, Richard, even in my dreams I wasn't this happy."

"It's like the perfect paradise," he admitted, a pensive look on his face.

She gave him a sidelong inspection. *Richard has changed.*

He had made peace with the endless questions that had plagued him on the river. This new Richard was reserved, quietly contemplative. The burning in his soul had quenched, replaced by a deeper introspection.

But then, he's not the only one who's changed.

She looked out at the world with a stranger's eyes. Little more than a year had passed since she wedged the body of her first husband and her son into the crack in the sandstone. Since then, she'd glimpsed four different worlds: Pawnee, White, Shoshoni, and the Land of the Dead.

Like Richard, I, too, have lost my innocence.

She noticed the tension in his face. "What are you thinking when you look like that?"

"Look like what?"

"Like that. With that ghost of a frown. I see a distance in your eyes. As if you don't see this world for the moment."

"I was thinking about my father. About Boston."

Dread spread through her. "Boston. If I could pierce it with an arrow, kill it, I would."

His frown deepened. "How do I explain this? My father sent me off to Saint Louis with a great deal of wealth. I was robbed, lost every penny of it. Then, to save my life, I signed on with the *Maria*. So, here I am, Willow, living in a kind of paradise I'd never dreamed. But my father lost thirty thousand dollars because I was a fool."

He pursed his lips, then added: "It's funny, but I never understood him until recently. I imagine him sitting behind his desk, looking miserable because he thinks I'm dead—or worse, that I've betrayed him and taken the money for myself. He never forgave himself for my mother's death, and he'll never forgive himself for sending me to Saint Louis."

"Your words frighten me."

"You?" he asked, arching an eyebrow. "Heals Like A Willow, who drove Packrat insane? The woman who killed so many Rees, and saved my life? The woman who crossed the wilderness, rescued White Hail from the Blackfeet, and dared to search the Land of the Dead for my soul? Is that the same Willow who now says she's frightened?"

"Don't joke. I'm afraid you will go to Boston and never come back."

That you will stay with this yellow-haired Laura you used to dream about.

"I haven't left yet."

"No, you haven't. But you're a man, Richard. Men always leave."

He glanced suspiciously at her. "But they come back, don't they?"

"Will you? Have you asked yourself that question? Where do you belong—here with me? Or in your Boston with its philosophy, and God in buildings, and women in houses with their children?"

"Willow, it's as if I was reborn when I awoke after the Land of the Dead. I don't fully understand this new life—where I'm going."

"But the old life still intrudes?"

"He's still my father. He thinks I'm dead. Thinks he sent me to that death. You lost a son. How much worse would it have been if you'd sent him out to his death? I think you understand the Power of guilt."

She nodded reluctantly. The mare stopped to rub her head on a propped foreleg. "Richard, do you *want* to go back?"

But he didn't have time to answer the question, for as they topped the ridge that led down to their wickiup, Willow spied two men sitting at the fire.

Richard reached out to stop her. "We'll talk of that later. Recognize them?"

From their sheephide coats they were *Dukurika.* She cupped hands around her mouth, shouting, "Who's there?"

The men stood, craning their necks. One shouted back, "Rock Hare and Eagle Trapper! Is that you. Sister? I know that horse! But who walks beside you?"

"His name is Richard!"

"Where is White Hail?"

"Back with the *Ku'chendikani*."

Willow strode forward until they were close enough for her to recognize them. Rock Hare had that superior air about him: the proud male in all of his magnificence. Eagle Trapper watched curiously as she and Richard picketed the horse and unslung the heavy pack full of grouse.

"Who are they?" Richard asked in English. "The Shoshoni was so fast, I missed most of it."

She pointed, saying slowly in Shoshoni, "Rock Hare, my brother. Eagle Trapper, my friend."

Richard stepped forward, extended a hand, and in passable Shoshoni said, "My heart is happy to meet you."

"He speaks like a human!" Eagle Trapper was staring as if seeing a new kind of animal. "He is dressed like a human!"

Rock Hare made a face. "He has skin like a corpse. And the hair—all over his face! Like a dog. Hyyyah! What they say about them is true. They all look this way."

"What's happening?" Richard asked, hand still held out.

Willow said, "Unlike so many of the *Ku'chendukani,* few *Dukurika* have actually seen a White man." She stepped forward to take Rock Hare's hand and place it in Richard's. To her brother, she said, "Shake hands. It's a White man form of greeting. Just do it. I'll explain later."

Rock Hare shook hands, but his heart wasn't in it.

Eagle Trapper adamantly crossed his arms. "I do not shake hands with a man who looks like a corpse."

In English, Willow said, "Richard, Eagle Trapper is frightened of you."

"And of his Power," Eagle Trapper added. "We have heard rumors. Stories that come from the *Ku'chendikani.* It is said that you have become a witch."

"What?" Willow's heart skipped, unsure if this was some sort of joke.

Rock Hare glanced around nervously, as if trying to see everything but his sister and the White man. "Well, it's a rumor, Willow. The story came to us that you had sent your *mugwa* into the Land of the Dead to find this White man. That you brought him back from the Dead, and in the process, angered the Spirit World with your pollution. It is said your *puha* has turned evil now."

She locked her knees to keep from staggering. An electric fear tightened in her chest.

White Hail might have been jealous of Richard, but he wouldn't have turned on her. She couldn't believe that. The only person he would have told would have been Two Half Moons, and Willow trusted her implicitly. But somehow, someone had found out. Who? *Red Calf!* Somehow, some way, she'd managed to learn the story and work her poison.

"What's wrong?" Richard asked.

"The *Ku'chendikani,* White Hail's people, are saying that by going after your soul in the Land of the Dead, I've become a witch."

Richard cried, "That's ridiculous!"

Rock Hare asked uneasily, "Is it true, Sister?"

"No," she said unevenly. "What...what does Father think?"

"He doesn't know what to think. He'll arrive tomorrow. We came ahead to scout the way. We didn't expect to find you here. We thought you'd run off to the *Ku'chendikani,* or the White men, or some such thing."

"I'm *no* witch," Willow insisted, "but that doesn't mean I'm not shaken to be accused of being one. Well, I can't fix that tonight. Come, help us pluck these birds. Then we can go and soak while they cook."

But try as she might, she couldn't dismiss the brewing worry; a cold wind of premonition blew around her souls.

CHAPTER NINE

If then the means by which the soul discovers truth, and generally discerns things unchanging or even those things variable about truth, are science, prudence, wisdom and intuitive reason, and if not one of the first three—prudence, science, and wisdom—is a means of grasping primary principles, our only possible conclusion is that they are determined by intuitive reason.

—Aristotle, *Nicomachean Ethics*

The wind came from the west, roaring down across the ragged plains from where the Big Horns thrust up like a humped giant against the horizon. It howled over the broken hills, around the lonely sandstone outcrops, shivered the sage, and whistled over the tilted shale beds of the Powder River basin. Heedless of the wind's cold caress, the land lay dormant under the frozen spell, numbed by ice, and as gnarled as the bent sage that trapped snow in pimpled drifts.

The long column of people and horses looked like

some mythical serpent winding through the snow-crusted valley, crossing the drainage, and winding through the drifted sage before climbing the other side.

"Never seen a winter like this," Travis growled wearily as he slumped on his horse. A heavy melancholy had settled on him; the relentless cold just pressed it down tighter around his soul.

"Nope," Baptiste agreed.

They were both warmly dressed in heavy hunting shirts and hairy buffalo coats. Fur hats covered their heads, and mittens protected their hands. Their legs were encased in thick leggings made from elk hide with rabbit fur sewn on the inside.

They rode side by side on mud-spattered horses, rifles resting on saddlebows. Ahead of them, Two White Elk joked with Lightning Bull, both of them bragging about the hunt they'd just finished. Behind them rode a knot of happy and tired warriors, blood-splotched and mud-smeared. Still farther behind came the women leading packhorses. The animals—piled high with chunks of freshly butchered meat—slipped and slid in the hoof-churned mud and snow.

A week ago, the weather had warmed above freezing during the day—just enough of a break in the deadly cold that the Crow had taken the opportunity to hunt. A band of winter-thin bison had moved into the Tongue River bottoms to avoid the deep snow on the ridges.

"Hell of a winter," Baptiste observed, as his little buckskin slipped and scrambled up the snow-packed trail beaten through the leeside drift. They followed the other warriors out onto a windswept ridgetop, studded as it was with scabby-looking sage and red shale. The wind worried their fur hats and hide fringes as the horses clopped across the flat ridgetop, thankful for solid footing.

"Worst in memory," Travis agreed. "Whoa up a minute."

He pulled his horse out of line and walked it to the side. There he squinted into the gale and studied the Big Horn Mountains, so majestically white against the clear sky.

"Yep, bad, all right." Baptiste slouched over his rifle, eyes slitted against the cold wind. "What's wrong, coon? You been too damned quiet and mopey. Even Two White Elk is getting fidgety, a-giving you that worried look. It's Moonlight, ain't it? She been a-prying at your soul, now ain't she? And Dick, too. You ain't figgered him fo' dead yet."

"Yep, I reckon ye read the spots on the cards, all right." Travis sighed. "Hell, every time I turn around, I expect ter see Calf in the Moonlight come walkin' around a lodge. I keep listening fer her voice, seeing her face in every young woman's. And, when I ain't doing that, I'm wondering about old Dick."

"He's dead, Travis. Shoah' 'nuff, you know how damn cold it got. Then the wind blowing the drifts around. Even if'n he'd a had a hoss, he'd a been lost and froze."

The cold wind made Travis's eyes water, and he blinked. "I gotta look, is all."

"Foah what? Bones?"

The Crow continued to pass, still laughing and talking, every last one happy about the fresh meat. During the relentless cold, people had reached deeply into their parfleches for pemmican and jerky. Folks ate more when it grew cold enough to make trees pop and spit crackle when it hit the ground. Nearly a quarter of the horses had died, some frozen solid on their feet. The worst of winter was past now. The thawing winds of March had come, and buffalo had been killed. Within weeks, all that would remain of the kill would be splintered bone—and that thrown out only after it was boiled for marrow butter.

"You been itching," Baptiste said. "I can see it in yore eyes."

"Reckon so." Travis cocked his jaw. "We got all the beaver we can trade fer hyar. We're just wasting time... eating their food."

"We done repaid that debt today." Baptiste jerked a thumb at the meat-laden packhorses that scrambled up through the beaten-down drift to clop across the ridgetop on shaking legs. "Ain't no red bastard heah shot more buff than you and me."

"That's a fact."

"So, why is you figgering to pull yor stick, foah God's sake? You got a nice warm lodge to live in, and young New Moon Rising a warming yor robes. Tarnal Hell, any damned fool knows that spring's the most miserable time fo' travel. The snow's melting, mud up to an elk's arse everywhere. Hellacious storms come a-rolling in and pile up—and then it rains on the whole shitaree and makes what's plain torment into pure misery. A feller can't keep his powder dry, and...and there ain't no place, for God's sake, where a coon can throw out his bed and be dry! Ain't nothing so horrible as spring travel."

"Reckon so." Travis snorted. The last of the packhorses had passed, the Crow women leading them only mildly interested in the whites as they stared off to the west.

"Then why, in sweet Jesus' name, would you be wanting to ride out in all that slop?"

Travis growled nervously to himself, then said, "Aw

hell, I reckon yer right, Baptiste. I'll give it another couple of weeks, then I'm pulling my stick. Ride or stay, it's yer decision, coon."

Baptiste slapped Travis on the shoulder. "I'll ride with you, old beaver. Head down to Rendezvous with you. But I just ain't a-going slopping through no mud. I done enough of that in Louisiana. I didn't like it there, and I'll tell you, coon, that mud whar a heap site warmer than this heah mud."

"Reckon so, but this mud don't have no snakes nor 'gaters slithering through it."

"Maybe, but Louisiana mud ain't sticky like this mud. Why, I seen it suck a hoss's hoof clean off'n the bone. Left that po' hoss a-stumping around with the damnedest gait you ever seen."

"So, are we gonna sit up hyar, freezing our pizzles off, a-lying about mud, or are we gonna go back and fill our gizzards with hot hump steak?"

Baptiste twisted his lips in disgust, spat downwind, and reined his horse around. "And I thought you was the one talking 'bout riding off all hellbent to slip and slide and sleep in the mud. Now yor talking 'bout hot food. You takes all, you do, Travis."

Travis shot one last look back at the Big Horns to the south, the peaks so white in the distance. "I reckon I do. Now, come on, let's catch them Injuns afore they eat all that meat." He let his horse follow the beaten track. The gelding slid down the pockmarked slope on braced legs.

I'm a-coming, Dick. And if'n I find yer bones...well, I guess I could scatter a little tobacco over 'em at least.

Loud whoops shattered the quiet night air as Richard walked along the curving edge of the steam-cloaked pool. The sound of violent splashing worthy of Perry on Lake Erie carried across the water; waves chopped at the shoreline of the hot pool. The high-pitched laughter belonged to Rock Hare, the deeper bellow to Eagle Trapper. Both *Dukurika* hunters were obscured by the thick plume of steam that rose in the moonlight.

Richard found Willow on the far side of the pools. She was standing on the bank overlooking the river. The *Pia'ogwe* had cut down through solid rock here, and below the jagged travertine banks the swirling black waters were moon-bathed in silver.

She'd wrapped her mountain sheep cape tightly about her shoulders, head back as she watched the starred heavens. With her long black hair streaming down and the gentle curves of her heart-shaped face caressed by the moonlight, she seemed like an exquisite sculpture, the sort Michelangelo would have crafted.

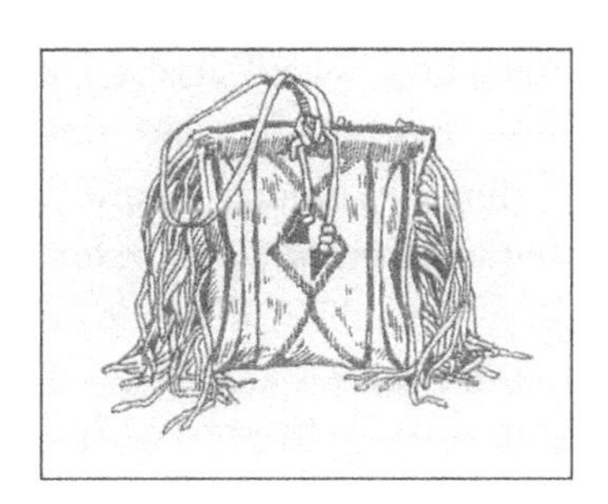

He walked up behind her, lacing his arms around her waist. His frosted breath hung in the stone-cold air. "I thought the pools were sacred. Listen to them; the splashes sound like cannon balls."

"The pools *are* sacred," she answered absently. "Is that any reason people can't enjoy themselves? That's another difference between my people and yours. To White men the sacred must be deadly serious, never room for laughter, jokes, or humor."

"It would be unthinkable," Richard agreed. "God—and holy things—are for serious contemplation."

She pointed across the distance. "You've seen the mountain we call Coyote's Penis? The story is that just after the Creation, Coyote was wandering around the land to see what he could see. One time, Coyote was sneaking along the *Pia'ogwe*, and he saw Wolf's daughter bathing on the other side. Being Wolf's daughter, she didn't like Coyote, wanted nothing to do with him. But he'd always desired her, and seeing her there in the water, he wanted her more than ever. He sent his penis swimming across the river to mate with her. Just as his penis was about to slide inside her, Trout rushed up from the bottom of the river. Thinking he saw a big worm, he bit Coyote's penis clean in two."

"That makes me cringe just to think of it."

"Oh, yes, and Coyote screamed in the most hideous fashion, for it hurts to have one's penis bitten off. Anyway, Wolf's daughter waded across the river to see what had happened, and found Coyote thrashing around in the brush, holding his bloody stump. The pain had dulled his wits so much that he told her how he'd tried to trick her, and how Trout had mistaken his penis for a worm and bitten it in two.

"Wolf's daughter immediately ran home and told Wolf what Coyote had tried to do. Wolf was infuriated. He called to Bald Eagle, who was fishing on the river, and told him: 'Coyote tried to sneak his penis into my daughter, and Trout mistook it for a worm and bit it off. Go and see if you can find it floating in the river.'

"Bald Eagle owed Wolf a favor and flew down the

river, looking for the penis. There it was, floating along, looking pathetic and limp, so Bald Eagle swooped down and grabbed it out of the water. He carried it high up on top of the mountain and left it there where Coyote couldn't reach it. It was so high up that it turned to stone, and you can still see it there today."

Richard gave her a quizzical glance. "You're right, a White man would never tell a story like that."

"But my people do. The lesson it teaches is that a man should be careful about letting his lust overwhelm his sense. But the other thing is, like all Coyote stories, it's funny. *Tam Apo* made people to laugh as well as cry. Often a joke can teach a holy truth better than a somber story. Someday I'll tell you about how Coyote faked his death, then disguised himself so he could marry his daughters and lie with them, and how they baked his penis in the fire when they discovered what he'd done to them."

Richard thought back to Wolf, nodding slowly. "Coyote. The root of all evil and mayhem. What does that say about the nature of the universe?"

"According to the stories my people tell, it wavers between Wolf's kindness and sense, and Coyote's cunning and trouble. One must always challenge the other."

He tightened his grip on her. "Then the transcendental dialectic is the only constant."

"What are these words?"

"It means the inevitable conflict of ideas coming from a common source. Good versus evil, or, in the Shoshoni case, Wolf versus Coyote."

"We call it 'opposites crossed.' That's just how the world was made."

Wild laughter exploded behind them; a body thudded into the water with a cascade of droplets hissing like rain.

"Willow, why are you out here? I thought you'd come back to the fire after we left the water."

She turned and looked up at him, moonlight revealing the desperation in her eyes. "Do you know what it means when Rock Hare says that people are calling me a witch?"

"I don't believe in witches. Rational people don't."

"My people do. What was the argument you made the other day when we were fleshing the buffalo hide? That human understanding is always colored by individual perception? My people perceive witches. They *want* to believe in them. Therefore, they do."

"But what people want to believe doesn't create truth."

"It doesn't have to, Richard. Your people don't believe a joke can teach a sacred truth. But it can."

"All right. Is witchcraft as serious a charge as say...a charge of murder would be among my people?"

She considered, finally shrugging. "I don't know your people that well. What if someone among your people accused someone else of having incest with their children? The children might deny it, but the suspicion has been planted. No one will look at those people the same way again. They've become *omaihen,* no matter what they protest."

"And you think that will happen to you?"

"It has happened," Willow whispered softly. "I'm sure it's a woman named Red Calf. She's White Hail's wife, the one he was going to throw away. I'm sure it's her. She tried to call me a witch after my husband died. People will remember. If White Hail cast her out, and if he told of me sending my soul to find yours in the Land of the Dead, it will confirm people's suspicions."

"Wait. Didn't you tell me that *puhagan* go after souls all the time, that your father, High Wolf, has sent his soul to the Land of the Dead?"

"He's a man, Richard. For a woman to become a true *puhagan* is *omaihen,* forbidden."

"I'm sorry, Willow. What can we do?"

"Nothing. What is done is done." She stared out over the river, where moonlight shone on the icy water. In the distance the buttes and hills rose in ghostly luminescence that contrasted with patches of shadow. She raised her hands, irritated. "And maybe it's true. Remember, I killed Packrat's soul. Drove him mad. I can't forget that. I have great *puha,* Richard. I can kill with it."

"I don't believe in witches."

"No, but Packrat did. My people do. Tell me, if a person believes, is that not his individual truth? Just as I called up the *Dukurika* version of the Land of the Dead?"

"Some would make that argument. But, Willow, you've always been a little hazy on how you drove Packrat mad."

"I was his captive. I didn't tell him when I began to bleed. Once, when he took me, he looked down and found his pizzle covered with woman's blood. I broke his Power, killed his soul."

He flinched. *She was a captive, Richard. Captors treat slaves however they will. And she paid him back for it the only way she could.*

He calmly said, "I didn't know that menstrual blood was that dangerous."

She laughed nervously. "Oh, Richard, I don't know what to do. And it's not just the talk of being a witch. It's as if I came home to people who had changed—and all the while it was I who was different."

"Different how?"

"One day, Rock Hare took the ax. He beat the edge off my ax. How? By hitting rocks with it to see the sparks fly. And then he wouldn't sharpen it. Instead, he went off to hunt. Then came all the unmarried men, coming to look me over, to see if they wanted to marry me. Why? They wanted the—how do you say?—prestige. Some thought I had a way with the Whites, special access to trade. If I'd wanted that, I could have married Dave Green and saved myself the hard work expected of an Indian wife.

"I'm not sure you will understand, but it was as if I didn't belong any more. My people, they didn't believe the stories I told about *Maria,* about the *engagés,* about killing the Rees. None of it. They listened politely, but I could see it in their eyes. They thought they were all just marvelous stories that I'd made up."

He nuzzled her neck, savoring the sulfur smell the water had left in her hair. "You've seen beyond the horizon. Willow. They're still innocent. Like Adam and Eve in our stories, you've bitten the apple, seen beyond the Garden of Paradise."

"Where do I go? Where do I belong, Richard? For the first time, I think I understand the Shoshoni women among the Mandan. I was very upset when they didn't want to return to their relatives. But now I see through their eyes. Unlike them, I have no place. Not among the *Dukurika,* not among the *Ku'chendikani,* not among the Whites, or Mandan. I've become like a tree that's fallen into the river. The current of life carries me along, but I can't find the right soil for my roots."

"We'll find it."

"We?" She turned, trying to read his expression in the moonlight. "You're going back to Boston, Richard."

"Willow, I never said a thing about—"

"You don't need to."

"I haven't made that decision."

She reached up to run a gentle finger along his cheek. "But you will, Richard. You don't know it yet, but you'll go in the end."

"That's silly."

"Say what you will. I'm cold and tired. Come, take my hand. I want to go back to camp. Then I want you to hold me all night long."

"Afraid you'll dream about being a witch?"

Her head bowed. "Yes. And I want to enjoy you all I can. Maybe tomorrow, maybe the day after, I will begin my bleeding."

"I'm not worried about it. I can still sleep with you, can't I, even if we don't couple?"

That familiar wry smile curled her lips. "Oh yes, I know. You're a great *puhagan,* without fear of pollution from anything so threatening as a lowly female's blood. Aren't you even a little afraid of me?"

"So much so that I'll just have to hold you even more tightly." He kissed the top of her head.

She gave him a saucy smile, took his hand, and led him back along the curving edge of the pond.

When High Wolf arrived the following day, White Rock's band accompanied him, bringing nearly forty people and close to a hundred dogs to the flats around the steaming *Pa'gushowener.*

Willow and Richard walked through High Wolf's camp as the people unloaded the dog travois and began building wickiups from poles, hide, sagebrush, and grass. To Willow's dismay, people greeted her with uncharacteristic reserve, watching uneasily from the corners of their eyes. She noticed that children were being kept at a conspicuous distance. Their reaction to Richard was one of wide-eyed amazement, and—in a manner most rude for *Dukurika*—they pointed at him behind his back.

They don't trust me—my own relatives!

Stunned and injured, she could imagine the whispered conversations passing from lip to lip.

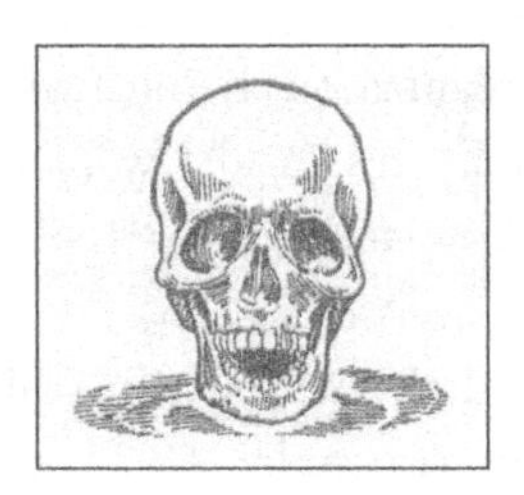

Richard watched with open delight, oblivious to the stares, as brush lodges were constructed on the grassy slope south of the hot pools. "Why don't they have tipis like the Crow and Sioux?"

"To haul such big tipis, you must have horses. White Hail's *Ku'chendikani* live in tipis," Willow told him, hiding the turmoil inside. "Sometimes we use small tipis that the dogs can haul. But why haul a lodge around when you can build one out of what's handy at the next camp?"

"A horse can haul more than a dog can. Think about how much more work they can do." He hooked a thumb back at their horse where it was picketed on grass beside the river.

When they passed old woman Yellow Tooth, she wouldn't meet Willow's eyes. "Horses need a great deal of grass, Richard. Those cakes you like so much? They are made from grass seeds we gather in late summer. Horses would eat that grass. In spring, we dig the roots of the desert parsley, and eat the leaves. Horses trample those plants. A horse can't walk through the dense timber where we hunt. Have you ever seen a horse jump from rock to rock on a mountainside? No? Well, a dog can, and my people often cross steep mountain valleys, and climb up and down cliffs. Horses are animals for wide plains and open trails, not for the places the *Dukurika* live."

"I guess I didn't think about that."

Willow's heart leaped when she saw High Wolf. Would he, too, turn his back on her? He looked fit and hale. His white-tanned sheephide coat accented his broad shoulders. High moccasins rose to his knees, topped by bands of wolf fur, and the sun glinted in the silver threads in his long braided hair. High Wolf was carrying armloads of sagebrush to White Alder, who wove the branches around the outside of a dome-shaped willow-pole framework.

Willow walked forward. "Greetings, Father." She hated the reserve in her voice, and the fluttering of her heart. Her nerves tingled anxiously.

If he doesn't acknowledge me, what will I do?

High Wolf dropped his load of sagebrush and turned toward her, smacking his hands. He cocked his head, inspecting her with those familiar bright eyes, then carefully studied Richard from head to foot, before saying, "So, this is your White man? I forget. Look at all that hair! And such a thin face—and those pale eyes. Can he really see through them?"

"Richard, this is High Wolf, my father."

Richard smiled, stepping forward and offering his hand. In carefully practiced Shoshoni, he said, "Greetings, High Wolf. I am called Richard Hamilton."

High Wolf contemplated the outstretched hand for a

moment, then took it in a limp grip. He glanced at Willow. "This is a White man's thing?"

"An offer of friendship," she said, as High Wolf withdrew his hand and inspected it curiously to see if there had been any change.

White Alder took a hesitant step forward, her body canted to the side, expression wary, as if approaching some exotic animal she couldn't be too sure of. "Willow? This is the White man? The one in your dreams?"

"He is. Richard, this is my mother, White Alder."

By now Richard had sensed the tension, giving her an uneasy glance as he offered his hand. Although White Alder had seen him shake High Wolf's, she held back. "Is he dangerous?"

"No," Richard replied. "I am happy to meet Willow's mother. I am Richard Hamilton—um, of Boston, madam. I assure you, I am a...a gentleman."

"He is a noted warrior," Willow supplied since her mother had no idea of the meaning of "Boston," "madam," or "gentleman."

In English, Richard asked, "Do they know we're lovers? Will that be a problem?"

"No," she replied tersely. Leave it to Richard to worry about trivia when witch talk was in the air. Then, trying to mask her desperation, Willow said too quickly, "Father, I know you are busy, but could I...?"

"Yes, yes." He turned to White Alder. "I think I must go and talk to our daughter. I will be back to help you as soon as I can."

White Alder's reserved gaze went from Richard to Willow. "Go, husband. Find out what all this foolishness is."

As they walked toward Willow's camp, Richard added nervously, "He's going to see only one bed."

"Richard, you are my husband. This is about witchcraft. And *puha,* and *omaihen.*"

"Yes, yes, I know. But you're still their daughter. And I'm essentially a stranger who's sharing your robes. I'd think they'd be a little more concerned about that."

"Why should they? Unless, of course, we're both witches."

"Both?" He raised an eyebrow. "Me—a witch? How irrational can you get?"

High Wolf feigned indifference as he walked, his curious study of Richard conducted as surreptitiously as possible.

At their camp. High Wolf ceremoniously seated himself cross-legged before the smoldering fire, took a deep breath, and propped his arms on his knees. "I have heard that White Hail went back to his people."

"He did."

"So, Daughter, what have you gotten yourself into this time?"

"You remember the dreams I was having in camp?" At her father's nod, Willow seated herself between him and Richard. She told of her travels with White Hail, of seeing the wolves and finding Richard. She related the steps she'd taken to save him, including sending her soul into the Land of the Dead; how she'd talked Richard into coming back to the living, and their journey.

When she finished, High Wolf leaned his head back and pulled his tubular stone pipe from the badger-hide pouch at his side. Tamping the bowl with kinnikinnick, he used a twig to fish around in the fire for an ember, and lit it. After making his offerings, and singing a prayer, he puffed and passed the pipe to Willow, who repeated the ritual, then handed the pipe to Richard.

High Wolf watched, expression pensive. When the

pipe was returned to him, he studied the curls of smoke rising from the stained end of the steatite tube. "I always knew you had great *puha,* and it frightened me. Daughter, you've always been different, a little odd, but that was all right because I'd looked into your souls and seen all that you were.

"I am relieved by some parts of your story, and even more disturbed by others. I am relieved that you escaped the Land of the Dead despite being *omaihen,* for that tells me that you have not been overcome by a *puha* too powerful for you to use wisely. Instead, it was this White man who saved you, and his *puha* must be very Powerful if he could help you find the way back. I am glad that you survived. I never thought that you were evil, Daughter."

"And what disturbs you?"

High Wolf puffed on his pipe and blew smoke into the air with solemnity. "What I see for you in this world, Willow. Now I know what happened—and that you have a Power greater than any woman I have ever known. Maybe you are blessed by *Pa'waip.* I do not believe you would misuse such great Power, but they"—he indicated the *Dukurika* camp—"do not know. The rumors have already frightened them. Many are thinking of leaving... of going as far from you as they can."

Willow had been translating for Richard, filling in the words he didn't know. As she spoke, her guts knotted and cramped.

"I will speak for you. But many will suspect my words since you are my daughter. They might stay if I ask them to, but if anyone grows sick, or has bad luck, they will blame you. I think you know that, don't you?"

She nodded, a hand held to her sour stomach. "I feared as much, but I hoped that...that..."

"Yes, I know." He gave her the old familiar smile that

had soothed her over the years. "I'm sorry. Daughter. It's not me, but the people who will fear you. You know people as well as I do. What they fear, they hate. What they hate, they finally destroy."

Willow drooped, soul-weary. "What should I do?"

High Wolf pursed his weathered brown lips. "Does this White man have a place? Will you go with him?"

Willow nodded. "I will."

But for how long?

High Wolf scratched his ear. "I always knew you would be trouble. You asked too many questions. You wanted too many answers for things that must remain mysterious. That was the *puha.* Had you been a man, you would have been the greatest *puhagan* ever. But now, I see you here, full of Power, with the haze of the Spirit World around you so strong that any normal person should fear you."

"But you don't?"

"No. We've seen the truth in each other's souls." He indicated Richard. "Are all White men as Powerful as he?"

"No." She took Richard's hand. "He is like me, Father. Among his own people, he asks the kind of questions that I do. It is only recently that he has begun to understand his *puha.*"

High Wolf nodded respectfully to Richard. "Take care of my daughter. She will need all of your skill and Power."

"I will," Richard replied, catching most of the meaning.

Will you? Willow questioned, looking into his soft brown eyes. *How can you, with Boston always calling?*

High Wolf sighed, slapping hands to his legs. "And that is that. If you decide to leave, I would go soon. Maybe even tomorrow morning. For now, I must go and help your mother. Explain what has happened. And perhaps we will come to your camp tonight. You can feed us, I hope? That dried buffalo meat back there—it's not for coyotes, is it?"

"No, Father." She patted his arm. "I think I could feed you with it."

He stood then, looking around, the sun glinting in his gray-streaked hair. Despite the slight stoop to his back, he looked weathered and powerful, the sort of elder anyone would look up to. "I think you should eat that horse. Dogs would serve you better. One of my bitches will whelp soon. I could give you some pups. They'll be good dogs. A person shouldn't live without dogs. It's not natural...or healthy."

Willow stood. "I think we'll keep our horse for a while. But if we need dogs, I know where to find the very best."

Richard arose and stood before High Wolf, offering his hand again. "You are welcome here any time, sir. My... uh, our camp is always yours."

High Wolf shook the hand, and for a long moment, stared into Richard's eyes, both of them locked, measuring. In the end, High Wolf nodded ever so slightly. "You are a good man. Not everyone has Wolf as a guardian spirit. He chooses carefully...as does my daughter."

Then he turned, walking purposely back toward the *Dukurika* camp.

"Quite a man," Richard mused. "So stately and possessed. I think I could come to like him a great deal."

"And he you," she said sadly. "But I don't think you'll get the chance, Richard. He's right. We must leave. Tomorrow, before trouble starts."

"Go where?' Richard wondered.

She sniffed the west wind, blowing mildly on this

warm day. "I know a place. Tonight we will feed my parents, and tomorrow we will cross the river and go to *Ainkahonobita,* Red Canyon Spring. It's just west—a half-day's journey."

"And after that?"

Suddenly desolate, she pulled him to her, hugging him close in an attempt to draw on his strength. "I don't know, Richard. For once in my life, I just don't know."

"I won't leave you, Willow. We'll find a way, somehow. You have my word."

And she did feel better—even if she knew he was lying to her...and himself.

CHAPTER TEN

> The essence of the spirit is therefore freedom—the absolute and negative identification of the concept with itself. It can remove itself, therefore, from everything external, and from its own externality as well as from its very being, and thus bear infinite pain, the negation of its immediate individuality; in other words, it can be identical to itself in this negativity. This possibility is the self contained being within itself, its simple concept, or absolute generality by itself.
>
> —Georg Friedrich Wilhelm Hegel, The Philosophy of Spirit

The Owl Creek Mountains ran east-west, separating the Warm Wind Valley and the *Pia'ogwe's* basin. *Ainkahonobita,* Red Canyon, lay in the foothills on the north slope of the Owl Creeks. Bright red sandstone rose in sheer cliffs that walled the northern side of the canyon, while to the south, the mountains drained into a creek that cut eastward toward the *Pia'ogwe*.

Ainkahonobita was an oasis. Its tall red cliffs caught the full measure of winter sun, and the surrounding heights protected it from the prevailing westerly winds so that the canyon remained warm and sheltered. The spring to which Willow had led Richard wasn't hot, but ran warm enough that the water didn't freeze, and green grass and rushes grew there throughout the winter.

The slopes were timbered in pine and juniper, firewood abundant in every direction. Here, too, the buffalo, antelope, elk, and deer came to drink. Sheer-walled side canyons acted as natural corrals for their horse, and forage was plentiful on the sun-melted slopes.

Willow's inclination had been to build a wickiup, but Richard insisted they elaborate. The construction took three days. They picked a place with southern exposure where the juniper-dotted ground sloped beneath the sandstone uplift. With digging sticks they excavated a waist-deep hollow in a space sheltered by the trees. The damp red dirt was piled to the sides. Then, on a much smaller scale than that used by the river tribes, four limber pine supporting posts were tamped into place in the lodge bottom, and stringers were run across the top to form a hollow square. With Willow's ax they trimmed juniper rafters to the right size, and laid stringers from the rafters to the ground. The whole was covered with rabbitbrush, hides, and sage, then overlaid with dirt.

"It looks like home." Richard had his arm around Willow's shoulders as they stood admiring their primitive house.

"So much work!" Willow rubbed the busters on her

hands. "You White men, always doing more than you need to."

"It will be warm, dry, and comfortable. You'll see."

As the cold spring storms roared down from the northwest and dropped successive snows, they remained snug in their haven, feasting on smoked meat and talking. By day, they explored the crimson sandstone that thrust up in layers around the valley; the color contrasted to the bright green of juniper and pine and with the enamel blue of sky.

One particularly warm day they took the worn game trail that followed a circuitous route to the canyon rim. Bright sunlight brought the colors out of the stone, glared off the patches of unmelted snow, and promised spring.

"I've never seen such a beautiful place," Richard declared as he climbed to stand on a spur of rock high on the canyon wall. Before him the cliff dropped away in a sheer fall that dizzied the senses. From the edge, he had an eagle's view of the layered sandstone beds, straight down to the broken red rubble sloping away from the base of the cliff. He could see for miles up and down the rugged canyon and out over the mountains beyond. "It's as if God lives here."

"God lives everywhere." Willow put her arm about his waist, long black hair teased by the gusty breeze. "It's only you Whites who have put him inside a building. You'll never be the same, Richard. Your souls *feel* now."

"I suppose. How odd. It's as if half of myself lay dormant until you brought me back from the Land of the Dead." He traced a finger along her cheek. "You made me whole."

She slipped around to draw him tightly against her. "Make love to me, Richard."

"Here? It's cold. The wind's blowing. Dear Lord God, we can be seen for miles!"

Her fingers began unlacing his buckskin pants. "We're dangerous spirits, remember? Filled with terrible Power. We'll blind anyone who watches except *Tam Apo* and *Tam Segobia*—and they made us to couple anyway."

He couldn't pretend to ignore his erection when her fingers found it. She'd stripped his coat and shirt off, dropping them in a pile before she drew her dress over her head. She stood naked, feet spread, head back proudly, hands raised to the sun. The chill hardened her nipples, and her sleek black hair curled around her narrow waist and muscular rump.

My God, she's beautiful.

She was laughing, white teeth shining between those full lips as he lowered her to the weathered rock.

Perhaps it was the sunshine, the invigorating chill in the pine-laden air, the dizzying heights upon which they lay, or the smile of God, but the climax consumed Richard's entire body, his cries mingling with Willow's. Spent and shivering, he looked down into her glowing eyes and kissed her.

I'm free! Free as I never shall be again. In all the world, nothing matters except man and woman, love, and sunshine, and the good earth. Thank you, God. Thank you for this single moment.

I am alive*!*

The nightmare was so vivid that Phillip bolted upright in bed. He gasped for air. Twinges of pain darted through his chest, and a curious numbness tingled in his left arm. Sweat beaded on his doughy skin, and he could feel each laboring beat of his heart as it hammered at his breast bone.

"Dear God...dear, dear God!" He blinked anxiously around the dark room, cocking his head. In the silence, he could hear the *tick-tock* of the ship's clock in his office next door, and the pop of a log in the bedroom fireplace.

The constriction in his chest was ebbing now, but his frantic fingers continued to wad his nightshirt, crumpling it against his breast

The dream: so vivid

He swallowed hard. He'd been standing on a dark and muddy shore. At his feet, murky water lapped the bank, the surface smooth and oily. Huge trees grew at his back, the branches overhead stretching out over the black water. What a dismal place. It stirred primeval roots of fear.

Phillip had turned this way and that, seeking the way to safety. With the brooding forest behind, muddy swamp to either side, and Stygian water before him, he could see no route of escape.

Something moved on one of the branches. He looked up, and made out the somber silhouette of a vulture. The carrion bird craned its neck, hopping out on a limb that hung low over the water.

A pale thing bobbed there. A bit of white flotsam that barely broke the surface.

Phillip squinted. Some sort of fish?

The vulture flapped scabby wings, and stalked lower on the branch. There it balanced precariously directly over the flotsam and pecked at its barely exposed target. No, not a fish, but some loathsome *thing*.

As the vulture's beak worried its prey, the white thing bobbed, sending slow ripples to wash at Phillip's feet.

But the vulture's actions were its own undoing, for

the questing beak imparted motion, and the thing drifted silently in Phillip's direction.

How slowly it came, like a man-sized snow lump submerged in the water. Phillip bent down, a curiosity as terrible as Oedipus's driving him.

Only when it lodged in the mud at his feet did the current finally spin it, turn it, so that Phillip could see Richard's water-blanched face. The eyes were staring sightlessly into the murk, the fine brown hair wavering like moss. His tender throat had been slit wide.

The pain had pierced Phillip's chest then, heart hammering as he tried to back away. The vulture gave an angry, croaking cry, and Phillip had stumbled backward, brought up short by the thick bole of a tree.

He'd fallen to his knees in the mud, hands clasped as he looked up into the sullen sky. There, out of the mist, her face had formed: delicate cheeks, high brow, and perfect jaw framed by lustrous hair; her curved lips and delicate nose; and her large brown eyes. Normally soft and loving, they were hard now, implacable with rage and loathing.

Such a terrible dream.

Phillip climbed out of bed, pulling his nightshirt straight. The floor creaked as he padded to the door, and then out into the hallway. The chill in the dark house dried his sweat and made him shiver as he tottered down the hall. The hinges creaked when he opened the latch on Richard's door. And the floor groaned as he walked over to the bed, reaching down to feel the cold, smooth covers.

"I'm sorry, Richard. My fault. All my fault." The sodden misery in his chest had eaten his insides, devoured all that had remained of him after Caroline's death.

What's left for me?

He blinked in the darkness. How many times had he walked in here since Eckhart's visit just to feel the fabric? As if the mere touch could bring his son back?

"You're a fool, Phillip Hamilton. Everything you've fought, schemed, and struggled for has come to naught" He cocked his head, aching at the emptiness in his soul. "What was it all for, anyway?"

He had no answer. Hollow. Empty. Silent inside. And oh, so tired.

Turning back from the bed, he could make out the dark frame for the doorway against the pale plaster walls. He felt his way back into the hall. Accompanied by the squeaking floor and the ticking of the clock, he made his way to his office, crossed to his desk, and opened a drawer.

The pistol fit his palm like an old friend, the smooth wood polished and cool in his hot hand. His finger found the trigger as he stepped out into the hallway and hitched his way down the stairs and through the French doors into the dining room.

He took a long splinter from the tin over the hearth, and lit it in the dimly glowing coals. One by one, he lit the wicks on the whale-oil lamps, and adjusted the flames. That done, he walked around the table and stared up at her portrait.

"Caroline, you were there, watching me." He'd never forget that loathing in her eyes. How she must despise him for wasting her only son. How she must hate him for everything—for the neglect during her pregnancy, for his absence during Richard's birth, and most especially for having to face death alone.

"You know about me, don't you?" He pulled out one of the chairs, and lowered himself. "About everything I've done. I'm sorry, Caroline. Sorry for all of it. Sorry for being unfaithful to you, for sneaking out in the night to all those women. But I was lonely after you died...and weak. So pitifully weak. You could forgive me for the frailties of the flesh, couldn't you?"

He glanced down at the pistol in his hands, then back up at the portrait. "It's Richard that you can't forgive. Well, I can't either. I tried, Caroline. I really did. I...I thought the risk...well, I was wrong again."

He crooked his thumb around the cock, listening to it click crisply, the sound loud in the quiet house. Her brown eyes were boring into his, reading every miserable flaw in his soul.

"Well, you can see that I've nothing to live for any more, beloved wife. Without you, without Richard, there's nothing left. It was for the future, you see. I did it all for the future. And I...I tried, waiting, praying for a miracle...that Richard was alive."

Her face had turned silver as the tears welled in his eyes. "The dream, Caroline. I can't stand the dream any more."

He sniffed, and tried to swallow the painful cramp in his throat. His hand was shaking as he lifted the pistol.

Dear God, this is hard...harder than I thought.

Why was he so afraid? It would bring peace, wouldn't it? The pain would be gone. All he'd have to do was explain himself to God, and then accept his punishment for all the things...

Suddenly the pistol was twisted out of his grip. Phillip jumped, startled half out of his skin. Sputtering, he jerked around, staring up wide-eyed as Jeffry carefully lowered the hammer to half-cock.

"Dear God! Jeffry? What are you doing up?"

Jeffry raised his eyes to the ceiling. "The floorboards, sir. You've grown moody over the last months. I keep track of which rooms you enter. I've noticed the pistol lying on your desk more often recently, noticed it was polished, loaded, and primed. You've always come down to speak with Mrs. Hamilton in the night, but only recently have you spent so much time in Master Richard's room."

Phillip sagged in the chair. Had he ever felt this listless and tired? "Why didn't you let me shoot?"

"Because in the afterlife, sir, you would have asked me why I didn't stop you."

"Afterlife? Do you think there's a heaven...or a hell?"

"Yes, sir. All men have souls," He indicated the portrait. "Just as Mrs. Hamilton did, and Richard, and my Betsy. Sir, you'll have plenty of time with Master Richard, Mrs. Hamilton, and God when you do finally die. In the meantime, here, in this life, you have work to do. God will call you when He's ready."

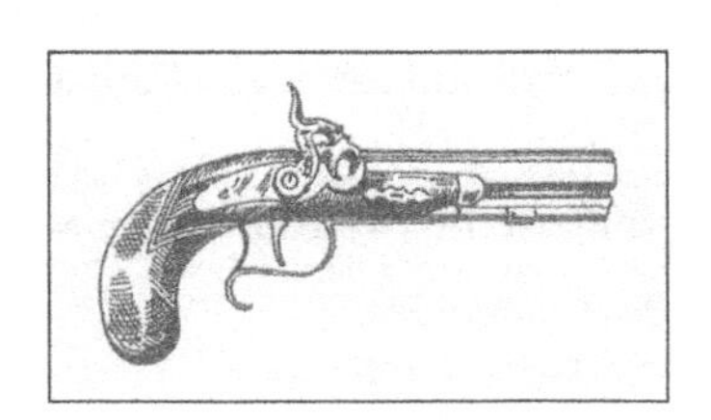

Phillip stared numbly at the carpet beneath his feet. "You can't stop me, you know. Not every time."

"No, sir." Jeffry patted him on the shoulder. "I can't. I pray, however, that in the future I won't need to."

Their bodies were locked together, lax in the honeyed afterglow of passionate union. The doorway hanging was hooked back, allowing a shaft of moonlight to silver the inside of their shelter. With a delicate fingertip, Richard traced the hollow curve of Willow's cheek. She sighed in contentment.

He whispered, "Never, in all of my dreams, did I understand it would be like this."

She patted his cold shoulders, and pulled the heavy buffalo robe up to cover them. "The world was made in a very clever way. A man's *we'an* fits a woman's *ta'ih* just so, and the pleasure makes us want to fit them together as often as we can." She grinned at him, teeth shining in the darkness. "Did you know that just after the Creation, Coyote was wandering around and saw a pretty girl? He tricked her into carrying him across a river, but as she swam along, he kept trying to slip down so he could poke his *we'an* into her.

"She realized what he was doing, of course, and threw him off in the water. She was so mad, she stomped all the way home. What she didn't know was that Coyote had climbed out of the river and raced like a streak to her house.

"Coyote found the pretty girl's mother there and tricked her into letting him inside their lodge. But even though he tried to disguise himself, Mother knew he was Coyote and up to no good."

"And when the pretty girl arrived?"

Willow stared up into his eyes as she ran her fingers around his ears. "Well, she was still storm-mad, and she told her mother all about Coyote trying to mate her in the river. 'Hush!' her mother said. 'Coyote is inside the lodge waiting for you, but he thinks he's disguised. He doesn't know about women, about how we take care of ourselves. Just let him try and slip his *we'an* into one of us. We'll show him.'"

"What does that mean, that he didn't know about women?"

Willow's grin widened. "Here's what happened: They finally went to sleep that night, and Coyote sneaked up next to the pretty girl. He reached down between her legs to find her *ta'ih,* but something snapped at him."

"What?"

"Oh, yes. You see, during the Creation, women were made with sharp teeth in their *ta'ih.* This was a real problem for Coyote because if he stuck himself in there, he was going to get his *we'an* bitten off."

"He has a real problem with that, doesn't he?"

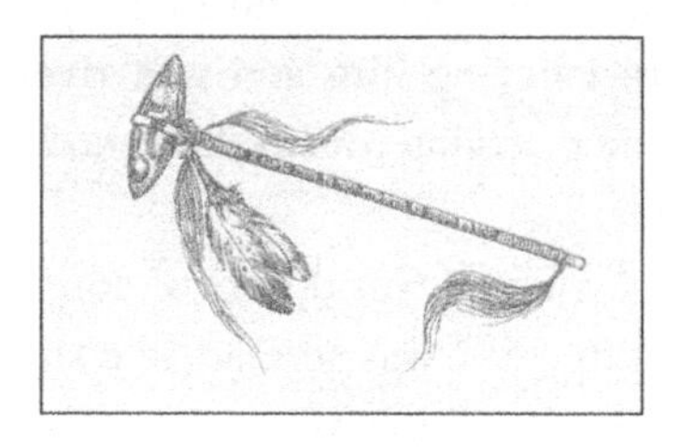

She lifted an eyebrow. "Most men do. But Coyote never gives up. He sneaked back outside and looked around until he found a *tsokkainompeh,* you know, the grinding stone. And with it, he tiptoed back into the lodge. He thrust it into her as if it were his *we'an.* This time, when the girl's *ta'ih* bit at him, the teeth shattered on the stone."

"So he got her."

"He got her. And, being Coyote, he used the rock to break the teeth out of Mother's *ta'ih,* and got her, too."

"Quite a fellow, this Coyote. He reminds me of Thomas Hanson. The rumor was that he'd stick himself into any woman who came along." Richard screwed up his face. "But teeth? That's a little ridiculous."

"Is it? I drove Packrat mad with woman's blood. Teeth come in many forms, Richard. But just so you won't worry. I happen to like your *we'an* right where it is." And she squeezed him with her vaginal muscles.

"So...what happened to Coyote?"

"He stayed there with the girl and her mother, until he drove them half mad with his demands and lazy tricks. One time they sent him for water, but Coyote spent the day playing. When he came back, the women had left, taking their children with them. From them are descended all the people on earth."

"Great! People are descended from *Coyote?*"

"Knowing people, do you doubt it?"

He watched the moonlight trace the delicate arch of her cheeks. "Willow, what if you conceive?"

"I don't know this word. Conceive?"

"What if, like Coyote, I give you a child?"

Her dark eyes seemed to expand, sucking him into their depths. "Then I shall bear it, Richard. I am strong and healthy. I bore my first without trouble. The first is generally the most difficult."

"I don't mean that, Willow, I'm talking about raising the boy, providing for him. What kind of life will he have?"

She frowned for the first time, and gently pushed him

off to one side so she could see his face in the moonlight. "What are you saying, Richard?"

"I'm saying that if I make you pregnant, we're going to have to figure out how to raise the child. I can't be Coyote. Do you understand? I don't want you to think that I'm going to run off like the Trickster, but, at the same time, I don't know where I'm going, what I'm going to be."

She sighed. "Boston again?"

"I don't know. Maybe. I'm torn, Willow. Half of me belongs back there. Half of me belongs here."

She laid her warm hand on his cool cheek. "Richard, until I returned to High Wolf's camp, I couldn't have understood. But you've stepped between worlds. Perhaps you could live in both?"

"Both?"

"If you must go back to Boston, go. Marry this Laura if it will help you in that world. She can bear your children in her house in Boston, and I will bear your children here."

The simplicity with which she spoke confused him. It wasn't a joke. She was serious. He muttered, "Sometimes I'm still not prepared for Indian logic."

"It's not a problem, Richard." She read his unease. "Unlike Whites, I don't have to be a prize. I am not a lady. I can provide for our children while you are away."

"Yes, I know you can. But, Willow, you'd accept me having another wife?"

"White Hail wanted me to be his second wife. Fast Black Horse wanted me to be his third. Had my husband lived, he would have brought a second wife to our lodge. Among my people, this is a normal thing. I didn't realize it would upset you so."

"Between two worlds," he whispered, and chuckled.

"It has possibilities—but Laura would have a fit if she ever found out."

"If she ever found out? I don't understand."

"No, forget it. I'm playing Coyote with myself." He paused, juggling these new ideas in his mind. What of jealousy? Just how differently *did* white and Shoshoni minds think? "You don't want two husbands, do you?"

She laughed. "Do I look crazy? You're trouble enough. I've heard of women taking two husbands—mostly among tribes where the women own the children. Among my people and yours where descent is from the man, how would a woman tell which man was the father of which child? I think it would cause too many problems. Especially with incest and inheritance."

"Is mating always so practical?"

"Of course not. We're talking about people, aren't we? I almost went crazy when all those *Dukurika* men came to marry me. I almost said yes when my souls were screaming no. Anything to be done with it." She snuggled against him. "Are you still convinced that I can't go with you?"

"Yes," he replied sadly. "Willow, please trust me about this. My people are unforgiving about many things, and intolerant of anything they can't understand."

"I trust you."

"You do?"

"Yes—but mostly because Travis, Green, and Baptiste told me the same thing." She gouged him in the ribs to make him squirm. "But in the meantime, Richard, your life is not the only one that has turned onto an unknown path. My future is as uncertain as yours. If some *puhagan* or *tekwhani* finally decides I really am a witch, they might hunt me down."

"And if they do?"

"They'll kill me, Richard. It's the only way to get rid of a witch who doesn't ask to be cured."

Long after she'd fallen asleep, he stared up at the dark rafters, trying to see into the future. What did a white philosopher do with an Indian wife and a half-breed family? He and Willow had tied their lives into a Gordian knot that he couldn't quite decide how to cut.

Willow in the West, and Laura in the East? Now, wouldn 't that be something?

But how could he make it work?

Sure, and you're Coyote all right. If Laura found out, her ta'hi *would have teeth, indeed. And in Boston you'll never find a grinding stone within easy reach!*

Travis checked the knots on his diamond hitch. Everything looked tight. The packs were loaded just so, balanced and mantied, padded to protect the horses' backs.

He looked up at the sky, squinting into the bright sun. The day was cold, cloudless, and breezy—the sort of deceptive weather that promised spring, then slapped a coon down with a hellacious blizzard.

Baptiste walked up, a braided leather rope coiled over his shoulder. Behind him, Two White Elk carefully inspected the horses, bending down every now and then to lift a hoof or feel a pastern.

"'Bout ready?" Baptiste asked. He'd pulled his wide-brimmed hat down low. His mane of thick black hair was tied in a tail behind his neck. During the winter he'd traded for a white coat with longer fringes than before.

"Reckon." Travis cocked his jaw, looking westward toward the Big Horns.

Two White Elk stopped before him, searching his eyes. "You do not need to do this. My lodge is always yours, Travis. You are my brother. Forever. What's mine is yours."

"Likewise, coon." Travis grinned, fingering his scars nervously. Two White Elk's wives had come, each bearing a pack which they tied behind the saddles of Travis's and Baptiste's horses.

Two White Elk patted his shoulder. "I have talked to New Moon Rising's people. If you were to stay, she would make you a lodge. For a couple of horses, she would be your wife. Her family would be honored. So would she."

"Aw, she's just a kid. You know—and I know—that she's not..."

"Not my sister?" Two White Elk grinned weakly. "Brother, she's long dead. Her spirit is gone from this world. We were close. I know how she thought, what she would say to this grief of yours."

"She'd tell this child he's a double-dyed fool," Travis snorted. "Hell, I reckon I know that. And, my brother, I needed this winter with ye. I just didn't know it. It ain't yer sister's ghost what's got me set ter go. It's the going, hoss. I lost that a while back. Wal, this hyar winter with ye put me right with my wife's death. Now I got ter see ter Dick, bury him. Ye savvy? Might be I'll be back next winter and see ter New Moon Rising. If'n she's still a-waiting, maybe I'll tie a hoss ter her lodge, send her folks some foofawraw."

"And this Bad-Lodge woman?"

"Willow?" Travis took up his reins, running them through his fingers as he thought. "It's me that's got ter tell her about Dick. It ain't right her thinking him a fool and dupe. She needs ter know about Green and the boat. It's just something I gotta do, Brother. Understand?"

Two White Elk's lips twitched. "White man's honor. I understand, Travis. But ride carefully. The Blackfeet have been bad the last couple of years. It wouldn't do to send your scalp home on one of their coup sticks."

Travis stepped into Two White Elk's arms, hugging him fiercely. 'Thanks, old friend. I'll be seeing ye. Walk with Power." Then Travis turned to Two White Elk's wives, hugging each one, kissing their foreheads as he thanked them for their hospitality. Walking to his horse, he vaulted into the saddle and took his Hawken when Two White Elk handed it up.

"So long, coon!" Travis waved as he kicked the gelding around. He looked back as Baptiste lined out the pack string. Two White Elk stood watching, a wife under either arm. Behind him, the conical lodges of the River Crow gleamed in the sunlight.

For a time Travis rode in silence, chewing fretfully at his lip.

"You all right?" Baptiste asked, dropping back.

"Yep. Plumb chipper." Travis cocked his head, looking sideways at Baptiste. "I can let her go now."

"Who?"

"Moonlight. I guess I been running from her ghost all along." He shrugged. "Wal, what the hell, let's see what comes of the Snakes."

"Willow and ye?"

Travis frowned. "She don't need the likes of me pestering her. Besides, I'd remind her of Dick. And she sure never warmed ter me like that on the river. Reckon I'm her friend, that's all."

"Sometimes, them kind of wives is the best," Baptiste remarked. He narrowed his eyes as they crested the first ridge. In the distance, the snow-capped Big Horns beckoned. "Just where at was you expecting to find Willow's band?"

"Beats Hob outa me. Ye and me, we're just gonna have ter shag up thar, and skin that beaver when we catch it"

"And hope we don't get no arrow shot through our lights in the process."

"Yep. There's always that. Shit, ye ain't figgering on dying old. are ye?"

The fourth moon—the moon of spring—had grown full and bright in the night sky. The world came alive again. The rich red soils of *Ainkahonobita* greened with spring grass. Phlox was blooming in star-shaped flowers of white and blue. Biscuit-root had leafed out in yellow-clustered flowers that signaled their root's freshness. Larkspur raised green-tufted heads above the bloodred dirt. The ragged cry of the red-tailed hawk sounded high above the twitter of grackles, finches, and siskins. Flickers called mating warbles to each other. In the brush, the rufous towhee skittered beneath the thicket of branches in search of hatchling bugs.

Willow had taken Richard root gathering that day, showing him how to lever biscuit-root from the damp soil with a juniper digging stick. She taught him the difference between wild onion and death camas. Under her tutelage he learned to sing the sacred song before eating the first flowers of the shooting star—a plant with the power to grant visions and to cure illness. From the spring-fed creek, she plucked the first mint leaves for tea. Together they boiled shoots of larkspur into a potent brew to kill lice and ticks in their clothing.

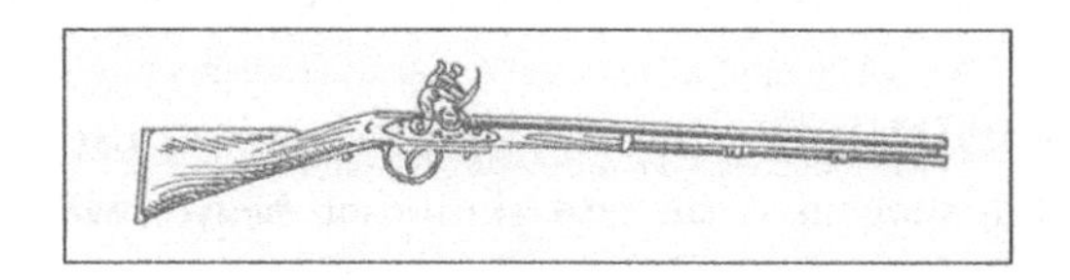

As evening extended fingers of shadow across the ocher cliffs, Willow bent over her *potton,* the grinding stone she'd made of hard sandstone. Richard sat beside the fire, watching dinner boil. First they'd dug a pit, lined it with hide, and filled it with water. Biscuit root leaves, mint, and small onion bulbs were added. Finally they'd lowered a buffalo tongue ceremoniously into the water. River cobbles had been placed in a hot fire, and when dropped into the water, steam exploded. One by one, Richard fished the rocks out, reheated them, and dropped them in again. The delightful aroma of cooking tongue and greens filled the cool air.

Willow tightened her grip on the *tsokkainompeh,* the hand-sized grinding stone, and used it to pulverize the roots against the *potton.* She ground them until she had a mush that she could flatten into patties to roast over the coals.

Richard was smiling to himself, eyes on the redtails as they circled in the late evening light, feet lowered in mating displays.

"Now, why would you be smiling?" Willow asked, her

grinding stones making a hollow *kok-rock-kok* sound. She wiped some of the thick root paste from one finger.

"Just thinking that this is a slice of Heaven," he told her. "I never knew that such a place could exist."

"Ah! Thinking again? That's only half of the way to truth, Richard."

"I suppose." He used wooden tongs crafted from limber pine branches to fish one of the hot rocks from the fire. "You know, they'd never believe this in Boston."

"I know." She hammered the root paste with renewed vigor. Boston—always Boston. But the evening softness, with its shadows and colors, the birdsong, and the gurgling from the spring-fed creek soothed her.

Perhaps Boston would remain forever over the horizon—the sort of a place a person always talked about going to, but never really meant to.

She glanced at the dugout shelter they'd made of juniper and pine logs. It was something new, half Indian, half White. More than a wickiup but less than a house. The place even had a pole doorway hung on rawhide hinges. Inside lay their bedding of freshly tanned buffalo hides atop mounded straw.

I could stay here forever, loving him. Tam Apo, *can't you make the world leave us alone? Is that too much to ask?*

As if in answer, a chorus of coyotes began yipping high up in the rocks, mocking her.

The wary manner in which Richard rose brought her to her feet; she followed his gaze down the canyon. Three horsemen were filing through the tall sagebrush. All carried rifles over their saddlebows.

"Visitors?" Richard wondered. "Friends or enemies?"

Willow shaded her eyes. 'Two White men and an Indian."

"And how would you know that from this distance?"

"Two riders have stirrups," she answered. "Indians don't use them."

Richard ducked inside the shelter, retrieving their bows and quivers. "I don't know what good these will do against good rifles. Let's hope we don't have to use them. Willow, before they get here, slip over the edge of the bank."

She nodded, heart skipping, and hurried into the screen of juniper, then circled to the side. Water that drained off one of the sandstone ridges had cut a narrow channel alongside their camp, and here she secreted herself, using one of the junipers for cover. From this ambush she could probably take one, or maybe two. And if not, she could wound the horses, affecting the riders' control.

Who are they? Why are they here?

Red Canyon was a favorite stopping place for travelers on the trail southward over the mountains. That none of the *Ku'chendikani* had ridden through made her suspect that stories about her and Richard had circulated among the bands—further proof of her spiritual alienation from her people. The thought tightened the fist of worry in her stomach.

She took a deep breath and checked her arrows. Each was tipped by a chert point carefully flaked to an edge sharp enough to sever a hair. Fletching made from sage grouse feathers had been painstakingly tied to the shafts at an angle to impart spin that stabilized the arrow in flight. With her Pawnee bow, she'd been able to drive such an arrow into a buffalo's chest until the point lodged in the far ribs. And it wasn't as if these strangers would kill any harder than Ree warriors.

The horsemen rode straight up the canyon, their

rifles at rest, and pulled up before Richard, who stood before the steaming stew.

"How!" the first called, pulling his horse up and taking stock of their camp. He wore fringed buckskins, had a dark brown beard, amused eyes, and a pug nose. Built like a bear, with broad shoulders and thickly muscled legs, he looked as if he could crush rocks with his bare hands. Atop his head sat a felt hat adorned with an eagle feather.

The second White man was thin—barely more than a boy—with the reedy look of wiry strength. Long blond hair flowed out from under a wolfhide hat. His sparse beard scarcely hid his pointed chin. He, too, wore finely crafted buckskin decorated in Pawnee patterns. Unlike his bluff companion, he glanced this way and that with faded blue eyes, then studied Richard with evident disdain.

The Indian was *Ku'chendikani,* his legs bent around the barrel of a ratty paint horse. He looked vaguely familiar to Willow, with a weasel-thin face and hooked nose. His hands knotted on the reins, and his nervous black eyes searched the camp warily, as if looking for...

Me? Willow wondered as the lead White raised his hands, making the sign for peace. Next his fingers traced out, "We come looking for a white man."

CHAPTER ELEVEN

I am ready to melt you and weld you together, so that you two may be made one, and as one you may join together as long as you live, and when you die, you may die together instead of apart, and be yonder in the House of Hades joined. Think of this as your passion, and if it will satisfy you to get this. If such a thing were offered we know that not a single one would object, or be found to wish anything else; he would simply believe he had heard that which he has so long desired, to be melted and united together with his beloved, and to become one from two. For the reason is that this is our ancient natural shape, when we were one whole; and so the desire for the whole and the pursuit of it is named Love.

—Plato, *Symposium*

Richard cocked his head as the bearded rider's hands made signs. "I'm sorry. I guess I've never learned sign talk."

"Hell!" the white roared, slapping his thigh. His horse started and pranced. "I mistook ye fer Injun."

"Richard Hamilton, sir. At your service."

The burly white laughed, kicked a leg over his saddle, and slid neatly off his horse. "Name's Fletch. Short fer Fletcher. And this hyar's Jonas Hayworth. That sneaky Injun yonder is Yeller Beaver. We're with Jed Smith's brigade. Over trapping the Green mostly, but we heard they's a white man hyar. And Yeller Beaver, he taken on an itch ta show us whar ye be."

Richard fingered the cool wood of his bow, frowning. "And why would you seek me out?"

"Wal, coon. Ain't that many white men out hyar. We run inter Jed Smith and Moses Harris. They's coming ahead of Gen'ral Ashley and the caravan. Smith figgered ye might have a way with the Snakes, since the story is yer living with one. He figgered it'd be worth our ride over ta see if'n ye could shanty some Snakes inter Rendezvous ta trade beaver. Figgered if'n ye'd have a mind, he might make ye an offer, buy yer plews, and see if'n ye'd represent the company with yer Snake friends."

"Represent the company? What company?"

"Ashley and Smith. Uh...ye've heard of us?"

Richard nodded, lowering his bow. "I have. Well, if it's trade you've come to talk, I take it you didn't come for war."

"Huh? War? Now, what kind of talk's that among white men?"

Richard gestured around. "Living out here alone, well, a man prepares for anything, and, to be honest, you might say I've been up the creek and over the mountain." He raised his voice. "Come on in. Willow, they're friendly."

Willow sighed, hating the premonition of trouble that crawled around her chest like a spider. She stepped out from behind the juniper, and watched Yellow

Beaver's interest sharpen. The White men's expressions changed as well. Jonas Hayworth let out a low whistle and said, "By God, what a purty woman. Hell, most Injuns is uglier than sin plastered over."

"Shut up," Fletch growled. Then added, "Got ta excuse Jonas. He's raised without no upbringing."

Richard fixed Jonas with a hard stare. "I'll let it pass —this time. But if he wants to keep his hair, he'll treat my wife like a lady."

Fletch studied Richard with a keen eye and nodded. To Jonas, he said, "Pilgrim, if'n I read sign, ye'd better keep a civil tongue in yer head, or ye'll be wolfmeat."

Willow walked up to stand beside Richard. Suddenly Yellow Beaver seemed interested in everything but her. The White men she understood: Fletch was a bluff, hearty trader. Young Jonas wanted to prove himself a man, and lacked any good sense about how to do it. But Yellow Beaver, what was his purpose here?

"Supper is almost ready, gentlemen," Richard said pleasantly. "Would you join us?"

"Reckon so," Fletch replied, taking in the sloping sandstone that rose behind their shelter, and the high white limestone cliffs west of the red caprock. "Right fine place ye got ta hole up hyar. Right fine indeed. She's some, she is. Purty as a picture—and they's a sight of purty country out hyar." Then he added, "Jonas, see ta the hosses."

Tin cups magically appeared as the men settled around the fire and evening deepened. Richard scooped the cups full while Willow took her place beside him, every nerve taut.

"You say you've been trapping?" Richard asked as they ate. "You haven't run into another white man? Travis Hartman?"

"Hartman?" Fletch asked, wiping droplets from his mustache. "Nope. Ain't seen him, but I've heard tell of him. Bear-scarred, ain't he? One of Lisa's men. Old-timer. He out hyar, too?"

"We were separated last winter." Richard paused. "I've been hoping he made it back to the Crow. Baptiste de Bourgmont was going to winter with them."

"Huh. I heard tell they's a black man wintered with the Crow. Ain't no telling fer sure, though. Could'a been Ed Rose. He's tight with Crow. I ain't been up with the Crows since last fall with Ashley—and nip and tuck it was. Them thieving skunks damn near robbed us blind, but Gen'ral Ashley, he seed his way through. Then we met up with Atkinson and O'Fallon, and the Gen'ral floated on downriver. Rest of the boys wintered down ta Willow Valley."

Willow studiously ignored Jonas's stare. He seemed entranced by her, sipping his stew, chewing, blue eyes never wavering. In contrast, Yellow Beaver never looked up, eating halfheartedly as if his stomach were bothering him. Why?

"We saw you," Richard said. "I was on a boat, the *Maria*. Dave Green was booshway. We were hidden off in a side channel when you passed."

Fletch raised an eyebrow. "A boat, ye say?"

"Green wanted to open trade with the Crow. He started a post at the mouth of the Big Horn. Blackfeet overran him, and he blew up the boat and as many Blackfeet as he could."

"Bug's Boys! Huh! And old Davey Green gone under? Well, Tarnal Hell, them's poor doings. Sorry ta hear it." Fletch considered. "And ye made do by yerself?" He glanced at Willow. "And right fine ye did, too."

"What of this rendezvous you mentioned?" Richard raised an eyebrow.

Willow finally had enough of Jonas's devouring stare. She met his eyes, called upon her *puha,* and aimed it like an arrow. To her satisfaction, Jonas swallowed hard and looked away. He flushed and scratched the back of his neck, as if suddenly uncomfortable.

Fletch continued talking like a man who couldn't get enough of it. "We got a caravan coming up the trail. She otta be down ta Willow Valley come June. Powder, shot, foofawraw, everything a coon needs. Ashley figgers he can supply his brigades out hyar, and trade fer plews with Injuns and free trappers alike. Then he caravans the plews back ta Saint Loowee."

"And takes a hell of a profit, I'd suppose?"

"I reckon, but fer most of us coons, why, we're fer the mountains, and hooraw ta that!"

Willow glanced at Richard, reading his intense expression. Her cold intuition, so often forgotten in the warmth of his arms, flowed again.

Now he will be thinking of Boston more than ever.

Better to immerse herself in the inevitable. "This caravan," she said, "it would be a safe way to travel back to Saint Louis. From there, you could return to Boston."

The trappers stared at her, surprised by her English.

Richard nodded, fingering his chin. "Fletch, do you suppose I could arrange passage? They'd value another rifle, wouldn't they?"

"Reckon so." Fletch glanced uneasily at Willow, catching the subtle undercurrents of the conversation. "Though God knows why ye'd want ta go back. If this ain't Heaven right hyar, this child don't know sign."

Willow gave him a surreptitious smile, then looked at

Yellow Beaver. In Shoshoni, she asked, "Why did you come here?"

Yellow Beaver avoided her eyes. "I came to see you, *Puhawaip*. You, and your Powerful White man."

"And why would you do that?"

"I have heard stories. I thought I would come to see if they were true."

"What stories?"

Yellow Beaver's eyes flickered, then he dropped them. "We will talk later, *Puhawaip*."

Richard had understood most of the exchange. He studiously ignored Yellow Beaver, perhaps because his mind was on the whites' caravan.

"How'd ye make do without a rifle?" Fletch was asking.

"Broke the cock in a fall," Richard answered absent-mindedly. "The bow has filled in."

"A Hawken's gun?" Fletch asked.

"Yes."

"We got parts. Ye still got the gun?"

"Parts?" Richard straightened. "With you?"

"Nope. But if some of the boys don't have one down ter Willow Valley, they'll be some a-coming with the caravan. Might take a bit of filing ta make 'er fit, but we can make her a daisy again."

Richard took a deep breath. "I'll admit, I've felt half naked without it. Having a broken gun is like having a friend with amputated legs."

"That's some, it is," Fletch agreed. "Wal, ifn yer of an interest, Rendezvous will be in the Willow Valley as soon as the caravan arrives. Maybe a month or so. Just about travel time ta get there."

"Willow Valley?" Richard shook his head. "I don't know that place."

Fletch took a stick to sketch in the dirt. "Hyar we be." He poked a hole. "This hyar's Wind River, what the Snakes call *Pia'ogwe*." He sketched in a line. "Hyar's the Wind River Mountains. West of them is the Green River. West of them is the Bear River draining inta Bear Lake. Ye follers that south inta Willow Valley." Fletch gave him a level glance. "Yer welcome ta travel with us, ifn ye'd like. We could use another gun."

Richard studied the map, that pensive look of opportunity in his eyes. "So could I, but it would need a working lock." He wanted to go, as plain as the sun in the sky; and with it, a conflict raged, his soul torn to stay with her.

Oh, Richard, why did these men have to come here?

The talk continued, stories about beaver, about Indians and cold snows, but not until long after dark did Yellow Beaver catch Willow to one side.

"I have come here, *Puhawaip,* to pay you to use your *puha.*"

Willow stopped short. He still refused to look at her, to meet her eyes. "What would you have me use *puha* for?"

He scuffed the grass with a moccasined toe. "It is said that you can do many things with *puha.* That you have traveled to the Land of the Dead in spite of being a young woman. It is said that you returned from there. This is true?"

"And if it is?"

"Then I would give you ten horses, ten buffalo hides, and anything else you wanted if you used your *puha* for me."

"And what would you have me do?"

"There is a man, his name is Slim Pole. I think you know him?"

"I do."

Yellow Beaver untied a little pouch from his belt, fingering it ever so carefully. "He is a very powerful man, and he does not like me. I wish to marry his granddaughter, but he has said no. When he speaks, people listen. This bag contains some of his hair, a bit of hide with his blood on it, and a bit of fingernail. It was all I could get. With it, you could use your *puha* to kill him."

Willow shivered, knotted her fists. Slim Pole? He'd never approved of her, but he'd been honest, and wise. A good man, and a *puhagan* who served his people well. With great deliberation, she said, "I am no *witch,* Yellow Beaver. You will leave this place. And you will never tell anyone why you have come here. Do you understand?"

He shrugged, crestfallen. "Perhaps if I made it twenty horses?"

"I said *no.*" She started to stalk off, then turned. "Wait. Who told you I was a witch?"

"A friend. Her name is Red Calf. She said you witched White Hail, hardened his heart against her so that he threw her out of his lodge. She had crept close to White Hail's lodge the night he threw her out. She heard the whole story when White Hail told it to Two Half Moons."

"Just *leave.* And tell people I am no witch." But as she walked unsteadily back toward her shelter, the relentless truth spread within her. Yellow Beaver would only be the first to seek her out. The charge had been made. Come what may, she would always be a witch to her people.

For hours she lay awake in the robes beside Richard, listening to the night sounds of owls hooting, the wailing chorus of the coyotes, and the burble of the creek. Outside, one of the White men, Fletch most likely, was snoring in his blankets by the fire.

Richard kept shifting and resettling himself.

"Are you awake?" she asked finally.

"Yes."

"This thing, this..."

"Rendezvous."

"Yes. I think we should go, Richard." A heaviness, like a terrible weight, pressed down on her heart. "It is a way for you to return to your Boston."

He remained silent for a long time. She could feel him turning the thought over and over in his soul. At last he asked, "What about you? About us?"

"Richard, you must go. It is within you. A thing you must do."

"You were upset when you came to bed. I heard Yellow Beaver call you *puhawaip*. A Power woman. What did he want?"

"Nothing," she lied. "Go to sleep, Richard. Tomorrow we will load the horse and start for this Rendezvous."

"I can hear the sadness in your voice. Why are you telling me to do this?"

"Because you are a warrior, Richard. And your *mugwa* will slowly sicken if you do not go back to Boston and settle this longing within you."

And I must risk the chance that you will never come back to me.

How had they accumulated so many things? Richard stared skeptically at the pack as he threw his diamond hitch over the buffalo-hide manty.

And we made most of it with our bare hands. The rope we twisted from juniper, the hides we scraped and tanned.

Willow's fleshing tool was made from the hock joint

of a mule deer. They'd sharpened the digging stick with quartzite flakes from the quarry high on the ridge, and hardened the tip in the fire. Together they'd dug the biscuit root that filled the net bags. Willow's agile fingers had woven the baskets. He'd made the stone hammer, using sharpened rabbit bones to sew green rawhide over the willow-stick handle before it dried tight.

Of his outfit, only his possibles and the broken rifle remained from the White world.

Beside him, Willow laced on her heavy travel moccasins, made from a buffalo he'd killed and prayed over.

The land provides.

Fletch and Jonas were already saddled up, their outfits little more than the blanket rolls behind their saddles and possibles hanging from their shoulders.

"Reckon we'll have ta steal ye some hosses," Fletch decided. "The two of ye walking, why we might be up and died of old age afore we get there."

"You could ride on." Richard looked up from his knots. "We'll follow behind."

Fletch had watched them pack, respect in his eyes. "Oh, I reckon we'll mosey along with ye. From the looks of things, Hamilton, there's a trick or two ye might be teaching us."

Me teach you?

That thought surprised him. For so long he'd been a student of the frontier. That a seasoned hiverner like Fletch would look to him brought a certain amount of amazement.

He took a long moment and looked around. So many memories were here. The shelter with its pole doorway had kept them warm in the worst of storms. The sloping ridges of red sandstone had awed him with their beauty—the shadows they cast forever changing with the light. He'd climbed to those spectacular high points with Willow, the two of them exploring, laughing, sharing their souls. Here they'd worked, played, and loved. The canyon had cradled them within its rocky womb, and now he was about to leave. To what end?

"Ready?" Willow asked, sensing, as always, his mood.

"Reckon so," he drawled in Travis's twang. "But my heart's a mite sad."

She smiled, patted his arm, and took up the lead rope. Without a word, she tugged to start the mare and followed in the wake of the trappers' horses.

"We'll come back here someday," Richard promised as he walked beside her. But his memory played with images of Boston, of his friends there, and shaded walks at the university. Most of all, he remembered every line in his father's face, right down to the red veins in his nose. Those terrible gray eyes had grown mild, warm and loving.

He thinks I'm dead by now. And the thought gouged him deeply. *Poor old fellow, all he ever wanted was a son to be proud of.*

Richard glanced down at himself, at the buckskin pants, the long fringes cut by Willow's careful hands, at the buffalo-hide jacket with its flowing fringe and the porcupine quills Willow had flattened and worked into intricate designs. Beneath lay his buckskin hunting shirt, with its brightly painted patterns.

I do look like an Indian.

Phillip Hamilton would still disapprove.

So, here I am. Richard John Charles Hamilton, squaw man, educated savage.

His coups, saved for so long in his possibles, had been sewn on the front of his jacket. Pawnee, Ree, and Blackfeet scalps.

I'm sorry, Father, but I'll not take them off for you. Nor for any man.

And how would Professor Ames interpret that?

"A man is only what he is," he muttered.

He glanced at Willow. Her smooth brow was lined with worry. What had happened between her and Yellow Beaver? Something about witchcraft, he supposed, for the *Ku'chendikani* had been gone before first light.

A squaw man? Charges of witchcraft? Once again, he'd dredged up the notion of taking Willow to Boston with him, but they'd crucify her. A white man married white; that, or he was the kind of human trash that decent people didn't associate with.

And how dare they think that about his Willow? She'd saved his life on the Missouri when the Rees would have killed him. She had healed the wound in his back when a white woman would have fainted at the sight of it. His Willow had crossed wilderness in the dead of winter and risked her soul to save him. How dare anyone condemn his precious woman who defied her people in the search for truth, and made sweet love on high rock pinnacles?

But destroy her they would—heedless of the beauty of her soul or the courage in her breast.

So, who's civilized, and who's a savage?

Something was skewed, turned at angles to itself. The civilized concept of justice galled the very notions it espoused, coming as it did from a Christian society.

No, what they needed in philosophy lectures was a Travis Hartman to debate ethics—as if they'd understand the scope of Hartman's perceptivity when it came to human nature. With that thought came the sudden illumination that most knowledge was predicated upon experience. Perhaps all of it.

He vented a bitter laugh, causing Willow to give him one of her knowing, sidelong glances. In response to her unasked question, he said, "I sure hope Travis is at Rendezvous. I miss that old coon. And Baptiste, too, ever so sure of himself and life and truth."

"You are back to worrying about Truth?"

"No. I was just wishing I could sit around a fire and talk to them one more time. I guess I'm a lot smarter now than I ever was."

Her smile was fleeting. "Travis would be proud of you."

"I hope so."

At least someone would be proud of me.

It prickled deeply within him that he wasn't so sure he could be proud of himself any more.

Travis crept carefully along. The slightest misstep meant that he'd fall to his death hundreds of feet below. The scary trail followed an undercut hollow beneath thick sandstone caprock. The overhang stuck out over the high valley, enough of it cracked and sagging that Travis's heart had a case of the grips. The wind roared in the conifers just above the rim, and tore through the brush clinging to the canyon below.

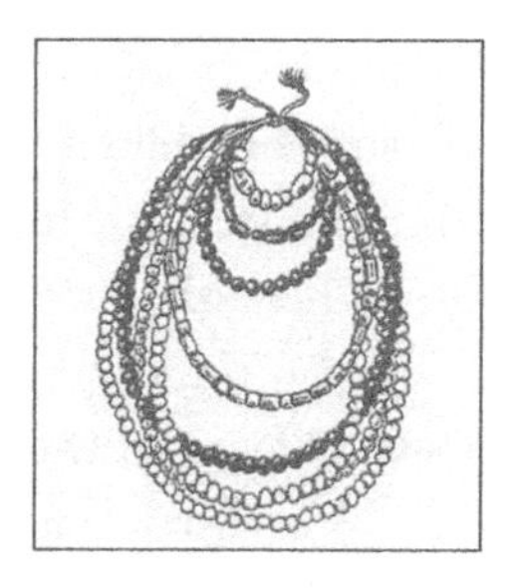

Tarnal Hell, what sort of damn fool situation did I get myself into?

He stopped, one hand braced on the rockface, his moccasins precarious on the angular rocks tumbled from the rim. He'd followed a trail marked by scuffed moccasin tracks down under the rock wall. What had started out looking like a game trail had ended up in a jumble of boulders that almost blocked the narrow ledge over a sheer precipice. From where he balanced, he could spit nearly one hundred feet down. He placed each foot with care to keep from falling, or from starting a landslide that would pitch him into the depths. Now, he paused, hefting the rifle in his free hand. From the rock he stood on, he'd have to leap half a body-length to the next.

And if ye miss...ye'll bust a leg sure, coon.

A feller could talk all he wanted about being a good hunter, but tracking down the *Dukurika* had challenged all of his and Baptiste's skills—and the closest they'd come was smoking fires and empty camps. The Sheepeaters had an uncanny sense, knowing by instinct that Travis and Baptiste were in the mountains.

But that had been the way of it. Living in the mountains—in terrain that a Natchez Trace Bald-knobber would salivate over—the Sheepeaters just melted away. In a sense it was more frustrating than being shot at.

"By damn," Travis muttered, looking up at the overhanging rock. "A Sheepeater would only need to roll a couple of rocks down, and this child would be wolfmeat."

He took a deep breath, steadied himself, and leaped. Windmilling, and using his rifle to balance, he caught himself short of disaster on the other side. And what if they hadn't come this way? What if they'd left a false trail and skipped off to the side just to sucker him into this dead end?

He hopped to the next rock, and then the next. If he fell, he'd break his neck.

And that'd serve ye right fer being a fool!

With his next leap, he came to a resumption of the trail: a narrow path that followed the edge of the rock before the slope fell away over the cliff below. There, to his relief, were more of the scuffed moccasin tracks—none more than an hour old.

Travis ghosted along, silent as death, head cocked, listening. The caprock bulged out here, and he stopped in mid-step, hearing the cadence of human voices. Someone laughed, a child from the sound of it.

Travis nerved himself and eased around the corner. They didn't see him at first, preoccupied with cutting up a grouse. Four of them sat under a rock overhang: a man, woman, and two kids. They were dressed in the most beautiful of white-tanned hides, all painted with colorful designs, fur-lined and tailored. The workmanship looked as fine as any Travis had ever seen. Five dogs were watching the grouse plucking with avid interest.

The chubby man had a bland face, almond eyes, and a thatch of braided black hair. As he pulled feathers from the grouse's breast, he chided one of the children. The kids were laughing, white teeth flashing, and the young woman with them was smiling, a sparkle of enjoyment animating her brown features.

They had set up camp in a big hole in the side of the cliff, rainproof, sheltered from the wind, dry and cozy. Firewood was piled to one side, and from the soot-stained soil the place saw frequent use.

"Excuse me," Travis said gently in his limited Shoshoni. "I am a friend. I apologize for interrupting, but I need to find a *Dukurika* woman."

They froze—the way deer did in that panicked instant just after being shot at. Then the dogs exploded in a frenzy of barking.

Travis laid his rifle to the side and raised his hands. The Sheepeaters stared at him in horror. The dogs charged back and forth, barking and growling with teeth bared. One, a big black-and-gray animal, kept leaping at him, snapping his teeth.

"I mean no harm. Do you understand?"

Hell, I hope that's what I'm saying. Even if I remember the words, my accent might be so bad I'm telling 'em I'll eat 'em fer supper!

He used his hands in sign language, repeating his words in case they couldn't hear him over the barking dogs.

"I'm Travis Hartman. I'm a friend of Heals Like A Willow. She's a woman of High Wolf's band. I've come to look for her."

That didn't cause them the slightest relaxation. The round-faced man began whispering to himself.

Instead of using them to talk, Travis desperately wished he had his rifle in hand in case he had to whack the dog before it took his kneecap off. "Do you know Heals Like A Willow?"

The man swallowed hard and glanced around as if seeking an escape. He contemplated the lip of the overhang—as if considering throwing himself over—then licked his lips. The woman was whispering frantically, pulling the owl-eyed children behind her.

"I know her," the man said, voice trembling, hands forming the signs. "She is not here. I have nothing to do with her."

"Do you know where I can find her?" The dogs were milling and growling now, hair standing on their backs.

"She is at *Ainkahonobita,* the Red Canyon. Please, do not harm us, spirit. My wife and I are good. My children are good. We pray, we..."

"Easy. Easy, there, hoss," Travis soothed. He signed, "I am no spirit. I am Travis Hartman. A white man. Who are you?"

Flashing hands accompanied the words, "I am Gray Moth, a man of White Rock's band."

"You seem uneasy about Heals Like A Willow. Is she all right?"

Gray Moth looked scared half to death. In the end, all he could do was shrug.

"Is there a white man with Heals Like A Willow?"

Gray Moth nodded, looking even more uneasy.

Travis knotted his fists and shook them in the sudden exultation—and the frightened *Dukurika* nearly darted to suicide over the ledge. The dogs began to bark and snap again. Damn them; if the mutts attacked, they could drive him right over the edge.

"It's all right," Travis crooned. "I will not hurt you, you are good people, a good father and mother for such beautiful children."

At that Gray Moth seemed to sweat relief.

"Where would I find Heals Like A Willow and the white man?"

"*Ainkahonobita*," Gray Moth said again and signed, "Red Canyon."

Travis frowned. "I do not know this place."

The man and woman looked at each other, slightly perplexed, as if they misunderstood, or might be entering some sort of trap. The man signed: "Spirits know everything."

Travis shook his head and sighed. "I am a man, Gray Moth, just like you. *Newe,* a man. *Newe,* ain't that the word?"

From the slight glazing of Gray Moth's eyes, he didn't believe it for a moment.

Travis signed, "Please, just tell me where to find Red Canyon."

"West, across the *Pia'ogwe*, at the foot of the Owl Creek Mountains. You will find red stone ridges. The witch and her White man-spirit are living there. At the spring. No one goes there now."

"Witch?" Travis cocked his head. "Heals Like A Willow is a witch?"

Gray Moth nodded fervently.

Travis made a face, grunted, and said, "Thank you for your help, Gray Moth." He fished into his possibles for a twist of tobacco. 'This is for you, for your help. May *Tam Apo* bless you with health and good hunting. Thank you. Travis Hartman is now your friend."

And with that, he picked up his rifle and eased back around the corner. Hurrying along the trail, he grimaced at the sight of the tumbled boulders. He glanced back at the way he'd come, half expecting Gray Moth to lean around the corner with his bow. The big dog was watching him, lips still curled in a snarl. The spot between Travis's shoulder blades prickled, anticipating an arrow's cutting bite. Heart in throat, he took the dizzying leaps.

"And those kids jump this?"

He trotted along the game trail, climbed up the narrow crack in the rock to the top of the rim, and met Baptiste, rifle in hand, keeping guard.

"Anything?" Baptiste asked.

"Yep. Willow's at a place called Red Canyon, west of the mountains. I caught a bunch of 'em. Pap, Maw, two kids, and a dog pack. Scairt holy hell outn 'em. But they fessed up. Told me where to go—and hyar's the best. She's with a white man!"

Baptiste scratched his black chin. "I'll be damned. Do you suppose?"

"Beats hell outa me. I'm just a-hoping. But, c'mon, coon, let's make tracks. I ain't sure I trust old Gray Moth."

"And why's that?"

"When I mentioned Heals Like A Willow, he damned near shit hisself inside out. I finally got it outa him that she's a witch."

"What? A *witch*? Willow?"

"How the hell do I know? But if the Sheepeaters think that, and I told 'em we're her friends, we might just want ter pound hooves off'n this hyar mountain. Folks think funny thoughts when it comes ter witches."

Baptiste rocked his jaw back and forth skeptically, then shrugged. "Yep, let's pull our sticks." He walked to his horse, untying the reins. "Witch, huh? Wal, I reckon everybody's got to do something with their lives—and she never was the sort to sit at home in the lodge."

"Do tell?"

CHAPTER TWELVE

And, in fact, we discover that the more a cultivated reason deliberately devotes itself to the enjoyment of life and happiness, the more a man falls short of true contentment. From this fact there arises in many persons, if only they are honest enough to admit it, a certain amount of misology: hatred of reason. This is particularly pertinent for those who are most experienced in its use. After cataloguing all the advantages which they draw—I will not say from the invention of the arts of common luxury—from the sciences (which in the end seem to them no more than a luxury of the understanding), they nevertheless discover that they have actually placed more trouble on their shoulders instead of gaining in happiness; in the end they envy, rather than despise, the common lot of men who are better guided by plain natural instinct, and who do not permit their reason much influence on their conduct.

—Immanuel Kant, *Foundations of the Metaphysics of Morals*

To the West, the Wind River Mountains rose into the spring-blue sky like ragged white teeth. At their feet, grassy bluffs stretched toward the river until they dulled into the baser greens of sage flats. Small herds of buffalo, like dark dots, accented the tan and white speckles of antelope that grazed in their midst.

Despite the clear day, a cold wind blew down from the mountains. Willow and Richard walked briskly to keep the chill at bay. Fletch and Jonas rode to one side, their rifles ready. Their route south followed the floodplain on the west side of the *Pia'ogwe.* They passed through stands of cottonwoods, their branches heavy with catkins and full buds. The entire bottomland had been grazed, old piles of horse manure turning gray in the sun.

"*Ku'chendikani,*" Willow explained. "These are their winter grounds."

"Friends of yers?" Fletch asked, an anxious set to his face.

"White Hail's people," Willow told Richard. To Fletch, she said, "Yes, friends."

I hope, Richard added mentally as he walked with his bow in one hand, his lead rope in the other. The furtive shape of a cottontail rabbit hid in the shadow of a sagebrush. No patch of brush or pile of deadfall escaped his scrutiny.

Fletch seemed just as keen, but young Jonas watched the hawks in the sky, or worse, rode with his eyes in an unfocused stare that irritated Richard.

He's going to be wolfmeat if he doesn't mend his ways.

At the thought, Richard smiled grimly.

"What is it?" Willow asked.

"I'm wondering why Travis never strangled me. The man has the patience of a saint."

Willow arched an eyebrow wryly. "He wasn't the only one."

Richard grinned at her. How beautiful she was, her

black hair shining. He wanted to reach out and caress the smooth curve of her cheek. As if reading his thoughts, her dark eyes sparkled, and she lifted a perfect brow in silent question.

If we just weren't with these two hunters, I'd—

"Know them folks?" Fletch asked, pulling up his horse. The first of the scouts came riding out of the trees, whooping and kicking their horses. The young warriors clutched bows and arrows, gaily painted shields on their arms.

Richard shaded his eyes. Six, seven, nine, the warriors galloped toward them. "Willow? Do you know them? Are we in trouble?"

"*Ku'chendikani*," she told him. "Slim Pole's band uses this country for the most part. I used to live in his village."

"Hot damn!" Jonas whooped as he clutched his rifle. "Fer a second there, I's figgering to shit myself inside out."

"Slim Pole?" Richard asked. "That's White Hail's village? The one he went back to?"

Willow nodded, face bleak.

"Reckon we need ta fort up?" Fletch checked the priming in his rifle as the scouts raced toward them. "Uh...they's friendly, right? I mean, Snakes and whites, we mostly get along. But they's some, like Mauvais Gouche, and that Iron Wrist, they's just as likely ta fight as look at ye."

"They'll be friendly." In Shoshoni, she told Richard, "I will do my best, husband. If there is trouble, it will be over me." Willow strode forward, raising her hands before her.

Richard called, "Is there anything I should do?"

She shot him a quick smile. "Just be rational."

As the warriors drew near, they suddenly crisscrossed in the maneuver that would have drawn cheers from any cavalry drill team. Dirt flew under racing hooves as the horses wheeled, cut at angles, and circled the party.

A tall warrior, older than the rest, rode up on his powerful warhorse. Richard took his measure. This man had a special grace, a keen glint in those black eyes. He wore his forelocks roached high over his forehead; a weasel-tail tie confined the rest of his long hair. A battered trade rifle was clutched in his hand.

"That's Fast Black Horse," Willow called back.

Richard studied the man with renewed interest. Fast Black Horse, the man who had wanted Willow for a third wife. That's where he'd heard of him before. Hostility bristled at the back of Richard's neck.

Good Lord, man, it was before your time. She didn't even know you then.

Willow stopped short of Fast Black Horse's prancing dapple gray stallion. He gave her a fierce scowl, until his eyes widened with recognition.

"Hello, warrior," Willow said evenly, and rested the tip of her bow on the ground before her. "Are you still interested in taking me for a wife?"

Richard narrowed his eyes to a predatory stare. She didn't have to bring it up, did she? It took all of his concentration to follow their Shoshoni, and the *Ku'chendikani* dialect was just different enough to challenge his ears.

Fast Black Horse used his heels to back his mount away, clearly wary. "A great many stories are told about you. Heals Like A Willow." He gestured with the rifle. "And now, here you come, followed by White men. Perhaps the stories are true."

"I haven't heard the stories, so I can't tell you which are true, and which aren't."

Fast Black Horse turned and barked a quick order; a warrior broke ranks, racing his pony back toward the village. Then he gave her a flat stare. "What are you doing here? Have you come to work evil among us?"

"No, warrior. We are only passing through, traveling westward to the White man's gathering. We mean you no harm and no trouble."

Fast Black Horse kept his distance, watching her with hard eyes. "I have heard that you are a witch. That you went to the Land of the Dead, and *Pa'waip,* took you as her own and gave you dark Power. That you couldn't control it and it made you warped and evil."

She crossed her arms. "Who says this? White Hail?"

"White Hail says little. His blood has become like water. But my wife would know these things. She has told me all about you, and the mistake I made in wanting to marry you."

"Ah, let me guess. You took Red Calf after White Hail threw her out. My sympathy, Fast Black Horse. You deserve better than her."

"A woman should know when to curb her tongue."

"So I have heard many times. But saying such things must not bother you, warrior, or you wouldn't have taken Red Calf into your lodge. Not only will she never curb her tongue, but she uses it to speak foolishness and lies."

Oblivious to the nature of the conversation, Fletch called out, "Will they trade fer a hoss?"

Willow translated, "The White man wants to trade for a horse. Do you think that would be possible?"

Fast Black Horse glanced around suspiciously. "Who would want to trade with a witch?"

"As *Tam Apo* is my witness, I am no witch." She raised

her voice so that the milling warriors could hear. "I am *no* witch!"

As far as Richard could see, no one looked convinced.

The rider dispatched to the village returned at a hard gallop, laid out over the neck of his pony as if one with the animal. He pulled up, sliding his bay on its hocks in the green grass. "Slim Pole would see Heals Like A Willow. He is preparing himself, and asks that Heals Like A Willow camp in the flats across the river from the village. No one is to see her until Slim Pole can talk to her. The Yellow Noses are to guard Willow's camp and make sure this is so."

Willow sighed and slapped hands to her sides in futility. "And how long is that supposed to take?"

Fast Black Horse chewed his lip for a moment, and studied her narrowly. 'That will be up to Slim Pole—and what the spirits tell him."

Willow marched back to Richard, Fletch, and Jonas. "We are to camp on the flats across the river from the village. Slim Pole, the *puhagan* here, wants to see me."

"Poohuggun?" Fletch made a face. "What's that?"

"Medicine man," Richard supplied. To Willow, he asked, "Trouble?"

She took a deep breath and said, "I don't know."

"Camp?" Jonas asked incredulously. "It ain't nigh ta midday! Reckon we could make miles yet. And who's these red niggers, a telling a white man what ta do? We're Americans, God damn it!"

"Shut up, kid," Fletch growled. "Don't mind him. He didn't get no ejication in his upbringing." He looked at Richard. "What do ye think, Hamilton? Buck the banshee and pull our sticks, or see her through?"

Richard turned to Willow. "What do you think?"

"I think we should see Slim Pole," she said. "He's a

wise man. He might stop this witching talk once and for all."

"Witch talk?" Fletch asked, perplexed.

"They think Willow's a witch." Richard was watching the sullen Fast Black Horse on the dapple gelding. "Or didn't you know that's why Yellow Beaver guided you to us?" His glance shifted to Willow. "That's what he wanted, wasn't it?"

"Yes," she said uneasily. "He wanted me to use *puha* to kill Slim Pole."

Richard cursed, then looked up at Fletch. "I think the best thing is to make camp. It will only cost a day or two, and if we can wrangle a horse out of it, so much the better."

"And if they don't cotton ta us?" Jonas asked, his thumb on the cock of his rifle.

"Then at least you'll be forted up," Willow replied. "Or would you rather build a post?"

"What's that mean?" Jonas demanded,

"It means, shut up," Fletch muttered. "Damn, boy, ye don't know shit!"

The horses cropped at the first spring grass while they waited under the spreading limbs of cottonwoods. The sap-heavy branches waved in the afternoon breeze. Bird-song rose and fell as the finches and juncos fluttered about. A mourning dove cooed in the distance. White masses of cloud formed around the Wind River peaks and sailed out to dissipate over the basin before they reached the eastern horizon.

All of Willow's attempts to prepare for the meeting ended in a rising anxiety.

What do I say? How do I answer him? Slim Pole never approved of me.

Like it or not, charges of witchcraft often hinged more on people's likes than on any evidence of witching.

"A witch, huh?" Fletch asked, rubbing his bearded jaw. "Naw, she looks too good ta be a witch."

Jonas grinned nervously from where he sat leaned against a cottonwood trunk and continued to whip the moldy leaf mat with a grass stem.

"It's a long story," Richard told them. "It seems that women shouldn't involve themselves in healing."

"Healing, huh?" Fletch studied Willow with thoughtful eyes. "Think ye could fix my back? I get a twinge of an occasion."

"I'll take a look when we have time." *If I live through this.*

Willow fingered her chin. What would she do if Slim Pole declared her a witch? She glanced surreptitiously at Richard. He'd fight for her, take on Slim Pole's village—and die in the process.

So, what do I do?

The only answer would be to accept whatever punishment Slim Pole decreed. For the first time, she regretted teaching Richard Shoshoni. He'd follow the conversation, understand enough to know what Slim Pole would do to her.

"Richard," she said softly, "I want you to do something for me."

He nodded, taking her hand. "Anything."

"Let me talk to Slim Pole alone. And afterwards, promise me that you'll do anything I tell you to. It may be more involved than a simple meeting. Do you understand? I may have to stay here for a while in order to bring an end to all this."

He studied her uneasily. "Is it that serious?"

"I have let it go too far as it is. I can't afford to ignore it any longer."

And I don't dare tell you the rest.

But as he looked into her eyes, she could feel him follow the tracks of her fear down into her souls. "I don't believe it. We're in the year eighteen twenty-six...and someone is going to accuse you of witchcraft? No, this has gone far enough."

She put a hand on his sleeve. "Yes, it has. But *I* must settle it—in my way. Do you understand? It's not a White matter. Anything you try will only make matters worse. You must trust me now, and do as I say. Will you?"

He nodded reluctantly. "If you think it best. I love you a great deal, Willow."

"Now, you must have faith in me." She took his hand, touching it to her lips. "Because I love you with all of my souls. And I'll do what I must do. For you, for me, for us. Do you understand?"

"I do." He smiled then, reassuring her.

"Hyar comes," Fletch called, rising, his rifle in hand. He stared down toward the crossing.

Slim Pole rode at the head of a group of warriors. Willow could see that his pony was wet up to the chest from fording the river. Slim Pole wore his hair in two braids confined by weasel hide—protection against evil, as were the eagle feathers stuck through the beaver-hide hat he wore. A long, fringed hunting shirt hung from his thin shoulders, the front and back decorated with quill-work. Water had darkened his moccasins and leggings.

Willow stood as the old *puhagan* pulled up and slipped off his horse. How curious: that face no longer cowed her the way it once had. She could sense his Power now, measure its limits. It was as if she saw him through different eyes.

Have I changed so much? Or is it him?

She gave Richard a last glance, an attempt to enforce her will that he stay out of it. Then she squared her shoulders and walked forward to greet Slim Pole.

"Hello, *Puhagan.* It's been a long time."

"Heals Like A Willow, you are looking well." He probed her with his old brown eyes. "My vision hasn't improved any since our last meeting, but I can see your *puha.*"

"Might we walk, you and I?" She thought of Richard. "It might avoid complications."

Slim Pole considered, thin brown lips pressed together, his weathered face wooden. "For what purpose?"

She lowered her voice. "My companions do not understand our ways, *Puhagan.*"

He blinked, squinting in Richard's direction. "A pace or two," he consented. "But not out of sight of my warriors."

His words stung. "Then you believe the stories? You believe I am a witch?"

He lifted his hands in supplication. "If there is trouble, you always seem to be in the middle of it. Why is this, Willow? I suppose now you are going to tell me with great energy and enthusiasm that you are no witch?"

She sighed wearily. "I'm tired of saying that, Slim Pole. I don't feel like a witch. I'll tell you what I've done, and where I've been. Then you judge. Maybe I am a witch...and if so, I don't know what to do about it. I don't feel evil, if that's important. I haven't shot magic into any of our people to harm them. And you must know this: Yellow Beaver rode over to *Ainkahonobita* offering horses and anything I wanted if only I'd kill you." She gave him a level stare. "I'd keep an eye on him, if I were you. He's no good."

Slim Pole stopped short, staring at her. "No, he's no good. How many horses did he offer?"

"Twenty, and all the buffalo robes and meat, and, who knows, maybe even the moon and stars had I asked."

Slim Pole chuckled. "Perhaps you should have taken the price. Then we would know for certain if you are a witch."

"He carried a little bag—hair, blood, a bit of fingernail. You might want to get that back."

"I will see to it." He paused. "Why do you tell me this? As proof you are no witch?"

"No. Well, perhaps. But mostly because I think you are a good man, Slim Pole. You lead your people well. And no matter what you decide today, I will bear you no ill will."

"You seem older, Willow. Almost a different person. What happened to you after you left? The stories say that you were taken by a Pawnee and carried far to the east, to the river there."

"I was. That story you may believe." She frowned. "Slim Pole, I have seen beyond the horizon. I traveled with the Whites, and now that I have returned, none of my people believe the things I try to tell them. They do not have room enough in their heads to understand about the giant boats and the White man's huge lodges."

"You saw these things in the Spirit World?"

"No, in *this* world. Things made by men." She stopped, puzzled. "But then, it's as incomprehensible for them as it is for me when Richard tells of ships, and boats that run with fires in their bellies."

"Boats with fire in their bellies?" Slim Pole's lips quirked at the notion.

Willow rubbed the back of her neck, shaking her head. "You must hear me, *Puhagan.* Listen to my words, and make them part of your soul. Great changes are coming to our People. They lie there, just over the horizon to the east. The Whites are coming here, to our mountains. And when they arrive, nothing will ever be the same again."

Slim Pole squinted eastward, deepening the wrinkles in his face. "Should we prepare to fight?"

"Can you stop the wind? Still the change of the seasons? No, *Puhagan.* This will not be a war of arrows and bullets. I've come to know the Whites. Heard their stories of war. They are like ants. Kick the anthill, and ever more come boiling out to fight. They will fight the way they work, with a single-minded determination we can't comprehend. For the sake of the People, Slim Pole, you must counsel them to bend with this coming wind. If they do not, the Whites will overwhelm them as a tornado does a tall pine. All that will be left will be a broken stump."

"Perhaps the Whites have done something to you, Willow. Is that it? Have they shot their Power into you, that you say these things? Are they like *Nynymbi*? Do they wield great Power?"

She shook her head. "Not like that. Their Power is called rationalism. With it, they capture souls, and lock them away like mice in pots." She quirked her lips. "I still have my souls, Slim Pole, so they did not work their magic on me."

His faded stare fixed on her. "When I look into your eyes, I see that you still have your souls. So...the stories say you were in the Land of the Dead?"

She steeled herself. "Yes, *Puhagan.* I found the way, and passed the guardians. But you should know that I would not have come back except for Richard. I would have become lost in the dark forest had he not sensed the right way."

He narrowed his eyes. "And which way was that?"

"Into the thickest tangle of the trees."

"You *have* been there." Slim Pole cocked his head. "Then that story is true. Did *Pa'waip* give you Power? Or perhaps one of the Rock Ogres? Or Water Baby?"

"None of the spirits gave me Power, Slim Pole." *I gave it to myself. And learned it from Richard.*

But aloud she said, "Perhaps it came from the journey, from the Pawnee I fought, or the Rees I killed. Perhaps it came from the river, or the mountains. My Power is different, Slim Pole. It comes from visions and dreams from far away."

"Such things can be very dangerous. *Pachee Goyo* discovered this when returning from Cannibal Owl's island. Remember all of the odd creatures he encountered on the way?"

"I do. And like the Bald One, I have returned safely through those lands," Willow countered. "Slim Pole, I will tell you this: I am no longer of the People. I have become someone different. Not *Dukurika,* or

Ku'chendikani, or White man. I have something of each people within me—but I am no danger to the People."

"Can you prove that?"

"How can I?" She pulled her hair around and twisted it into a thick braid, walking slowly beside the *puhagan.* "I can tell you over and over, but a witch would lie. You could look into the eye of my soul, but a witch would use just such a trick to capture your soul. Am I missing anything?"

"I could kill you, and burn your body so the ghost couldn't come back and haunt us."

"That wasn't what I had in mind."

"But what do I do with you, Willow? I have heard you speak, listened to the truth in your voice. You *are* something different. But what? I think you are too Powerful to roam loose and commit any mayhem you choose. I have told you before, spirit power is not meant for young women."

"I am nothing more than *Tam Apo* made me." On sudden inspiration, she stopped. "We think too much like Coyote, and not enough like Wolf. Humans always look for tricks when Power is involved."

"With good reason, girl."

When Willow pulled her knife, Slim Pole stepped back warily. Deftly she rolled up her sleeve to cut a small piece of skin from the inside of her elbow. Heedless of the stinging pain, she handed it to Slim Pole.

He stared thoughtfully at it, refusing to take the severed flesh. "What is that?"

"Proof," she said, holding it out to him. 'The only thing I can offer. A piece of myself. Take it. Do with it what you will. Would a witch offer you a piece of herself?"

His eyes narrowed. "Perhaps you seek to distract me

with some trick." He shook his head, answering himself with: "It's a piece of herself, a handle on her *mugwa.* A witch wouldn't dare offer such a prize to an adversary."

His hand trembled as he reached out and took the slip of bloody skin on his palm. "If you are a witch, Willow, you're the most foolish one who has ever lived."

"Foolish witches don't live long." She ignored the trickles of blood running down her arm.

"And what will you do now? Follow your White men? Go back to the mountains?" He paused. "I don't want you in my village."

She laughed bitterly. "None of the People want me, *Puhagan.* I will not be returning to your village, or any other for that matter. Like the Bald One, I still must search to find my place. And like him, I still have several challenges to face."

Slim Pole tightened his fist on the bit of skin. "You don't seem nervous for a woman who has just given a *puhagan* a piece of herself."

"I have nothing to fear from you, Slim Pole. You are Wolf, not Coyote. A man of honor and integrity. I have always respected your wisdom."

He looked away to the west, toward the mountains his failing vision could no longer see. The breeze teased loose strands of white hair that had pulled free of his beaver hat. Afternoon light played on the delicate brown skin of his wrinkled face. "I think I will tell my people to let you and your White men go. If you stayed away from my *Ku'chendikani* for a long time, I might be tempted to think I'd made the right decision."

"I will do my best"

As the old man turned, Willow added, "*Puhagan,* I told you the truth about the Whites, about their boats and ways."

He glanced back, looking frail and old. "I heard your words. I cannot see over the horizon where you have looked. I can only hope such things are in a place I will never go." And with that, he walked carefully toward where Fast Black Horse and the warriors waited.

Pensive, heart heavy. Willow walked out of the trees. Slim Pole was talking to Fast Black Horse, his old hands moving like brown birds to accent his words. The warriors clustered, to listen intently.

Richard and the Whites waited among the trees, anxious attention on the Indians. Willow gave Richard a smile and walked over to where they waited. The horses still cropped contentedly, but Fletch and Jonas held their rifles ready. She took Richard's hands in hers and met his worried brown eyes.

"It's all right. Slim Pole and I talked. He will not call me a witch, but my *puha* worries him. It is something he doesn't understand."

"Then you're free?" Richard asked.

She hesitated, and shook her head. "No, Richard. My people will never trust me again. I am different, changed. Like a white rock among black stones, I no longer have a place."

"Then, what will we do?"

She exhaled wearily. "I don't know. I'm still a tree lost in the river."

"You're bleeding."

She glanced down and shrugged. "I gave Slim Pole a piece of skin. Nothing else would have convinced him."

"Reckon we'd best pull our sticks." Fletch cast uneasy glances at the warriors. "I'd hate like hell to have them change their minds."

"It's me they'd want," Willow told him. "Had anything

gone wrong, I would have offered myself to them. You would have been free to go."

"Willow!" Richard cried.

"I told you to trust me," she reminded. "You do not know these people or their ways."

"Maybe not." Richard didn't look convinced as he turned to the packs. "Jonas, give me a hand loading the mare."

At that moment, an old woman appeared from the crossing, her dress wet to the waist. She hobbled through the warriors, leading a string of three horses.

"Wait." Willow reached out and caught Richard's sleeve. Then she hurried forward, a warmth stirring the empty feeling inside.

The sun glinted in Two Half Moons's silver-shot hair as she padded through the grass in soggy moccasins. She stopped before Willow, her lively old eyes gleaming like pebbles of obsidian. A young sorrel gelding, a bay mare, and a dappled gray were tethered together at the end of the lead rope.

"So," Two Half Moons said. "In trouble again, Heals Like A Willow? Look at you! Can this be the same woman I found freezing on the ridgetop? Now I can only wonder about what you have become."

Willow took the old woman in her arms, holding her close the way she would something delicate and precious. She could feel her aunt's bones through the thin doehide dress. "Hello, *napia*."

The reedy arms tightened, the old hands patting Willow fondly. Then she pushed back, inspecting Willow with pensive eyes. "You still look sad, girl. But now I see a strength in you that defies anything I have seen in a woman before. Can these stories White Hail tells me be true?"

"That depends on the stories."

"You have gone to a distant land and, like *Pachee Goyo,* you've come back changed. I think White Hail is right. You have found great *puha*."

"White Hail is well?"

"He is. He has changed, too, Willow. Become a thoughtful and sober man where once there was only a wild youth. For the first time, people come ask his opinion about things. He has told me all about his adventures with you. About the things you told him, and the White man you saved in the Land of the Dead. Something in his souls changed. This is good. One day, I think he will become a great leader."

One of the horses, the young sorrel gelding, tossed his head and pawed at the grass, jerking at the lead rope the old woman held.

Willow smiled. "Tell him I am glad."

Two Half Moons glanced suspiciously at the Whites. Her skeptical expression deepened the wrinkles in her brown face. "Doesn't matter that I know John Tylor and the Cunningham. They are still ugly men, girl. What do you see in them? This Power that the Whites are said to have?"

"They are just men, Aunt. Come, I would have you meet them."

"No." Two Half Moons shook her head. "I have no need of their kind. It was you I came to see. To tell you that no matter what is said, you still have a place in my lodge."

"And you in mine."

"Here, take this. That ornery sorrel will pull me over if you don't. Then it will take all day to get me picked up again." Two Half Moons offered the lead rope to Willow. The braided leather was the same color as the old woman's age-knotted hand. "People in the village are saying that you wished to trade for horses. I have brought you three. They are a gift."

"I cannot take such a—"

"Hush, girl. You will need them. When you no longer do, bring them back to me."

"Aunt, I can't."

"Still arguing! And after you ignored my warnings the last time. Look where that got you. Listen to your elder for once. Take the horses." She made the sign for finality. "Willow, I am old. Pains come in the night, and my legs have lost the strength they once had. I think this might be my last summer."

Willow's heart ached as if to burst. She studied Two Half Moons's face, trying to memorize every wrinkle. "I hear your words, *napia,* but I don't believe them. You are good for a great many summers yet."

The thin brown lips bent in a wry smile. "Do not try to fool me about life, Willow. I've lived too much of it for silly talk and lies. Coyote made sure we die when our time comes. I have cheated death many times. This time, I will not. And, to be honest, I am tired of the aches and hurts. The winters are colder, the summers too hot."

"Isn't White Hail caring for you?"

"White Hail takes good care of me, and he's been talking to young Split Antelope. I think she will come to the lodge soon. She is a lot like you, that girl. She will be what she wants to be. I think his lodge will have more children soon."

"All the more reason for you to live. *Napia.* Those children will need you. Someone must see that they are raised properly."

As I wanted you to help raise my son.

Two Half Moons made a gesture with her birdlike

hand. "My world was different, Willow. I see changes coming—like your White men, here. First it was the Astorians. Then John Tylor. Now I hear they have been all over the country. And I have heard more are coming. The *Pa'kiani* are growing stronger, and the wind tells me that my time is over."

"Wasn't it you who once brought me down from the mountain? Perhaps you need me to do that for you."

Two Half Moons smiled to expose toothless pink gums. "When I brought you down from the rim that day, you were empty. When my *mugwa* leaves to travel to the Land of the Dead, it will be full. But, tell me, you've been to the Land of the Dead. Is it like the stories say?"

"Yes, Aunt." Willow jerked the pliable lead rope when the sorrel pulled against it.

The old woman nodded with a weary contentment. "Then I shall see many old friends. The hunting will be good, and there will be no talk of changes. I can gamble at the hand game, tease the children, and tell your husband what has become of you. I look forward to seeing him again."

The dapple gray mare stamped at the season's first flies, and the bay shook her head.

Two Half Moons scowled at Willow's expression. "Oh, stop that! You look as if the sun had just gone black. The world is the way it is, girl, and nothing can stop the turning of the seasons. Now, I will wish you well and leave."

"Are you sure you won't stay? Eat with us? Maybe spend some time talking about better things?"

Two Half Moons cocked an eyebrow. "Last time, it was me pleading with you. Why should I do what you wouldn't that day I put the pack on your shoulders? No, girl. I want it this way. To say goodbye and go back to my lodge."

"I—I understand."

"Ah, good. You're showing sense for once. Now, take the horses, and go to this meeting of White men that people are talking about." She reached out, laying a frail hand on Willow's shoulder. "Be all that you can, girl. That is all I have to say." With that, she patted Willow's arm one last time, love swelling in her old eyes. Then she turned and walked back toward the river without a backward glance.

"Who was that?" Richard asked as Willow led the horses back to the camp.

"A very dear old friend." She lowered her head, her heart like a stone.

I am slowly losing everything I love. My people, Two Half Moons...and finally, Richard.

"You look so sad," Richard said, taking her arm.

"The sun just turned black," she whispered.

"What was that?"

"Nothing." She stiffened her resolve. "Come, let's pack these horses. We can go far before night falls."

CHAPTER THIRTEEN

For example, let the question be: May I, when in distress, make a promise without the intention to keep it? I easily distinguish between the two meanings which the question can have, viz., whether it is prudent to make a false promise, or whether it is implicit to duty. The former can, without doubt, often be the case; however, I see most clearly that it is not sufficient merely to escape from the current difficulties by this means, but that I must consider whether much greater inconveniences than the present one may not later arise from this lie. Even with all my cunning, the consequences cannot be so easily anticipated

—Immanuel Kant, *Foundations of the Metaphysics of Morals*

Rain fell from the solid bank of oppressive clouds. They hung so low they devoured the high ridges of Red Canyon. At the wispy fringes of gray, the ghosts of limber pine and juniper lurked, appeared, and were engulfed by the mist.

"We missed 'em," Travis declared sourly as he sat his

horse and stared up at the water-slick layers of canted sandstone. The shelter, its doorway black and vacant, seemed to stare forlornly at them, echoes of loneliness in the cant of the logs.

"Well, hell," Baptiste muttered. He cocked his head so the rain dripped off the brim of his black felt hat. He glanced around at the spring-fed creek and the cropped grass. Here and there piles of horse dung were dark and unbleached by the sun. "We're close ahind 'em, Travis. The grass is still mashed flat. I'd say they's only a couple of days ahead of us."

"Reckon we'll make a camp of it hyar." Travis wiped water from his ruined face. His leather clothing was soaked, and his skin chafed. "This child's about half-froze fer a hot fire and a drying. Reckon that shelter looks plumb chipper fer an old beaver like me."

Baptiste gathered a handful of fringes and wrung them out. "Yer not the only one, coon." He worked his mouth distastefully. "I done started to think I's back in Louisiana."

"Then camp it is. Hell, this hyar little canyon makes a right fine hole. Old Dick done hisself slick, I tell ye. Yes, sir, slicker'n Hob."

Baptiste dismounted and took a halfhearted step, as if testing his land legs. That, or the cold water had picked a new path to run down inside his leathers. "Reckon she'll be a mite tough to sniff out their tracks after this rain."

"Maybe so." Travis swung a leg over his saddle and dropped to the ground. He shifted his rifle from one hand to the other, working fingers that had stiffened around the cold gun. "But, then, I figger ter be a fair sniffer when it comes ter tracks. Tarnal Hell." He winced. "My arse aches, I'm telling ye, hoss. Got prickles in my hind end like ants."

"Yor getting old, coon." Baptiste gave him a big grin. "Now, haul yo' rickety bones inside that shelter and clear out the buzzworms whilst I see to the hosses."

Travis hunched down at the doorway, studying the inside. The place looked neat and trim. Several hides still lay on the floor. Travis scented the air for some trace of Richard or Willow. Only the tang of smoke, juniper, and old leather rewarded him.

"Hell, Dick. I don't know whar yer off ter this time. Tarnation, Doodle, ain't I never gonna catch up with ye?"

The journey to Willow Valley would remain with Richard forever. He marveled at the expanses and colors of the Green River basin. They trotted their horses through undulating waves of sea green sagebrush. Paintbrush bloomed red and yellow. Purple dagger-pod vied with clumps of sagebrush violets. Sun yellow daisies and buckwheats splotched the stands of tall grass in color. And in the distance, mountain ranges capped with pristine snow rose above turquoise sage flats. The hills consisted of banded clays, many eroded like the cathedrals of old. Herds of antelope coursed like schools of fish through the verdant grasslands. Bands of humped buffalo grazed the lush grass, clumps of shed fur hanging like moss from their sleek hides. Tan calves bounced behind the protective screen of cows who snorted at the sight of the riders, lifted their tails, and finally wheeled to dash away in a clicking of hooves.

They rode through it all: four people alone in the majesty of the wilderness.

On the banks of the swollen Green River, Willow and Richard crafted a bull boat out of willow stems, and covered it with hide. As Fletch and Jonas swam the horses across, Willow and Richard paddled their possessions to the west bank.

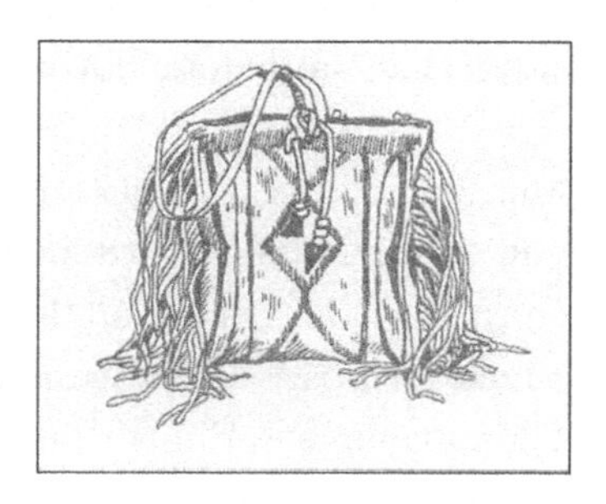

They climbed the long ridges to the west, winding through sagebrush and patchy stands of mountain mahogany. In the hollows, freshly budded aspens quivered in the breeze. The land might have been painted by the hand of God: thick-leafed balsam displayed a wealth of nodding yellow flowers as they passed. Larkspur bloomed so blue it hurt the eyes, and daisies painted patterns of soft purple, white, and yellow. Stands of lupine knit a tapestry of sky-blue accented by the yellows of desert parsley and red spots of biscuit-root. Onions lifted crowned flowers everywhere.

On the highest ridges, Richard was surprised to find oyster shells eroding out of the limestone beds.

"What does it mean?" he asked, looking back across the basin to the east as he fingered the shells. "How could they be here?"

"What are they?" Willow gave him a curious look. "Rock is rock, isn't it?"

"These are oysters. Shells, like the ones the Shoshoni trade for. A creature that only lives in the sea," he answered. "How did they get here? We're a good half mile higher than the basin—and thousands of miles from the ocean."

"*Tam Apo* works in mysterious ways." Willow shrugged. "In some of our legends the world was once covered with water. That was before Coyote and Wolf. A long, long time ago."

"Noah and the Flood," Fletch replied in awed tones. He picked up an oyster shell. "Hard ta figger. I ate oysters in Virginny as a kid. And hyar they be. Hell, I wonder if'n Salt Lake ain't part of the ocean maybe."

The following morning a spring storm rolled in and they rode in the rain. They crossed a misty divide and dropped down through valleys lush with cottonwoods and willows, the streams thick in beaver.

"Wisht ta hell we could trap some," Jonas lamented. "We'd make nigh a hundred in a week."

"Ain't got traps," Fletch growled. "An' the plews ain't prime."

In the marshy flats below the mountains, chirring red-winged and yellow-headed blackbirds perched on new shoots of cattails. When they paused, Willow waded out to dig some of the cattail from the muck, later making sweet cakes from the starchy roots. Nor did the delights of the wilderness stop there. Biscuit root, onions, parsley, sego lily, bladderwort, and blazing star added taste to the meat they shot.

"Tarnal Hell," Fletch exclaimed. "A white man'd starve ta death atop all these greens, and right smart they is, too!"

Jonas nodded as he fished another of the biscuit-root cakes from the roasting stones in their fire.

They skirted the curiously green waters of Bear Lake, and climbed southward into Willow Valley. Sheer mountain walls rose on either side, the heights clad in velvet forests of pine and fir. The air seemed to have taken on a crystal purity.

For all of that, a knot had formed in Richard's belly. That night, lying under the robes, he stared up at the myriad of stars. How clear they were in the cool black sky.

A terrible decision is coming. How will you choose?

He chewed on the nagging problem of Boston, and his father.

How can I give this up? Dear Lord God, I have everything here. Freedom, Willow, and a wonderful life spreading out before me.

Assuming, that was, that some Blackfoot didn't lift his hair.

And, at the same time, the terrible weight of responsibility pulled relentlessly at him.

No, I've got to go back. If only for a week. I have to see Father. Tell him what happened. Maybe make peace. Then I can come back.

"You are worried." Willow propped herself on her elbow beside him. With a slim hand she pulled back her hair. Despite the darkness, he could feel her sober stare.

"I don't know what to do." He sighed wearily. "I don't want to go back."

"Then don't go."

He reached out to finger her glossy hair. "He's my father, Willow. I owe him something. It's a matter of responsibility. Do you understand? My father gave me great wealth—and I lost it. Think of it like a thousand horses, and I was to drive them to the Missouri. But when I got there, they were stolen. By now, my father thinks I'm dead, and no word of his wealth—or his son—has come back to him."

He could barely make out her pursed lips as she watched him. "Was it your fault?"

"Yes." He pinched the bridge of his nose. "I was a fool, Willow. I never believed the world was real. Thirty thousand dollars. Think of it. More money than most people make in a lifetime. What could my father have been thinking when he sent such a foolish boy on so important a journey? Why didn't he hire a real man to make the trip?"

"Eventually, every father must let his son become a man."

"And a son owes something to his father. Willow, look at me, living in a paradise. Here I am, as happy as I've ever been, and he's back in Boston grieving. I have a duty to him, to myself."

"I don't know this word."

"Duty: an honorable responsibility. That's what I'm struggling with now. It's one thing to read about duty and discuss it in class as if it were an idea; and it is yet another to accept real responsibility...where fortunes, or even lives, can be won or lost. What a weight Dave Green took on when he risked everything with *Maria*. Looking back, I wonder why he didn't shoot me that day on the river."

"You have told me that Travis saved you. Maybe he understood what your father did."

Richard's thoughts went back to that night in Boston. To the dinner table, and Jeffry serving up one of Sally's masterpieces. Phillip's stern eyes burned in Richard's memory. "Did he? I wonder. Knowing what I know now, *I* wouldn't have sent me."

He frowned up into the sky. Responsibility—what an awesome thing.

So what will you do now? You have two responsibilities: one to your father in Boston, and another to Willow. How can you meet both?

The world had laid an ethical trap for him, and now he was caught. Damned either way. Two people, in two different worlds, depended on him. He could not take Willow to Boston, and he could not bring Phillip Hamilton to the mountains. Oh, he could send a letter, but his conscience demanded that he see his father face to face. Anything else would be a dereliction.

Willow asked, "What would you have become if you hadn't come here? Who would you be, Richard?"

"A silly student carried away with dreams about Truth and the nature of mankind."

"Would you have liked who you became?"

The distant yipping of coyotes carried on the night. "As I am now? No. I'd have despised that man, so pompous with his conceptions of life and nature. And he would have despised me, called me an animal and brute. So here I am, a savage who wears men's hair as a badge. And what has happened to my belief in rationality? Where did it go? Why was it such a flawed concept? Men aren't rational. They steal each other's horses, kill each other. No, not rational at all. Just —chaotic."

"I think *all* men are rational," she challenged. "Each does what he thinks is best. *Dukurika* avoid fights with others, and hide in the forest when danger is close. That's rational. According to the *Ku'chendikani,* a rational man steals as many horses as he can, because by doing so, he makes his people stronger. His children will have full bellies. His prowess as a warrior enables his people to keep their enemies at bay."

"That's not rational. That's pragmatic."

"I don't know that word."

"Pragmatic. It means doing what makes the most sense at the moment."

"Isn't that rational, Richard?"

"You're setting me up for epistemological tail-chasing." He paused. "Tell me, do you think Green was rational when he blew up *Maria*?"

"Yes. You told me the *Pa'kiani* would have taken everything."

Richard squirmed uneasily under the blanket and raised up to see that the horses were still standing at their pickets. He listened intently to the soft whispers of the night, until satisfied that all was well with the camp. "Does that mean that everything depends upon an individual's perception?"

"We are all like Coyote," she replied. "A man can't know more than what he sees. We make decisions, like Coyote when he went to steal Sage Grouse's eggs. He wanted to eat the eggs, but when he found Sage Grouse's nest, all the eggs had hatched into chicks. He was so mad he kicked dirt all over the chicks and urinated on them. To him it seemed right because he was hungry. Then he killed the chicks. And forever since. Sage Grouse goes out of her way to fly up and scare Coyote.

"The point of the story is that Coyote was doing what he was supposed to. Trying to fill his belly. And he's been suffering ever since because Sage Grouse always tries to ruin Coyote's plans."

"Maybe that's why I have to go back." He shook his head. "I don't want to be like Coyote, Willow."

"You can't fix what is already done."

"No. But Coyote would shirk his duty, wouldn't he?"

"Yes."

"Would Wolf?"

"No."

"A Sioux *wechashawakan* said that I came up the river as a dog, but that I would turn into either a coyote or a wolf. I am no longer Coyote. I can't shirk this duty."

She bit her lip, then grasped his hand. "You have already been Coyote, Richard. You said you would stay with me. Let me go with you to this Boston."

He closed his eyes, rubbing his thumb on her hand. "Do you remember when Slim Pole came to see you? You asked me to trust you? *If I* decide to go back, I'll need you to trust me. Going to Boston would break your soul, Willow."

"It didn't break yours."

"I was born to it—like a Pawnee chief—by station and birth. I wasn't Indian." He vented a dry laugh. "How funny. Back on the river, dreams of Boston kept me alive. I walked the streets, longed for it with all of my soul. And now, as we get closer to this rendezvous, the more I dread leaving you, leaving the mountains. To hell with duty."

"Then you must go."

At the despair in her voice, he said, "I haven't decided."

"Richard, listen to me. This duty, this worry about your father. If you do not go, you will never know if it was right or wrong. No matter what you once were, you are a warrior now. A man. A part of you will never be complete unless you go to this Boston."

She snuggled into the hollow of his arm, and he tightened his hold on her. The stars slowly slipped across the silent sky, but no answer came to him.

———

As they rode south along the Little Bear River, Willow cast surreptitious glances at Richard. He'd withdrawn into himself, struggling with his soul. He rode head down, a frown lining his brow.

Fletch and Jonas noted his preoccupation, and directed more of their talk to her, asking about the plants, about the game, and different tribes of Indians. She told them what she knew about the beaver streams, and about *Tssa'shogup:* the land to the west and south.

Richard barely noticed the green meadows of tall grass that rippled like waves on a lake. His eyes were blind to the majestic mountains that rose to either side. He had removed himself from this world in an attempt to find the answer that she already knew.

She studied him from the corner of her eye. *Could Boston be such a terrible place? Would it be as bad as Richard says?*

Puffs of cloud drifted eastward across the sky. Along the river, cottonwoods had leafed out and the land breathed and flexed itself for summer. In the backwaters, ducks guarded nests full of young. Willow's heart had always lifted in spring, enjoying the rebirth of *Tam Sego-bia.* This year, she entered a summer of dread.

Richard would go, and her love with him, heading for a place she could neither comprehend nor understand.

And then what will you do. Willow? Where will you go? Unlike Richard, who has two places, you have none.

She was still a tree adrift in the current—and one by one, her roots were being broken off.

She saw them first: Riders in the distance like dots on the grass. Five of them, leading more horses packed with meat. Even before Fletch whooped, she'd identified them as Whites by the way they sat their horses.

"Let's go!" Jonas crowed. They kicked their animals to a run, pounding across the grass. Fletch raised his rifle, firing a shot into the air. Willow tucked against her mare's neck, racing with the rest toward the Whites who'd pulled up to watch.

When they were within shouting distance, four of the five riders trotted to meet them. The remaining man held the packhorses as they whinnied and jostled.

To Willow's surprise, four of the strangers were Indian, but of a people she'd never seen before. In some ways, they reminded her of Pawnee with their shaved heads, but the decorations on their buckskins were unlike anything she'd seen.

The White man was small, whip-thin, with long brown hair and beard. She instantly liked his soft brown eyes. He sat his horse as if part of the animal, a use-polished Hawken across the saddle. His buckskins were shiny with fat and blood, half the fringe missing.

"Fletch!" the hunter cried. "Hell, coon. I figgered you for dead! And who's this with you?"

"Jonas Hayworth." Fletch pointed. "And this hyar's Richard Hamilton, and the squaw's Willow. Hell, Tylor, it'd take a heap of grizzlies and a passel of Injuns to raise this child." The two rode close to clasp hands.

Jonas had a silly, uncomfortable grin on his face as he shook Tylor's hand. Richard rode close and shook hands, saying, "Richard Hamilton, sir. I'm pleased to meet you."

A curious light shone in Tylor's sharp eyes. "John

Tylor, at your service. I assure you, sir, the pleasure is mine."

Willow studied him with greater interest. So this was the John Tylor everyone spoke of?

Richard straightened. "Indeed. And where are you from?"

Tylor's eyes veiled. "The East. A long time ago." He turned to Fletch. "Is the caravan coming?"

"Hell, we thought they'd a beat us hyar." Fletch scratched his ear. "And who're these coons?"

Tylor looked back at the Indians. "Iroquois. They, er, joined us. Nor'westers originally. Some of Ogden's brigade who decided to cast their lot with Americans rather than British. Not an unseemly choice, given their history. Meet Smokes His Pipe, Fights the Huron, and Calumet. Tall Fire's back there holding the horses."

The Iroquois nodded, taking their measure with hard black eyes. Willow bristled as they stared at her with open interest. Instinctively, she pulled her mare closer to Richard's mount.

"How far ta camp?" Fletch asked. "What's news?"

Tylor had heeled his horse around, resuming his interrupted travel. "About three miles. We just went out after meat. Most of the boys are waiting, gambling away their winter hunt. By now, each man jack of them has won and lost a fortune five or six times. A band of Snakes are camped with us. Gray Bear's band. My wife's people."

The Iroquois snagged up the lead ropes from Tall Fire, and fell in behind.

"Yawhooo!" Fletch whooped. "We're damn near there! Hot damn, coons, she's a long way from Saint Loowee!"

"When would you expect the caravan?" Tylor glanced over. "Moses Harris and Jed Smith came in a couple of weeks ago. They said General Ashley was on the Platte."

"That's where Jonas and me left him." Fletch pointed to Richard. "Heard tell of a white man living with the Snakes up on the Wind River. Jonas and me went ta see, and Hob take us, we found old Richard, hyar."

"Indeed?" Tylor asked, speculative eyes on Richard.

"It's a long story." Richard continued to give Tylor a thoughtful study.

Willow placed her horse on Richard's far side, doing her best to ignore the rapacious glances of the Iroquois. Hadn't they brought any women with them?

I wouldn't trust them any further than Coyote!

Maybe they, too, carried two penises.

"I don't suppose you've had word of a Travis Hartman?" Richard asked.

"Hartman?" Tylor lifted an eyebrow. "No. Last I heard he was on the Missouri, hunting for one of the Company posts."

As she glanced at the Iroquois, Willow stiffened, a crawling sensation in her gut. Mean lust reflected in their eyes—and even Trudeau hadn't sent such a cold shiver down her back. In Shoshoni, she asked: "Who are these Iroquois?"

To her surprise, Tylor answered in her tongue, "Indians from far to the east. They live in the forests of northern New York. Many have joined the Canadians."

"They have no women?" Willow asked. "From their looks, their blankets have been empty for many moons."

Smokes His Pipe laughed. "I speak your tongue. Perhaps you come to my bed, eh?"

Richard answered with frost in his voice, but smiled in a disarming way. "My wife's bed is full enough with me in it."

Tylor chuckled and gestured for the Iroquois to back down. "Coons, I think the woman is spoken for. And I think you'd best look elsewhere unless you're anxious to find the Village of Souls."

The Iroquois grinned at each other, but the Coyote look still filled their eyes.

John Tylor gave Richard a surreptitious study. "Tell me your story, Mr. Hamilton."

As Richard talked, Willow did her best to ignore the Iroquois. The grass had been grazed off here, old piles of horse droppings already sun-bleached. By the time they reached the camp, Richard had outlined his adventures.

The camp sat in the flats under the trees, a series of tents, tipis, and shelters dotting the flattened grass. In the distance a horse herd grazed under the watchful eyes of Indian guards.

Men gathered as they rode in, all calling questions about the caravan. Mixed among them were Shoshoni peoples that Willow assumed were *Agaiduka,* the Salmon-eaters who lived west of the mountains.

"Ho! Fletch!" a buckskin clad man called. "Welcome to Rendezvous, coon!"

"Indeed," John Tylor agreed. "Welcome to Rendezvous. Mr. Hamilton, my camp is over there to the west. On the small rise by the creek. If you'd like, you and your wife may establish yourselves there. It may be days yet before the caravan arrives, and Mr. Smith, our booshway, is out on an exploration. I would appreciate your company in the meantime."

"Thank you," Richard responded, inclining his head. "We accept your hospitality."

"Tarnal Hell," Fletch cried. "Somebody fetch this coon a cock fer his rifle. And a file." The burly trapper winked. "We'll fix ye up, Hamilton. Make a white man outa ye again."

Make a White man out of him,

Willow thought to herself, glancing around at the hairy men in their grease-stained leathers. One or two were accompanied by bead-covered *Agaiduka* women. Most of the rest were staring at her, sizing her up with hungry eyes that seemed to look right through her dress. Some were shuffling, pushing each other to get a better look.

Richard, I don't like this place. If only we could go back to Ainkahonobita *and act as if Fletch had never ridden into camp. I would give my* mugwa *for that.*

John Tylor had laid out a neat and spare camp. His little lodge was made of cured buffalo hides tied over a pole A-frame. Richard sat with Willow at his side as the first bowl of tobacco he'd had in months sent ribbons of blue smoke into the cool air. A haunch of elk meat roasted on the evening fire.

A brilliant sunset illuminated the mountains east of them with an ethereal glow, and cast the western peaks in dark shadow.

Tylor studied Richard thoughtfully. Finally he asked, "What brought you to Rendezvous, Mr. Hamilton? Just the need of a cock for your rifle?"

"I have a choice to make. My father thinks I'm dead. He entrusted me with a small fortune. I lost it all when a boatman called François robbed me. I think my father deserves to know what happened."

Richard frowned at the fire while meat sizzled; burning wood popped sparks and flared with dripping grease. Colors waned as the evening sky dimmed; orange-streaked clouds turned rose, and then maroon, before fading into deep purple. The night calls of the robins joined with those of the nighthawks, and the bedding finches. Out in the distance, coyotes raised their pointed noses in jocular chorus.

The trappers camped just beyond them sang "Yankee Doodle" and followed with various drinking songs around their evening fires. The *Agaiduka* sang their own songs about Coyote, Cottontail, and Chicken Hawk. As the singing rose on the night, trappers hooked arms and danced, stomping around in moccasined feet.

Tylor pulled thoughtfully on his pipe, a vacant look in his brown eyes. "You said you came upriver with a boat. You're a learned man, Mr. Hamilton. Not the sort one expects to find in the West. There's more than you told me on the ride in."

"Yes, I suppose there is." Richard gave up his pipe, and used a file to square out the rough hole in the new cock for his Hawken. As he filed, he told about François, and Travis, and Dave Green.

Willow sat close beside him, her shoulder touching his, as if she savored even the slightest contact. Behind them, they'd built a shelter from one of the buffalo hides and spread their sleeping robes on the sweet-smelling grass within.

Tylor listened carefully as Richard talked, his soft eyes thoughtful. Every now and then he nodded. The fragrant tobacco in his long-stemmed pipe added to the aromas of woodsmoke and cooking meat.

"And now," Richard concluded, "I'm here. I'm told I can accompany the caravan when it returns to Saint Louis."

Tylor considered him for a moment, then glanced at Willow. "From the tone of your voice, I'm not sure that you really want to go, Mr. Hamilton."

Richard inspected the curved metal of the cock and wiped silver filings from his hands. "I don't, Mr. Tylor. But I have a duty to my father. One I never understood when I set out on this adventure." He glanced at Willow, who was trying to hide the sadness in her eyes.

Tylor watched the curls of smoke rise from his pipe bowl. "Duty can become a terrible tyrant, indeed. And God knows, finding one's way through the maze of life is mostly the chore of sorting out what you owe to whom." Tylor glanced at Willow. "Obligations have a habit of sneaking up on us, entwining themselves with our lives. What with them, and dreams and ambitions, it's a wonder that any of us remain sane. I don't envy you your choice. But, if I might ask, what are your plans if you stay in the mountains? How will you employ yourself, and is that what you want out of life?"

Richard glanced at Willow, meeting her liquid gaze. "I hadn't thought that far ahead."

What do *you want, Richard?* he asked himself. *You can't have the parlors of Boston with refined discussions and fine brandy and have* Ainkahonobita *at the same time.*

Willow said, "We can live well. *Tam Segobia* provides all that we need. We can find food, make clothing, and have a house anywhere. If Richard stays, he will not starve, Mr. Tylor. He is a hunter and a warrior."

"Indeed, Willow, I can see that." Tylor glanced at Richard and lifted an eyebrow. "You know, some of the trappers in our party have taken wives among the

Agaiduka. I'm married into Gray Bear's band. It wouldn't be a bad life. A living can be made here."

Richard smiled self-consciously. The file whispered as it shaved metal from the cock. Willow was right. The land provided. But what about security? Who was to say that the Blackfeet wouldn't ride into Red Canyon and kill them both?

Richard drew breath. "It seems that as Hobbes noted, life is a compromise. Within society, a given amount of security is granted in exchange for compliance to the social contract. If our civilization has done anything worthwhile, it is that. But it takes so much from us by our agreement to conform to its ways. If I go back, I can't take Willow with me. You know how they'd treat us, Mr. Tylor. A white man doesn't marry an Indian—not in a city like Boston. And Willow would die there, from disease, from confinement, or from the acid in people's looks and actions."

"Indeed she would," Tylor agreed.

"I am willing to take my chances, despite what Richard tells me. I know Boston would be hard for me. But I—"

"Your courage isn't at issue, Willow. You don't have to put your hand in fire to know it's painful. Boston would be like that for you, for me." Richard gave her a reassuring smile. "How can I leave you? It's not just a matter of what I'll do. What about you? You can't go back to your people. You've said over and over that you don't fit. Not even High Wolf can make a place for you."

Willow shrugged. "I will make do, Richard. I always have. If you go, I will be waiting for you when you return."

Tylor gave her a knowing squint. "Some men would give anything for a woman like you." And he glanced away, not quite managing to hide the sudden pain in his eyes.

Richard quickly said, "That makes my choice a great deal more difficult."

"Loyalty, in wives or friends, is the rarest of virtues, Mr. Hamilton." Tylor knocked the dottle from his pipe. "Before you make your final decision, I suggest that you weigh that fact very carefully." He paused, staring absently into the distance. "Sometimes a man never knows what he has until he's lost it."

Richard took Willow's hand. An awkward silence followed. What had the man lost that hurt him so? A woman; position? What drove a gentleman like Tylor into the wilderness?

"I know what I have." Richard tightened his grip on Willow's hand.

Willow's smile was fleeting as she wound her fingers into his.

Tylor stood suddenly. "If you would excuse me for a moment, I'll take a quick look at the horses, and then we'll eat."

Richard watched him walk quietly away. "A most interesting man." In the dusk, he could see Tylor by the horses, head back as he looked up at the sky's evening glow.

"I like him, Richard." Willow gazed at the fire. "Perhaps you can be thankful. Unlike Tylor, you can go back."

"You think he can't? Do you know something about him that I don't?"

"I can see it in his soul. A thing beyond words."

"I'm sorry we hurt him. When he returns, we'll ask to hear his story."

"You may ask, but I don't think he will tell."

Richard took a deep breath and watched the sparks

twirling up into the night. "No, I suppose he won't." He paused. "I'm stuck, Willow. I'll worry about you the whole time if I go. If I stay, I'll worry about Father. Given a choice between worries, I'll stay here."

"Is that easier?"

"It is. My father knew the risks when he sent me west. And I can write him a letter explaining what happened to me. Send him my apology. At least he'll know I'm alive. That's the lesser of the evils."

"But you would rather tell him face to face, wouldn't you?"

Richard stared at the cock, warm from his touch and the rasping file. "I owe it to him. The things I have to say to him should be said man to man."

She lifted an eyebrow and shrugged. "Then you should go, Richard. What if he dies? What if you never have the chance? Your soul will ache forever, knowing that you could have gone."

"And if something should happen while I was in the East? What then? What if you were killed? What if I could have made the difference?"

"You are trying to guess the future." She lifted his hand, brushing it against her lips. "I took a risk, too. I took it when I fell in love with you. I knew then that you would go back to your Boston. Half of my soul tells me that you will not return. The other half insists that you will."

"Where do you get the strength to tell me to go?"

"My people are different from yours. Every time a man leaves his lodge, a woman knows there is a chance that he will not return, whether it is to fight *Pa'kiani* or to hunt buffalo. Nothing is given to us forever, Richard. I have lost one husband and a precious child. My people are lost to me—even the camp of my father. I will never see Two Half Moons again. My old world is dead. I have survived these things. If you never come back, I will survive that, too."

But would she? The fire popped and flared as grease dripped into the flames.

CHAPTER FOURTEEN

By our continual and earnest pursuit of a character, a name, a reputation in the world, we bring our own deportment and conduct frequently in review, and consider how they appear in the eyes of those who approach and regard us. This constant habit of surveying ourselves, as it were, in reflection, keeps alive all the sentiments of right and wrong, and begets, in noble natures, a certain reverence for themselves as well as others, which is the surest guardian of virtue.

—David Hume: *An Enquiry Concerning the Principles of Morals*

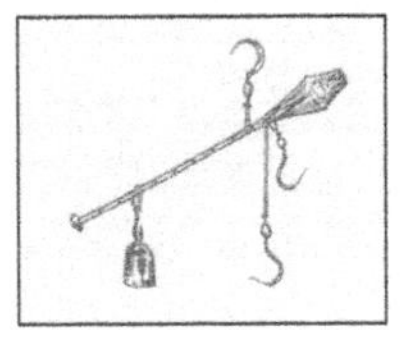

Travis and Baptiste had crossed the divide into the Bear River Valley, and were following the ridges down toward the river when they found William Ashley's caravan.

The supply train—a long line of pack animals and men—was crossing the sage flats beside a small creek. The animals were tail-hitched in groups of five, each string led by a man on foot. They proceeded at a fast walk, trampling the sage and grass into a churned trail.

Travis raised his rifle and fired it into the air. His horse pranced sideways, startled by the shot. For a moment, Travis had his hands full with the animal. In the valley below, the outriders stopped and turned their horses to look up the cobble-strewn ridge.

"Thought fo' a second that ragtail you ride was gonna pitch you on yo' head," Baptiste jested.

"Huh! Not this old Pawnee nag. She's the best out of old Half Man's string."

"Could have traded fo' one of Two White Elk's good hosses."

"Me and this old wolf bait knows one another."

"I reckon...a knothead foah a knothead."

Travis kneed his horse down the steep slope. Hooves slipping on the rounded rocks, the animal uprooted sage and sent cascades of dirt flying. Their pack animals followed, nostrils wide and ears pricked. The packs rocked, but stayed, a test to Travis's genius at hitches.

Ahead of them, the caravan of horses and mules had come to a stop, the weary animals hanging their heads while the riders walked their horses out to meet the newcomers.

"Ashley, by God!" Baptiste whooped. "And a fair sight if'n I do say so!"

"Better hope they ain't none of 'em from Louisiana, hoss, or they'll raise yer fuzzy hair fer the bounty."

"Ain't no white coon born can raise hair off'n Baptiste de Bourgmont."

Travis loped his horse across the blue-green sage, Hawken held to one side, the wind whipping his beard and hair. Closing on the riders, he pulled his animal up and brought it to a stand, blowing and sweat-streaked.

Travis relaxed into his favorite slouch and studied the buckskin-clad men. "How do? I reckon this hyar's Ashley's caravan fer Rendezvous."

"Ye reckon right, stranger," one of the young men said as he stared wide-eyed at Travis's scars. "And who might ye be?"

"Travis Hartman, and this hyar wolfmeat with me is Baptiste de Bourgmont. Come down from the Crow country, we did."

"Name's Bill Smith, and this long-legged coon's Cub Davis." The young man wore a felt hat that barely contained his long black hair. Cub Davis didn't hardly look old enough to be off the teat—until a man looked into his dark eyes and saw the soul-gaunting of hard travel.

"Reckon ye wouldn't mind if'n we rode along with ye?" Travis asked. "We figgered ter head fer Willow Valley." He jerked a thumb at their loaded packhorses. "Got plews ter trade."

"Best rustle on up yonder," Smith gestured toward the column's van where a knot of riders had pulled up to look back. "The General's up there with Campbell and the others. Reckon he'll make ye right welcome."

As Travis prodded his horse forward, he heard Smith whisper, "What on earth happened to that face of his?" So he rode with his head tilted up, letting the sun bathe the scars.

Trotting past the line of animals and men, he couldn't help but wonder at the amount of goods they carried. Tins of whiskey, powder kegs, boxes, and bales were outlined under the manties. The lot of it couldn't have been loaded into *Maria.* No wonder the critters looked worn. But, then, so did the hollow-eyed men who watched him pass. Like their animals, they were dusty, mud-spattered, and hard used.

"Looks like a tough trip," Baptiste noted in a low voice. 'These coons ain't green no more."

"Come on, men!" a hale voice shouted from ahead. "Let's go! Move out by the mess!" The speaker was a patrician-looking fellow who waved his hat as he shouted orders. He rode a big bay horse—a quality animal that didn't look nearly as ragged as the rest of the cavvy.

Reining out from the main party, he gave curt orders and turned his gelding to meet Travis and Baptiste. He pulled his sun-bleached and water-stained hat down over curly brown hair. His buckskin jacket was finely tailored, but showed the strain of wind, rain, and weather.

Travis pulled up in front of him and met those sharp eyes with his own, measuring, and liking what he saw. "Gen'ral Ashley. How do. I'm Travis Hartman, and my partner hyar's Baptiste de Bourgmont."

"Got plews to trade," Baptiste added and stuck out his hand to shake.

When Travis followed suit, he found the general's grip firm, a match for that penetrating stare. "Hartman and de Bourgmont. Your reputations have preceded you. Mr. Hartman, I'd have recognized you from the scars. Word is that you're good men, solid and reliable. That said, you are more than welcome to accompany us." He studied them thoughtfully as they walked their horses alongside the moving train.

The rest of Ashley's crew had fallen in, watching curiously. How young they seemed to Travis's veteran eyes. Mere youths. Here and there, old canvas clothing, mostly turned to rags, hung on their lean frames. Some had crudely tailored hide shirts or breeches, the leather rough-tanned at best. Their moccasins were even cruder, as if they'd been making clothes on the trail. All but one, and he rode along in worn broadcloth.

"Where are you from?" Ashley asked. He cast appraising eyes on their pack string with the bundled plews.

"Wintered with the Crow," Baptiste replied. "Heard tell from Long Hair's camp that you was holding a trade fair, so we come to see."

Ashley lifted an eyebrow. "Ah, the Crow. Still thieves, I presume?"

"Hell, Crows is always that." Travis laughed.

"And you got away with your outfits? You're doing better than my brigade did last fall."

"Wal," Travis said carefully, "Baptiste and me, we got kin among 'em. 'Course, that didn't stop 'em from lifting our hosses down below the Cannonball last summer. Had a right pert chase ter get 'em back."

Ashley gave Baptiste a long look. "I suppose you're a friend of Mister Rose's?"

Baptiste's expression turned sour. "Reckon not, General. Him and me's been crosswise since the start. I reckon if'n I had to put it to words, I'd say we didn't agree with each other."

Ashley's smile broadened. "In that case, you're more than welcome in my camp. And forgive me for any suspicion, it's just that Negroes and Crow—well, enough said."

Baptiste quirked his lips. "I see a couple of black folk riding with ye."

"Indeed." Ashley squinted at the horizon where a herd of elk spooked and vanished over a ridge. "Riding yonder is Jim Beckwourth. But if I might offer a word or two of advice, take what he tells you with a grain of salt."

"Or a whole sack," the thin man in broadcloth said. He had ridden his pinto bone-pile alongside. The tired horse bobbed its head with each step. "I'm Robert Campbell, clerk for this expedition. If you need anything, powder, tobacco, or such for your outfit, I'm the man to see."

"I see you've had good trapping," Ashley noted, eyeing the packs again.

"Traded mostly," Travis told him. Then he related the story of Dave Green and the *Maria.* "What we saved from the wreck gave us an outfit. Come midwinter, the Crows was right fond ter trade. We got beaver, Crow-tanned buffalo robes—some of 'em's line blankets—fox pelts, and mink. Prime, all of it."

"I don't suppose any of that beaver bears my mark? Perhaps from the packs I couldn't recover after the Crow stole them last year?"

"Reckon so." Travis lifted a questioning eyebrow. "We traded fer what we could get. If we hadn't a got 'em, ol' Jim Kipp or Josh Pilcher would'a."

Ashley waved it away. "Well, Mr. Hartman, since you didn't steal them in the first place, I'll give you fair price for my plews: three dollars a pound. I suppose it's better to buy them back than to have Missouri Fur profit from them."

"I reckon we figgered it the same," Baptiste replied. "Why, some plews gets traded around worse'n hosses these days."

"That they do," Ashley agreed. "And people, too, I might add." He studied them thoughtfully. "You both started with Lisa, didn't you?"

"Yep." Travis pulled the stopper from his powder horn and began reloading his rifle with practiced efficiency. "I come upriver back in eleven." He short-seated a ball. "Seen the tough years after eighteen and twelve. Wintered with the Sioux when that British coon, Dickson, was trying ter turn 'em against us. I reckon I been over the mountain and down the creek a time or two. Same with Baptiste hyar. What I don't know, he does."

"Perhaps I could make you an offer. Look around. Most of these young men could benefit from your experience. They're tough and able, ready to take on the wilderness. But they could use a knowing hand to teach them the ways of the land and Indians."

"Uh-huh? And what would y'all have in mind?" Baptiste cocked his head.

"Trapping parties, Mr. de Bourgmont. My brigades move into a river valley, then split up into little groups. Instead of trading with the Indians for the plews, we trap them ourselves. To do so, I need men who know the country and how to survive in it. I'll outfit you, supply you with everything you need. In return, you receive a percentage on the plews you bring in and reduced rates in trade for luxuries and foofawraw."

Travis glanced at Baptiste, who grunted uneasily and said, "Funny thing how a man's life changes. Last summer, I's hunting fo' the Company. Green comes along, and I's a partner in *Maria.* The Blackfoot blows up the boat, and I got me my own outfit from what's left of the wreck. I don't know, Gen'ral. What's in them packs yonder, why, half o' it's mine. I just ain't sure I want to go back to working fo' somebody."

"That's prime, that is," Travis agreed. "Fat cow, if'n I do say so. Hell, Gen'ral, I reckon I got the bug ter be free fer a while. Reckon I might just foller whar my stick floats fer a change."

"Fair enough," Ashley agreed genially. "In that case, I can offer you my services. I'll trade with anyone, and save you the hazards of the journey to take your catch to market. Consider this: In the past, furs had to be taken to posts. On the way, theft, raiding, weather, and every other disaster could befall a party—as it did to mine among the Rees back in twenty-three. A man spent most of his time carrying furs to market and obtaining supplies. But now, gentlemen, you can trap and trade the year through. Concentrate your efforts on what you do best, and bring your harvest to Rendezvous. You need never leave the mountains again."

"Huh," Travis said. "Then this hyar's gonna happen again next year, and the year after that?"

"Absolutely." Ashley slapped his thigh. "I call your kind Free Trappers, and unlike the companies on the river, welcome your business. Why should the fur hunter go to a post? Bring the post to the fur hunter. Far more efficient, wouldn't you agree?"

Travis looked at Baptiste and shook his head, grinning. "Old Manuel Lisa would be a-spinning, wouldn't he?"

Baptiste scratched his neck. "Reckon so. 'Course, Gen'ral, he'd a beat you heah by a month and done had yor trade."

Ashley raised an eyebrow. "Perhaps. But not even he could have anticipated this last winter." He gestured toward the men. 'The snows caught us near the Pawnee villages. Even the old women among them hadn't ever seen snow so deep. Things got so bad we had to mount a relief expedition for our relief expedition."

"Yer men look a mite worn, all right," Travis observed. "But they march like an army."

"Thank you, sir." Ashley inclined his head at the compliment. "Discipline on the trail is the only means of survival out here. Some chafe and rebel. Nearly forty men deserted, but these, the ones who stuck it out, they're men, sir. And with them, I shall conquer the mountains."

"You just might at that," Baptiste agreed. "Reckon the Shining Mountains ain't never gonna be the same."

"Nope," Travis replied thoughtfully, remembering his dream out on the prairie north of Fort Atkinson. Lisa had come to him and told that the river was dying, and that the mountains would follow. "Old Lisa was right. Ain't none of it gonna be left. All gone dead, just like the river."

"What's that?" Ashley asked.

"Ruminating, Gen'ral. Just ruminating."

Riders from the caravan began to trickle into camp, and excitement grew among the trappers waiting for Rendezvous. At the current rate of travel, talk said, Ashley and the supplies would arrive the following evening.

Richard's anxiety grew as the inevitable decision loomed. He sat that night, smoking his pipe and cleaning his neglected rifle. With the new cock, she shot again, and just as straight as before despite her rust pits and nicks.

If only his own life could be as easily fixed. He sighed as Willow came to crouch beside him. She fed wood into the fire where a pot boiled. Dinner would consist of buffalo, yampa root, sego lily, wild onion, and spicy beeplant flowers for seasoning.

"What's the word in the *Agaiduka* camp?" Richard asked as he watched her pull back a shining strand of black hair with a slim hand. How beautiful she was, and the brave expression she'd adopted made his heart ache. Did it have to be so hard on her?

Willow shrugged, checking the stew with her knife.

She gave critical inspection to the starchy water steaming on the blade. "These Fish-eaters, they are a different people. The same, you know, but different." She said neutrally, "I could stay with them while you are gone."

"Yep." Richard lifted an eyebrow. "I guess you could. If I didn't know you better, I'd never guess that you were lying."

"Oh, Richard. It will be all right. None of them have ever heard anything about me. They don't know any of the stories the *Ku'chendikani*—"

"They'll hear," he answered, steepling his fingers before his chin. "It's inevitable, Willow. People—red or white—tell stories, especially about things as interesting as witchcraft."

John Tylor appeared in the company of two trappers. One was a young man with red-brown hair and serious blue eyes. He walked with an athletic grace, his slim build belying a wiry strength. His reddish beard had started to fill in over a pointed chin. The second man was older, perhaps thirty-five, with a keen gaze that took a man's measure at a glance. The breast of his fringed buckskin shirt was decorated with elaborate beadwork done in a fleur-de-lis pattern. The man's haunted amber eyes spoke of terrible secrets.

"Mr. Hamilton, I would like you to meet two of my

associates." Tylor indicated the young man. "Captain Thomas Fitzpatrick, one of General Ashley's most able brigade leaders."

"My pleasure," Fitzpatrick said with a faint Irish brogue.

"And Mr. Weberly Catton," Tylor continued.

"Mr. Catton." Richard took the older man's hand in a firm grip. "The pleasure is mine. And this is my wife, Heals Like A Willow."

"Pleasure, ma'am," Fitzpatrick said agreeably as they seated themselves. Catton nodded pleasantly at Willow as he settled himself beside Fitzpatrick.

Tylor squinted into the boiling pot. "I hope the two of you don't mind, but I took the liberty of inviting Messrs. Fitzpatrick and Catton to dine with us. I believe we have enough to go around."

"We do." Willow, too, watched Catton with a certain fascination. The man drew attention like a magnet. Something in his manner set him apart, an indefinable suggestion of tragedy, and greatness.

He has a puha *all his own,* Richard decided, hardly aware that he now accepted such irrational intuitions without qualm.

Tylor broke out his pipe and shaved tobacco into the bowl from the remains of a twist. "Thank God, caravan's coming," he groused. "This is my last carrot of tobacco. Lord knows, I've stretched it enough with red willow and kinnikinnick as it is."

"Aye, caravan's coming," Fitzpatrick said with a smile. "I can tell ye for a fact, John, there's tobacco a-plenty for all."

The magically ubiquitous tin cups appeared in eager hands as Willow ladled out steaming stew. Tylor laid his pipe aside and ate with the rest.

Fitzpatrick smiled at Willow as he sipped the steaming broth. He glanced at Tylor. "If she can cook like this, I want her."

"Want her?" Richard asked warily. Dear God, they didn't think he'd sell her, did they? "Mr. Fitzpatrick, my wife isn't—"

"I believe I've stepped ahead of meself"—Fitzpatrick chuckled in embarrassment—"or at least, ahead of John Tylor." He wiped his mouth with a leather sleeve. "'Tis me understanding that ye might stay in the mountains with us, Mr. Hamilton. As one of Ashley and Smith's captains, I come to see if ye'd consider j'ining the Company."

Tylor sipped at his stew and added, "I realize you haven't made any decision yet, Richard. I thought, however, that I'd offer you some alternatives. Please, we're not trying to press you into anything unsuitable to your situation. But there are choices available." He smiled. "And we'd like you to know that you have a place here. With us."

"And you've choices beside the Company." Catton's cool gaze shifted from Willow to Richard. "Myself, I have a lovely wife in Missouri. We love each other a great deal, and she's borne me two wonderful sons. I believe John's purpose in asking me here is that I have experience with the benefits and tribulations of living between the frontier and the wilderness. It can be done."

Richard met Willow's inquiring eyes, then said, "Very well. Let's talk about these choices."

Fitzpatrick took another tin of stew, saying, "We're trapping in small bands, and I'd have no objection to yer wife and ye traveling wi' us. I think it's the way o' the future, Mr. Hamilton. The advantage being that ye'd have the protection of a large party when it comes to Blackfoot and Bannock raiders. In the meantime, a man can make himself a fine life oot hyar."

"I see," Richard said guardedly.

"Mr. Tylor wanted me t' meet the two of ye, get to know ye, and let ye form yer own opinion of me. I don't think a man should jump blind into a situation afore seeing as many sides of it as he can—though I myself be a bad one fer doing just that." He laughed, blue eyes shining. "Times are changing for fur hunters. Ye seem like a good man, Mr. Hamilton. If'n ye decide t' stay, the two of ye have a place in me party."

"And you, Mr. Catton?" Willow asked.

Catton studied his stew for a moment, then glanced up with that unsettling amber gaze. "My wife is one of the bravest women alive. For various reasons I am forced to leave Laura in the settlements. Living in such circumstances can be extraordinarily difficult. We manage, but then, Laura is a unique woman."

Willow hesitated, then asked, "Can you not overcome your White ways? A woman doesn't *need* to live in a building. If Indian women can stand the wilderness, can't an American woman?"

Catton smiled thinly. "I was raised among the Iroquois, ma'am. Not all of my ways are White." He gave her a quizzical study. "Laura has traveled the west with me. But she comes from a respected Kentucky family. She stays in Missouri because that is what is best for us. As I said, I have a variety of reasons for living as I do. My point in being here is to say that it can be done."

"In other words," Richard said, "I could travel back and forth. But, Mr. Catton, a wife in a settlement is in a different situation from a Shoshoni woman living in the wilderness. Your wife has a militia to protect her and her property. The institutions of civilization provide security."

Catton nodded. "That is true. But believe me, not all dangers come from savages and wild animals."

Richard laughed ironically. "Yes, I know. The streets of Saint Louis are filled with threat enough."

Catton stared absently at the fire. "Safety is only an illusion—be one a king or Digger Indian. That reality eludes most people. One can be blinded by walls, streets, and an abstract promise of social contract."

"Your Iroquois gave you a most interesting education," Richard observed.

Catton studied him thoughtfully. "If a man lives at all, Mr. Hamilton, he cannot help but be exposed to certain fundamental truths. *Tawiskaron* lurks in every shadow."

"Who?"

"*Tawiskaron.* A Huron equivalent to Cain. The chaos that mingles itself with the good things in life."

"Coyote," Willow supplied.

"Aye, the Devil," Fitzpatrick said absently. "Even hyar, in this beautiful land."

As the fire popped, Richard turned the options over in his mind. Would it be so bad to stay? He could post a letter with the caravan and accompany Fitzpatrick. Traveling with a fur brigade would allow him to stay with Willow, provide a place for both of them. A few of the trappers here already had Indian wives. What would it be like, just traveling around the wilderness? He could trap, hunt, and Willow would be with him.

"I'll give it some thought." He glanced at Catton, and then at Tylor. Two of a kind, each burdened by some terrible secret that neither was keen on discussing. What had driven them here?

The talk turned to beaver, the coming caravan, and

the fierce winter just passed. For the most part Richard and Willow sat silently, listening to the talk of Hudson's Bay trappers, Blackfeet depredations, and the recently negotiated peace with the *Agaiduka* Snakes who now camped with them.

When Richard finally walked out into the night, Tylor followed him.

"I hope I didn't make you uncomfortable, Mr. Hamilton. I didn't wish to intrude into your affairs, but I wanted you to know that other solutions to your problem might exist."

"You didn't intrude."

Tylor crossed his arms. "Mr. Hamilton, I want you to think very carefully about this. If I could, I would save you from making a terrible mistake."

"And that would be?" Richard looked up. The air was so clear that the myriad of stars seemed like a gray haze. Until he'd come to the West, he'd never seen the whole immensity of the night sky.

"I don't usually tell people this." Tylor hesitated. "I left a woman once. At the time, I was carried away with ideas of duty, a misplaced loyalty, and blind ambition. I was gone from my home for more than a year. She was beautiful, vivacious, and attractive. When I returned, all was in ruins. Everything."

"I'm sorry to hear that. And I will keep your confidence."

"Thank you." He paused. "I often wonder what would have happened had I stayed where I belonged and acted the way a proper husband should. As it was, she turned to one of my enemies. Betrayed me and my plots. I hated her once; but time has ameliorated that. With the years has come understanding. If I could offer a bit of advice, Mr. Hamilton: Don't awaken some morning, years from now, suffering from the realization that you let something beautiful slip through your fingers. I can tell you, you'll never recover it."

At that, he turned and walked away into the night.

In the bright midday sun, Richard scowled at the yellowed paper. On John Tylor's advice, he'd gone to a young man named James Clyman, who kept a journal. After Richard explained his need, Clyman had parted with a clean sheet from his precious book, and loaned a quill and ink bottle.

With birds singing in the cottonwoods, and the excited shouts of mountain men and Indians for a background, Richard labored over the words, scratching out text in the dirt beside him with a stick. Despite all the papers he'd written on philosophy, this was by far the most difficult screed he'd ever attempted.

He frowned and resettled his back against the cottonwood log. He had so much to tell his father, and so little space to write it all. How did one apologize for being a fool, for losing a fortune, and at the same time justify the decision to remain in the wilderness with an Indian wife to a man like Phillip Hamilton? How did he put all of that on a single sheet of paper?

After hours of labor, he had managed to write:

> June 1826 Willow Valley
> Dear Father:
> I am alive.

And there it ended. He plowed the dark soil beside him with flowery prose, direct statements, and intricate arguments, only to wipe them clean and start again.

This is insane!

But the compact eloquence he desired eluded him.

Willow hummed the Cottontail song as she walked up from the creek with a load of firewood over her shoulder. The collection of sticks and branches was bound, Indian-fashion, by a single cord. The load clattered as she dropped it and smacked her hands authoritatively. She glanced around the camp, satisfied that all was in order, and lifted an eyebrow as she noted his pinched expression.

"You have finished?" She walked over to inspect his paper.

He sighed, placing the sheet to one side and weighting it with a stone so the breeze wouldn't whisk it away. "No. The words escape me." He rubbed his forehead and stared at his fingers, now damp with sweat.

Come on, Richard. You can do this. They're just words on paper.

She settled beside him and frowned curiously at his most recent scratchings in the dirt. "I think you are making the wrong decision, Richard."

He'd told her last night, holding her closely after they'd made love. *I'm not going.* The words had brought relief, and a terrible sense of injustice.

"Are you that anxious to be rid of me?" With a finger

he replaced long strands of her black hair that the breeze had teased.

"No, Richard. I want you with me forever." She kissed him tenderly. "I would never part with you—but I think you will regret staying here."

"I don't know what I'll regret any more." He balled up a lump of dirt and tossed it away. "Tylor's a cunning fellow. He knew that I'd be sorely tempted by Fitzpatrick's offer. It solves so many problems for us. We'd have a place, Willow. Traveling with a band of trappers would be like traveling with *Maria.* We'd have the safety of numbers. We could build a lodge, have our own home. Think of it as a new society for you, one where no one would care if the *Ku'chendikani* called you a witch. Whites and Indians, living together. Fitzpatrick offers us everything."

She ran her fingers down the side of his face. "And what of your father? What of your Boston?"

The dream image where his father looked at him so sadly filled his mind. To blank it out, he looked up at the mountains that rose like a wall to the east. "Willow, in life, we all must make choices. If I've learned anything, it's that the world isn't perfect. Oh, sure, I'll regret that I never told my father the things I want to tell him. At least, not man to man. But I'm not the first man to have regrets. I doubt I'll be the last."

"Did John Tylor tell you that?"

"He told me I'd be a fool to leave you." *And, God knows, I would be.* But that wasn't the issue, was it?

She glanced away. Four riders were racing horses across the open grasslands between them and the Indian camp. The riders hooted and whooped, quirting their horses. A large white stallion took the lead accompanied by cries of encouragement from a group of onlookers who waved their favorites forward.

"Look closely, Richard." She sighed. "Look into Tylor's eyes and see the regrets that linger in his soul. Would he go back if he could?"

Richard tapped his stick on the dirt. Yes, he'd seen that longing in Tylor's brown eyes. "I think he would."

"I think he left the Whites because he had no choice. You have a choice, Richard. In the end, it will make it worse for you."

"But what if I go, and when I come back, you're not here?"

How could I endure that? I'd blame myself for the rest of my life—worse than I blame myself for letting Father down now.

"Then Coyote will have acted. What if you stay, and something happens anyway? What if your father dies in the meantime? Then it will be too late."

"What if, what if!" He chuckled ironically. "This is pointless, arguing in circles."

"Travis would tell you to go."

He hung his head. "Would he?"

"I think so."

Richard sighed. "I wonder. I sure miss him."

"Me, too."

"If I stay, we could go look for him."

"He would have gone back to the river, Richard. And from there maybe to Saint Louis."

He searched her eyes, so large and dark, looking for an answer. "You're just telling me that."

"Maybe."

"Ah, Willow, how I love you."

Her smile warmed him. "Perhaps as much as I love you, my man."

How was he supposed to turn his back on her? He'd have to be a worse fool than Coyote.

To the north, popping sounded—rifles being fired into the air—and faint cries carried on the wind. The horse racers stopped short, all heads turned toward the north.

Richard climbed to his feet, staring off up the valley. Joyous shouts broke out from the surrounding camps: "Caravan's a-coming!" "Caravan!" "Rendezvous!"

Men leaped to their horses, flying northward in a rush of pounding hooves. "Caravan! Rendezvous! Hyar's to the mountains, boys!" Another staccato of shots filled the air.

Richard took Willow's hand and exhaled. "Well, I guess the time's come—one way or another."

CHAPTER FIFTEEN

> If the object of our moral purpose is that which, being within our power, is the object of our desire after deliberation, it follows that moral purpose is a deliberate desire for something in our power; for at first we deliberate on a thing and, after reaching a decision about it, we desire it in accordance without deliberation.
>
> —Aristotle, *Nicomachean Ethics*

During the first night after the arrival of the caravan, the revelry never let up. Loud screams punctuated by gunshots might have led one to believe he heard a massacre rather than a gleeful celebration. Giant bonfires illuminated the camps, and around them, black silhouettes of trappers could be seen dancing and cavorting.

Willow lay with her head pillowed on Richard's chest and listened to his deep breathing and the rhythmic thumping of his heart. The insects made their nocturnal whizzing and clickings despite the human uproar.

Would it be so bad to go off with Tom Fitzpatrick?

The notion stuck to her with the persistence of warm pitch.

I would have a place, a people.

Living with the trappers wasn't such an alien idea after a summer with Green and the *engagés.* And other trappers already had *Agaiduka* wives. How curious it was —this need to belong. Rejection by her people had cut so deeply; that wound might never heal.

With the trappers she wouldn't have to worry about some frightened Shoshoni sneaking up behind her with a war club. And organized punishment for witchcraft was painful at best: A witch was tortured first, beaten and burned in an attempt to drive the evil away. If that didn't work, a hideous death followed.

Willow, be honest with yourself. Eventually, someone will die in strange circumstances. When that happens, the family will blame you.

She was so weary of the ways of people.

How wonderful it would be to ride off with the trappers. She and Richard, together for always. Images mingled in her dream soul: They walked hand-in-hand through a warm spring morning; sat side-by-side before a crackling fire; laughed at stories while the firelight played on the tan walls of a tipi; and lay together under the robes, naked bodies moving as they made love.

Her fists knotted in a vain attempt to strangle her frustration. If only she could draw all of him inside her, make him a part of her. But the womb only worked one way. In the beginning times. Coyote had seen to that.

I can keep him. The notion drew her on, teased the

aching part of her souls. *All I need to do is plead with him to stay—and he will.*

Such ideas came upon a person in the depths of the night when the hours were the longest.

You lie to yourself. Willow. He must go. And you know it.

If only he didn't have to go right now. If, perhaps, he might go next year.

What a fool I am.

She could feel the pulsing of her own heart, matching his in its misery.

It must be now. I'll never be strong enough to let him go again.

Into the aching loneliness of love came a naked grief. It devoured her, sucking away her souls, crushing her with its bruising weight until tears ran hot from her eyes. Thus she passed the night, drifting in soul-pain, her grief wetting his rising and falling chest.

Morning sunlight shot golden rays across Willow Valley. Richard took a moment to enjoy the view. He gazed up at the snow-capped peaks to the east, wondering at the steep slopes that rose so precipitously from the flats. Such contrast—the soft green of the valley, forgiving, fruitful, and lush, gave way so quickly to the vertical wall of gnarled stone that thrust up to tear at the sky with jagged summits.

He settled himself before the fire and used his knife to spear one of the long strips of meat they'd been roasting for breakfast. He blew to cool it, wincing as the smoke turned in his direction and finally drove him to his feet.

Willow squatted opposite him, a vacant expression on

her delicate face, eyes puffy and lifeless. Richard watched her warily as she chewed, a piece of meat clutched in greasy fingers. Something had cracked her defiant courage.

Richard washed the last of the smoke-flavored elk down with water from his tin cup. Wiping his greasy hands on his pants, he stared pensively at the ash-white wood burning in the firepit.

"How about walking down to the traders?" he asked. "Tylor said they'd be set up by this morning. Let's go see."

She smiled up at him, the effort forced, as if only raw will animated her full lips.

Hand-in-hand, they strolled across the flower-sprinkled grass toward the distant knot of lodges and tents that marked Ashley's camp. She remained silent, even distant.

"Are you all right?" he asked. *Come on, Willow, tell me what's wrong.*

She nodded, eyes downcast.

"Bad dreams?" he suggested. "Want to talk about them?"

"No, Richard. I just...I'll be fine. I'm tired this morning, that's all. I didn't sleep well."

"Me neither," he admitted, trying to break through this new awkwardness. "I had horrible dreams. I was standing in my father's office. He was lying on the floor, gasping, dying. He kept reaching out to me, but I couldn't move, couldn't call out. I was paralyzed, my arms and legs too heavy to lift. As if—well, I'd been turned to stone." He forced a chuckle. "Imagine, me, a rock ogre? What do you think? Am I one handsome *Pandzoavits*?"

Her smile faded too quickly. "You wouldn't have dreamed such a thing if you hadn't decided to stay, Richard. Your soul is telling you to go to your father, now." She glanced off at the mountains. "If you don't, you will live that dream for the rest of your life. It isn't wise to ignore your *navuzieip.*"

"Why are you so insistent?"

"Because I must be. How can you live if your souls are sick? I know these things, Richard."

"And what if my leaving makes your souls sick?"

"I will heal them. Besides, it's only for a short time. You *will* come back." She sounded as if she was trying to convince herself.

They walked in awkward silence, approaching the shouting men who stood around the tents. Like the trade around *Maria,* this, too, consisted of utter disorder, men yelling and gesturing as they crowded around. Necks craned as men tried to see over their companions' shoulders. Some sat atop horses for a better view, and called out information to the fellows on the fringe.

Richard spotted Web Catton at the periphery and turned in his direction. Catton leaned on his rifle, an amused look on his sun-browned face. The beaded fleur-de-lis on his chest sparkled in the morning sunlight.

"Quite a mess." Richard pointed at the mob.

With forced gaiety, Willow said, "They remind me of children when the first fat is fried from the fall buffalo hunt."

Catton chuckled. "Reckon they do. 'Course, there's ways to get what you want without fooling with that mess. In fact, here he comes now."

A tall young man walked out from behind the tents, passed the armed guards who watched over the piled packs of trade goods, and headed toward them. He carried a large tin cup, balancing it, his tongue out the side of his mouth as he concentrated.

"Took you long enough, Jim," Catton announced.

"Reckon so, Web. Tarnal Hell, that's a damn riot yonder." The strapping young man handed Catton the cup and glanced curiously at Willow and Richard. Thoughtful brown eyes, a long nose, and broad mouth dominated his thin face. In spite of unruly brown locks and obvious youth, he had a seasoned look. "Reckon I don't know ye. Come with the caravan, did ye?"

"No, arrived from the north. I'm Richard Hamilton, and this is my wife, Heals Like A Willow."

He bobbed his head as if uncertain as to the social graces. "'Bliged, I reckon. Ma'am. I'm Jim Bridger, uh, one of Gen'ral Ashley's captains. Been out with Jed Smith scouting west and south for the last month."

"And, let me guess," Catton said wryly as he sipped at the liquid in the cup, "you found salt, sand, and desert." His face twisted bitterly. From the drink, or his description of the land, Richard couldn't tell.

"Reckon so," Bridger agreed. "Got my fill o' that country, I'll tell ye. 'Course, Jedediah, he figgers ta go back after Rendyvous breaks up. Figgers there's got ta be a way down ta the ocean, and maybe beaver on the other side of the desert."

Catton shrugged, took another sip, and passed the cup to Richard. The clear liquid was straight alcohol, and Richard supposed his own expression mirrored Catton's.

Willow barely sipped, wrinkling her nose. In Shoshoni she muttered, "For outside the body only," and passed the cup to Bridger.

"What happens next?" Richard asked, as Bridger took a big swig from the tin and passed it back to Catton.

"Most everybody gets drunk as the whiskey is poured." Catton grinned at Bridger. "Me, I didn't want to fight all the elbows, so I sent Bridger into that mess for me."

The tall young man grinned, scuffing the ground with his moccasin toe. "Wal, ye see, ain't so many around as can say they done favors for Web Catton." He gave Richard a conspiratorial glance. "Reckon ye'd be plumb smart ta listen ta anything old Web tells ye. He done wrassled bears and treed painters out hyar when the rest of us was sucking a teat—and that's fat cow."

With a nod to Catton and Willow, Bridger turned, padding back past the guards to disappear among the packs.

"Good lad," Catton said. "He's got a way about him. I figger he'll make a right fair trapper if he lives long enough. Too bad that Hugh Glass hangs like a shadow over him."

"Hugh Glass...the man who got bear-chewed." Richard recalled the story. 'Took him months to crawl into Fort Atkinson."

"That's him." Catton indicated the direction Bridger had gone. "Young Jim and old Fitzhugh were supposed to stay with Glass until he died. Problem was. Glass wasn't dead when they left." He shook his head. "Be a hell of a thing if that's all Bridger was ever remembered for." Catton offered his cup again.

"No. Thank you, Mr. Catton. I think we'll walk around, see the sights."

"You won't get close to the trade, not today. Them coons will be mobbing them kegs until they drink her dry, or pass out. Whatever comes first."

As they walked off, Richard wondered, "So, that's it? Just liquor?"

Willow shrugged as she watched the milling trappers and their Indian cohorts. Men would slip out of the crowd, tilting battered tin cups to their lips before they hollered to friends. Immediately they'd be mobbed by backslapping bear huggers until the tin was empty, then another hardy would take the tin and dive back into the writhing mass for a refill.

Richard caught the barest glimpse of a familiar black face in the seething mass of humans, but he couldn't be sure. A handful of Negroes were in the crowd, but he had yet to find Baptiste among them. "Come on. I thought I saw..."

"Saw who?"

"Well, maybe Baptiste."

Richard towed Willow behind him as he ducked past drinkers, periodically jumping up in an attempt to see, wishing he were taller.

Richard caught a glimpse of the black man again, and shoved to reach him, calling, "Baptiste!"

The man turned, his face unfamiliar. "Sorry," Richard wilted. "I thought you were someone else."

"Yassuh, dat happens. I's Peter Ranne, of Jed Smith's party, suh." The black man smiled, nodding. "Shoa pleased to meet you."

"Richard Hamilton—and this is Willow, my wife."

"Pleased, ma'am," Ranne replied. But by then the shoving had become unbearable and Richard slipped back toward the fringes.

"Sorry," Richard told Willow as they broke free from the fringe of drinkers. He shrugged, relieved by Willow's understanding nod. "I'm trying too hard, I guess." He looked around. "Desperation. It's running through me like creek water."

She patted his hand. "I know, Richard. Let's leave this place. Some man in there grabbed me. I was packed in so tightly I couldn't pull my knife and cut him."

Richard took her arm in his and had just turned back

toward camp when a burly man pushed his way out of the press and called out, "Hey, squaw!"

"I think he is the one who grabbed me." Willow dropped a hand to her knife, glaring at the man.

The trapper tottered forward, a tin cup in one grimy hand. His wispy mustache was wet, and spilled drink had dampened the thin red beard growing from his blocky jaw. His glazed blue eyes were fixed on Willow. "Hey! Squaw!" Thrusting out a fist, he offered several hanks of glass beads: yellow, blue, and red. "You take these, huh? You know, 'Fuck me'? You know them words?"

Richard pulled Willow behind him before she could strike. His voice dropped to a sibilant threat. "Get away from her. You leave my wife alone, or by damn, you'll—"

"Who the hell are you?" The trapper stopped short, blinking in confusion.

"Her husband, sir. And you'll offer an apology to my wife."

"Wife?" The big man laughed, taking another drink from his tin. "What white man's got an Injun *wife*? Hell, mister, if I can have her for a couple of hours, why, I'll give ye a hoss. Yep, a hoss! Ain't seed such a purty woman among these hyar Snakes. I reckon she'd put a hell of a squeeze on a man's pizzle. How 'bout that, coon?"

For a moment, Richard wasn't sure he understood; then something let loose within him. The frustration and anger, the indecision and reeling sense of loss were swept away on a tide of single-minded rage. The burly round-faced trapper filled Richard's world as he coiled and struck.

His first blow bent the man double, then he skipped in to hammer an elbow to the side of the neck. With a quick pivot, Richard back-heeled the man and threw him down. He was ready to drive a knee into his victim's stomach, when two trappers grabbed him from the side and flung him away.

Richard staggered to catch his balance. A ring had formed around them, men shouting and cheering, waving fists and dancing from foot to foot. Willow circled warily, body in a crouch, her gleaming knife tucked in, ready to strike.

The two men who'd thrown Richard off checked their companion. He moaned on the ground amid a scatter of broken beads and spilled whiskey. One, black-haired and wiry, rose and dusted off his hands, flexing his fingers. "Reckon that flat warn't called fer, coon. Ye'd have kilt him. I saw it in yer eyes, ye Injun-loving white nigger."

"Come on," Richard rasped. "Both of you, damn it! I'll whip you both, hear?"

The black-haired man indicated Willow. "She ain't gonna stick me. That ain't fair."

To the delight of the assembled trappers, Willow hissed, "Come die!"

"Oh, Gawd," the downed man moaned. "I feel plumb awful." And he rolled on his side to vomit.

"Ain't gonna be no cutting hyar," a familiar voice called from behind Richard. "C'mon, coons, back ter drinking and fun. This squaw's off limits! Go, boys. Hyar's fer the mountains!"

Like a tribe of banshees, a series of wild shrieks and war whoops split the air as the trappers turned back to the trade tent. The downed man was picked up by his two friends, clapped on the back, and led off.

Richard took a deep breath, and turned, grinning. Travis Hartman watched him with twinkling blue eyes. The hunter's ruined face was one of the most beautiful sights Richard had ever seen. He leaped, hugging Travis as if to crush the life out of him. Willow had vaulted onto the both of them, shrieking. Round and round they went, like some huge awkward three-headed dancing bear.

"Yer some, Dick," Travis declared, "Hell, I figgered ye'd jist up and philos'phy him half ter death. But ye give him what fer, knuckle and skull, instead. What'd Willow feed ye all winter ter put the bark on ye so?"

"Blessed Lord God! What a relief! Travis, I thought you were dead!"

"Easy, coon. Don't bust me ribs!"

"What happened to you? Where did you go? Where's Baptiste? Where have you been all winter? How'd you get here?"

"Whoa up, lad! One thing at a time."

"We've missed you, Travis!" Willow was crying, as she clung to him.

Richard kept grinning like an idiot, checking the hideous scars to ensure that no new ones had appeared. The blue eyes still had the devilish gleam that laughed and warned at the same time.

"My God," Richard repeated, "it's so good to see you. You wouldn't believe the things we've been through."

Travis chuckled, gaze drifting from Richard to Willow. "Wal, I reckon at least the two of ye finally got the robes straightened out. 'Wife,' ye said, just afore ye lit inter that poor pilgrim!"

Richard lifted an eyebrow. "What of it?"

For the barest second, Travis gave him an iced look that chilled the guts. Then he grinned and bent over to kiss Willow on the cheek. "Fat cow, coon, that's what!"

Willow was prodding Travis in the ribs, laughing, saying, "Where have you been, Bear Man? I feel fat on your ribs. Have you taken up with some woman?"

"Me? Hell, no. Wal, at least, not fer permanent. Them Crow, they fed me right pert, they did." He winked at her. "'Course, once a coon crawls under the robes, they try and work it outa ye, too!"

"Hah!" Willow challenged, slapping him on the shoulder. "An *A'ni* woman couldn't tire a dead man. You need a real woman, Travis."

Travis glanced at Richard. "And what if them coons would a tried ye, just now?"

Richard gave him a crooked smile. "I'd a whipped 'em both, damn it. Hell, Travis, what do you think? I'm some kind of Doodle what don't know shit?"

His arm still around Willow's shoulder, the scarred hunter threw his head back and laughed until the tears came.

Travis puffed at his pipe, savoring the tobacco he'd traded for that afternoon: not quite Saint Louis fresh, but close enough by mountain standards. He cocked his head at a shouting match a couple of camps down the way. Someone else broke out into guffaws, and the babble of talking men was everywhere. Hard as it might be to believe, the second night of Rendezvous was even louder than the first. Travis sat in Richard's camp with his back to the log and listened as Richard told him of his winter adventure.

Baptiste sat cross-legged, nursing a whiskey head, slitted eyes watching the coals burn down in the fire. Willow and Richard were seated the way lovers ought to be, their shoulders touching, hands held in every spare moment.

Hard to believe that ol' Dick's the same coon what François sold me fer a penny in Saint Loowee. Travis took this new Richard's measure: broad-shouldered, firm of eye, and easy in his movements. His nose and cheeks were mottled from frostbite, but those scars were easier to bear than Travis's. Something in Richard's core had toughened, and from the tale he'd just told, it wasn't any wonder.

"So, we ended up here," Richard finished, thoughtful eyes on Travis. "And I guess here is where I'll stay. Maybe join Tom Fitzpatrick's party and go fur hunting. We've talked about it. He's more than willing to have Willow along."

"Uh-huh." Travis knocked the dottle out of his pipe and shaved more tobacco into the bowl. He fired it with a twig and puffed blue smoke like a chimney. "If'n ye decide ter do that, Dick, latch onto Tylor, hyar, or ol' Catton if'n he's gonna winter over. Them coons can teach ye things this child ain't larned yet."

"I doubt that." Richard cocked his head. "They are interesting men. Real mysterious, both of them."

"I reckon," Travis said as he propped his arm on a knee. Willow was too sober, worrying herself about something. "They don't talk much, leastways, not about themselves. Tylor, hell, he come upriver with Lisa back in eighteen twelve. Then, when he got upriver, old Manuel give him and Will Cunningham hosses and let them go.

Cunningham showed up next season, but Tylor disappeared inta the wilderness fer nigh onto two years. From time ter time he'd fetch up at a post, spend most of the winter a-yarning, resupply, and light out again fer who knows where. Thing is, Tylor always has his books. I remember a time or two where he'd send a paper downriver on a pirogue ter Lisa, and all it'd have on it was the names of books. And sure enough, next summer, they'd be packed away until the expedition met up with Tylor somewhere. One thing's plumb prime about him: he's a gentleman, he is—and his word's good."

"And Catton?" Willow asked.

"He's an odd coon, I'll tell ye." Travis considered his pipestem, then broke a piece off and flipped it into the fire. "There, that's a mite sweeter smoke. Where was I? Oh, Web Catton. Wal, I don't know a heap about him, neither. Reckon we shared a camp hyar and there over the years. He's married to a right fine gal back in America. A plumb proper lady, she is. Comes from the Bragg family of Kentucky. Real white-china folk with lots of land, hosses, and slaves and such. Old Web, he's white, I figger, but he's Injun-raised. Iroquois, I recall—and never a squeak of how that come about. Anyhow, he met this Laura Bragg, married her, and had a real tussle with her paw. Kilt him dead with a sword in a duel, he did.

"Web, he's a mite like Tylor. Travels the wilderness when and where he pleases. He's made peace with most of the Injuns, especially down south around Santy Fe."

Richard was fingering his chin, vacant stare on the fire. "What drove them out here?"

"How in hell should I know? Maybe they let some ornery coon run off with their pap's money?" At Richard's sour scowl, he added: "One thing's sure, neither one talks about it."

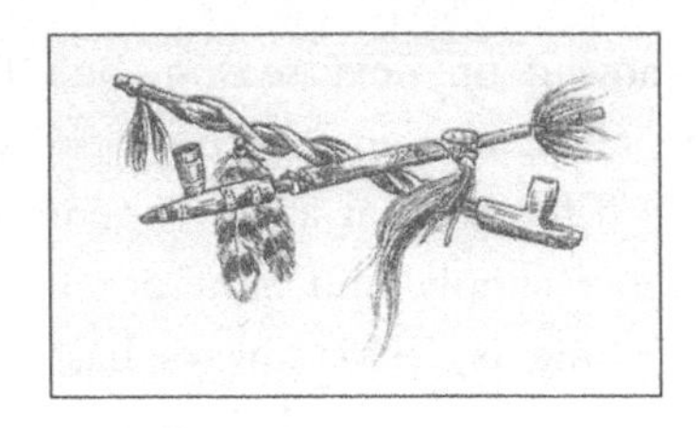

"And some folks shouldn't otta ask," Baptiste reminded darkly. "Folks has got their reasons foah leaving the States."

Richard nodded soberly. "Yes, they do."

"Now, then," Travis asked, "are ye sure ye wants ter string along with Ashley's brigade? Hell, Dick, me and Baptiste would be right tickled ter have the two of ye join up with us."

Willow straightened, lifting an eyebrow. A spark of hope kindled in her dark eyes.

"And we don't care that Willow's no witch," Baptiste added. "And if'n she were, I'd figger she could cure this heah whiskey head right quick." He gave Willow a pleading look.

"Spirit water is for the outside," she said bluntly.

Baptiste groaned and carefully lowered his head to his knees.

"You and Baptiste have an outfit, Travis," Richard reminded.

"And you and Willow have the perfect place ter winter," Travis responded. "We seen that Red Canyon. Them springs is some, they is. And from there, a feller can trap the Big Horns, Owl Creeks, and west clean up inta the Yellowstone high country. Hell, Dick, throw in with us." Travis grinned. "Truth of it is, we got ter missing yer company. And Baptiste and me ain't doing so good on our writing no more."

"You don't need me to teach you writing."

"Wal, who's gonna philos'phy us half ter death? A coon never knows in this country. We might get surrounded by Blackfoots and need ye to give 'em a batch of Rousseau, or some such thing."

Without raising his head, Baptiste added, "Ain't no campfire quite right 'thout ass-spitology and he-pissed-'em whatever it was."

"Eschatology and epistemology." Richard's face softened as he looked at Willow. "I could go back to *Ainkahonobita.* Couldn't you?"

She gave Richard that familiar probing gaze. "What of your father, Richard?"

"My father." Richard slumped, expression glum. "I'll write the letter, I promise."

Willow turned to Travis. "Will you tell him? He has been worried about me. You and Baptiste are here, Travis. I can go with you while Richard returns home. I know where streams of beaver can be found. I can take you there, and next year we can meet Richard someplace."

Travis sucked at his pipe. Tarnation! A year alone out in the wilderness with Willow? She might be his good friend, but damn it, pretty as she was, she'd drive him half berserk. He glanced at Richard. How torn he was. Willow was giving him a pleading look, tearing her heart out while she begged him to go.

By God, she loved him so much. It brought an ache to Travis's soul. He'd seen a look like that once, that pleading love in Moonlight's soft gaze.

Damn it, ain't many men got the chance to have women like her and Willow.

Aw, ter hell with it! If having Willow around brought on dreams of soft warm bodies, he'd just shinny over ter the River Crow and buy hisself a wife.

"Go, Dick." The words came to Travis's lips. "Do what ye must. Baptiste and me, we'll see ter Willow. My word on it."

Richard nodded, a distant look in his pained eyes. He said nothing, but rose and walked away from the camp, head down, shoulders sagging.

Willow struggled to keep from clinging to Richard as the long days of summer began. Together they watched the races, and shouted for their favorites. They attended the shooting matches, making private wagers over who would win. They went dancing with the Shoshonis in their camp. They shouted encouragement to the mountain men who wrestled with each other, screaming and yelling, their bodies thumping on the hard-tramped grass.

Rendezvous was like nothing she or Richard had ever seen. Games of euchre, monte, and poker were played on blankets, and every possession under the sun was wagered, lost, and won again. *Agaiduka* men hired out their women for powder, beads, shot, and whiskey. Brawls broke out, blows landed, then peace was made between the bloody, bruised antagonists.

Arm-in-arm, they watched it all, living as if each moment was forever. At night they sat around the fires, listening to tales of bears, Indian fights, and beaver. Outright lies mingled with hilarity as one man or another tried to outyarn his comrades. Interlocked in the tales were nuggets of information on rivers, the land, mountain passes, and places to camp.

And when the stories were finished, Richard and Willow twined their bodies together under the robes. They joined themselves with fierce passion one time, and tender caress the next. Each bout of lovemaking was driven by a subtle desperation, as passionate as if the last on earth.

But all things finally end.

The alcohol had been drunk. General Ashley's packs, once full of coffee, bolts of cloth, powder, and lead, now held beaver plews, a hundred to a pack. The summer sun burned down hot and brassy; the solstice came and went.

Word passed from man to man that Ashley and Smith had sold out to a new firm, Smith, Jackson, & Sublette, and that the General was packing to leave.

"I will miss you with all of my souls, Richard." Willow ran her hands down the sides of his face as they lay entwined in the blankets that last night.

"And I you," he told her.

She smoothed the brown curls around his ears. "Richard, you've told me about Boston, and your father, and his business. I don't understand all of this, but I know what I learned from Green. If you have to stay for a while, I will understand."

"Willow, I'm not going to—"

"Hush. Hear me, husband. Listen to my words."

"All right."

"You might not be able to come back as soon as you plan. What if your father is sick? What if he needs you?"

"He might just throw me out on my ear."

"And maybe you can fix things between you and him. If it takes a while, I will wait. And Richard, if it is necessary, and if you still wish to, marry this Laura Templeton. I'm not a White woman. My people take second wives all the time. I will understand."

"She won't."

"That is up to her. But if you need her for the White world, marry her."

"Willow, that's completely—"

"Richard, I will wait for you. I have nothing else."

"How precious you are," he whispered. "I'm coming straight back to you."

"Yes, I know. But this is Coyote's world. What we plan doesn't always happen. Things go wrong."

"What if I get killed on the way?"

She considered. "If you are not back in two years, then I will know that your Boston has won...or you're dead."

"I don't kill so easily."

Neither does your Boston, Richard.

She closed her eyes as he kissed her neck, nuzzling the hollow of her throat. She tightened her hold on him, straining, as if by sheer strength she could impress him upon her soft flesh. "Come back to me. Please, Richard."

Tam Apo, *let my* puha *be more powerful than his Boston.*

The dawn came too soon. Richard climbed out of their blankets as gray light outlined the high mountains to the east. While Willow attended to nature, he opened his pack and placed each article with great precision: pemmican, jerky, some of Willow's biscuit-root cakes. A spare elk-hide jacket she'd made for him, and three pairs of moccasins. He wanted to take everything, his digging stick, bow, arrows, net bags—all things he shared with Willow. But that was foolishness.

He stuck with necessities, then seated himself and poked at the fire as she prepared their final meal.

Richard watched her from the comer of his eye. *How carefully we move, so painfully aware of each other.*

Travis and Baptiste appeared out of the gloom.

Robins and finches were greeting the morning, and the insects had begun to stir. John Tylor, his body still rolled in a brown blanket, called out, "Take care, Richard. Give my regards to the East."

"I will. And thank you for your friendship, John."

"Hyar, Dick," Travis said, handing Richard a small cylinder wrapped in buckskin.

"What's this?" Richard hefted it, surprised how heavy it was.

"Twenty-dollar gold pieces, coon. Ten of 'em. I done sewed 'em inta that hide and let her shrink down tight. Kept 'em in the bottom of my possibles."

"What's it for?" Richard looked perplexed.

"How ye figgering to get boat fare to Boston, coon?" Travis lifted a grizzled eyebrow. "I been saving it in case trouble come along. Pay me back when ye can."

Richard shook his head, handing it back. "I can't take this, Travis. I'll make do."

"Nope." Travis stood firm. "We're partners now, Dick. Have been fer a spell. And, wal, ye'd do 'er fer me." He grinned. "'Course, it ain't thirty thousand, but I reckon ye'll keep it this time."

Richard took Travis's hand in a firm shake. "Thanks, Travis."

"Reckon it's my pleasure, Dick."

Baptiste appeared, leading Richard's horse, the animal saddled and ready. "Heah you be, coon. Fat and sleek." Baptiste offered his hand. "Take care, Dick. Come back to us safe and healthy."

Richard took his hand, then hugged him close. "You, too. And watch your topknot."

"Ain't no red Injun getting my wool."

Finally, Richard turned to Willow. Her eyes were shining, saying more than words. "I love you, Willow."

"And I you, my warrior." She hugged him one last time, tracing his face with her fingertips. "Go, Richard. I will wait for you."

He kissed her then, holding her until she finally pushed back. To his surprise, a tear had escaped her swimming vision and tickled its way down her cheek. He wiped it away with his thumb. God in Heaven, how could he leave?

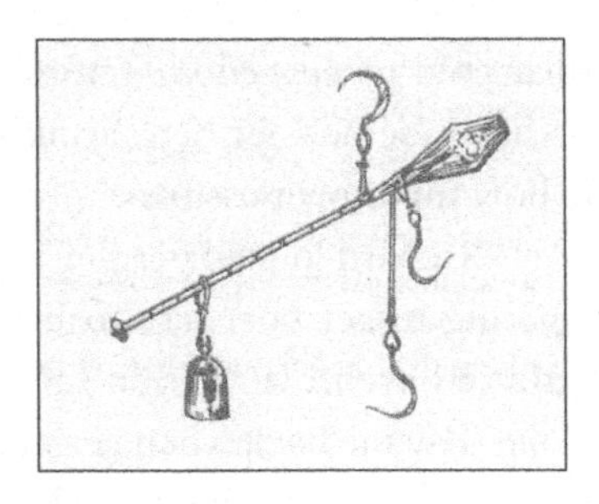

Richard turned quickly and stepped into the saddle. Travis handed up his rifle.

"Mind yer hair, Dick. Ashley's a-waiting on ye."

"Mind yours," he rejoined. He reined the horse around, walking the animal northward toward Ashley's camp. He kept looking back, waving. Willow stood there, chin up, back straight, the first rays of morning sunlight gleaming in her long black hair.

Damnation, he could just turn around.

I don't have to do this.

But despite the wrenching in his soul, he finally turned his head toward the north. While, inside, a voice kept telling him, *This is a mistake—a horrible mistake.*

She stood in silence, watching him, barely aware that Travis had placed a reassuring arm around her shoulders. Baptiste sighed, watching with sad eyes. One by one, she returned Richard's waves, each more distant than the last.

"Yes...you'll be back, my man." She placed a hand to her stomach, pressing to still the terrible ache.

CHAPTER SIXTEEN

I am first affrighted and confounded with that forlorn solitude, in which I am plac'd with my philosophy, and fancy myself some strange uncouth monster, who not being able to mingle and unite in society, has been expell'd all human commerce, and left utterly abandon'd and disconsolate. Fain would I run into the crowd for shelter and warmth; but cannot prevail with myself to mix with such deformity. I call upon others to join me, in order to make a company apart; but no one will hearken to me. Every one keeps to a distance, and dreads that storm, which beats upon me from every side.

—David Hume, *A Treatise of Human Nature*

Richard sat up late that first night, and watched the fire bum down to red embers. Around him, the men in his mess snored and wheezed, rolled in their blankets. The hum of mosquitoes and night insects mingled with the far-off cries of the coyotes and wolves.

He looked eastward at the dim black shadows of the mountains, but felt no relief.

Willow was a day's ride south. He could be there by morning, enfold himself in her arms, and spend the rest of his life there.

He closed his eyes, recreating her face, every detail of her hair, eyes, and smile.

Dear Lord God, this is going to be horrible.

"It's not forever," he whispered under his breath. And tried to turn his thoughts to Phillip, to what it must feel like to be a lonely old man leaving nothing behind him.

Reckon I'm glad yor going, Baptiste had told him. *You fix things with yor pap. It be the right thing. And don't you fret none fo' Willow. Travis and me, we'll keep her plumb safe. You got my word, Dick.*

How his world had changed. He'd entrusted the love of his life to an ax murdering escaped slave and an uncouth ruffian. And each would hold that trust inviolate. To the death, if necessary.

And I thought I understood ethics?

He stood then, walking out to the edge of the camp where Ashley's pickets watched the darkness. The night was star-filled, clear, and cool. Was Willow staring up at the stars right now? He could feel the longing in her heart.

"I could be there by morning."

But, he had come to understand, there were times when a man had to do unpleasant things. It wouldn't take long. Race to Boston, tell his father what had happened, and race back. He could be back in *Ainkahonobita* within ten months.

Wasn't that what he'd told himself the last time?

Two years. That's how long she'd said she would wait.

High in the sky, a shooting star streaked the darkness,

and just beyond the fringe of sagebrush a coyote racked the night with a mocking howl.

"I reckon they's done crossed the Green by now," Baptiste said as they rode out of Willow Valley.

"Yep." Travis had a chew juicing and spat. He glanced at Willow. "How ye doing, gal?"

"Sad, Travis. The same as yesterday, and the day before." She took a moment to look back. If she never returned to Willow Valley, it would be fine with her.

"Why'd you let him go?" Baptiste asked gently. "You coulda throw'd a fit and kept him heah. He'd a stayed if'n you'd asked him."

She'd been asking herself that same question over and over. "He's a warrior, Baptiste. He must return to his father, settle this thing between them. He must choose between me and Boston."

"And if it's Boston?" Travis asked, grabbing at a pesky fly.

She twisted her mare's mane in her fingers. "A woman must let a warrior face his challenges. Do you think life is ever safe? Too much of Coyote is in the world."

"He'll come back." Travis gave Baptiste a crafty squint. "Reckon I'll bet ye a pack of plews."

Baptiste narrowed an eye and rocked his jaw back and forth. "Travis Hartman, yor a black-hearted son of a bitch."

"Ye gonna take her?"

"Hell no!"

Richard called the mare Pia, the Shoshoni word for mother. She was really Willow's, a gift from Two Half Moons. But over the long months, Richard had come to think of her as his own. And, unlike his stiff-gaited old white mare, this dapple gray could move like the wind.

An early October frost lay on the ground. He watched the horse's ears swiveling as he walked her down the rutted wagon road. To either side, farms had been hacked out of the trees. The crops were in, the fields gleaned of their produce. Each squat cabin had a plume of blue smoke rising from the clay-coated chimney. Sometimes a buckskin-clad farmer would wave, and more than one had offered his hospitality, corn, and pork in return for tales of the West.

And what tales I can tell.

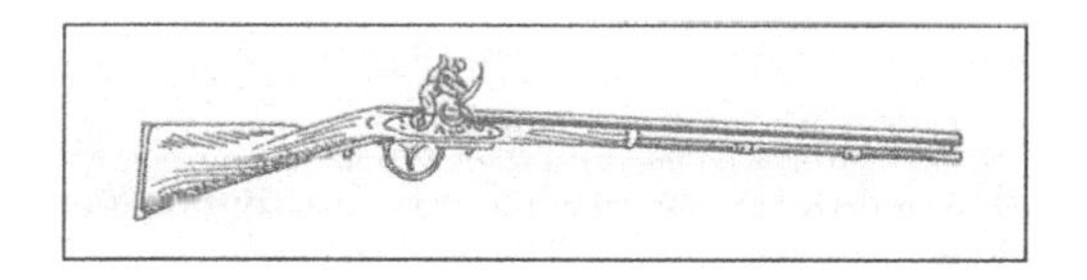

Just like his horse. Funny how things went round. The animal had come from Willow's first husband's family—actually from White Hail's herd—then it had gone to Two Half Moons, and then to Willow.

Now, here we are, halfway across the world, and both longing for Ainkahonobita.

The first July days with Ashley's caravan had been long, hot, and dusty. But then Richard had worked his way into Ashley's circle. On many a night they'd sat at the fire, discussing philosophy, the role of the state, and government. Ashley had the politician's bug.

"I'll tell you, Hamilton," he'd said one night, "my future is in government. Missouri may not look like much now, but we're building. I can see the day when

Saint Louis will be the largest city in the country—bigger than New York, Philadelphia, or any of the other cities. Even bigger than your Boston."

"And why is that, sir?"

"Because of the location, Hamilton. Saint Louis controls the rivers."

Well it might,—some day in the distant future—but as Richard rode past the outlying plantations, he had trouble making the outskirts of Saint Louis appear anything like those of Boston.

He reined Pia to one side to allow a squeaky wagon to pass, then trotted her on toward Saint Louis. He broke out of the last of the trees to encounter cleared land, most of it littered with stumps and piles of burned logs. Fences were going up here and there. In the distance he could see the two-story houses of the city's wealthier citizens.

Ashley was one of those now. He'd floated down to Saint Louis by boat with his bales of fur. Richard, hating to part with Pia, had ridden in, making no more than twenty miles a day.

He'd paralleled the route he'd poled and cordelled up with the *Maria.* Along the way, the ghosts of Trudeau, Toussaint, Green, and Henri had called to him.

"But here I am," he told Pia's patient ears. "Saint Louis again."

They clopped through the outskirts, and into the heart of the city, following Ashley's instructions. He found the street that would take him to Ashley's office—and then turned toward the river.

He knew the place by the signpost over the door: "The Green Tree Tavern." That's where Richard stepped down and tied Pia off. He hesitated at the door and took a deep breath.

Are you ready for this?

No, probably not. But all those long days on the trail, he'd promised himself to see this through. He'd studied on it, and decided to do it the way Travis Hartman would have. Nerving himself, he entered the grimy interior.

It took a moment for his eyes to adjust. Boatmen sat at the tables dressed in white cotton shirts, belted at the waist with bright red sashes. He walked to the first and rested the butt of his rifle on the stained hardwood floor.

The three boatmen looked him up and down, no expression on their faces. In French, Richard said, "I'm looking for a man. A cutthroat and thief. He's big. Blue eyes. His name is François. He used to run with a man named August. Do you know him?"

Glances were exchanged, and one man shrugged. "Why would you want him?"

"I've come to discuss a little business with him."

"You are too late." The second man watched Richard through half-lidded eyes.

"He's dead," said the third. "Found floating in the river with his throat slit." He ran a callused and dirty finger across his throat.

"And August?" Richard asked.

"Shot...when?" The first frowned. "Over a year ago. I think at the same time François was killed, *oui*?"

The second nodded. "Just before. François shot him. This I know for a fact. They argued over a woman." He glanced sidelong at Richard. "It was Lizette, you know? The whore. That's who they fought over. François had money—a lot of it. And Lizette had François."

"She killed François," the first said. "Cut his throat and rolled him into the river. You know how I know? Because he had a ribbon tied on his penis. That was her sign."

"And where is she?" Richard arched an eyebrow.

"Who knows? Some say New Orleans. But I have been there and heard no word of her. She is the kind of woman who is talked about. No, I think the ones who say Paris are right. You want my guess, *mon ami,* she killed François and August, took their money, and poof! She is gone."

"A smart one, that," the third man agreed. "But if François is no longer of help, perhaps..."

Richard sighed wearily. "Sorry, boys. *Merci beaucoup.*"

He plucked up his rifle and headed for the door. Outside, in the fading twilight, he glanced down at the river, visible through a gap in the buildings.

"Ah, hell, it was worth a try." But then justice had always been a thing for the gods.

He untied Pia's reins and stepped into the high Shoshoni saddle. As he rode away, the three boatmen stepped out to stand before the Green Tree, the question lingering in their eyes.

The sun hadn't cleared the summits surrounding *Ainkahonobita* when Willow stepped out of the shelter. She placed a hand to her stomach as her careful gaze surveyed the surroundings. Wisps of smoke still rose from the firepit. The woodpile looked like a gray jumble in the dawn. The junipers and limber pine stood like silent sentinels against the fading night.

Travis's and Baptiste's bedrolls had already been rolled. They had risen even earlier, taken their rifles, and were hunting the juniper breaks beneath the rimrock in hopes of killing meat.

Reassured, she made her way on careful feet to the

draw and followed the trail down to the rocky bottom. To still the queasy tickles in her stomach, she sucked in the chilly air. Eyes closed, she propped one hand on a cottonwood trunk and fought the growing nausea.

Willow bent double. In a violent fit, her stomach pumped the last remains of last night's supper onto the tumbled red rocks. She spit, and wiped off her mouth. Sure that it was over, she straightened to catch her breath.

The chill braced her, cold air soothing her hot throat. High overhead a flock of blue herons fluted calls as they winged south across a golden sky. Two Half Moons had once told her that the second time wasn't as bad as the first. Grimacing at the taste of bile in her mouth, Willow wasn't sure.

Feeling better, she kicked loose soil over the damp stains and squatted to relieve herself. By the time she climbed out of the wash, strength had returned to her legs. The rapidity of her recovery always surprised her.

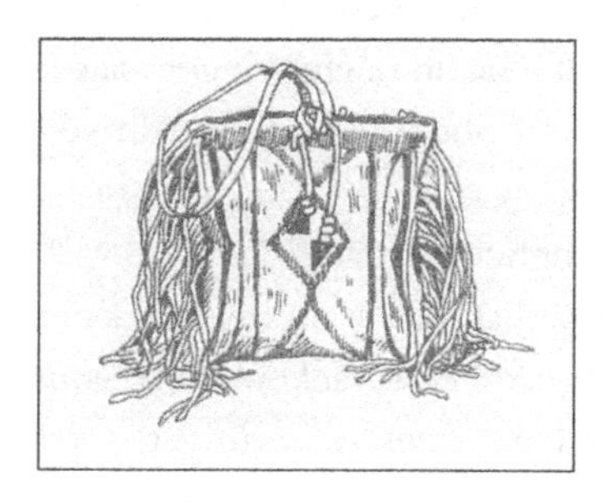

She crossed the camp to the spring and drank deeply before rising. She'd plucked several pieces of wood from the pile when Travis stepped out from behind one of the junipers. He fixed her with a hard stare and came striding across the beaten grass. His Hawken hung from one hand, the tight grip purposeful.

"Good morning," she said.

He stopped before the fire, a sour look on his scarred face. "Been sick, ain't ye?"

She bent down to hide her face and stirred the fire for hot coals. Prodding them into a mound, she placed her firewood atop them and blew them to life. As the first flames leaped up, she said, "Something I ate."

"Not fer two mornings, Willow." He squatted down to her level, refusing to be put off. "Ye've missed yer bleeding, too, ain't ye? It's nigh on two months now since Dick left, and yer putting on fat, gal."

She bit her lip, flashing him a hot glance. For a long moment their eyes held, and she nodded in defeat. It wasn't as if she'd hide her condition for much longer.

Travis lowered his eyes to watch the fire. At last he reached up and scratched his ear. "Baptiste, he done noticed first. He's a keen old coon, he is. Wal, I reckon it ain't that much of a surprise."

"I'll be fine, Travis. I've done this before, you know."

"Yep." Then he grinned. "Why, Tarnal Hell, gal, this means this child'll be an uncle! Figger that fer beaver."

"Uncle Travis?" She lifted an inquisitive eyebrow. "And Uncle Baptiste?"

Then she laughed.

Travis fingered the cock on his rifle as he looked up at the brightening sky. Nutcrackers were squawking in the trees, their raucous cries drowning the trill of a chickadee. "What about Dick? He otta know."

She shrugged. "He will find out when he finds out, Travis. What can we do? Nothing, and even if I could send word, I wouldn't. He has to make choices without my interference."

"Interference? Waugh! They's a child involved, Willow. Dick's got a right ter know. It's his kit, ain't it?"

"If the child is born, and lives, it will call him *appi*."

Travis was pulling on his beard now, frown lines wrinkling his scars. "Reckon I could go ter Boston and tell his sorry arse he's a pap. Painter crap! This coon don't hanker fer them doings. Not by a damn sight."

"Travis, if he comes, he'll know soon enough. The child won't be old enough to know a father until two years have passed anyway. And what if you ride off and tell Richard, and then you come back and the baby is dead? You know that happens. My first died like that."

"Yer fibbing ter yerself, ain't ye? Think, Willow. Ye knows Dick, how his head works. Hell, if'n anything happened, why he'd skewer hisself with guilt till Christ hisself couldn't fergive him."

Travis lowered his voice. "'Sides, girl, they's more to it. He told ye about his pap, didn't he? 'Bout how the old man was gone when his wife died? And how he never could face Dick again? Ye want that?"

Willow sighed wearily. "I'm no White lady." She smacked her hips. "See? Like a good mare, I can drop a child without dying. *Dukurika* women are like that. And this stomach? It's strong..." *When it's not throwing up.* "It can push a child out, and I can still cook supper that evening. Or breakfast the next morning, if the child comes at night."

Travis suddenly rubbed his face, an odd fear in his eyes. "Nope, this coon's a gonna go fetch Dick from Boston."

"Travis, what is it? You tell me."

He started to stand, but she grabbed a handful of his shirt, twisting him back to face her.

The muscles in his face twitched and made the scars seem to writhe. "Aw, it's nothing. Seeing inter the past is all. Seeing..."

"What? This is Willow you are talking to."

His lips parted, the pain in his soul open to her. "I had a wife once. Crow she was."

"I know this."

"Uh-huh, but what ye don't know is that she's kilt by the Blackfeet. Pregnant. When they caught her, she couldn't run. Not heavy like that."

Willow released him and shrugged. "These things happen, Travis. Coyote made the world that way."

"I warn't thar, Willow. I's out hunting with Two White Elk. Warn't a damn thing I...I warn't thar, is all."

She nodded then. "Ah, so now, Dick must be. This is not a thing I can talk you out of, is it?"

He gave her a weak smile. "Nope. I reckon not. Not this time."

"But you don't want to go. I can see it in your soul, Travis."

"There's things a coon's gotta do, Willow. Just like Dick's a-doing now. Now, I ain't gonna lie and tell ye I'm just chipper ter go and...and...Hell, I *hate* the East."

She laughed, kicked at the dirt, and gave him a sidelong glance. "No wonder you come here to find Injun women. Without them, you White men will all die."

"I don't see whar yer stick floats."

"If you must do this thing"—she gave him a smug look—"I know a way to tell Richard without you going to the cities, Travis. You know it, too."

"I do?"

"Come, we will find the things we need."

William Simon was more scared than he'd ever been in all of his life. He hadn't come that far, he just knew it. But no matter which way he looked, all he could see were trees. Under his feet the carpet of leaves crackled and felt spongy, but study as he might, he could see no imprint of his small boots to tell him which way he'd come.

In the streets of his native Philadelphia safety lay in any direction, no farther than the closest door. He need only cry out for help. But here, lost in the forest, he felt as if something was watching him, stalking in those shadows.

"I gotta get back," he mumbled to himself as a tear streaked down from one eye. He sniffed, trying to be brave, and shouted, "Mama! Father!" He'd shouted before, but the endless trees seemed to swallow his words.

He ran, panicked. They had so little time at wood stops, and he'd just walked into the forest to see. That's all. He'd dreamed of the forests, of Indians, and hunting, just like the frontiersmen.

The *Sultana* would be leaving any minute now—and it would do so without Willy Simon.

I'm lost! Oh, please God, don't let me die here!

"Mama, Papa—help me!" As he charged through the trees, he tripped, falling into the leaf mat.

In the distance, he heard the shrill steamboat whistle.

"They're leaving," he mewed piteously. Which way had the whistle been? Sound changed here in the forest, and he'd crossed a couple of small ridges.

Breath tearing in his throat, he ran for all he was worth, and heard the whistle again, but which way was it?

"Mama! Father! Help!" A vine slapped him across the face, and he splashed through a shallow stream. Shivering from fear and exertion, he blinked down at the water. Had he crossed it before?

He couldn't remember. "Help me!" Then he prayed

out loud, "God, don't let them leave without me. If You do this one thing, I'll be good, I promise! I'll never be bad again!"

"That's always a good policy," an amused voice answered.

Willy nearly fell over from fear. There, standing up the slope from him, was an Indian!

"Don't kill me—I'm only ten! I'm lost! Help! *Father!*"

"Whoa now." The man stepped out further, and Willy could see that while he wore buckskins, he was a white man with a beard, and a big rifle. "You're fine, Willy. I've come to find you."

"The boat's going to go, and I'm going to die here! I want my mama and papa."

"The *Sultana*'s not going to leave without you. Your folks told the captain you were missing and there's men combing these woods for you."

Willy felt a little better. The whistle sounded again, and the man cocked his head. "Sound plays tricks on you down in this little valley, doesn't it?"

"Yes, sir."

"Come on. It's this way." The man gave him a smile and started up the hillside.

Willy gulped, took his chance, and charged after him. "You're sure that's the way?"

"I am. Willy, remember, you can always follow the streams if you get lost. They'll take you back to the river."

"How do you know that?" Willy was eyeing the big rifle. It was scarred, weathered, the kind of rifle that had seen a lot of Indian battles.

"A man told me once, just like I'm telling you."

"Then, why aren't we following that stream back there?" He pointed at the brook they had just crossed.

"Because this way we cut the corner off the angle. Think. If you crossed all the streams, and water was running to the left, which way would you be from the boat?"

Willy put it together in his head. "Downstream. West. Because we're on the north bank."

"You've got it."

Willy trotted to keep up with the big man's steps. He got a closer look at the worn leather clothes. The buckskin was black and shiny, and bits of hair had been sewn into the seams. Colored quillwork made designs on the sleeves and chest. Here and there, a tear had been stitched with thongs from the long fringes.

Willy said, "I'll bet you don't get scared in the forest."

The man smiled. "Were you scared?"

"Yes, sir. I could feel eyes on me, like animals or monsters that would get me." He winced. "That must sound pretty silly to you."

"No, not silly at all." He winked at Willy. "You know why? Here, stand still for just a moment. There, now. Listen. Feel with your soul. Do you know what that is?"

Willy did, uneasy at the lurking presence. "I feel it. No, sir. I don't know what it is, like a haunt!"

"You're from a city, aren't you?"

"Yes, sir. Philadelphia."

"It's the land, Willy. It has power, a soul all of its own. That's what you're feeling." He glanced around, brown eyes serene. "I was just like you, once. The first time I felt the way you do now—that *things* were watching me. But do you know what?"

"No, sir."

"The land becomes your friend when it knows you." And he smiled.

"Willy!" Father's voice shouted from somewhere in the trees.

"I've got him!" the man called back.

"Father!" Willy's heart felt like it would burst from his chest. He charged headlong, arms out, never so happy in all his life. His father's strong arms plucked him up and hugged him to that familiar cloth-covered chest.

"The lad's all right," the stranger said. "Just lost his way."

"I, uh...thank you, sir," his father said uneasily.

As Willy was lowered to his feet, he noticed the strained expression on his father's face as he took in the bearded man's dirt-streaked leather clothing, and the battered rifle. Next to his father's fine suit, the stranger looked wild and unkempt, the kind of man Father would never acknowledge on the streets of Philadelphia.

"My pleasure. Richard Hamilton, sir. At your service." The dirty man offered his hand.

For once Father didn't shake, but clung to Willy's shoulders with both hands. "John Simon. Thank you. Thank you again, Mr. Hamilton. Come, Willy. We're late. Holding up the captain. Come on. Let's hurry." And his father dragged him off so fast that Willy had to run to keep up.

Willy threw a quick glance over his shoulder; the wild man followed behind, an ironic smile on his lips.

Men greeted them at the plank, most making jokes about his getting lost, or captured by Indians, or eaten by a bear. But his father laughed them off as they boarded and he pulled Willy toward the stairway. "Quite an adventure, eh, son?"

"Yes, sir. Who was that man?"

"Some frontier ruffian. He's riding down on the lower deck. Rabble, son. A fur hunter from out west, they say.

But, son, you must always remember that you are a gentleman."

"Yes, sir." Willy glanced back down the stairs just as the wild man waved goodbye to him. Later, in their stateroom, he watched the forest pass slowly by as the *Sultana* steamed up the Ohio for Pittsburgh.

The soul of the land. That's what I felt out there. How brave Mr. Hamilton must be. But Father is right. A gentleman should only associate with other gentlemen.

Veils of misty rain marked the river with interlocking ringlets that danced on the waves. Richard leaned on the rail just below the driver as it rose and fell, in the endless cycle of powering the huge paddlewheel. Each revolution was accompanied by clanking and rattling and the endless *shish-shish-shish* of the paddles biting into the river. To block the noise, Richard imagined a perpetual waterfall, droplets cascading down just for him.

The dark, forested bank slid past, scarred here and there by farms. The water swirled and sucked from the bow wake and the ripples generated by the hull. This was the Ohio, the water dark by its very clarity. A tame river, soothing to the soul.

How unlike the Missouri, which always waited to kill the unwary.

Only on rare occasions did the silent and deadly embarras come corkscrewing down the current. Here, the sawyers and planters were marked, mostly unchanging.

An irregular patch of cleared land was momentarily visible through falling curtains of rain. In the center of the newly cleared field, a pall of blue smoke issued from a smoldering pile of burned limbs. The farmers set fire to the litter created by their clearing. For days, the smell and haze of smoke never dissipated.

What of the forest's spirit? He shifted, a lonely sadness within. *We're killing it. Breaking the Power of the land.*

Richard twisted his head to see the gallery above him. No one stood out in the rain today. They were all huddled around the warm stoves inside. He could imagine the cigar and pipe smoke, the clatter of pasteboards at the card tables. The talk would be of business, politics, and market prices.

Here, on the cargo deck with the other cheap fares, Richard lived under his blanket shelter. He'd come downriver in the *Virgil*, a gentleman with a stateroom, a grip full of a fortune in banknotes and a satchel of philosophy books. Now, a year later, he was going upriver as a laborer, working off his passage as a deckhand, loading firewood and freight, doing menial chores on the boat.

He thought back to the Richard Hamilton who'd once traveled down this river, so certain of his own invincible truth.

Was that really me?

He'd understood John Simon's reluctance to shake his hand that day the boy had gotten lost.

I'd have done the same thing, once.

That led him to think about François. Blessed God, how ironic fate was.

It was he, not I, who ended up in the river with his throat cut.

Coyote pranced in the most curious of places.

A glass bottle floated past, bobbing in the *Sultana's* wake, only to be scuttled by the thrashing paddlewheel.

Fate brought people, events, and goals relentlessly back to their starting points. Damp and cold, he squinted out at the drizzle. On the *Virgil,* he'd longed for Boston. Now, on the *Sultana,* his heart ached for Willow and *Ainkahonobita.* He shrank from the inevitable arrival at his destination.

No matter how many times he played out the meeting with his father, it was like an actor on a stage, the lines rehearsed. The real meeting would be so different.

How will he react? Richard winced at the thought of those gray eyes, and his father's unforgiving face.

Father, for God's sake, let's make this pleasant.

Coyote would grant him that, wouldn't he?

The difference is that this time, I will understand you, Father. This time, I don't have anything to prove to you.

A flight of ducks darted past, swinging wide of the *Sultana.*

The future would always have to be faced; and face it he would. If he reached Boston, he and his father would either repair their differences or they wouldn't. He would see Will Templeton, and Professor Ames. They would ask him what had happened, why he had changed so.

And what can I tell them?

Nothing—at least, nothing they could understand. Anything he said would be illogical without the rational foofawraw to back it up.

As the rain fell, Richard stared down into the water, heart heavy with longing for Willow. Since he'd left her, he'd had no one to talk to. No one who understood his heart.

He absently fingered the hard roll of gold coins sewn into his jacket seam. The circles of fate. Once again he carried another man's money. The accumulated savings of Travis Hartman's hard life: in its own way, another fortune.

But, Travis, I'm going to hand it right back to you one day. I swear that before God.

And he smiled wryly at the rain. This was a very different Richard Hamilton to whom Travis had entrusted his gold.

He always felt a warmth when he pictured the expression on Travis's face as he handed that roll of coins back. An offer given, a debt repaid, and a man's proof that he could face the world on his own merits.

That narrowing of Travis's hard blue eyes could speak more eloquently than Shakespeare's sonnets.

Life's circles: always ironic, always humbling. He reached up to flick a bead of water from the brim of his worn felt hat. The last time he'd passed these shores, he'd been dreamy-eyed with infatuation for Laura Templeton. Giddy fantasies had filled his head, visions spun of himself and Laura, hand-in-hand, gazing rapturously into each other's eyes.

Now, whenever he closed his eyes, he was with Willow—seeing the gleam in her dark eyes, feeling her touch, hearing her words. Sometimes they talked under the night sky. Other times their bodies locked together in that ultimate piercing unity of man and woman. However she appeared, she dominated his heart, body, and soul with a captor's totality.

It won't be long, Willow. I'm coming back—just as soon as I can.

But then, he'd promised that to Laura the last time he'd traveled this river. Circles. Forever haunting. Endlessly mocking.

CHAPTER SEVENTEEN

Art goes yet further, imitating the rational and most excellent work of nature, man. For by art is created that great LEVIATHAN called COMMONWEALTH, or STATE, in Latin CIVITAS, which is but an artificial man; though of greater stature and strength than the natural, for whose protection and defense it was intended.

—Thomas Hobbes, *Leviathan*

Travis pulled his hat off and stared up at the morning sky. A light breeze was blowing from the west, as if urging him eastward. It whispered in the dry grass, rustled the yellow-brown leaves. The distant chirp of a horned lark was the only other sound. The soul of the land soothed, the aches of the body nettled. From long habit, his gaze went first to the horses who watched him with half-lidded eyes as they stood, heads down, and hobbled over close-cropped grass.

He threw the blanket back, grunted as he climbed

stiffly to his feet, and stretched to loosen the weary ache of muscles, bones, and joints pushed too far.

To still the gnawing ache in his belly, he chewed a strip of jerky, then rolled up his blanket. The saddle leather was cold against his fingers as he threw it onto the dapple gelding and tightened the surcingle.

He walked off several paces to attend to nature, knowing full well that the gelding had swelled his chest against the cinch. Finished, he casually cinched up the slack, and stepped into the saddle. The lead ropes in hand, he resumed his race to the east, walking the horses into a trot, and holding the pace.

As he limbered to the saddle, the pains stitched through his body.

Getting too old fer this, boss.

Hell, how did age creep up on a man so? Time was, he could have ridden like this for days, and nary a complaint once his body warmed to the strain. But this time the ache hadn't left his bones and stringy muscles.

As the sun climbed the sky, he maintained the distance-eating pace, stubborn will overcoming the resistance of his flesh.

Today, like the day before, and the day before that, he'd switch off one horse for another. The trick was to balance the horses, and himself: endurance against time and distance. Changing off three mounts was about the best a man could do; more horses meant more cussed trouble to keep the cavvy together.

And it's still a gamble, coon.

He kept throwing glances back, forever expecting to see riders racing up his backtrail. The rifle in his hand reassured him. A lone man with three horses made an all-fired tempting target.

Travis kept to the uplands, paralleling the Platte.

When possible, he trailed through the hollows, off the skyline. Miles passed with the hours, an endless race across waving grass, crumbly stone, and dark patches of prickly pear. Hooves pounded across bleached buffalo chips, and crushed an occasional dry bone.

Why in hell are you doing this? The question rolled around in his fatigued mind. The answer haunting him: *For Moonlight. For me.*

And damn it, just because it could be done and it otta be done.

Wasn't that what a man was made for? Doing things? Accepting challenges?

If'n not, he repeated over and over, *ye might just as well be dead.*

Down in the root of his soul, he could see Willow's face. Well, by God, if she could be so damned brave about bearing a child by herself, he could see to it that Dick got word.

If I could just see his face when he hears.

Travis chuckled. Yep, that would be some, it would. The Doodle would get that stunned look, as if the world had just come unstuck again and turned upside down. Old Dick, just like always, would torture hisself right miserable.

And when ye hears, coon. Ye'll come. I know ye will, 'cause yer more a man than ye ever knew ye was.

And Boston could just damned well rot itself.

Filling his lungs, Travis was on the point of howling. Then he topped the ridge. Looking back, he could see them, a line of riders following his tracks.

He pushed his horses across the ridge and into the swale on the other side.

Wal, coon, what're ye a gonna do now? Fort up and wait it out, or take a chance on losing them red bastards?

From the angle of the sun, he had about three hours to darkness. If he could outrace them into the night, he just might be able to lose their sorry carcasses.

"Ho, Hamilton! Time to get off! We're here," the wagon driver called.

Richard blinked and yawned. He peered owlishly out at the foggy gray morning. The wagon had ceased to rumble, bang, and lurch. Boston, at last.

He unrolled from his blanket and sat up on the unforgiving crates. The cries of gulls, the salty smell of the harbor, brought a deep contentment to his soul. He quickly rolled his blanket, grabbed up his rifle and possibles, and stretched.

When he jumped stiffly to the cobblestones, he needed a steadying hand on the wagon box while his legs firmed up. The wagonmaster had climbed down, and stood with his fingers shoved in his belt as he looked at the gray wooden doors of the warehouse. "Ain't that just fine," he muttered. "Locked. And all that worry and fuss about making time."

Richard rubbed his neck to kill the ache. "Well, Mr. Jones, thank you for the ride. I do appreciate your kindness."

Jones cocked his head. "Pleasure's mine, Mr. Hamilton. You more than repaid me with all them stories about the western lands." He paused. "You gonna walk through the city—looking like that?"

Richard glanced down at his buckskins, black and shiny with dirt. Some of the fringe was gone, and holes gaped here and there. "It's all I own."

"God keep you, sir."

"And you, Mr. Jones." Richard hefted his rifle, hung his possibles on his shoulder, and slung his blanket on his back. Then he walked out into the morning fog. He could see the masts and spars of the ships. Jones hauled freight from Boston to Rhode Island, making a trip a week down south to Providence where Richard had managed to find passage from New York.

His moccasined feet scuffing the damp cobblestones amused him. "I left in a carriage and returned in a freight wagon." He shook his head, stepping out onto Sea Street, took that west to Essex Street, and then turned onto Boylston.

Little had changed during his absence. Mystification filled him. How can I be so different—and Boston remain so carelessly eternal? He quoted to himself: "What a vanity is man's that he expects the world to notice his achievements, and to marvel at them, when in reality, the world, if it so much as pays the slightest attention, will only yawn, and then with but the briefest of enthusiasm."

His nose wrinkled at the acrid smells—smoke, urine, manure, rot, fish—borne on the early morning air. He grimaced at puddles of water, and the greasy scum that coated the cobblestones. He cringed at the filthy dampness soaking into the soles of his moccasins.

Cats slipped away into shadows, and the rats scurried into drainpipes and holes under foundations. Pigeons clucked and cooed from the rooftops, flapping as they sailed down to inspect the streets for garbage.

Richard passed shop windows, staring at the goods displayed. In the dawn twilight, Boston was just stirring, flexing its muscles for the day ahead. In a few hours, these streets would be crowded, the shops open for business. The several people he'd passed had gaped at him, as if seeing some sort of freak.

Never mind. You're home.

He rounded a familiar comer, and the Commons stretched before him. The trees were leaf-bare for winter, but the grass hadn't surrendered entirely. It still held a shade of green.

"What in hell?" a passing man asked, taking in Richard's skin clothes, the rifle, and his beard. "It's Daniel Boone!"

Richard glared, but managed to throttle the desire to feed the bastard the butt of his rifle. He hurried on self-consciously, stung by the derision.

He stepped out onto the Commons. Here he'd played as a boy, chasing bushy-tailed squirrels, running to and fro in the attempt to catch fall leaves as they fell. Here he'd made his first snowball—and thrown it at Jeffry.

He could see the house now, and slowed, a sudden constriction in his throat. He took a deep breath. Torn, he walked toward his home, his father, his past, and his future.

The first knock had been timid, and Jeffry barely heard it. He'd just stepped out of the kitchen and into the hallway when the knocker hammered more insistently.

"I'm coming," Jeffry growled, as he hurried past the hall chair and checked himself in the mirror. Early as it was, it wouldn't do to appear disheveled. The door knocker clanked again, demanding this time. Jeffry pulled himself straight and opened the door.

A vagabond stood on the step, his back to the door. Jeffry's nose wrinkled at the odor. And then, to his horror, he noticed the heavy-barreled rifle resting butt-down by the intruder's leg. Beyond him, three or four of the neighbors had gathered, staring, some pointing.

"Looks like an Indian," Jeffry heard a man say to his companion.

William Pembroke, an associate of Master Hamilton's, had come to a stop, surprise on his face. Pembroke dealt in cotton and textiles. "I say," Pembroke called out, "you there. That's Phillip Hamilton's house. Have you business there?"

The vagabond rested his nervous hands on the muzzle of his rifle and called back, "Indeed I do, Mr. Pembroke. But none that concerns you, sir. If you have nothing better to do than stand about the streets gawking, I'd suggest that you'd be better employed counting cotton bales in your warehouse."

At the ragamuffin's voice, Jeffry froze, a hand half lifted.

Laughter broke out, and Pembroke reddened. Calls of "Who is that?" went back and forth.

No, it couldn't be!

Jeffry cleared his throat. "May I help you, sir?"

The vagabond turned, bearded, dirty, with long greasy hair hanging over his leather collar. Jeffry's hand went to his throat.

"Jeffry? It's me. I—I'm home. Is Father..."

"Richard?" he asked in a hoarse whisper.

"Yes, Jeffry, It's Richard. Richard Hamilton."

"You? You're...dead." Jeffry's mouth dropped open—a slow shake of the head expressing his disbelief. He collected his swimming senses, swallowed hard, and glanced at the knot of watchers. "Come in, quickly, sir. But I don't...I mean. Why on earth are you dressed like... like *that?*"

Richard stepped inside, looking grateful when the

heavy door clicked shut behind him. He sighed wearily. "Thank God." He leaned the rifle in the corner before he dropped his blanket and a heavy hide bag on the tall-backed hall chair. "It's a long story. Tell me, how is Father? He's all right, isn't he?"

Jeffry's instinct was to dance and shout. "His health is fair, Master Richard, although his soul has withered over the last year since he received word of your death."

Richard glanced around, as if cataloguing the familiar artifacts of the hall. "I'm sorry, Jeffry. There was no way to send a message. I would have if I could." He placed his hands on Jeffry's shoulders. "My God, but you're a sight for sore eyes."

"And you, too, Master Richard." Jeffry's nose wiggled. "As soon as I inform Master Phillip of your return, I'll heat water for a bath, sir."

"Jeffry." Richard studied him from the corner of his eye. "What will...? I mean, how...? He hasn't disowned me, or anything, has he?"

Jeffry allowed the faintest quirk of the lips. "Oh no, Master Richard. Quite the contrary. In fact, well, he might even forgive the way you're dressed—um, assuming, you *meant* to arrive this way."

"I had no choice. I need to tell my father—explain to him, if you will."

Jeffry's eyebrow arched. "Master Richard. Please, sir —" But how could he give advice? *Don't hurt him again, Richard Not after what he's been through. Just once, be kind to him.*

With cold formality, he said, "I will tell him you're—"

"Jeffry?" Phillip called from above, and a band like iron clamped on Jeffry's heart. "Who was that pounding on the door at this time of morning?" And Phillip hitched his way out onto the landing at the top of the stairs. He peered down, squinting. "Who is that? Who's there?"

Before Jeffry could get his breath, Richard called out, "It's me, Father. It's Richard."

"Richard?" Phillip's fleshy face faded from florid to gray. "Richard? My...Richard?"

He grabbed for the banister. Jeffry started forward, but Richard beat him to the stairs, taking them three at a time. On the landing, he reached out, taking Phillip by the shoulders. "It's me, Father. Alive and well. I've been on the frontier. Gone places...and seen things."

"The frontier." Phillip's mouth worked, his gray eyes seeming to lose focus. "Dear Lord God, boy, it's you! Alive!"

And for the first time in more years than Jeffry could remember, Richard took his father in his arms and hugged him. For long moments they stood, unwilling to relinquish their hold. Jeffry climbed partway up the steps, hesitating.

Finally, Richard pushed back, and Phillip fingered his buckskin jacket. "You smell of woodsmoke and sweat. And what's this...this long black hair? Some kind of animal?"

"They call it...a fetish." Richard took a deep breath. "Father, come, let's go into your office. I have some things to tell you, and, well, they're not pleasant."

Jeffry turned. They would want coffee, and he'd tell Sally to make enough breakfast for two. Richard, home.

Thank you, Lord, for such a miracle.

But who was this strange Richard, so smelly and ragged, somehow wild? And so oddly sure of himself?

Phillip felt better once he'd seated himself behind the cherrywood desk. The thumping of his heart eased slightly. Was this lean man really his son? He looked like Richard, talked with his voice, but everything else about him was wrong. Right down to the filthy leather clothing.

But it is Richard, and he's alive!

And for that, Phillip could only praise God. He scratched his fleshy nose to hide the fact that a tear was trickling down his face.

For the moment, all he could do was stare. *When did my son become this man?*

Muscles packed his shoulders, and the almost predatory way he stood before the desk set Phillip back. Richard's face, despite being browned by the weather, had a mottled look. His expression had been honed. Even the wild cut of his clothing seemed to fit him now.

Richard was looking him straight in the eyes when he said, "I was robbed in Saint Louis. I'd had words with a man named François. He and several boatmen jumped me while I was walking through Saint Louis." Richard squared his shoulders. "The fact is, it was my fault, sir. I was careless and irresponsible. I'm sorry. So sorry. I came to apologize." He hesitated. "It seems that I've let you down a great many times over the years."

Phillip fiddled with the articles on his desk, and ended up twirling the officer's brass button. *My God, how do I tell him all the things I want to? What can I say?*

"You're alive, Richard. That's all that matters."

"But, *thirty* thousand dollars!" He spread his arms wide. "Father, how can I ever pay that back?"

Phillip braced his arms on the desk. "Oh, dear me, Richard. Do you think I'm a fool? I insured it, of course. And, beyond that, I sent along an agent, a man named Eckhart, to watch after you."

"Eckhart? Charles Eckhart." Richard lifted an eyebrow. "With the cigars and the card games?"

"Yes, the Virginian. You don't think I'd send you off alone and helpless, do you? He told me you acted very responsibly, didn't socialize, didn't do anything to jeopardize the banknotes. He said that you were a model courier for the money, close-mouthed and discreet. He lost you at the landing, waiting by your luggage, but you never arrived at the carriage hired to take you to the hotel."

"I...I wanted to walk. All that time on the boat..."

"The money was insured, Richard."

"Thank God!" Richard seemed to relax as he gripped the handle of his knife with a brown hand. "Upon reaching Saint Louis, I scoured the place, looking for any sign of François. General Ashley used his offices, as did General William Clark, but all we could discover was that several days after *Maria* left upriver, François was found floating in the river. It seems he'd shot August the night before in an argument over a woman, a Creole of rather dim reputation. The facts of François's death are rather peculiar. He was found naked, his throat cut, and, well, a red ribbon was tied around his penis. The rumor is that this, er...courtesan had the quirk of tying up her business with a bow."

"And the woman?"

"Disappeared completely the day after François's death. Rumor says she booked passage on a boat to New Orleans, and then to Paris."

Phillip scowled. "And if you'd caught this François?"

Richard's lips thinned. "I'd hoped to beat the hell out of him and dump him on General Clark's steps—alive or dead."

Phillip gasped, then shut his mouth with an audible click. Was this Richard talking? "I see. Enough of this for now. What's happened to you? Where have you been? Why are you dressed in such outlandish clothing?"

"It's a long story. Father."

Jeffry knocked, waited for Phillip's call, and entered with a tray holding a steaming pot and two cups. "Master Phillip, I would imagine Master Richard is famished, sir. I have informed Sally to set another place."

"By all means," Phillip was sniffing, struggling to keep tears at bay. "Come, son. Let's eat. You can tell me your story over breakfast."

"Should I clean up first?"

"Oh, dear Lord, no. That can wait. Yes, let's eat. There shall be time enough now for many things, my boy. Today, Richard, I am a young man again. And life has meaning once more. Yes, indeed, young as sprat, I tell you."

Richard took his father's arm, steadying him as they descended the steps together.

Richard studied his father as the fire popped in the tile-lined hearth in the parlor. Phillip stared down at the amber reflections in his brandy as he swirled it. Behind him, row upon row of books made a suitable backdrop. While dying in the snow, Richard had dreamed this very scene, and now here it was, almost as he'd imagined. Richard chafed in his broadcloth suit and sipped from his own snifter as he sought to place this world against the one that existed so far to the west.

The week had fled on frantic wings. Time was so different here. The flames danced on oak logs. Somewhere, Willow was watching fire, too.

Blessed God, how I wish I could talk to her. She'd love to hear how this has turned out.

Each night of the week they had sat by the fire, sipping brandy. Phillip—and Jeffry invited in—had listened, rapt, as Richard talked, his eyes half-glazed with memories. In the mornings, they lingered at the table over tea, eggs, and bacon, Richard telling his father of the Indians, and the river. They talked in the office, in the drawing room, and in the carriage.

Phillip had gasped at the scar on Richard's back; and Richard knew he'd come to suspect the long black patches of hair sewn into the buckskin jacket, but couldn't quite bring himself to ask. Nor was that the only secret between them. About some subjects, Richard couldn't talk.

"I don't know what went wrong," Phillip said suddenly. "Between you and me." He swirled his brandy. "It was as if a distance was forever between us. I couldn't..." He frowned, lost for words.

"I know, Father," Richard said. "In the last two years, I've come to understand. About you and me—and Mother. I was as blind as you were. I didn't help matters any, bullheaded as I was. I got straightened out on the river, I'm afraid."

A faint smile bent Phillip's lips. "And I, by reports of your death. I want you to know, Richard, that I'm very proud of you."

Richard chuckled. "Risks must be taken." And a melancholy pang lanced his chest.

But we're still living in different worlds. My truths are beyond your comprehension.

The thoughts of Willow, of her body intertwined with his on a rocky spire, sent honeyed sensations through his heart.

I'm married to a savage, Father. If you knew that, it would break your heart.

"But for the sense of courage and honor you taught me, I'd have died on the river. I learned more from you than I ever knew, or could admit."

Phillip's face twitched as he battled to keep his expression neutral. "What about the West? What would you advise? Surely some aspect of the fur trade should prove profitable over the next ten years?"

Richard fingered his beard; not for love nor money would he cut it. "Fifty percent of the fur trade is capital, Father. Another fifty percent is the caliber of the people you employ. The final fifty percent is sheer blind luck."

"That's one hundred and fifty percent, Richard."

"Yes, sir. And men who don't understand those mathematics are headed for disaster. Dave Green did everything perfectly—and in the end he blew up his own boat. Had the Blackfeet come a week later, we'd have fought them off, and Green would now have a foothold in the Crow and Snake trade."

"Could this be done again? With you and this Travis Hartman as booshways?"

"I wouldn't want to try it. I've gained an understanding of my capabilities. I don't think I'd make a good trader. I don't have the patience to stay at a post."

"I was thinking more in terms of administration, Richard. Overseeing the stocking of those posts, and the factors we'd employ. It would mean traveling back and forth from Boston to Saint Louis, and then into the wilderness."

Richard smiled. "A partner in the fur business?"

Phillip put down his snifter and rubbed his eyes. "I'm no longer young, my boy. Someone must take over the business. What you learn in the fur trade will prepare you to take my seat when my health... What's the matter? Not philosophy, again?"

Richard bit his lip, then took a deep breath.

"Tell me, son," Phillip asked gently. "Are you in some sort of trouble? I have means of dealing with such things, settling any ruffled legal feathers."

Richard laughed, amused. "No, nothing like that. I broke no laws, committed no offenses." He cocked his head, as if amused by his own words. "Or, perhaps I have, in the eyes of some."

"Is this the big dark secret you've been so careful to avoid?"

Richard gave him a level stare. "Father, I have my—"

"Richard, please!" Phillip slapped the arm of his chair. "Just once, I would like to be your father. In all ways. Do you understand? We've a second chance here. Is it so impossible for us to trust each other?"

Richard steepled his fingers, eyes level. His heart skipped, nerves prickling.

Tell him, Richard. Eventually he'll have to know why you're returning.

"Very well, sir. I have a wife."

"A wife? But, why didn't you say so before?"

"Because she's *Dukurika,* Father. Shoshoni, Snake Indian."

Phillip leaned back, struggling to understand. "You mean, you..."

"I do. I can't bring her here. Not to Boston. Men like your friend Pembroke would delight in the torment they could dish out over such an irresistible bit of gossip."

"But, a *savage*, Richard?"

He gauged Phillip's level of incredulity, and chuckled. "No more than I, Father. I've spared you many of the details of my survival in the wilderness. Do you seriously want honesty? Very well, that's what I'll give you. Morality is dictated by time, place, and necessity. Do I love her? Yes, with all my heart. As much as you loved Mother."

"Richard, surely—"

"Wait, Father. I can hear your protestations: It's undoubtedly something that will pass; a young man's first infatuation; the sort of fling a young man needs before the responsibilities of marriage preoccupy him. Were she a courtesan, I might agree, sir. But she's not. She's Heals Like A Willow. The woman who cut the arrow out of my back, who kept me from freezing to death, and helped me discover who I am."

"Richard, you're a young man of standing, worth nearly five hundred thousand dollars!" Phillip placed a hand to his heart.

Richard shook his head slowly. "Father, dear Father, I could try to explain from now until Hell freezes over, and you would never understand." He glanced toward the door. Jeffry stood there, silent, a stricken look on his face. "Jeffry, you might. You see from different eyes."

"Yes, sir," Jeffry replied mildly.

"What's this?" Phillip wondered.

Richard sipped his brandy. "Think about it, Father. Could you tell Pembroke that your slave is your best friend? Your confidant? The two of you don't fool me, not any longer. You play the roles so well, but you're just like Baptiste and Travis. Well, Father, I can't play the game."

"So you'll go back to your *Indian* wife?"

Richard nodded, gaze unwavering.

"Richard, you must think this—"

"My choice is *made.* That's all there is to it."

Phillip sighed, and Jeffry stepped forward to refill his glass. In the strained silence, the fire crackled. Phillip's face was a mask, frown lines cut deeply into his forehead. Then he said, "It is not unheard of. More than one prominent man has had a white wife—and a woman of standing, I might add—in the settlements, and an Indian squaw out beyond the frontier."

"Yes, sir. But it would not be right for me."

Phillip shrugged, eyes narrowing. Richard could hear the thoughts behind that shrewd face: The boy is young yet. And besides, time will do more to overcome Richard's notions than any argument.

Ah, Father, plot and scheme as you like. This time, I've lived that other life. And I accept it with humility.

Phillip glanced at Jeffry. "By the way, Richard, I have received word that your young friend, Will Templeton, is planning a reception for you."

Richard cocked his head. "I wasn't aware that he knew I'd returned."

"Oh, Richard, all of Boston knows."

CHAPTER EIGHTEEN

The most perfect philosophy of the natural kind only staves off our ignorance a little longer as perhaps the most perfect philosophy of the moral or metaphysical kind serves only to discover larger portions of it. Thus observation of human blindness and weakness is the result of all philosophy, and meets us at every turn, in spite of our endeavours to avoid it.

—David Hume, *Skeptical Doubts*

Autumn leaves had fallen from the oak, hickory, and beech trees to form brown drifts around the corners of the buildings. The day was warm enough, sunny, with a hint of November breeze blowing across the Charles River from Boston and into Harvard.

Richard and Professor Ames strolled past the chapel, the soles of their shoes tapping on the stone walk. Two years might have been yesterday as far as Ames was concerned. He still wore his black frock coat and slim trousers. His white head had lost no more hair, and the thoughtful expression remained as Richard related his experiences.

Richard clasped his hands behind him as he looked up at the pale autumn sky. How he missed the bright blue of the high mountain West. Was Willow looking up at it, even now? Wondering where he was?

"A most extraordinary adventure, Richard." Ames glanced at him with questioning eyes.

"And very difficult for me, Professor. I kept trying to fit everything into a rational framework. I was an enlightened man, sir. But one by one, the arguments proved hollow in the end."

"Indeed, Richard?" Ames raised an eyebrow.

Richard knew that look. "Sir, would you say I was an intelligent and competent student?"

"You've a keen mind, Richard. One of the best I've ever had the pleasure to instruct."

"Thank you, sir. Given that, I can't *tell* you why the arguments are flawed, because in some situations, they aren't. For example, Immanuel Kant creates a rational argument for Truth as it exists within his university in Prussia. When we read and debate his ideas, we do so within the framework of our own intellectual experience. We share social, intellectual, and historical bonds with Europe."

"Generally speaking, we do."

"Sir, knowledge is experience. You've read the same books that Kant has, so your knowledge comes from the same roots as Kant's. Therefore, you both perceive a similar framework for Truth derived from a Northern European perspective that traces its origins back through the Reformation to the Roman Church, to the Greeks and Hebrews before them."

"That is civilization, Richard."

"From our perspective, sir. I was cast out into the wilderness looking for ultimate Truth. My experiences have taught me that while it may exist in some abstract, we've leagues to go to reach even a fundamental understanding of what it might be."

"Richard, two thousand years of critical philosophical examination have led us to our current state of knowledge. Do you discard that?"

"No, sir. Not completely. Experience is necessary for knowledge, but not sufficient. Philosophers write from the culmination of their experience, but for no man can it be sufficient to find Truth."

"And why is that, Richard?"

"The world is too immense, too diverse. Once we saw God as a paternal Creator. Now we think of Him as a sort of watchmaker who's invented a perfect machine. The notion works well for the rational mind. But, sir, I experienced things out there that are not rational, not mechanistic."

"Then what is God, Richard?"

"In all honesty, I have no idea. Perhaps, as Spinoza proposes, we are indeed nothing more than modalities. I can tell you that one truth I've experienced is that each of us must find his own way to whatever element of truth he discovers—and in your analogy of the building, it won't even be a wall that we see, but most likely, only an individual brick in that wall. If we're lucky."

Ames raised a white eyebrow. "You've become a pessimist, Richard."

"Quite the contrary, sir. The difference is that I've seen through other eyes, glimpsed different sides of the building. I'm smart enough to begin to recognize just how big the building is, and how limited my experience has been."

Ames walked in silence, head bowed. "You seem very sure of yourself, Richard."

"I'm only sure about my own ignorance, sir, and how little I understand about God, nature, and reality. You could create clever arguments that could destroy every observation I've made. But, if you did, it would be through syllogistic tail-chasing, because I've been there, and you haven't."

"For instance?"

"For instance, I can tell you that you can think about God, but you can never think your way *to* God. Or that people may believe in concepts, things, or phantoms because they *want* to believe in them. Or that a perfect argument for, or against, something cannot be constructed because the initial conditions are constantly changing."

"Your universe sounds like chaos, Richard."

"It is, sir. I fought that acceptance until the very end. It was only after the last of the veils of illusion had been ripped away that I could truly see how ridiculous I'd been. How arrogant I was in my knowledge of that one brick in that one wall."

"Tell me what you saw, Richard."

He shook his head slowly. "I can't, sir. No more than you can tell me the smell of cinnamon, or the color of violet. Imagine yourself in intense cold, starving in the snow. Now, describe the odor of hot antelope blood. Impossible, you say? Indeed. Some things can only be experienced, not communicated. But, once experienced, they are nevertheless known."

"Hence experience is necessary, but not sufficient for knowledge." Ames grasped his lapels, his face a study.

They were approaching the library now, passing occasional students. 'Tell me some of these things you experienced."

"As a people, we're as deficient as any other, Professor. Our perceptions of the universe are only male, when half of the world is female. You are familiar with Latin and Greek that have male, female, and neuter cases. Did you know some people speak in languages that deal with the animate and inanimate? What does that say about the human mind's ability to perceive?"

"And Rousseau?"

"Dear Lord God, Rousseau! He wrote a fantasy, sir. I've witnessed man in a state of nature, or at least as close as you can get. There is no innocent Eden out there among the savages. It's self delusion to think there ever was. Anywhere. Rousseau just rewrote one of our fundamental myths. Once you see past the differences in primitive society, people are the same everywhere. No better and no worse. We all want the same things—health, a mate, shelter, food and water, and to understand the universe."

"But we are civilized, Richard. And they are not. Civilization does better the human condition."

Richard clasped his hands behind his back. "In some ways. We have our books. Our provisions for the common defense. On the other hand, we have insulated ourselves from reality. We're killing the soul of the land, removing ourselves from God, and veiling ourselves with illusions about life until we're half blind to truth. Tell me, has God ever laughed? Does He have a sense of humor? Perpetrate a joke?"

"God, laugh? No, not to my knowledge."

"Then why does laughter exist in the universe? Humor plays an important part in Indian religion."

"Humor isn't suited to the sacred."

"Why not? Be careful, here, sir. You'll fall into a syllogistical trap if you don't think this through. Is it because humor *can't* teach a sacred truth, or because our theology is flawed? An artifact of omission due to historical processes?"

"I see," Ames mumbled absently, his mind gnawing on the problem.

Richard shot Ames a look from the corner of his eye. "I was told by a frontiersman that people in Boston were like caged bears. It's true, sir. We only know the reality of our cage. We perform our tricks, and we're fed, sheltered, and cared for. We've given up our freedom in return for security, you see."

"I don't understand the cage, Richard. I'm free here, able to go where I want, think what I want, write what I want. Isn't that freedom?"

"As you know it, yes. I'm going back, Professor." Richard tilted his head. "I suppose of all people you might be able to understand. If I'm so free here, why can't I bring my wife to Boston? Or one of my best friends?"

"I don't know, Richard. Why can't you?"

"Because my wife is an Indian, sir. And the friend to whom I refer is an escaped Negro slave."

Ames studied him through wide eyes. "You? Married to an Indian? A savage?"

"A savage. Illiterate, unschooled in the Classics, but she and I have argued endlessly, night on end, about the nature of God, and why the universe was created the way it was. She stunned me the other day, proposed that nothing could have existed until God split into two to create duality. Only when the Godhead had broken into male and female could it begin to define itself. It has interesting possibilities, since only in duality can identity be measured against something else."

"What you are saying is heresy. It wasn't so long ago that people were burned for such crimes."

"Yes, sir. But you're not one of those people. You once said in a lecture that the search for Truth will take you into dangerous country. It does. In ways you can't imagine. It's a damning thing to say, but Harvard isn't ready for my ideas. It may never be."

Ames paced for a while, hands clasped behind his back. "A savage, you say?"

"Yes, sir. My wife and I would not be received in any decent home in Boston. Therefore, I will ask you to keep this between you and me. Rather than be branded a freak or a madman, rather than be scorned and spit on in the street, I'll return to my wilderness and the ability to associate with whom I choose."

"You don't sound like a madman, Richard." Ames puckered his lips, then said, "What you tell me is provocative, dangerous."

"Most people don't like dangerous ideas."

"But I do. That's what led me to philosophy in the first place. These ideas of yours must be fleshed out, placed into an orderly whole. It is the nature of philosophy to question, and you've unique insights I'd like to see developed, Richard."

"It would take a lifetime."

"That's how long it takes most philosophers." Ames gave him a sidelong glance. "You seem terribly confident, Richard. What if I can disprove everything you say with a logical argument?"

"What if you can, sir? In the final analysis, I know what I know, and it's based on what I've experienced. There are two sorts of people with whom you can never win an argument: those who base their belief on absolute faith, and those who know something by experience."

Ames was still frowning, his lower lip stuck out in a way that Richard had rarely seen, and then only when Ames was particularly engrossed in an idea. "I'm serious, Richard. I think you have something unique and wonderful. An insight into life and philosophy that will challenge and inspire students for generations to come. Philosophy isn't stagnant, and I think it could use a gadfly like you." He lowered his voice. "If you're willing to pay the price."

"I'll see, sir. Like I said, I have—"

"If you develop these ideas, organize them, I would recommend a lecturer's position for you. Of course, in the beginning you'd have to be careful. Challenging rather than offending. I'd begin by picking at the flaws in the epistemological framework. Omit any references to God for now—Harvard being what it is. In a few years, once you were established, you could advance your more radical arguments." Ames watched him with steely eyes. "I believe you know how important such an offer is to a student, Richard."

Lecturer? His heart skipped, an excitement brewing in the depths of his soul. Everything he'd ever wanted, just handed to him?

"You would be taking a risk by recommending me, sir."

Ames shrugged. "Cultivating dangerous ideas takes risk. I'm an old man. They can't hurt me. Can I be any less courageous than Socrates was?"

"That's within you, sir. But remember, they executed Socrates for speaking his mind."

Heals Like A Willow dropped her pack of wood and straightened slowly, awkward with her swollen belly. She winced and placed a hand on a nearby juniper for support. The red rocks of *Ainkahonobita* were maroon in the predawn light. A thick layer of frost had coated the brown grass.

Overhead two falcons soared through the chilly morning sky, twisting and turning before swooping low over the grassy flats under the canyon rim.

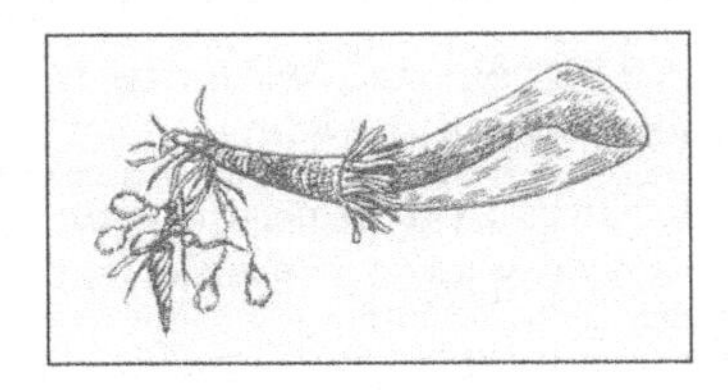

As she drew the cold air into her lungs, the rich odors of juniper, pine, and sage filled her nostrils. The child sapped her reserves, and she had to rest more often.

"Y'all all right, Willow?" Baptiste asked as he rounded the corner of the shelter. His black face was pinched with worry.

"Yes, fine. I just needed to catch my breath."

Baptiste lifted the bundle of wood by its leather strap. "You carry all that? In yoah condition? Come on, now, inside where it's warm. I got a stew on. Rabbit, just like you wanted." He glanced down at her belly. "He kicking in there yet?"

"No. It's early for that. In a couple of months. Travis is still asleep?"

"Yep. I don't know how that coon did it. Crossing all that country. Dodging them Pawnee and all. Reckon he's about as crafty as a raven around a fresh carcass."

Willow stopped short, breathing deeply. Baptiste

rocked from foot to foot, his dark eyes narrowed with worry.

"It is all right," she told him, amused by his concern. "I would think you were my mother. You should be off with the Crows, not wasting your time here."

"No, ma'am. Not with you in this condition. I don't know much about it, but Baptiste'll stay with you. And Travis, too. Leastways, till Dick comes back."

She glanced away, hoping her eyes wouldn't betray her.

"He'll come," Baptiste said gently. "He'd a never left if'n he knew he'd planted a child in you. Dick's a man, gal. And don't you never ferget it."

She nodded, starting for the shelter again. "And this paper?"

"Travis done delivered it. It'll be a-heading right down the river slick, I tell you."

"He should never have ridden off like that. I must have been hydrophobied to think of such a thing. Fort Atkinson is too far for a man to ride alone."

"Dick's gotta know. And, hell, Travis probably enjoyed the ride. He snuck through Pawnee country like a snake through the grass. Them coons is still chasing around trying to find his sign."

But she knew how risky the trip had been, and what a toll it had taken on Travis. He'd ridden in two days ago, his three horses worn down to bones, and Travis himself looking little better, with hollow eyes. He'd slept like a rock since his return.

"Dick will come," Willow told herself.

And to her child, she added, *He's like Wolf, little one. You will be proud of your father.*

Richard stood with his back to the piano, a glass of fine brandy in his hand. Almost two years had passed since the last time he was in Will Templeton's parlor. Around him, the room was crowded with old friends, but they seemed so young, so innocent.

He'd come to Will's house, uncertain, half anxious, half dreading. So much had changed since the last time he'd stood in this parlor. Right here he'd bragged to them, desperate to hide his dismay at being forced to take his father's money west. Here, his infatuation for Laura Templeton had been born from a touch of her slim hand, and a promise in those startling blue eyes.

She watched him now, from an overstuffed chaise on the opposite side of the room. Unspoken questions reflected in her charming eyes, inquiry in the tilt of her pink lips. Her hair was curled, bedecked with ribbons, and a pale blue velvet dress caressed her delicate body.

Why do I still find her enchanting?

Richard gave her a quick smile, and continued telling the company his story about being lost, starving, and seeing visions of Professor Ames.

"I clung to the rifle, you see. That was all that made me human after the last veils of illusion were torn away by hunger and pure animal survival. For the first time, I could see myself clearly. All that I'd been, all that I could be." He turned the glass. "We spend a great deal of time fooling ourselves about what's real, what's important."

Will, attentive as ever, said, "There's more, I dare say. You're not telling us everything, Richard."

No, indeed I'm not.

The West was so far from here—from the garlanded wallpaper, the gleaming crystal goblets, and finely upholstered chairs. Soft rugs cushioned his feet from the hardwood floors, the wood polished to perfection. The dark furniture gleamed, and the bright damask upholstery looked French—imported, no doubt.

George Peterson watched him curiously. Somehow, word of the lecturer's position had already spread. Behind his handsome face, Thomas Hanson's resentment festered.

Richard lowered his gaze to his brandy and nodded. "You've always known me too well, Will."

"Then tell us!" Templeton cried.

"I can't. Not in words. Until you live it, feel it in the gut, you can't comprehend. Until you've stood on the same mountain I have, you have no comparison with which to measure yourself."

Hanson, in bitter tones, said, "You expect us to sit here, accept your declarations on face value? An appeal to authority is worthless, Richard! Come on. You've had Professor Ames in a tizzy since he talked to you. He's been hammering on and on about epistemology and the assumptions we make about ourselves. What have you discovered?"

Richard lifted an eyebrow. "That you have to be very careful about how you know what you know, and what you accept on face value. As philosophers, we do entirely too much tail-chasing in the epistemological rafters, and not enough inspection of the stones from which we build the foundation."

"This is nothing more than...than rubbish!" Hanson stood and stretched, a smirk on his handsome face. "Wasn't it you who stood there once and bragged about taming the wilderness? Going off to become 'The Sage of the Frontier?" The 'real' is the 'rational'? I don't know what happened to you, Richard. But if you call this philosophy, you're a fool."

"The only fool, Tom, is one who proclaims knowledge when he has none."

"And now you do?"

"Now I know how little I really know. My blinders have come off. How about yours?"

Hanson stepped close, his slitted eyes inches from Richard's. Richard smiled then, letting his gaze bore into Hanson's. "I think you're nothing more than a charlatan, a cheat. Mountain sage? How about just a common liar?"

Richard heard gasps around the room.

Hanson glanced at Laura, as if to assure that she was watching, and thrust his face forward, the dare in his eyes.

Richard's wry smile bent his lips as he met Hanson's stare. "Don't even think it, Tom. You're not up to my kind of trouble."

Hanson broke then, Richard saw that sudden fear in the man's eyes. That he'd crossed a line from which he could never step back. Dropping his eyes, Hanson stepped away. In a last effort to save face, he stated, "I think I'm going for a walk. Laura, would you care to accompany me?"

"Thank you, Tom. But I think I'll stay for the moment."

"Laura?" Hanson's voice raised the slightest bit.

"You heard her." Richard narrowed an eye.

Hanson fidgeted for the moment, then slipped out the doorway.

Richard watched him go. "I'm sorry, Will."

Templeton took a deep breath, leaning back in his chair. "Richard, in your travels, you have changed. I thought for a moment Tom and you...well, what would have happened if he'd pushed it?"

"Nothing, Will. It wouldn't have been worth disrupting a charming evening."

"You've grown wise, Richard, and that is a gift rarer than knowledge."

"Indeed? I don't feel very wise. If anything, I'm more adrift than ever."

Peterson, looking nervously after Hanson, asked, "Tell us one of these truths, Richard. You seem so sure of yourself."

He rocked his brandy back and forth, watching the patterns of light. "If there is anything common to the condition of mankind beyond the obvious physical needs, I'd have to say it is responsibility." He glanced at Will. "I tried so hard to make the world fit what I had learned. I looked for rationality—and found it; but at cross-purposes with itself. And Truth? What is true for us, here, in Boston, is incomprehensible beyond the artificial construct of our society. What is rationally moral to us is immoral to others."

"I've never really thought about it in those terms." Will laced his hands over his knee. "And, while I can't agree, I'm loath to disagree because I don't understand exactly what you are saying."

Richard sighed. "You have to step outside of your reality, Will. Let me elaborate in a very personal way. As a philosopher, I ask you to listen, to think, and to make no judgments until you consider carefully what I have to say. This"—he gestured around the room—"all of it, is illusion. Our civilization has generated its own artificial reality."

Will frowned. "I think I understand."

"Do you? I have argued every nuance of philosophy with men you'd consider illiterate. And, if you'd believe it, with an Indian woman, too. We have debated morality, human responsibility, duty and honor. We have discussed the place of man in the state, the nature of integrity, and the condition of the soul in all its variations."

"Variations? Isn't a soul just a soul? A spark of God given to Adam?"

"It is an argument a little too sophisticated for most Americans. Those discussions caused me to revise my notions of society and civilization completely. As a result, I have been exposed to flaws in our logic that I never would have suspected. Isn't it curious? Most people in our fair city would say that a savage woman isn't ready for our society. The irony for me is that Boston isn't sophisticated enough to understand her. So, tell me? How did we become so blind?"

Peterson shifted uncomfortably. "Are we blind, Richard? Or do we have Truth that the savages can't conceive?"

Richard glanced up, meeting Laura's eyes. She'd been sitting demurely, watching every move he made. She cocked her head inquisitively, measuring him, waiting.

"The problem is epistemological. While men like Hume have questioned the mechanics of epistemology, no one has seriously questioned the effect it has upon us as a society. We believe the way we do because we have always believed that way." His gaze bored into Laura's, seeing the excitement in her eyes.

Peterson frowned. "Give me an example."

"Would you publicly debate a woman on the role of man in the state?"

"Of course not! That's preposterous. A woman doesn't have the faculty of mind to comprehend even the basics of the question."

"Ah! Is it because she doesn't have the ability, or is it that she's never been taught?"

"She doesn't have the ability."

"I can only retreat to my first position. There are things I can't tell you because you don't have a framework for understanding them. And here the debate must end, because I have had such a discussion with a woman, and you have not. To take it any further will end in frustration for both of us, for we have no common experience upon which to examine the question. Think of it as a frontier too far."

Peterson gave him a sour look.

"George," Richard raised his hands, "I am not trying to irritate you. Only to illustrate my dilemma. Philosophy, when pursued diligently and fearlessly, is the most dangerous of businesses. If Socrates was put to death for being a gadfly, what would my society do to me? I ask the most dangerous of questions. I challenge the roots of our mythology. And worse, I don't do it abstractly. I've seen beyond the horizon, but no one wants to accept what I have to tell them. We believe what we believe because we want to. It's comfortable, familiar. And no one wants to think that it could all be wrong since what little we know looks right."

"So, what will you do next, Richard?" Will asked. "I understand that your father has offered you a position in his firm. You are to be in charge of his western operations. At the same time, the rumor is that Professor Ames is offering you a position at Harvard."

Richard took a deep breath and drained his glass. "I don't know."

Laura's attention had wavered during the philosophical discussion, but now she straightened. If anything, she'd grown more beautiful during the last couple of years. Her pale skin had a radiant flush, and her smile charmed.

"Well, enough of this," Will said, aware that Richard had locked eyes with his sister. "Come, George, let's see if Jonas has managed to browbeat the servants into setting the table." He glanced at Laura, and then Richard. "We'll be right back."

Richard had to admit, it was smoothly done. He doubted that Peterson even knew he was supposed to beat a hasty retreat.

They'd barely left the room when Laura said, "It must be very rewarding, Mr. Hamilton. How splendid to have been offered a lecturer's position at the university, and a position with your father's firm."

He smiled. "I suppose it is, Miss Templeton."

"I kept all of your letters, read them over and over. When you stopped writing, I was dismayed. When word came that you were missing, well, it nearly broke my heart."

"I'm sorry if I caused you any distress. At times, your memory kept me alive, gave me something to cling to."

She flashed him a radiant smile. "Thank you, Mr. Hamilton. That's one of the most flattering things I've ever heard, and from the direct way you said it, I think you really mean it."

He met her challenging gaze and said, "I suppose I've lost the ability to dissemble. I should have gone a little easier on Thomas. Forgive me. I was a bit boorish."

"I'm not used to seeing him back down. It's not in his character. He believes himself the most dashing man alive. He thinks he's won me. Does that interest you, Mr. Hamilton?"

"I think you could do better than Thomas Hanson. He wouldn't make much of a husband. But that's just my opinion. Outspoken lout that I am now."

"I see." She blushed and smiled at him self-consciously. "I think the West sounds very exciting. Tell me, what is Saint Louis like? What do the ladies wear?"

"Oh, about the same as they wear here."

"Fine dresses from Paris and London?"

"Yes, indeed. Saint Louis is far from isolated. The steamboats tie Saint Louis to New Orleans, and from there, to the world."

"It sounds like a very interesting place. Will you go there for your father?"

"I would have to. The fur trade can't be run from a distance. The competition is of a fierce nature, and the demand for goods changes constantly."

She tilted her head. "I remember the last night you were here, so shy and self-conscious. You almost threw up after you kissed my hand. You're so different now. You're like no one I've ever met. Dangerous...somehow, exciting."

"I've never thought myself exciting or particularly dangerous."

"You don't see yourself as I do, from the outside. You're like a wolf, sir, trying to associate with a pack of hounds. You smile at them, but all the time, you're masking your teeth. And when you met the pack leader, you needed but a stare to send him slinking away with his tail between his legs."

"That doesn't sound particularly flattering, Miss Templeton."

She stood amidst a whisper of velvet and walked up to him, her blue eyes penetrating. "Perhaps some women would prefer a wolf to a dog."

"Spending time around a wolf can make you a little uncomfortable. A dog is a good deal more predictable and safe."

She stood so close he could smell the gentle scent of

lilac as he looked down into her eyes, reading her soul. Like Willow, she looked back fearlessly, telling him so many things. Her lips parted to expose delicate white teeth, and the pulse at her neck betrayed her excitement.

"I'd thought you'd already be married."

"I've been looking for the right man."

Richard, you've got to tell her. You owe it to her.

"Laura, you'd better know. I have a wife already."

Her eyes narrowed, head tilting so the lamplight glistened in her blond locks. "In Saint Louis?"

"In the mountains. Far to the west."

"I've heard there are no women beyond a few settlements outside of Saint Louis."

He shrugged, watching her put the pieces together.

Laura said, "She's Indian, isn't she? Not a proper wife at all."

"As you can see, I wouldn't be a suitable choice for a lady like yourself."

She took a deep breath, swelling her ivory bosom, and paced thoughtfully toward the piano. She turned back, watching him through half-lidded eyes. "And to think I only found your letters forward and bold. Are you this honest with all the women you meet?"

He smiled wryly. "It's a fault I've developed. I just thought I'd avoid any misunderstandings before they'd—"

"I'm still interested, Mr. Hamilton."

"Miss Templeton, I'm not the pampered rich boy who left here two years ago. Not the boy who wrote you all those silly letters on the river. I've killed men. Fought with my bare hands. Lived like an animal. I'm married to an Indian woman whom I love. She'll probably bear my children when I get back to the mountains. And I *will* go back."

"You *are* a gentleman, aren't you? Honorable to the core."

Richard shifted, suddenly wary. Who was this Laura Templeton? What game was she playing? "I must admit, I didn't anticipate your reaction. I'm telling you the truth. I'm going back to Willow."

"You'll go back as your father's partner, Mr. Hamilton." She stared thoughtfully at the rug, then raised her eyes. "Very well, let's be honest. Marriage doesn't always have to do with love. Sometimes it's a partnership. I'm not a fool, Mr. Hamilton. I trust you, and Will trusts you, so I'll tell the truth, too. We put on a pretty good show here. But this is Boston. My father is a ship's captain. My mother was an indentured woman. Despite all of my brother's friends, I've turned nineteen and never fallen in love. The way you talk, I'd think you, of all people, could understand a pragmatic woman. I'll go to Saint Louis with you."

"How do you know what kind of man I am?".

She stepped close again and took his hands. "By looking into your eyes, by the things you just told me. You're honest, Mr. Hamilton. And I can see the interest in your eyes. You're tempted, aren't you?"

Tempted? He looked into her blue eyes, aware of her beauty and the challenge she radiated. "I'm not an oak tree, Miss Templeton. Just frail flesh and blood."

She smiled at that, a delicate eyebrow arching. "That makes two of us, sir."

"Yet you'd know I was with another woman."

"Most men are. Even my father. I suppose that's the price a woman pays when she marries a wolf. But at least I'd marry a rich one."

At that Will arrived, leaning in the door. "Come, all. Supper is ready, and what a feast it is!"

CHAPTER NINETEEN

Very well, so far we are agreed, Glaucon. The state which is to be arranged in the best possible way must have women in common, children in common, and education in common. So also, its practices must be common to all, both in war and in peace. Kings among them must be those who have shown themselves best both in philosophy and warfare.

—Plato, *The Republic*

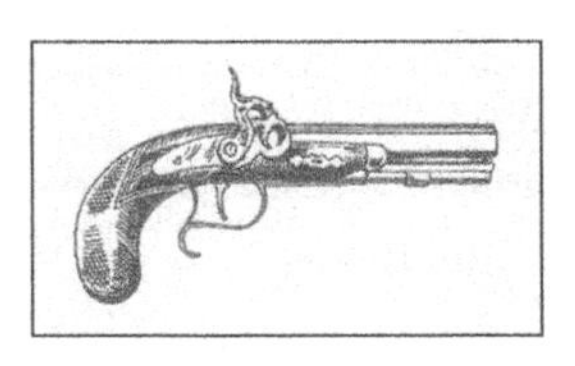

Richard was in his father's office, compiling lists of trade goods, things in constant demand on the frontier. As he finished list after list, Phillip would take them, squint through his glasses, and periodically grunt a question.

"Tin cones, Richard? What are these?" Phillip asked.

"Just what it, sounds like. Tin rolled into a narrow cone. They hang them on moccasins like little bells, or they can be used for horsehair tassels."

"I see. Made locally in Saint Louis, I suppose? Labor

and materials would be cheaper here. Perhaps some sort of machine could stamp them out?"

Richard nodded, rubbing his forehead. His mind was awhirl with so many things: trade, a lecturer's position, Laura Templeton—and Willow. So much to consider. Too much, really.

Jeffry stepped into the office, an eyebrow raised. "Master Richard, sir, a note has been delivered."

Richard opened the small white envelope, reading:

I'll be walking in the Commons at 2:00.
Laura

Richard glanced at the clock. The time was a quarter till.

Phillip was watching with mild curiosity. Richard chewed his lip, then said, "I think I'd better attend to this. It won't take long."

He nodded to Jeffry, tucked the note into his pocket, and headed down the steps for his hat and coat. The afternoon was chilly, a breeze rolling in off the harbor. Richard's boots clicked across the cobblestones and onto the browning grass.

He walked with his hands jammed into his pockets, the tall beaver hat pulled low on his head. How did he sort this all out? With so many directions, how did he choose?

"Mr. Hamilton?"

He glanced up as a carriage pulled even with him. When it stopped, Laura stepped out. She was dressed in a light pink satin dress that billowed under a gray wool coat. Richard recognized the carriage driver as the Templetons' house servant. He would watch from a discreet distance as they walked.

Richard bowed as Laura curtsied. “Miss Templeton. Good afternoon.”

They fell in step, walking side-by-side. Richard gave her a curious sidelong glance.

“I wanted to talk,” she said. “I wanted to elaborate on some of the things I said last night.”

“It did seem a bit risky for a lady.”

She chuckled. “Oh, Mr. Hamilton, you’ll keep my confidence as I will keep yours.” She gave him a sly glance. “So, what are you going to do? Become a professor? Go to Saint Louis for your father? Run off to the mountains? What?”

He watched the leaves crush under his boots as they walked. “I don’t know yet. It’s all happening so quickly. Everything I ever dreamed has come true. All I have to do is reach out and take it.”

“You told me you dreamed about me.”

“I did.” He studied her for a moment, dropping all pretense. “Why, Laura? What’s this all about?”

For a moment, their eyes met, hers challenging. “It’s about escape, Mr. Hamilton. Two years ago, just after you left for the West, my mother died. I took over the running of the house. At the same time, Will took over my father’s financial affairs. Will isn’t a businessman. He’s a philosopher at heart, interested in ideas, not figures.”

“I see.”

“Will and I have always been close. I began to advise him on business decisions and started keeping the books. I discovered that I have a head for it. That year was busy, needless to say. When I should have been looking for a prominent man to marry, I was involved in tariffs, debits and credits. I doubled my father’s profits in the last two years. About a month ago, he discovered that I, not Will, have been making many of the buying decisions. Since it’s improper for a lady, I no longer have that privilege. More to the point, he is adamant that I marry. He favors Thomas Hanson, especially for the social and business benefits such an alliance would bring."

Richard puffed out a breath, seeing the faint white haze on the air. It brought memories of snow, of cold mountains and hunger. "I see."

"In the parlor last night, you said that Boston was a big cage. I don't mind marriage, but I want more. I thought if anyone would understand, you would."

"To be a partner?" Willow's words echoed from the past.

She gave him a level-headed stare. "Yes. I can do it, Mr. Hamilton. I want the chance. Is Saint Louis such a place?"

"All this, just from last night?"

"I liked the way you looked at me. Challenging, as if asking what I was worth to myself. Would you accept a woman as a partner?"

"I already have. Her name is Heals Like A Willow."

"Will you bring her to Saint Louis?"

"No. Saint Louis isn't that much different from Boston, at least, among the upper classes. And Willow wouldn't like Saint Louis. The Power is wrong there."

"Power?"

"Spirit, if you will. The soul of the place."

"You wouldn't have to come back, Richard. You could stay out there, with her. You could tell me what goods are in demand, and I could forward your orders to your father here. You'd be free."

"What on earth makes you think you could live that way?"

"I'd be doing what I want to do."

"And when you get lonely? If you took a lover,

someone would find out. They always do. The scandal would ruin you."

"I don't know." Then she put her hand on his arm. "Mr. Hamilton, I want the chance to do something with my life besides be a gentleman's wife, bear children, and keep a house. I'm willing to take risks."

It was in her eyes, something unquenchable, and a burning spirit that touched him. "Let me give it some thought."

The note would never qualify as great literature of the Western world. In roughly formed block letters, it stated:

> DICK:
>
> Willow is pregnant Cum kwik. Yer kid xpected maybe April. WER camped at Red Canyon til rondeeyvu. Cum kwik. Willow KIN make a koon krazy. All well.
>
> TRAVIS

"Dear Lord God," Richard whispered as he stared at the rough paper. "How on earth did he ever get it here?"

Phillip sat behind the cherry wood desk, staring up

at him over the nose-pinch glasses. The ship's clock tick-tocked on the mantel. In the corner, the old Charleville musket stood in mute testament to another age.

"I've got to go." Richard tapped the paper with his finger as he paced. "That settles it."

"Go? Back to the wilderness?"

Richard lifted an eyebrow at his father's disapproval. "She's going to have my baby, Father. I *need* to be there, for both of them."

Phillip rubbed his face, rearranging the fleshy jowls. "Richard, I have tried to understand. I really have. But I—"

"You don't need to understand." Richard leaned over the desk. "You must only accept. Our worlds have always been different. I suppose they always will be."

"Richard, your place is here. This is your world." Phillip gestured out through the window at the Commons. "You belong here, among educated Americans. This Indian woman, I assume she's a good woman, but you have a future here. You can send her support, an allowance to raise the child. But Richard, find yourself a white wife, one who can keep your house, provide me with grandchildren."

"Laura Templeton?"

"Discreet inquiries have been made. Her family is not opposed to such a union. Her father has been after me for years to employ his ship in my trade. She is a beautiful young woman, Richard. I hear that the two of you get along famously."

"Indeed? 'Famously'? Yes, Father, she's beautiful."

"A woman doesn't need brains, Richard."

"I suppose they don't. Not here. But Miss Templeton, it seems, has them anyway."

"Then marry her and stay! Or take her to Saint Louis and establish my office there."

Richard stopped short, half frantic, but the pieces began to fall into place. "How much are you willing to invest in this office in Saint Louis?"

"How much would you need?"

"Five thousand."

"I'll give you ten."

"I don't need ten. Five will be more than enough for what I have in mind. Father, I want total freedom to do this my way. Hire my people. Call it a...a challenge. You wouldn't want me to take over the company without having proved myself. All right. This is my chance to do it."

"And the Indian woman?"

"I'll deal with her in my own way."

"But, Richard... All right. Yes." Phillip placed his hands flat on the desk. "Very well, I suppose you're a man now. I'll admit, I had a few...er, relationships before I met your mother. It's to be expected. This will pass."

"Perhaps, sir."

Phillip laughed ironically as he reached back and pulled the bell cord. "I heard an old saying once: 'I am a soldier in order that my son can be a farmer, in order that his son can be a poet.' Well, so be it. I was a soldier so that my son could be a merchant. Instead, I got a philosopher with queer ideas. But more than that, I fought so that I, and my kind, would be subservient to no one. In that, I can take some solace, even if it didn't work out as I dreamed."

"No, sir. But then, life rarely does. The five thousand will allow for the establishment of a Saint Louis office and capital enough for an initial investment in trade goods. I think, working with my agent, I can double it within two years."

"Now you're talking like a businessman. You have a plan, I take it?"

Richard gave him a crooked grin. "Yes, I think I do."

Phillip reached into the desk drawer as Jeffry entered. "Richard needs to return west with as great a haste as possible. Could you pack his things?"

"Yes, sir." Jeffry bowed and left.

Richard stared thoughtfully at the door. "You should free him, you know."

Phillip cocked an eyebrow. "Richard, it's in my will. And, Richard, if I should die before he does, don't make him miserable. Don't tell him, 'Go be free,' and cast him out on the street."

"No matter what, he has a home here until he dies, or he decides to leave on his own. I give you my word, sir. Oh, and Father, one last thing."

"And that is?"

"Uh, that pistol. You don't suppose I could take it with me this time, do you?"

"A caller, Miss." Jonas handed Laura a card imprinted with Richard Hamilton's name. She put her needlework to one side and rose, checked her hair in the mirror, straightened her collar, and went down the stairs.

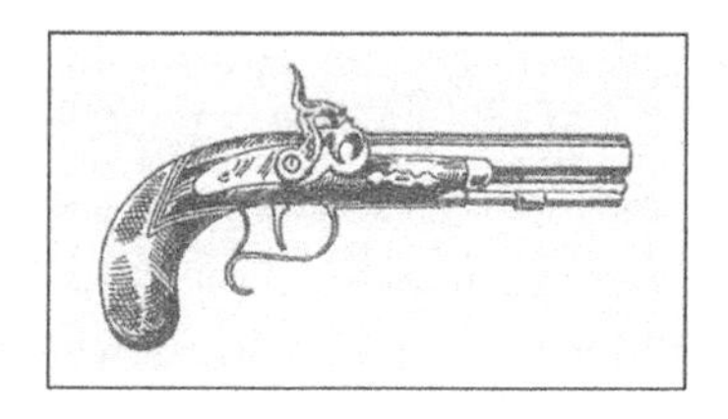

Richard was looking out the window at the misty rain falling on the street. His cloak draped his shoulders and he held his hat in one hand.

"Mr. Hamilton? You look as if you're in a hurry."

He turned, that daring smile on his lips, and kissed the back of her hand when she offered it. Then he looked significantly at Jonas.

Laura nodded at Jonas, knowing he'd go no farther than the hallway.

Richard stepped close. "I have to go. I just received a note from Travis. Willow's pregnant. I must leave as soon as I can. It's a long journey and I may not make it in time as it is."

She studied him, trying to read that glint in his eyes. "I see. Well, I wish you a safe and speedy journey, sir."

"Thank you." He paused, curiosity in the slight arch of eyebrow and the set of his lips. 'Tell me, how serious were you when you told me you wanted more?"

She steeled herself, fists knotted. "Very."

He handed her a brown paper packet tied with string. She hefted the brick-sized bundle in her hands, light for its size. "And this is?"

"Those are banknotes. Two thousand, five hundred dollars' worth. Half of my father's investment in the Saint Louis trade. I'm taking the other half with me for initial expenses. Your travel to Saint Louis shouldn't cost more than two hundred dollars. That's standard fare for a lady to take a steamer to New York, a coach to Pittsburgh, and a steamboat to Saint Louis. You will travel as my fiancée. It will give you greater latitude in your dealings with men along the way and in Saint Louis."

"Mr. Hamilton, I—"

"When you arrive in Saint Louis, contact General William Ashley. The General will tell you where your office will be. By the time you arrive, he'll also have found suitable quarters for a lady. He will give you an envelope from me containing a list of goods to procure. That you will transmit to my father here in Boston. After that, we've two years to double the investment."

"But, how are we...I mean, goodness, my head is spinning!"

"I'll send you reports from the interior, as well as things for the trade that will give us an edge on the competition. In the meantime, you'll run the Saint Louis office."

Laura took a deep breath, suddenly unsteady. She blinked, clutching the packet to her breast. "And I will marry you there? In Saint Louis?"

"Only if it's necessary to keep the business solvent. I'm a pragmatic man, Laura. Know in advance, however, it will be a marriage in name only."

"Why, Mr. Hamilton? Why are you doing this?"

"Something I saw in your eyes the other day. Let's just say I want to see the bear outside the cage."

"I don't understand."

"One day, perhaps you will. Now, I must be going. I'm leaving for New York tomorrow morning at first light. On the way I'll organize as much as I can so you won't be completely lost upon your arrival in Saint Louis."

"Wait! My God, Richard. How do you know I won't just—well, not appear?"

For a long moment his brown eyes burned into her soul, sending a thrill through her blood. "Won't you?" And then he stuck out his hand. "To Hamilton & Templeton."

"To Hamilton & Templeton." She shook, straightening, chin up. "I'll see you in Saint Louis, Mr. Hamilton."

Phillip stood on the top step, Jeffry behind him. The carriage clattered off into the morning fog that drifted across the Commons to obscure Beacon Street. His stiff leg ached, and his soul weighed heavily. Damn it, the frontier was so far away, and dangerous.

If I just had more time to talk him out of this foolishness! What would his mother say? Dallying with an Indian woman! Isn 't his own kind good enough for him?

The mist closed behind the carriage, until only the clop-ping hooves could be heard on the cobblestones.

"If I'd only had more time," he repeated aloud.

"Time, sir?" Jeffry asked.

"With Richard. He's got to come to his senses, that's all."

Jeffry nodded, expression stony. "Yes, sir."

"Does he do things like this just to torture me? Is that it?"

"No, sir."

"What is it, then?"

"You know, sir. He's your son. Like you, he's fighting another kind of revolution. The problem is, no one is on his side."

And were it I, a young man with a wife about to bear a child?

How many times had he wished he could have changed the past? Been there at her side? He swallowed hard, Caroline's eyes softening in the shadowy sconces of his memory. The best a father could hope for was that his son wouldn't duplicate his mistakes.

"Another kind of revolution. Huh! Well, I pray to God that he makes it safely."

Go with my blessing, boy. Don't live your life as I have.

"He will, sir. He's got the fight in him. Just like his father. That comes out in the blood, sir."

Phillip nodded wearily, hitching around on his bad leg. He paused as Jeffry opened the door. "Then why do I feel so damned old?"

"Perhaps you're not looking hard enough for Master Richard's frontier, sir."

Richard himself had said it was too far—even for a man like Ames to see.

So, why should I be different?

"Oh, I'll find it. After all, I've got the sprat involved in the trade, haven't I? And he's become quite a man. The sort for an old man to be proud of." And at that, Phillip limped into the house, toward a satisfaction he couldn't completely comprehend.

EPILOGUE

Feathery snowflakes sifted from the dark sky. They spiraled and tumbled in the heavy air, and began to mound on the clumps of dry grass. Those that landed on rocks and soil melted at first, darkening the earth. But before long pebbles, clods, and weed duff whitened, then the shadowed patches, and finally even the hard-beaten paths.

Willow had seen many spring storms like this. She walked slowly, heedless of the flakes that landed so gently on her robe-covered head. When she stepped on the cropped grass, the thin crust of snow groaned, moisture soaking into her moccasins.

The baby had been upset, kicking and squirming within her belly. Since sleep was an impossibility, Willow had climbed to her feet, massaged the small of her back, and draped a robe about her before ducking into the night. She prowled through snow-frosted junipers and hesitated to look eastward down the canyon.

How many times had she stopped here on moonlit nights? On clear days and cloudy? She knew each crevice in the high red rock wall. The patterns of sage on the amber grass had impressed her souls, until even now, in the darkness of this spring storm, she could see them so clearly.

Where are you, Richard?

Flakes tumbled before her, their hiss on the ground barely audible. From old habit her hands went to her protruding belly. The child kicked, pressing perilously on her bladder.

"Soon, little one. Is that what you're trying to tell me? Is that why you won't let me sleep tonight?" She took a deep breath, ambling down into the canyon.

To one side she heard the warning cough of a mule deer, followed by the chunk of hooves as the herd bounded away. The sound of their passing was finally eaten by the silence of the night, the snow, and the comforting rock walls.

Until now, the pregnancy had been easy, almost second nature. She'd gone on about her tasks despite Travis's and Baptiste's constant harping. In self-defense she'd finally lit into Baptiste, scolding him unmercifully. To her dismay, he'd stiffened, wide-eyed, and avoided her for the rest of the day. The following morning when she'd gone to apologize, his bed had been missing, his horse and outfit gone.

"He went fer the Crow," Travis had replied laconically.

"I drove him away, didn't I?" And a horrible guilt had hollowed her souls.

"After a fashion, I reckon." Then Travis had turned into the wary male: he who dared not speak lest he say the wrong thing.

Contrite, Willow had reined in her surging emotions, attended to chores, and allowed Travis to handle those jobs he felt compelled to undertake on her behalf. At the same time, Travis had built a third lodge out of juniper, rock, sage, and earth.

A month later, in the middle of the deep cold, Baptiste had ridden in with two *A 'ni* women: New Moon Rising and Makes Antelope. New Moon Rising had moved into Travis's bed, while Makes Antelope and Baptiste took up the new lodge.

Relations with Willow had been cool at first, but over the last weeks an equilibrium had been achieved.

"Tarnation, gal," Baptiste had said. "You ain't figgering on Travis and me birthin' no baby! Why, I done brung these heah gals fo' you. They got a sense foah such doings."

"And your blankets are warmer now," she'd told him wryly. "They've a sense for those doings as well, I'd wager."

Baptiste gave her a wide grin in response.

Who am I to deny them the chance to be men?

But the arrival of the Crow women had irrevocably shifted the tenuous balance in Willow's life. Where once she, Travis, and Baptiste had stood like a tripod, now she felt odd, uncomfortable, as if intruding on their affairs.

It's just the baby. Willow. Soon it will be over. A woman with a child in a cradleboard isn 't as dependent as one with an infant in her belly.

The silence of the night pressed around her, cloaking her in the solitude of snow. The ache in her lower back was nagging again, and pains picked at her pelvis.

The faintest of breezes stirred the flakes into a slow dance. What a cold, wet night. How good to have a snug shelter so close by. Spring was a miserable time for travel.

Richard would probably arrive with the summer caravan. As Travis explained it, by the time the note made it to Boston—if it made it to Boston—and Richard traveled to Saint Louis, the caravan would be leaving for Rendezvous.

And he will come to me there.

She smiled into the storm, picturing Richard's face as he met her, and this child. What a joyous day that would be.

The wind tugged at her. She started to turn, ready to retrace her way to the shelter. But the baby thrashed within her, causing her to gasp and suck shallow breaths as she cradled her belly.

"Easy, little one. You'll have plenty of time to use your legs and arms once you're born. There's no need to wear them out now." What she really needed was to go back to the fire and warm up.

She took a step and the child kicked again. Frowning, Willow gritted her teeth and stopped. What could possess the child to...

The muffled clink of metal carried through the curtains of falling flakes.

Willow cocked her head, staring off into the snow-grayed darkness of the canyon bottom. In the time she'd stood there, a finger's depth had covered the ground.

Willow, it's just your imagination. No one would travel in weather like this.

She turned once more, only to have the baby squirm uncomfortably. "Enough," she growled, starting resolutely up the trail. Her baby thumped her with enough vigor to make her draw breath.

She massaged her belly to still the child. "It's snowing out here. And I'm getting cold. We must go back to..."

She heard it again, a muffled *thump* down in the valley.

Willow turned, staring into the storm-blurred night until her eyes ached.

They might have materialized out of nothingness, little more than moving shadows that appeared and blended back into the darkness and snow, a phantom in motion with the storm.

Real, or dream? Willow blinked hard, vaguely aware that her baby had gone still as the night. A swirling wall of white engulfed the apparition.

Just your imagination, Willow. A quirk of pregnancy.

She took a deep breath. Foolishness! She wanted him so badly that she was spinning his image out of the night.

She turned—but when the horse snuffled, she froze, heart leaping in her breast.

Careful, Willow. You don't know who this is. Perhaps some Pa'kiani *riding through with murder on his mind.*

She stepped closer to one of the junipers, blending her form into the tree's.

Like *Pandzoavits* from mist, snow-caked and hunched, he rode out of the night. Pia plodded in a stumbling walk, head down, her gait that of a horse nearing exhaustion. A second animal followed on a lead, also white-backed and weary.

He was almost abreast of her when she said, "Richard?"

He pulled up, snow clinging to every fold of the robe he'd wrapped around him. In the darkness, his frosted beard was all she could see of his face.

"What are you doing out here?" he asked. "It's the middle of the night."

"The baby wouldn't let me sleep. It knew you were coming."

"Then I'm not too late?"

"No, husband."

He almost collapsed when he stepped down out of the saddle. She caught him, the two of them teetering together for a moment, and then his arms went around her.

"Blessed God, Willow, I've missed you!"

"And I you, my warrior!"

"Are you all right? Is everything all right? The child...?"

"We are all fine. The baby can come any time now."

Bone-deep weariness echoed in his hollow chuckle. "Well, by God, I beat old Coyote this time, didn't I?"

"I think you've become Wolf, Richard. Now, come. Let me warm you, feed you, and make you a bed."

"Wind's blowing a mile a minute out in the flats. I'm half froze, Willow. But this time, you won't have to go clear to the Land of the Dead to find me."

"Only as far as Boston?"

He laughed again, tightening his hold on her. "I think Boston's dead—just the same as Cannibal Owl was for the Bald One. It's all worked out, Willow. I fixed everything—made peace. Now I can stay home."

This time, the child didn't kick as they turned toward their lodge.

Richard smacked his fist into his palm as he paced back and forth. This was miserable, just waiting and waiting. Behind him the fire popped and spat. Lazy snowflakes drifted insolently down. The clouds masked the red stone of *Ainkahonobita* and hid the sentinel pines that guarded the heights.

"Easy, coon." Travis sat on a log before the fire. "Could be worse. These Snakes, they make the man grunt and groan when the child's born. They claim it makes the birthing easier, shared, ye see."

"I'm not Shoshoni."

"Reckon even a blind buffler could see that." Travis ran a patch down the Hawken barrel as he cleaned his rifle. "How ye feeling?"

"About got my land legs back. I think Pia's going to be all right. By the time we got here, I was half afraid I'd broken her down."

"Naw, she's a tough one, she is. She's coming round." Travis glanced at the lodge.

Willow gave a muffled gasp. New Moon Rising and Makes Antelope spoke in low voices.

"That was sure a shock to ride in here and find three lodges," Richard admitted.

"Baptiste and me, we just got lonely." Travis scowled at a powder-stained patch. "And, wal, truth be told, it was getting ter be plumb hell a-watching Willow all the time. A beaver's got needs."

"That he does." Richard paced some more, arms crossed. His frosty breath rose in the cold air.

Baptiste appeared out of the trees leading a horse packed with firewood. He walked the animal up to the fire and untied each load. Then he pulled the halter from the animal and slapped it on the rump. "There, reckon that'll keep the fires going fo' a day or two." He walked up to the firepit and extended his hands. "What's the word on Willow?"

"Still waiting," Richard said.

"Birthing takes a while." Travis shifted. " 'Course, any coon what goes inter business with a woman fer a partner, why, hell, he'd best be waiting fer Christmas come July."

"She'll make it," Richard said absently. Then he

turned a narrowed eye on Travis. "I'll bet you. Five packs of prime plews."

"I'd like some of that." Baptiste's face lit up. "Ain't no woman gonna make it in no business."

Travis squinted skeptically at Richard. "Naw, I ain't having none of it. Not with Dick looking that a-way."

Willow lay back on the blankets and let the sweat dry on her hot flesh. She blinked her eyes in the darkness and let her thoughts float. Childbirth was that way. The terrible wrenching pain, the feeling as if one's guts were being pulled from the body, and finally, after the delivery, the foggy feeling as the body forgot the agony.

Perhaps *Tam Segobia* had made the world that way, so a woman would forget, lest she refuse to undergo such a horrible ordeal again.

New Moon Rising knelt beside her, wiping the blood and fluid from the squalling infant. The baby was changing color from blue to pink, a sign of health. New Moon Rising's hands were quick and sure, her care of the baby one less thing for Willow to worry about. She might have been *A'ni,* but at least she was a woman.

I'm still Dukurika *down in my souls. I couldn't have stood to have Richard, Travis, or Baptiste here.*

Willow cramped again as the afterbirth passed. Makes Antelope had placed a hide to catch it, and now carefully folded the hide, binding it tightly with thongs. Willow would have to bury it with appropriate ceremony. That would be later. For now she was happy to let her weary body rest.

To Willow's relief, New Moon Rising had followed instructions, dipping the child *Dukurika*-fashion in warm water to clean it. Now she finished rubbing the baby clean, and bent down, chattering in her *A'ni* tongue. Willow smiled, and took her child. So, she'd borne a girl.

She pulled the blanket back, and nestled the little round head against her breast. As the tiny mouth found her nipple and began sucking, Willow closed her eyes, savoring the sensations that stimulated her milk.

For the moment, she could float in this sense of euphoria. Her daughter was born. Richard had returned from Boston. She'd won. *Tam Apo* had smiled on her.

She would see Richard soon, in spite of the *Dukurika* warning about seeing a husband too soon after a birth. Together, they would raise this new daughter. Their girl would learn the ways of the *Dukurika* and of the Whites. Born into two worlds, she would be the first of a new tribe. In the distance, she could hear the wavering howl as a wolf cried its Power into the spring storm.

Richard stood on one of the worn sandstone boulders and watched evening come to *Ainkahonobita.* The sky was touched with hints of salmon pink that reflected on the melting snow. The junipers and pines stood in stark contrast to the pristine white. The air had warmed, promising a turn in the weather. Spring was like that, cold and snowy one day, warm and pleasant the next.

He recognized Willow's dainty step, but remained as he was, staring up at the sky while she stopped beside him and twined her arm with his.

"How's little Caroline?" he asked

"Little White Alder," she corrected gently, and poked him in the ribs. Then she said, "You have that look in your eyes."

"Just thinking about how I got here. Father sending me West, the trouble I got into with François, getting sold onto the boat. And you, your husband and son dying, your being captured by Packrat and taken East. So many little things, all leading to Caroline being born."

"*Tam Apo* made the world to work like that." She shrugged. "This bothers you?"

"I'm still looking for purpose, I guess. It all seems like chaos. François, August, Trudeau, and Dave Green, all of them dead. Yet here I stand, with you. Who would have thought that I, the least suited of all to survive, would have lived through it?"

"Perhaps it was you, Richard. You've never known the strength of your *puha.* You came looking for Wolf, and you found him. The others, they looked for what they wanted...and could not reach out with their souls to grasp it."

"Or they just didn't have the luck." He smiled weakly. "Luck and chaos are twins, you know."

"And what does that mean?"

"It means we had better live our lives with all the passion we can. If there is a truth, it's that this, like all things, will pass. The Blackfeet could come tomorrow, or the small pox, or a bad fall from a horse. Assuming there is an ultimate truth, it is that all is chaos."

"Only half," she corrected, placing soft fingers to his lips. "For everything Coyote did wrong, Wolf did something right. The world is made that way. Now, come with me. Those pesky *A 'ni* women have been roasting hump meat all day. I think it's ready to come out of the pit."

He nodded, and together they turned, picking their way through the rocks toward home—for however long it would exist.

SELECTED BIBLIOGRAPHY

Baldwin, Leland D. *The Keelboat Age on Western Waters.* 1941. Reprint. Pittsburgh: University of Pittsburgh Press, 1980.

Billon, Frederic L. *Annals of Saint Louis in Its Territorial Days from 1804 to 1821.* 1888. Reprint. New York: Arno Press & 77K; *New York Times,* 1971.

Bradbury, John. *Travels in the Interior of America in the Years 1809, 1810, and 1811.* 1819. Reprint. 1904, Thwaits edition. Lincoln, NE: Bison Books, University of Nebraska Press, 1986.

Bowers, Alfred W. *Mandan Social and Ceremonial Organization.* Chicago: University of Chicago Press, 1950.

Brown, Joseph Epes. *The Sacred Pipe: Black Elk's Account of the Seven Rites of the Oglala Sioux.* Norman, OK: University of Oklahoma Press, 1953.

Clokey, Richard M. *William H. Ashley: Enterprise and Politics in the Trans-Mississippi West.* Norman, OK: University of Oklahoma Press, 1980.

Denig, Edwin Thompson. *Five Indian Tribes of the Upper Missouri.* Norman, OK: University of Oklahoma Press, 1961.

Dominguez, Steve. "Tukudeka Subsistence: Observations for a Preliminary Model." Unpublished manuscript, 1981.

Dorsey, George A. *The Mythology of the Wichita.* Norman, OK: University of Oklahoma Press, 1995.

Fletcher, Alice C, and Francis La Flesche. *The Omaha Tribe.* Vols. I and II. Reprint. 1906, Bureau of American Ethnology Report. Lincoln, NE: Bison Books, University of Nebraska Press, 1992.

Frazer, Robert W. *Forts of the West.* Norman, OK: University of Oklahoma Press, 1965.

Frey, Rodney. *The World of the Crow: As Driftwood Lodges.* Norman, OK: University of Oklahoma Press, 1987.

Gale, John. *The Missouri Expedition 1818-1820: The Journal of Surgeon John Gale.* Norman, OK: University of Oklahoma Press, 1960.

Garrard, Lewis H. *Wah-to-yah and the Taos Trail.* Norman, OK: University of Oklahoma Press, 1955.

Gilmore, Melvin R. *Uses of Plants by the Indians of the Missouri River Region.* Lincoln, NE: University of Nebraska Press, 1977.

Gowans, Fred R. *Rocky Mountain Rendezvous.* Provo, UT: Brigham Young University Press, 1975.

Hafen, Leor R. *Broken Hand: The Life of Thomas Fitzpatrick.* Reprint. 1931. Lincoln, NE: Bison Books, University of Nebraska Press, 1973.

Hultkrantz, Ake. *The Religions of the American Indians,* trans. Monica Setterwall. Berkeley: University of California Press,1967. *Native Religions of North America.* San Francisco: Harper & Row, 1987.

Shamanic Healing and Ritual Drama. New York: Crossroad Publishing Company, 1992.

Hunt, David C, et al. *Karl Bodmer's America.* Lincoln, NE: The Josyln Art Museum and University of Nebraska Press, 1984.

Hyde, George E. *The Pawnee Indians.* Norman, OK: University of Oklahoma Press, 1951.

Klein, Laura F., and Lillian A. Ackerman, eds. *Women and Power in Native North America.* Lincoln, NE: University of Oklahoma Press, 1995.

Larson, Mary Lou, and Marcel Kornfeld. "Betwixt and Between the Basin and the Plains: The Limits of Numic Expansion," in *Across the West.* David B. Mad-son and David Rhode, eds. Salt Lake City: University of Utah Press, 1994.

Lauer, Quentin. *Phenomenology: Its Genesis and Prospect.* 1958. Reprint. New York: Harper Torchbooks, 1965.

Lavender, David. *The Fist in the Wilderness.* Albuquerque, NM: University of New Mexico Press, 1964.

Lowie, Robert H. *The Crow Indians.* 1935. Reprint. Lincoln, NE: Bison Books, University of Nebraska Press, 1963.

Luttig, John C. *Journal of a Fur Trading Expedition on the Upper Missouri.* 1920. Reprint. New York: Argosy-Antiquarian, Ltd., 1964.

Meyer, Roy W. *The Village Indians of the Upper Missouri.* Lincoln, NE: University of Nebraska Press, 1977.

Miller, Wick R. *Newe Natekwinappeh: Shoshoni Stories and Dictionary.* Salt Lake City: University of Utah Anthropological Papers, no. 94, University of Utah Press, 1972.

Moore, Michael. *Medicinal Plants of the Mountain West.* Santa Fe: Museum of New Mexico Press, 1979.

Morgan, Dale L. *Jedediah Smith and the Opening of the West.* Lincoln, NE: University of Nebraska Press, 1953.

Moulton, Gary E., ed. *The Journals of the Lewis and Clark Expedition.* Vols. II and III. Lincoln, NE: University of Nebraska Press, 1986.

Nute, Grace Lee. *The Voyageur.* 1931. Reprint. St. Paul, MN: Minnesota Historical Society, 1953.

Oglesby, Richard Edward. *Manuel Lisa and the Opening of the Missouri Fur Trade.* Norman, OK: University of Oklahoma Press, 1963.

Powers, William K. *Sacred Language: The Nature of Supernatural Discourse in Lakota.* Norman, OK: University of Oklahoma Press, 1986.

Primm, James Neal. *Lion of the Valley: St. Louis, Missouri.* Boulder, CO: Pruett Press, 1981.

Rogers, Daniel J. *Objects of Change, the Archaeology and History of Arikara Contact with Europeans.* Washington, DC: Smithsonian Institution Press, 1990.

Ruxton, George F. *Life in the Far West Among the Indians and the Mountain Men. 1846-1847.* 1849. Reprint. Glorietta, NM: Rio Grande Press, 1972.

Schlesier, Karl H. *Plains Indians, A.D. 500-1500.* Norman, OK: University of Oklahoma Press, 1994.

Shimkin, Dimitri B. *Some Interactions of Culture Needs and Personalities Among the Wind River Shoshone.* Ph.D. dissertation, University of California Library, Berkeley, 1938.

———. *Wind River Shoshone Ethnogeography.* Berkeley, CA: University of California Anthropological Records, no. 5 (4), 1947.

Smith, Anne M. *Shoshone Tales.* Salt Lake City: University of Utah Press, 1993.

Steffen, Jerome O. *William Clark, Jeffersonian Man on the Frontier.* Norman, OK: University of Oklahoma Press, 1977.

Thomas, David, and Karin Ronnefeldt, eds. *People of the First Man.* New York: E. P. Dutton, 1976.

Trenholm, Virginia Cole, and Maurine Carley. *The Shoshonis: Sentinels of the Rockies.* Norman, OK: University of Oklahoma Press, 1964.

WarCloud, Paul. *Sioux Indian Dictionary.* Sissiton, SD: Paul WarCloud, 1971.

Weeks, Rupert. *Pachee Goyo: History and Legends from the Shoshone.* Laramie, WY: Jelm Mountain Press, 1981.

Weltfish, Gene. *The Lost Universe: Pawnee Life and Culture.* 1965. Reprint Lincoln, NE: Bison Books, University of Nebraska Press, 1977.

A LOOK AT: BIG HORN LEGACY

***New York Times* best seller W. Michael Gear presents a family saga of the old west with richly drawn characters and portrayals of life in the era.**

When the father he never knew was gunned down in the New Mexican high country, Ab Catton swore to unite his estranged family–five brothers and one sister–in order to avenge Web's murder and claim his legacy of gold. Now the feuding clan members have to bury their own differences in order to bury their father's killer and take possession of the inheritance that is rightfully theirs.

Hot on their trail and eager to disrupt their plans is their sociopathic uncle Branton Bragg. He hated Web, and he hates the children just as much.

Overcoming the difficulties will prove a challenge, but Ab and his siblings are willing to risk it all to test the bonds of family and blood.

AVAILABLE NOW

ABOUT THE AUTHOR

W. Michael Gear is the New York Times and international bestselling author of over fifty-eight novels, many of them co-authored with Kathleen O'Neal Gear.

With seventeen million copies of his work in print he is best known for the "People" series of novels written about North American Archaeology. His work has been translated into at least 29 languages. Michael has a master's degree in Anthropology, specialized in physical anthropology and forensics, and has worked as an archaeologist for over forty years.

His published work ranges in genre from prehistory, science fiction, mystery, historical, genetic thriller, and western. For twenty eight years he and Kathleen have raised North American bison at Red Canyon Ranch and won the coveted National Producer of the Year award from the National Bison Association in 2004 and 2009. They have published over 200 articles on bison genetics, management, and history, as well as articles on writing, anthropology, historic preservation, resource utilization, and a host of other topics.

The Gears live in Cody, Wyoming, where W. Michael Gear enjoys large-caliber rifles, long-distance motorcycle touring, and the richest, darkest stout he can find.

Made in the USA
Monee, IL
26 June 2023